The Hidden Legacy

The Hidden Legacy

Carrie Sue Barnes

Bold Vision Books
PO Box 2011
Friendswood, Texas 77549

In honor of my grandmothers:
Esther, Evelyn, and Thresa.

For Jessica, who never doubted since page one.

Table of Contents

I

September, 2000

Laurel Thomas shut the door against the raindrops slapping her skin. Water dripped from her jacket to the faded peach tiles beneath her feet. She hung the jacket in the closet on the same plastic hanger as yesterday. Then she used the edge of her t-shirt to dry her face and neck.

She walked the hallway to the master bedroom and greeted the home's sole resident. "Hello, Grandma!"

"Hello, Laurel! I thought I heard you arrive." Annie Walcott lifted her face toward her great-granddaughter.

Laurel settled into the rocking chair next to the bed as she had done countless times in recent months. She caught a glimpse of herself in a mirror on the bedroom wall, her black hair damp and tangled.

"How's the day treating you?" she asked, looking away from her reflection.

"Quite well now that you're here." Grandma smiled, papery wrinkles fanning from the corners of her green eyes.

The 103-year-old woman sat against the oak headboard, supported by pillows and covered by a tatty afghan that matched the red poppies on her nightgown. She removed her reading glasses, set them on the open book at her side, and tucked her short, white hair behind her ears.

Between the bed and the rocking chair stood a small table topped with a curious pattern of ceramic tiles in yellows and blues. Laurel couldn't recall anything else ever sitting on that table except the present items: a dog-eared edition of the Psalms, a thin anthology of Irish poetry, and a framed photo of four generations. The photograph of her great-grandmother Annie, her grandmother Megan,

9

her mother Erin, and Laurel's five-year-old self testified to a similar curve in each of their smiles.

"Why has this book of poetry always been on this table instead of with all the books in the living room?" Laurel asked with a surge of curiosity.

Grandma Annie turned her hunched shoulders toward the bedside table, the quietest sigh slipping between her lips. She closed her eyes for a long moment before reaching for the book. "No one ever asked before you."

"I have wondered before but it didn't seem important."

"It stays in here because it is important," Grandma Annie replied before handing Laurel the book opened to its title page.

Laurel read the words handwritten there, "'To Annie, with all my love between the pages.'" She lifted the book to her face, peering over its worn edge. "Grandma, there's no signature."

Grandma Annie feigned surprise, "No?"

"Who gave it to you?" Laurel asked with a laugh.

Grandma Annie took the book, holding it tightly and stroking the spine. She neither answered the question nor refused it.

"Was it my great-grandfather?"

Grandma Annie met Laurel's gaze as if pondering the inquiry.

Hesitation coursed through Laurel, opportunity staring her down like a dare. During the numerous drives from her apartment to this house, she committed herself again and again to ask the questions no one in her family had asked her great-grandmother. Like every instance before, she felt tonight's resolve ebbing away. She grabbed the last sliver before it escaped completely. Laurel looked again at her reflection in the mirror. Twenty-four, single, and only a few years into her career; she was barely an adult. Who was she to coax out answers hidden for eighty years? The resolve settled back in as Laurel wondered how many more chances she might have to ask. She pulled her fingers through her hair and refocused on Grandma Annie.

"Who was he? Mom said that Grandma Megan knew nothing about her father except that he was Irish, and you met during the war."

"Well, that is all I told Megan."

"Didn't she ever ask to know more about him?"

"Other than when she was a young child, only on the day she married your Grandpa Lee. I knew better than to delve into that story hours before the wedding. I decided to tell her the next time she asked, when we had enough time to discuss it." Grandma Annie's eyes lowered.

"She never asked again, did she?"

"No, and I didn't broach the subject." Grandma Annie wove her fingertips through the stitches of the afghan.

Laurel swallowed hard, certain she was about to cross a forbidden line. "Would you tell me?"

Grandma Annie's white eyebrows arched. "Well, Laurel, I'm not sure. I have spent so long avoiding that story that I am uncertain how I could tell it."

Though Laurel's disappointment was surely apparent, she was about to say she didn't want to pry. But then her great-grandmother clicked her tongue and added, "I can try to tell it. I just don't know how it will go, Laurie Bean."

The childhood nickname delighted Laurel, although she only ever let Grandma Annie get away with using it. She leaned over the arm of the chair. "You'll really tell me? You've no idea how badly I've wanted to ask."

Grandma Annie's voice grew solemn, "Where to begin? Laurel, you put fresh water on for tea and let me think a moment."

"Chamomile or lemon?" Laurel paused at the door but received no answer.

The water heated to a boil while she considered the questions Grandma Annie had surprisingly agreed to answer. In her twenty-four years, she'd only inquired after her great-grandfather a few times, such as when she studied World War I in grade school. Her mother encouraged her to ask Grandma Annie about Annie's service as a nurse in that war. Laurel did ask, for the sake of a history report, but she heeded the unspoken family rule to not ask about matters beyond that.

Laurel poured the water into two mugs and added tea bags. "I made one of each. Which would you like?" she asked as she reentered the bedroom.

"Lemon, please. It's a bit more energizing for the task."

The pair sat in silence, toying with the strings of their steeping teabags.

"Grandma, do you want to tell me?"

"I thought you said you want to hear it."

"I do, but I won't make you share something you'd rather keep secret."

Grandma Annie reached over to pat Laurel's knee. "Oh, you wouldn't be able to make me."

Laurel chuckled, but her great-grandmother remained pensive.

"I was thinking over why I never told anyone. I had good reason while Megan was young. But once she grew up I really should have explained things. The longer something is kept to yourself, the more uncomfortable the idea of sharing it becomes. I doubted that the truth would give Megan any comfort, or that she could be happier for knowing." Grandma Annie shifted her shoulders against the pillows. "I was just making excuses though, wasn't I?"

Laurel kept quiet, letting Annie sort through her thoughts.

"I'll begin at the beginning," Grandma Annie declared, "when we met. I remember nearly everything about that day. It was early October in 1917, and I was serving at a small hospital in northern France. That morning, once the frost had melted, I spent a long while meandering the wooded trails behind the nurses' dormitory. After the better part of a year at that hospital I knew those trails by heart.

"Though I tried not to stay very long each time I went out, I enjoyed the trails so much that I was afraid my mind would wander too far from my work." Grandma Annie tapped her finger on her temple. "All that wretched shock after arriving in France and starting as a wartime nurse never fully left my head. The leaves lining the trails and the bark under my fingers could have been from a tree at home, you know, where there was peace. Living over there during war, it immortalized home."

Laurel tucked one long leg beneath her and used the other to push her rocking chair into a slow rhythm while Grandma Annie continued.

"I've probably made it more impressive in my memory, but the hospital was housed on a sizeable estate. Since the start of the war, the doctor gradually lost his gardeners, maids, and other staff. A butler and a cook remained to keep up the mansion which served as the hospital. The old butler had proudly pointed out the hunting trails to us nurses. When I headed for the trails on my free mornings I felt separated from the hospital, from the other nurses, and from the hurting soldiers. During the first few months I spent a lot of the time out there thinking about Samuel. I was afraid of forgetting his face, his voice, everything."

"Samuel." Laurel tested the name on her tongue. "That was his name?"

"I'm simply trying to get my bearings." Grandma Annie lifted the cup of tea to her lips, sipped and set it down again. "Samuel was my fiancé, you see. More often than not, I recalled him at the docks in Boston. When I left home in January of 2017, his expression had such a pitiful mixture of gloom and...," she searched out the right word, "exasperation. I wish I'd had some comforting words for him, but I was so preoccupied with fending off my own nerves that all I could do was kiss him goodbye."

"What was Samuel like?"

"Handsome, tall, charming," Grandma Annie murmured fondly. "Samuel was a banker, like his father. He already owned a fine house in Boston and had become quite successful in the early years of his career. Samuel had a way of making me feel cared for and safe. He had such plans for us, all laid out and decided."

"He sounds wonderful, Grandma. It must have been hard to leave."

"The truth is I was itching to disturb the routine of my days. I can admit now that restlessness was my true motivation for heading overseas. I'm not sure I really knew the significance of the war except that it was memorable and entirely outside ordinary life. In my mind, at twenty years old, it was unfathomable that someone might not feel some urgency to be a part of it."

"Did you love Samuel?"

Grandma Annie bit her lip and nodded. "Yes, I believe I did. At least the person I was before going to France loved him. Our wedding was set for the coming June. He wasn't thrilled with my decision to serve as a nurse. I left for France in January, 1917 and remained long past our intended wedding date."

2

October, 1917, 83 years earlier

Annie left her beloved trails behind to return to the hospital. She was due to relieve Meg Dupree, a young nurse from Toronto.

Meg welcomed her to the main ward with a tired smile. "Is it really two o'clock already?"

"It is. How was the morning, Meg?"

"Splendid, as far as a war hospital goes." Meg winked.

Annie squeezed Meg's petite shoulders. "You look worn out from all the fun."

"Nah, I'm fine. It is Tuesday, after all."

"And Tuesday means what?"

"I have no idea." Meg rolled her brown eyes. "But it sounded good, didn't it, to have a day mean something different than all the rest of the days?"

"Whatever you say." She threw a hand in the air, impressed as usual by Meg's deep reserve of good humor.

After their arrival ten months prior, she and Meg became fast friends borne of both mutual fondness and necessity. The other nurses at the remote hospital were matronly, with respectable backgrounds in medical care. Meg at eighteen and Annie at twenty were by far the youngest and least experienced women on staff.

"What's hiding in the kitchen for us?" Meg asked. "I'm famished."

"Potatoes and biscuits left from lunch."

Meg shook her head, blond curls swinging. "You ate that. I imagine Madame Adele has tucked away a warm plate of chicken parmigiana with pasta and buttery toast for me. Perhaps some strawberry tarts for dessert."

"Be a good friend and imagine two plates, Meg."

Annie tied a white apron over the modest gray dress worn by all the nurses. Her black hair was pinned up in a thick bun at the nape of her neck. Before leaving, Meg updated her with the latest improvements and setbacks amongst the patients.

To start her shift Annie made rounds, walking the rows of iron-legged beds and smiling at any of the soldiers who acknowledged her arrival. Her mind collected critical details: who was napping; who exhibited pain; who had lacked the appetite for lunch; who was in high or low spirits. With these observations in tow, she saw to the men as thoroughly and cheerfully as she could manage. Some patient needs were simple, but she could never call the work easy. Since beginning her post in January, she realized speedily how unprepared she was for the depth to which the men would affect her. From every age and every stage in life, the men had become captives to pain, reshaped by loss of limbs or by the humiliation of depending on someone to clean up their blood, vomit, or soiled sheets. Yes, she arrived in France unprepared for these realities. Nevertheless, she met the challenges with greater willingness and dedication than she knew she possessed. Pouring herself into the work meant the shifts were not just physically trying but emotionally exhausting too.

This night proved no different. Eight hours in, she was weary on her feet where she stood beside a surgical table, offering consolation to a semi-conscious soldier and aiding Dr. LaCroix as he worked on the man's left arm. Longing to let her eyelids close, she waited for the clock to strike eleven, so she could walk to the dormitory and collapse into bed.

This week's ambulances arrived at the hospital doors with increased frequency. Dr. LaCroix's estate, with its eighteenth century mansion, adjacent servants' quarters, and large acreage stood on the outskirts of a village west of Arras. Arras, a city in northern France, repeatedly changed hands as the warring militaries gained and lost ground. Most citizens of the surrounding countryside fled, but the unmarried, forty-five-year-old physician Paul LaCroix stayed to offer both his home and his medical skills.

Watching Dr. LaCroix's precise movements, Annie thought for the ten hundredth time how strongly the doctor reminded her of her father. He had the same professional yet approachable demeanor, same height and slim build, and same dusting of gray in the dark mustache.

"Nurse Walcott, hand me fresh gauze," Dr. LaCroix requested without looking up from the wound.

By now, Daddy probably has much more gray in his mustache. Ignoring the dull ache for her family, Annie traded the doctor for the bloody gauze to toss in the waste basket.

"The arm can't be saved, can it?" she whispered. She'd learned to interpret the doctor's expressions in the silence of surgery.

"The damage is bad. Two tendons are nearly severed." He pointed at the worst of the wound. He spoke English well, although his accent required attentive listening. "We will wait until the morning to decide, when the bleeding slows enough for a better look. You must tell tonight's nurses to wake me if it does not slow. He has lost a dangerous amount of blood."

Annie nodded. It didn't matter how common amputations were here, she could not escape the horror that came with each one.

She saw to the last of her tasks once the surgical room was sanitized, providing a modicum of relief to men wishing for just enough comfort to sleep. Her vision zeroed in on the opposite wall and the tall wooden door leading to the gardens. She craved a moment in the fresh air away from the sights and smells of the ward. Once the notion arose, it would not leave her mind. The cadence of her boots quickened on the hardwood floor until she reached and opened the door.

The odors of blood, sweat, and antiseptic were instantly swallowed by the cold night air. Goosebumps prickled over her legs when she sat on the stone steps. From the east came the intermittent boom of artillery. A mile up the road, the village was asleep.

"I don't remember nearly so many stars at home," she marveled aloud. She craned her neck to see as much as she could of the celestial display then closed her eyes. The crisp, clean air filled her lungs.

As she exhaled, she was knocked down, her back hitting the hard step. A man fell into the door behind her, tumbling in his haste. He slowly raised his tall frame and rubbed his forehead, then he bent to reach Annie. His hand cupped her elbow, helping her to stand. She stared openly.

"This is the hospital, right?" His deep, anxious voice was thick with an Irish brogue. His hand remained on her arm as he peered at her in the darkness.

"Excuse me?"

"The hospital. Do you work here?"

She glanced down at her bloodstained apron, put on a polite smile, and replied, "Yes, I do."

"I'm sorry. Were you hurt?"

"Only stunned."

"Good." He dropped his hand to his side. "I believe my brother is here. A man on the train said it was the most likely place. He was shot in the leg." His eyes returned to the door as he added absently, "My brother was shot, not the man on the train."

She suppressed a smile at the unintended joke.

"I got a telegram a few days ago. I knocked at the front but after no answer I didn't want to just walk inside. I thought I'd try the side here."

Annie spoke up, "We'll go in at the front. Come with me."

She led him into a small, lamp-lit room adjoining the foyer. The former parlor had been converted into a makeshift office for the hospital.

"If your brother is here he will be on this list." She indicated a thick pile of papers. "Do you know when he arrived?"

"I think a week ago, maybe, or a little longer."

"His name?"

"Chet. Well, I suppose he's registered as Charles. I always call him Chet." He spoke to the room at large as he took in the menagerie of medical supplies and stacks of patient documents.

"I need a last name." She straightened her posture and attempted a business-like tone.

"Of course, I'm sorry. His name is Regan, Charles Regan. He's with the Irish Guards."

She flinched at the name and had to force a neutral expression while flipping through the registry. Her thoughts reverted back to a morning more than a week past.

It was the only morning they could call slow in the past month. Very few new patients, no major surgeries, and most of the soldiers were napping as they waited for lunch. The calm meant the battles had shifted closer to a different hospital.

Then Annie heard shouting. The front door swung open and banged the wall. She dropped the sheets on the bed she was stripping but before she could reach the front hall a soldier fell into the ward. His right leg was a mess of blood and dirt and his hair above the right temple was also matted with dried blood. Another man, a civilian, saw Annie and helped the soldier toward her. The civilian kept shouting, "Help! We need a doctor! Help!" In French, of course, but Annie certainly knew those words.

She noticed the Irish Guards insignia on the soldier's filthy shirt. He had collapsed and she rushed over to kneel beside him. He trembled, squeezing his eyes shut and grabbing at her apron. He tried to speak. He opened his eyes and those eyes took Annie's breath away. They were a shade of silvery blue she'd never seen before, radiant even during all their pain.

"Just breathe," she said. "It's alright now."

"You'll help me. You'll help me, right? You'll help me."

She assured him she would. Another nurse found Dr. LaCroix and they brought a stretcher. The doctor asked the soldier his name.

"Regan," he said before he lost consciousness.

Annie's thoughts returned to the man standing near her. She stopped fumbling with the registration papers. He had turned away so she took a moment before speaking. A wool newsboy cap was twisted in his large hands, first one way then the other. His youthful features indicated he wasn't much older than her own twenty years. He was tall, six-feet-three or six-feet-four inches. Dressed in plain, practical clothing, his frame was solid, his arms and shoulders thick with muscle. Barely perceptible waves gave texture to his short, dark hair. A shadow of whiskers testified to the long day or more of travel he'd endured.

Annie's breath caught in her throat when he turned to face her. The same incredible eyes as she'd seen in his brother's face stared back at her now. "If you just follow me, we'll find Dr. LaCroix. He will give you the details on Mr. Regan."

"So Chet's here? I've found him?"

"Yes, you have." She couldn't help but smile. The brother spoke like he'd won a prize.

His voice thickened, "Thank you, ma'am."

Finding the doctor, she explained their visitor's presence. With only minutes remaining in her shift, she could have excused herself but she followed as they walked to a bed at the center of the long ward.

Dr. LaCroix lifted the blanket above the soldier's bandaged leg and spoke to their guest, "The gunshot wound was not severe enough to call for amputation and the leg is healing well now. It will be some time before your brother can use his leg, but it will function again. The loss of blood was our greatest concern. Between his leg wound and the shrapnel wound on his head, your brother's had to fight to regain his strength."

Dr. LaCroix assured the younger man that Chet would make a full recovery but needed at least a few weeks to rest. Chet's brother wordlessly accepted the chair Annie pulled up to the bed.

She spoke gently, "Sir, stay as long as you like. Please let me or the other nurses know if you or your brother need anything."

"Are you leaving?" His eyes remained on his brother's face.

"Yes, but I'll be back on duty again tomorrow."

"Thank you for your help." He lifted his gaze to her now, laying his hand on her arm again. "Please, call me Kyle."

She nodded. "Goodnight, Kyle."

3

October, 1917

With only occasional wakefulness, two days passed before Chet fully realized his brother Kyle's presence. In less time though, Annie grew fond of the pair. Chet attempting a smile as he began recognizing Kyle's face, and Kyle endeavoring to assist in his older brother's care, built up a store of affection in Annie. These encounters, with their mixture of sadness and hope, chipped away at the numbness she'd welcomed months ago. They triggered a return to life in Annie.

Once Chet grew more alert, Kyle's residence in the bedside chair grew livelier. He entertained his brother with animated conversation. Every subject inevitably wound its way around to home, a farming village on the western coast of Ireland. One morning, a creek and the fish that eluded their hooks occupied their memories. Another day, Kyle caught Chet up on news of the cousins they used to visit outside Kilarney. Annie wordlessly gathered details as she worked, her mind soaking up the images painted by Kyle's stories: the creek frozen over each winter and perfect for ice skating; summer visits with the cousins spent cliff-diving or training rambunctious pups into hunting dogs. Whenever Chet had the energy, he brought Kyle to tears with impressions of their curmudgeon uncle or the village's absentminded priest.

To Annie's pleasure, eavesdropping couldn't be helped. Most of her working hours were spent in the main ward where Kyle's voice carried easily down the rows of beds. Customary small talk with the patients became frequently unnecessary. Many of the soldiers began telling their own tales to each other. A few would call Kyle over to their beds, eager to coax a story from him or to tell him a memory that surfaced after overhearing the Regan brothers' stories. To each soldier, Kyle was an obliging listener, and Annie saw the light of gratitude in the men's eyes.

Ten days after Kyle's arrival, Chet had improved remarkably. However, because he'd started from the brink of death he still had miles to go. The trauma and the days of recuperation had lined Chet's handsome face to look older than his twenty-seven years.

Annie was securing the last corner of a new bandage on Chet's leg when he held out a pocket-sized, leather bound book. She finished the bandage, then accepted the book, examining its worn cover.

"The Psalms," he informed her.

"You would like me to read them?"

"To me, yes." Chet slid himself into a sitting position and she moved his pillow between him and the wall. "I tend toward extremes. I finally don't need to sleep all day, but now I can't sleep much at all. When I needed to settle down in the trenches, I read the Psalms. Maybe they'll help again."

"Maybe they will." Sitting down in Kyle's usual chair since he had left for the night, Annie thumbed through the pages. "Should we start with the first one?"

"Oh, no. The Psalms are poetry, each enjoyed individually."

"I see."

"Tonight, I would like to hear the Thirty-Third Psalm."

She began slowly, letting her voice slip into the rhythm of the words. She felt the syllables swell in the final verses:

> "*For our heart shall rejoice in him,*
> *Because we have trusted in his holy name.*
> *Let thy mercy, O Lord, be upon us,*
> *According as we hope in thee.*"[1]

Chet closed his eyes. The muscles in his face and neck twitched as relaxation took hold. "Words to sleep by," he whispered when she finished.

She stood, placed the book on the chair and moved away.

"Thank you, Annie," he called after her. "We should do this again tomorrow night. Same time, same place?"

She turned in time to catch Chet's wink before he closed his eyes again and slipped down beneath the wool blanket. She shook her head, still mulling over what she read. She had heard the Bible numerous times at Sunday services, funerals, and weddings, but had not read it herself. Unlike Chet, the verses stirred rather than calmed her. Annie's emotions were like the exultant feeling she remembered having after a symphony concert in Boston.

Her enjoyment of the Psalms grew as Chet made the reading a nightly ritual. Other soldiers gathered on the edges of the nearest beds to listen. Eventually, Annie stopped waiting for Chet's invitation, and simply came to his bedside when her last rounds were finished and Kyle was gone for the night. She endured her lengthy shifts with greater energy, knowing they would end in such a manner.

More than a week after that first reading with Chet, dense clouds hung low around the hospital all day. When night arrived, the day's rain intensified to a roaring downpour. It hit the walls of the mansion at a sharp angle while the wind hunted out every crack it could whistle through.

Annie listened to the rain's percussion on the window panes. The day had been exhausting. A caravan of ambulances arrived at two A.M., bringing forty-three new patients. Several nurses, including Meg and herself, were called from their sleeping quarters to assist the night shift. Then during the course of the day, seventeen of the wounded died. It was an uncommonly high number for a single day at their small facility.

"You know, in the last war that one wouldn't have stood a chance," said a recovering senior officer, gesturing to the young private Annie tended to in the bed next to him.

"What war was that, sir?" she asked.

"Between the North and South. You are American, aren't you, miss?"

"Yes, I am." She studied the officer's face. His skin was ruddy and weather-beaten, his nose misshapen by old breaks. A white scar crossed his right eyebrow and a fresh bandage covered his left eye. "You couldn't have been more than a child during that war," Annie observed.

"Sixteen when I joined up. Mother cried for days, but I knew I'd survive," he asserted loudly.

"Well, she must have been relieved that you did."

"Might'a been, but she died birthing my sister while I was away."

She moved to the man's side, laying her hand on his shoulder. "Your mother would've been proud. I'm sure of it."

"Thank you, miss."

A gust of wind amplified the rain against the windows and she shivered.

"It'll pass, this storm," the officer assured her with command. "Everything does, miss."

Before she could respond, the unconscious patient she'd stepped away from began thrashing, throwing the blanket off his body and exposing multiple sutures and bandages. He jerked himself in one direction, then the other. His mouth opened and closed in a futile effort to cry out.

To protect the soldier, Annie held him down against the mattress with all the force she could muster. Her hands were no match for the soldier's frenzied strength.

"He's hallucinating, miss. I've seen it plenty of times. Just wait it out with him."

She glanced at the senior officer. "He'll hurt himself even more. I can't keep him on the bed."

The officer tried standing up but sunk back onto his bed. His hand went to the wound around his eye. "I'm sorry, miss. I'm not yet steady on my feet."

Glancing up and down the ward for another nurse, everyone appeared to be with the more critical patients in the surgical area where, incidentally, the sedatives were kept as well. Her mind raced. *Just keep him in the bed. Don't let him fall.* Mere minutes felt tripled as the strength drained from her muscles.

The soldier's fit went on, but Annie realized he was being held firmly within the borders of the bed. She let go. With arms shaking at her sides, she looked up to see Kyle Regan on the opposite side of the bed. She hadn't heard him sprint across the ward, nor noticed his presence until he draped his upper body across the bed's width to straddle the patient, his hands gripping each side of the mattress.

He looked her over. "Did he hurt you, Annie?"

She shook her head.

"Good. Not that he would have meant to."

The soldier's face was contorted in pain. His eyes opened, filled with terror, then snapped shut again.

"Talk to him, Annie," Kyle directed.

At the head of the bed, she leaned near the man. "You're safe and being taken care of. No one is going to hurt you here. Breathe. Take a deep breath and open your eyes." She heard the tremulous breaths inhaled and released. "Go ahead, you're safe. You can open your eyes."

The soldier's muscles relinquished their fight. Kyle rose from his position, keeping one hand on the man's chest, and nodded at her to continue. After a few more whispered entreaties the soldier opened his eyes. They darted frantically around the room before fixing on Kyle.

"She's right, you're safe," Kyle confirmed. His hand remained on the soldier's chest, which rose and fell rapidly.

"Can you tell me your name?" Annie asked.

The answer slipped out with one of the breaths, "John Kessel."

She stood but bent close to his face. "John, I'm Annie. I'm a nurse. You're in the hospital. Do you remember why you're here?"

Private Kessel's eyes squeezed shut again while he nodded.

"Good, then you know you were hurt. You need to let us take care of you."

His face turned from Annie to Kyle with a questioning look.

"I'm Kyle." He smiled.

Annie winced when she relaxed her fists. Nail marks were visible in her palms. The cloth bandage securing Private Kessel's injured ankle had loosened so she turned her attention to rewrapping the foot.

"My mouth's awfully dry. Could I have some water?" Private Kessel spoke up in an English drawl.

"Absolutely. I'll be back in a minute."

She walked from the ward with haste. The echo of Kyle's shoes on the tiled floor didn't register until she turned a corner and Kyle's height filled her peripheral view. She stopped until he caught up. When they reached the kitchen, Kyle picked up a glass as she did the same. He filled it at the sink and traded her for the empty one she held.

"It's for you," he said.

"Oh, thank you. I appreciate it."

He leaned against the porcelain sink, waiting as she sipped the cool water. It mercifully soothed her dry throat as she watched Kyle over the rim of the glass. The concern he'd shown at Private Kessel's bedside still creased his brow. The light drumming of his fingertips on the edge of the sink calmed the pace of her thoughts.

"I'm sorry I didn't help sooner. I wasn't facing you and that patient, but Chet noticed it."

She shook her head, wondering at the apology. "You came just in time. I couldn't have kept him on the bed any longer."

"I'm glad to help, but I think you could have continued. Necessity would have made you strong enough."

She doubted Kyle's claim but didn't argue. Pointing to the glass of water he held, she said, "I better bring that to him."

"Of course." Kyle handed the glass to Annie and followed her out of the kitchen. Once they entered the ward, he returned to Chet's bed.

She was glad to see the older American officer sitting up, telling a story to Private Kessel. She gave the glass of water to the private and he squeezed her hand. The officer prattled on, keeping the young man occupied while she finished wrapping his foot. Private Kessel appeared relaxed now, but Annie told him to let her know if he had trouble sleeping. She had a hunch he would need a sedative to get any rest tonight.

At the close of Annie's twenty-hour shift, she decided to sneak out before Chet could catch her for a reading. She found there was no need to sneak though. Chet was still deep in conversation with Kyle.

Lingering in the doorway of the ward, Annie reflected on the differences between the brothers. Kyle had his back to her. She pictured his face at the same time as she observed Chet's.

Chet was the more handsome of the two. Despite the gauze wrapped tightly around his fragile head wound, his dark hair lay smooth and shining above a face worthy of the silver screen: defined cheekbones, chiseled jaw, and of course, those striking eyes. Chet stood a couple inches shorter than Kyle, or would when he could stand again. Even after weeks in bed, it was apparent that he was blessed with an athletic physique. Then there was his easygoing charm that fit seamlessly with his appearance. It was common to hear Chet speak to a nurse with flirtation in his voice, and he always had a ready joke when conversing with other soldiers.

On the other hand, subtlety characterized Kyle's best traits and his looks. He carried his height and rugged build effortlessly. She'd noticed at their first meeting the strength of his upper body and was once again thankful for it when he restrained Private Kessel today. The waves in Kyle's dark hair were thick and looked soft. And when he smiled...she felt a smile come to her lips at the thought. Kyle's smile was friendly and wholehearted. It reached her like warm sunlight. Annie had the impression that he reserved that smile, and his resonant laugh, for moments that truly deserved them.

Kyle conversed carefully, choosing his words well. When he was the listener in a discussion, he appeared determined not to miss a word the other person said. In fact, everything from his mannerisms and courtesy to his warm, friendly interactions testified to his goodness.

Annie had given little thought to Kyle's life prior to arriving in France and now had a strong urge to ask what he'd set aside to come to Chet. Still, her craving for sleep prevailed. She left the shadow of the doorway and bundled up against the wind and rain, hurrying along the path to the dormitory.

4

September, 2000, 83 years later

Laurel found herself leaned forward, intently listening. She'd planted her feet on the floor, elbows on her knees, and chin in her palms.

"You haven't touched your tea, Laurel," Grandma Annie pointed out.

Laurel had forgotten the mug sitting on the bedside table. She lifted it toward her lips, inhaling its soothing scent before setting it back down without a taste. "It's cold now."

"What are you thinking, dear?" Grandma Annie asked with a small smile.

Laurel tried hard to picture her great-grandmother in that hospital ward. The image came out black and white with fuzzy edges on the faces and furniture.

"How did you handle it all, Grandma?" she eventually asked. "I mean, everything you experienced as a nurse." She doubted she could have endured it. Even visiting Grandma Annie these past months had been a struggle at times. There was no avoiding the older woman's gradual deterioration. Even so, the visits – the time in her great-grandmother's presence – had become an essential part of her weeks.

"I think Kyle was right. Necessity brings out strength," Grandma Annie said as she handed her empty mug to Laurel. "The prospect of adventure may have prompted me to cross the ocean to be a nurse, but necessity became my motivation once I arrived. I saw how much I was needed."

"Well, I'm not sure I could have done it."

"Of course you could have," Grandma Annie answered quickly. "Laurie Bean, you're the most self-sufficient person of our four generations. And you can match your mother's strong will any day."

"I can't deny the strong-willed part," Laurel admitted with a self-conscious smile. "But the rest of it is more show than anything else."

"As it is with most of us." Grandma Annie shook her head. "Don't underestimate yourself."

Uninterested in her cold tea, she brought their cups into the kitchen then returned to the bedroom. "Are you tired, Grandma? It's almost nine."

"Not at all, Laurel. All this reminiscing has wakened me."

"Well, your doctor won't be happy if I don't let you get enough rest."

Grandma Annie waved her hands, scowling. "That doctor ought to know a woman will sleep when she's good and tired. Besides, I'll have all day tomorrow to nap."

Laurel laughed under her breath, "All right, I'm not ready to stop hearing your story anyway."

Grandma Annie nodded, her smile lifting her wrinkled cheeks.

"Did you ever find out what Kyle left behind in Ireland to come to France?" she asked.

"Yes, but not right away. It took some time before I felt I knew him well enough to ask."

October, 1917, *83 years earlier*

In her exhaustion following her 20-hour shift, Annie forgot to draw the curtain closed in her bedroom. She woke reluctantly when the sun found a path through the dissipating rain clouds. Breakfast hours were nearly over and the trails were bound to be nothing but mud, so Annie stayed in her room until her shift began. She combed her hair out of its tousled braid, noticing how long it had become. It reached halfway down her back, uneven from no proper trimming since she left Boston. She pictured herself a year ago with a light swipe of rouge on the apples of her cheeks, rosy lipstick, and black hair shining with the ends curled. The remembered image felt distant and surreal.

She bathed in the nurses' shared bathroom. When she returned to her room, her foot nearly slipped when it kicked two envelopes across the floor. One was thin with tight printing, the other thicker and addressed in wide, feminine writing. She scooped both into her hands and plopped happily onto her bed.

She opened the thicker envelope first. It was from her sister-in-law Joanna and included two colorful drawings from her nephew. George was only three and she couldn't be sure what his pictures portrayed, but she treasured them. One had the appearance of a boat with large red sails. The other was a collection colorful circles in no particular pattern. Joanna's enclosed letter was lengthy.

> *Annie,*
>
> *I do hope you are well and safe. George asked that I send these to you. He is fascinated by colors and drawing, spending all his indoor playtime at the table with his crayons. I tried to ask for an explanation of the picture with the circles, but he only said he wanted to send you all his colors.*
>
> *Your mother and I have hosted several luncheons for the Red Cross. Mrs. Thompson attended the most recent one with her sister, visiting from Atlanta. What a storyteller that woman is....*

The letter went on with an abundance of local gossip, including a full description of the wedding of a former classmate.

> *Annie, we must be sure not to have quite so many flowers at your wedding. They could barely stand at the altar without disrupting the arrangements of roses.*

Joanna finished by sending regards from her husband, Annie's brother, Lee. Annie shook her head, realizing she had yet to imagine how the church would be decorated for her wedding. She spread George's drawings in front of her on the quilt and tried to picture how much the dear boy had likely grown since she last saw him.

Laying her head on her sun-warmed pillow, she reached for the second letter with a pang of guilt. She hadn't written to her fiancé Samuel in two weeks. When she arrived in France, she began a habit of two letters each week, one to her family and the other to Samuel. Lately, it was an effort to write one in as much time. Though the mail delivery was inconsistent, the postmarks told her that Samuel wrote her weekly without fail.

She felt the glue give way to the pressure of her index finger sliding beneath the flap of the envelope. Samuel's printing stood in precise rows on the bank's stationery. She tried to summon Samuel's voice with the first words of the letter. She willed the familiar flip in her stomach to come. His voice was elusive, and her stomach was still. She bit her lip as she began to read.

The first paragraphs varied little from his previous letters: assurances of the bank's thriving business, greetings from a few mutual acquaintances, and comments on recent social engagements. It then went on:

> *On Saturday last, I brought your nephew to the harbor. He was in such an excitement over the colors of the leaves that I feared he would miss what we actually came for. An immense merchant schooner, the "Glory of Portugal," had arrived in the harbor and the townspeople were gathered in a large celebration. The schooner docked in the harbor unscathed, despite fears of the Germans' unforgivable attacks on merchant and passenger ships. Well, the sight of that ship did capture George's attention once he looked away from the trees.*

I do wish you would return home, An-nie. I know I've asked you before, but ha-ven't you had your fill of this adventure? I don't know why you insist on remaining. Surely you could be released by now and allowed to return to your responsibilities. Your mother insists I am right in suggesting this.

Until I see you again, I remain yours devotedly,

Samuel

Annie's fingers squeezed into a fist, crumpling one edge of the paper. Adventure? Released? Did he suspect her of being on holiday in France? Could he not see that she was needed here? Doing essential work? She gave the letter a second reading and then wished she hadn't. Her consideration of exactly what responsibilities she might be neglecting at home was interrupted by a soft knock at the door.

"Come in," she called.

Meg poked her face into the room. "Oh good, I was afraid you'd still be sleeping." She seated herself on the bed, picking up George's drawings. "Are these from your nephew?"

Annie nodded.

"Adorable!" Meg's face lit up. "That means mail arrived."

"I think they brought it yesterday. I just didn't find mine until this morning," said Annie, pausing to glance at the grandfather clock in the hallway. "Aren't you on duty, Meg? Do they need me to start early?"

Meg tucked a stray curl behind her ear. "No, I slipped away for a minute. I needed fresh stockings. Mine were soaked through by the time I walked from the dormitory this morning. I didn't think the rain would ever end. Dr. LaCroix said not to call you in. He said to let last night's girls get some extra rest. Even so, if you wanted to start early, we could certainly use the help. I don't know where we'll put new patients if any arrive in the next couple of days. Hopefully some of the units' officers will come for transfers and discharges.

There are several who could travel away from the front to finish healing up."

"Have you changed your stockings yet, Meg?" Annie interrupted the rapid chatter.

"Right!" Meg laughed, "I better do that and get back."

She rose to leave then spoke again from the doorway, "Chet asked after you. He was pouting that you left last night without reading to him. Honestly, Annie, you've enchanted that poor man."

"Really, Meg," she scoffed but her friend was already halfway to her own room.

Slipping her shoes on, she decided to volunteer a couple hours before her shift began at noon. The letters lay open on the bed and her eyes blurred with tears as she thought of her nephew remembering her while he colored his pictures. She didn't linger when her glance moved to Samuel's letter. Instead she strode from the room, pushing his comments to the back of her mind.

A transport did arrive in the afternoon for transfers and discharges. Some soldiers were relieved to be sent closer to home to finish recovering, while others did their best to convince the superior officers that they were well enough to return to the front lines. Medals of honor and courage were awarded with small ceremony. To those unlikely to recover, the medals were preemptive memorials pinned to their chests; something meaningful to send to the family with the letter of condolence.

With the transport's departure, a dozen beds were reopened and ready to be sterilized. Annie pulled a wide basket behind her as she made quick work of stripping the sheets.

"He sure put up a fight," Private John Kessel said from his reclined position on his bed.

The empty bed she was working on had been occupied by the weathered American officer she met the day before.

"Did he?" she asked as she disinfected the bed frame.

"Yes, ma'am," the youthful British soldier answered. "They brought him one of those silver stars you Americans have, and congratulated him on his years of soldiering. He never even said a word of thanks. Just argued with the colonel, saying they were wasting a man with plenty of years left in him."

"I'm surprised they sent him home."

"Doctor said he wouldn't see out of that left eye anymore. Apparently he was already half blind in the other eye from an old injury."

"Oh, that is too bad." She empathized with the man's dismay. "I doubt he'll know what to do with himself apart from the army."

"You're likely right about that. Said he would rather have died in the trenches," Private Kessel went on. "Before he left, he gave me a loud lecture. Told me to get back out there and kill a few extra for him. Also said to bid you goodbye, ma'am, and tell you he was grateful for your kindness."

Annie smiled and thanked Private Kessel. Her fiancé's request for her to return home flickered through her mind as she moved on. *No, Samuel, I cannot be released yet.* Her chin lifted a little higher and she began working in earnest on the next empty bed.

5

October, 1917

Wednesday was errand day so Annie and Meg set out to walk the dirt road into the village for supplies. Their list included bread, eggs, dried pork, and pencils, as well as the precise quantities needed. The staff at the market's supply counter would precisely measure those quantities.

"What does your family think of you being a nurse over here? Did they mind you leaving?" Annie asked Meg as they walked the road together.

Meg didn't answer immediately.

"Meg?"

She was about to repeat herself when Meg looked up from the grocery list with a bright smile.

"Mother and Father are great," Meg said, nodding her head. "Really supportive. They worry, of course, but they were excited when I told them I was going. My father's family came from France. That's how I know some of the language, and he's proud that I'm here."

"That's wonderful."

"I had a letter from Father this week, in fact. He's always so encouraging."

They walked in silence for a few minutes. Annie was in no mood to match Meg's eager pace, so she lagged behind for the last quarter mile. The dirt road transitioned to rough cobblestone at the edge of the village. They had the road to themselves. Most of the residents were elsewhere now with the men fighting and the families removed to safer regions. A few dozen people remained: the man who ran the market store, a woman who owned the café, the priest of Saint Genevieve parish, and others who decided they would rather be in danger at home than be safe in a strange place. Dr. LaCroix liked to call them les fidèles. Annie dubbed them the stalwarts.

It was not the villagers who filled her thoughts now, but her family, and particularly Samuel. She'd begun to evaluate her anger over Samuel's letter. He suggested she return to Boston in nearly every letter he wrote. The particular way it infuriated her this time puzzled her.

In the first months of her absence, his words worked to motivate her. Annie tackled her work energetically in those early days, determined to prove her worth. Over time, her steady dedication to the work did not wane, but her fervor for convincing her loved ones did. In off-duty hours, loneliness threatened to take hold.

"My parents aren't like yours," Annie said to Meg as they entered the market and scanned the stacks of goods. "Mother spends all her spare time volunteering for Red Cross functions, but she couldn't comprehend why I would leave home to help the war effort."

"What about your father?"

She paused in her perusal of the shelves.

"Daddy never said if he approved or not. He barely said anything. I took it that he was mad, but I could be wrong."

"Why would he be mad?" Meg called from the next aisle.

Annie caught up to her and answered, "Maybe for interrupting Mother's perfectly laid plans, disrupting his impeccably run household. Mostly I assumed he was angry that the wedding would be postponed. Postponement never looks respectable."

"Yes, respectability is a prized possession in my family as well." Meg said, with a sharp tone that she dropped with her next question. "Has your father written at all? Told you to come back home?"

"Daddy usually just sends his love with Mother's letters. Asking me to come home has become Samuel's job."

"It must be sweet to be missed."

"It's hardly sweet," Annie said as she shook her head and continued, "Samuel has actually talked with my mother about it. I can picture them discussing me like I'm a runaway child."

"I'm sure they don't think of you that way," Meg argued.

They signed for the rations and supplies and secured the bags in their arms.

Meg returned to the topic as they stepped out of the store. She asked, "Have you ever explained what it's like here, Annie? Have you told Samuel the details of your work?"

"I've told him," she said, "but he's not hearing me. If he was, he would have no doubt that we are needed over here."

Meg opened her mouth to reply only to close it as Kyle Regan stepped into the road alongside them. He relieved each of them of a sack of goods, a warm smile lighting up his face.

"I'm guessing we're headed in the same direction. Do you mind if I join you?"

"Certainly not. Thank you so much. Those potatoes are heavy," Meg gushed.

"You're welcome." Kyle turned to Annie, but she avoided his eyes. "I hope I'm not interrupting."

"No, you're not interrupting at all. We were just returning with groceries for Madame Adele, our cook," Annie replied, hoping he hadn't overheard her perturbed declarations.

The trio walked together, silent but for the soft crunch of dirt and gravel beneath their feet. Meg eventually broke the quiet with a happy remark on how much snow Toronto would be expecting next month. She described her hometown's tradition of skating on wide, frozen stretches of the river running through the city.

Kyle asked a few questions about Canadian winters.

"Where are you coming from, Kyle?" Annie inquired at an eventual pause.

"From La Porte Rouge." His Irish lilt faltered over the pronunciation. "The Red Door. It's the café across from the market. A couple of nights ago, I checked out of the inn and leased a room above the café. Madame Chappelle, the woman who runs it and owns the rooms upstairs, agreed to let me pay by the week."

"So, you're staying a while longer?" Meg tilted her head to look up at him.

"I'll stay until Chet is well enough to return home with me."

Annie lifted her eyes from the road.

"That's kind of you. I'm sure Chet appreciates it."

Kyle shook his head.

"Truthfully, I've been meaning to thank you, Annie, for the care you've given my brother." He shifted the bags in his arms. "Taking the time to read to him each night seems to encourage him forward."

"I'm grateful to hear that," she said.

Annie caught Meg smirking and hoped her friend would keep her teasing thoughts to herself.

They rounded a bend that brought the LaCroix property into full view. From the road, the estate projected dignity and wealth. The ground beneath the gray stone mansion had been built up to raise the house above the surrounding land. Long, evenly spaced windows lined the width of the mansion along the upper and lower floors. The lower row's pattern was accented by ornate bow windows on each side of the front entrance. Stone pillars atop the front steps framed the heavy, black door.

Groomed hedges, seven feet tall, stretched along the sides and rear of the main house, with one hedged wall opening into a grove of trees and flowering shrubs. The gardens had been thick with blossoms in the spring, but now the trees stood starkly empty at autumn's culmination. Waist-high shrubs marked out the gravel path to the servants' quarters that were now the nurses' dormitory: a simple, two-story structure enhanced by front pillars and a black door that paired it with the mansion. This dormitory building stood behind the southeast corner of the main house and was backed by towering pines at the edge of the hunting grounds.

Annie and her companions squinted in the brilliant sun as they reached the front drive. A smile pulled at her lips. Something in the wind hinted at her beloved ocean, and home. She could almost hear the waves from somewhere beyond the trees. With a deep, slow breath, she imagined a taste of salt in the air.

"All things considered, it really is a beautiful day," she murmured.

Kyle and Meg glanced her way. About to share her thoughts, Annie instead halted and cried out. She discarded her parcels on the ground to run up the driveway, Kyle close behind her.

Private John Kessel made an unsteady descent on the front steps of the mansion. A crutch was tucked beneath his left shoulder and he kept most of his weight off the broken ankle. His right arm clutched his side as he flinched with each step. The four stone steps were steep with no railing for support. He managed not to collapse until he reached the bottom and stepped over to a patch of grass. Annie watched helplessly as he mistakenly stepped forward on his left foot instead of leaning on the crutch. His leg buckled and he crumpled to the ground.

When Meg caught up, Annie directed her to fetch Dr. LaCroix and asked Kyle to take care of the bags they'd left at the bottom of the driveway. She knelt on the grass next to Private Kessel to wait.

"I could carry him in," Kyle offered.

"It's safer to wait for the stretcher. When the doctor brings it, you can help carry him."

Annie turned to Private Kessel. The color was draining from his cheeks yet a shaky smile appeared when he looked up at her.

"Hadn't seen the sun in a while." The soldier's chuckle sounded like a broken cough. "I could see it through the windows. I thought it might be warmer out here. I suppose it's just for looks this time of year."

"Who gave you the crutch?"

"I swiped it." His smile widened. "Don't be mad. I'll put it back."

She tried to smile in return. "Shame on you."

He closed his eyes, sucking in the fresh air with rapid breaths. His body relaxed a bit as he stretched his arms beside him on the grass. She gasped when she looked at his side. Blood slowly spread down his cotton shirt as the underlying bandages failed to contain it. She hesitated only a moment before placing her hand firmly against the wound.

"Ow!" Private Kessel's eyes flew open, bulging with pain and surprise. "What are you doing?"

"You have some bleeding and I need to apply pressure to the wound. I don't know what you were thinking," she scolded him. "You are in no condition to be out of bed."

Annie refused to meet his eyes, hoping he couldn't see the fear in hers.

She softened her tone, "We'll need to reset that broken foot and check all of your bandages."

Private Kessel's face continued to lose color while her hand was red with blood, useless to stave the flow. Dr. LaCroix, Meg, and another nurse arrived with a stretcher. The doctor frowned in acknowledgment when Annie lifted her hand slightly from the wound.

He placed his hand over hers. "Keep it there."

Kyle and Dr. LaCroix loaded Private Kessel onto the stretcher, doing their best to move him both quickly and gently through the ward to a surgical table. The doctor ignored the ankle for the time being, stripping the soldier's shirt and the soaked bandages from his torso.

Annie moved to the head of the steel table where she was instructed to keep Private Kessel awake. His eyes were glazed, failing to focus as he clung to the edge of consciousness. He nodded as Annie reassured him that Dr. LaCroix was fixing everything and he'd be on the mend again soon.

Fear appeared to maintain a resilient hold though. Annie saw the same panic in his roaming eyes as when he was delirious with flashbacks. He began mumbling incoherently and he seemed paralyzed by the surrounding commotion.

"What's the first thing you'll do when you get home, John?" She couldn't keep the tremor out of her voice as she tried to focus his attention on her. "You're from England, right?"

He managed half a nod.

"I've never been to England. Are you from London?"

No response.

"I'll bet you're from the country; some place with a lot of open land and friendly people."

Another effort to nod.

"That must be wonderful."

The distraction was working. Private Kessel's eyes stopped their frantic darting around the room. He stared at the ceiling as she made guesses about his home and family. When she asked about a girl waiting for him, he managed a small smile that nearly dismantled her fragile grip on her emotions.

Two worrisome hours later, Dr. LaCroix didn't hide his relief as he finished the sutures and taped a wide square of gauze over the wound.

"The doctor's finished," Annie told Private Kessel. "You've made it through."

Annie trembled with adrenaline and relief. Another nurse, Nora, had covered the ward for Annie during the surgery and offered to stay a while longer if Annie needed to rest. She accepted the offer, trudging to her room after Private Kessel was settled in his bed. She smiled to herself as the experienced American officer's prophetic words came back to her. That one wouldn't have stood a chance.

Her heart swelled with pride. In her mind, she began a letter to Samuel, detailing Private Kessel's ordeal and all they were able to do to preserve his life. Surely such details would help Samuel understand why she stayed in France.

For now, she needed a nap. The letter would wait.

6

October, 1917

Annie awoke from her nap disoriented. She rubbed her eyes to see the hall clock which read 5:30. Three hours had passed since she left the hospital. Tossing the quilt aside, she twisted her braid into a fat bun and headed back for the remainder of her shift.

The sun was nearly set and a mixture of aromas floated from the kitchen where Madame Adele prepared her next masterpiece. Annie made a mental note to ask Kyle if the morning's groceries were ever delivered to the cook.

Nora was glad to see Annie return and informed her of a few changes with the patients.

"You should check on Private Kessel," Nora added after untying her apron.

Annie looked at the other nurse warily. "Did he ask for me?"

"He may have, I don't know. Chet Regan's brother has been with him since the surgery."

Her curiosity turned to trepidation when Nora avoided her eyes. She hesitated, turning in every direction before pointing her feet toward the kitchen.

Madame Adele was at the stove, her broad shoulders hunched over a steaming kettle. Several strands of gray hair escaped the red scarf around her head. Annie giggled when the woman jumped at the tap on her arm.

"Bonté divine! Goodness gracious!" Madame Adele wiped perspiration from her face with a handkerchief. "Mademoiselle, you are sneaky."

"I'm sorry," Annie apologized with another laugh. "What are you stirring there?"

"C'est une soupe de pomme de terre...ah, potato soup."

"It smells delicious."

"You taste?" Madame Adele's eyebrows rose in two little hills, rolling her forehead into soft folds.

"Yes, please." Annie sipped from the offered spoon of hot soup. It tasted even better than it smelled. "Thank you. You do great things with the little you have to work with. I came to check on the groceries. Did you get them?"

"Gro-cer-ies?" The French cook struggled with the syllables.

"The food." Annie gestured as if her hands could translate. "The bags of food, did Kyle bring them to you?"

Madame Adele nodded vigorously, "Oui, Monsieur Regan, he bring them."

Annie then noticed the partially unpacked sacks on the butcher block counter.

"Monsieur Regan is a kind boy, très gentil."

"Yes, he is."

The warmth in her cheeks brought on by the woman's comment unsettled Annie.

"And handsome," Madame Adele added with a wink. "Mais, he is sérieux. He look so sad for the poor soldier."

"I'm sorry, but I need to go," said Annie trying to regain her composure. "I'm on duty."

Her emotions were a brick on her chest. She rushed from the kitchen, leaving Madame Adele to her soup.

Grabbing an apron from the closet, Annie had it tied on by the time she reached the main ward. Kyle was at Private Kessel's bedside. He'd carried his chair over along with a second chair empty next to him. She lowered herself into that second chair. Kyle's eyes were on Annie but she focused on the patient in the bed, assessing Private Kessel with a trained eye.

Private Kessel was unconscious. Sweat saturated his hairline, running down his neck onto the pillow. Despite this, he shivered without interruption, reminding Annie of a bathed child waiting for a towel. She lifted his hand and squeezed his palm. Private Kessel didn't respond. His fingers, clammy and cold, remained limp.

She laid Private Kessel's hand back on the sheet and turned to Kyle. "When did this start?" she whispered.

"An hour ago."

"And before that?"

"He was awake; in a lot of pain but awake. He had quite a few lucid moments."

"But that was an hour ago?" she asked, leaning back against the chair, setting her mouth in a frown.

Kyle nodded.

"We saved him." The words stung her ears.

Kyle ran a hand down the back of his head. The action loosened his hair, which had grown the last few weeks into short waves over the edges of his ears and forehead. The extra length lent softness to his face.

Her green eyes burned with the effort not to cry. "I'm going to speak with the doctor."

Marching away from Private Kessel's bedside, she wanted to sob, to shout at someone for not waking her when his condition worsened. How foolish she felt for supposing they had worked a miracle for their patient.

She shook her head, shoving aside all these thoughts before approaching Dr. LaCroix. He was restocking the surgical supplies, so she picked up a box to help.

"What went wrong, sir, with Private Kessel?"

"Ah, that was a difficult one," Dr. LaCroix said, his tone full of regret. "I'm afraid it was beyond repair."

"Even with the surgery? I thought you stopped the bleeding."

"I did, at least temporarily. He'd already bled so much internally and externally, and it may have begun internally again. It's nearly impossible to know for certain."

"If the bleeding has restarted, you could stop it again," Annie replied with raw desperation.

"No, Nurse Walcott, we cannot," Dr. LaCroix said gently. "Cutting him again would only kill him more quickly."

Annie emptied the rest of her supply box onto the shelves. With a weary heart she returned to her rounds in the main ward. She found the checklist of wound dressings and picked up where Nora had left off. The hours dragged on in a slow march. During medication rounds, she approached Private Kessel's bed. Kyle asked if he could do anything for her.

"No, thank you." She would not risk losing her composure by meeting his eyes.

She ended the night with her usual reading with Chet. The words of Psalm Sixty-Nine rang in her ears.

Let not the waterflood overflow me,
neither let the deep swallow me up,
and let not the pit shut her mouth upon me.
Hear me, O Lord;
for thy lovingkindness is good:
turn unto me according to the multitude
of thy tender mercies.[2]

Annie's eyes fell on Kyle's back. He had not left Private Kessel's side, not even for dinner with Chet.

"He'll stay there until you ask him to go," Chet said, following her gaze.

"Why?"

He shrugged. "That's Kyle. Once he starts to care, he doesn't stop."

"He must be a wonderful brother to you," she commented absently.

"I have my good points too." Chet did his best to look offended. "Well, at least we balance each other out. That might be the truer way to put it."

Annie nodded, knowing she ought to laugh, then she bid Chet goodnight.

Sleep was held at bay by every creak on the stairs, each drip of a faucet in the corner bathroom, and low voices occasionally rising from the parlor below. The boom of artillery took its turn next, cracking the quiet of her bedroom from miles away. Tension crept up Annie's back as she lay flat on her little bed in the darkness. When the cacophony of shots subsided, a chorus of crows sounded from the shelter of the pines behind the dormitory. Annie rolled out of bed and opened her door just enough to see the clock. 1:25. She could hear the procession of the seconds: tick, tock, tick, tock, tick, tock.

Annie ran her hand along the wall to find the switch for her room's lamp. Dim as it was, her eyes still squinted at the sudden light. She changed from her pajamas into a skirt and blouse then wrapped herself in a long, wool shawl.

The front door moaned into the hollow silence of the dormitory. Outside, the air was still; no wind from any direction. Annie's eyes were on the woods as she walked. The pines reached until their peaks blended with the blackness of the sky. The crows' incessant calls were the only proof of their presence in the boughs.

Back inside, she paused in the foyer, cupping her gloved hands to catch the warmth of her breath. The lamps lining the walls of the main ward were dimmed to leave only enough light to safely walk the aisles between the beds.

A few patients were awake. "Couldn't sleep either?" one whispered.

Annie shook her head.

Kyle sat exactly as she had left him. His long legs were stretched out until his feet were hidden beneath Private Kessel's bed. Back straight, fingers tapping his thigh; exhaustion was evident in his face. Annie saw his lips moving. He seemed wholly occupied by words she couldn't hear but her arrival broke his concentration. Kyle gazed up at her. Puzzlement, then relief, and lastly sadness flickered in turn across his features.

"What were you doing?"

"Praying."

His answer did not surprise her. Annie sat in the other chair and folded her hands in her lap. "Has there been any change?"

"He isn't shivering."

So, he stopped fighting the fever.

49

Kyle stretched his arms over his head and a yawn escaped.

"There's no reason for you to stay. You might as well have some sleep tonight."

He shook his head. "If I go now, I'll wake Madame Chappelle at the café. No, I'll stay."

"The ward has empty cots."

"Thank you."

Kyle didn't move though, and she had no wish for him to go. She kept her focus on Private Kessel while Kyle looked over the long room.

The main ward was formerly the ballroom of the mansion and she surmised its grandeur from the remaining hints of beauty. The once gleaming hardwood floor, now scuffed and stained, was hardly visible anymore with three rows of metal beds lining the length of the room. However, the marble walls were still beautiful, especially when the sun came through the many window panes. Each long, narrow window was framed by white stone carved in intricate patterns of rosettes and fleurs-de-lis.

"Parties here must have been quite something." Kyle's blue eyes traveled up to the arched marble ceiling.

"I've wondered about them sometimes. Did balls go out of fashion long ago, or did grand parties and dances take place up until the war?"

"Can't you just hear the string quartet playing the waltzes?"

They smiled at each other's shadowed faces.

She added to his building the scene, "The women in their finest gowns and the couples dancing."

"The men talking politics and land prospects. Same things they talk about at the pub."

"Exactly."

"You've been to parties like these?"

She nodded. "I have. In books, they're fun. In real life they're tedious and sometimes boring."

"Molly, my niece, loves to dress up in her mum's old dresses. Is at least that part fun?"

"Dressing up?" She recalled the last dinner party she attended with Samuel. Hosted by the bank's president, they were joined by the board of directors and their wives. Not only had the conversation nearly put her to sleep, the peach silk gown she wore required a corset, only tolerably comfortable if she were standing up and holding still.

"No," she answered finally. "It's a lot of work and the dresses can be rather uncomfortable."

Nora and another nurse passed them as they checked on their resting patients. Somewhere in an upstairs room, a clock struck the two o'clock hour.

"It's only eight at night back home." Her voice broke into the silence that had settled around them. "No matter how long I'm here, that thought is odd to me. It is as if I've already lived a time that my family has yet to see."

"And on the ship home, you'll gradually relive that time. I know a good number of people who might envy that opportunity," Kyle mused.

"Only if they could pick the day to relive," she said. The notion intrigued her. "What day would you choose?"

Kyle's brows drew together. He inhaled, closing his eyes. When he slowly exhaled, she saw his shoulders relax against the chair.

"I know the exact day. Would've been before my ninth birthday because Nana, my grandmother, was still alive. Nana volunteered that year to provide the bread for our church's annual festival. She decided she needed an assistant and she chose me." Kyle rubbed the back of his neck, a contented smile on his face. "You didn't say no to my grandmother, although I tried. Spent an entire day, from dawn until past my bedtime, in that hot kitchen with her. She had me kneading the dough for loaf after loaf. In spite of myself, I enjoyed it!"

His choice of day and experience brought a smile to Annie's face.

"I'd gone to her house that morning planning to be angry the entire day. I think I was most angry with my baby sister for not being old enough to help yet," he added. "Turned out, I had more fun

51

and laughed more with Nana that day than I ever did with any of my friends. My Nana was all wisdom and wit.

"And she could sing," Kyle added, throwing his hands in the air. He lowered his voice again when a nurse gave him a sharp look. "She taught me all her favorite songs that day. I didn't want her to ever stop singing. I would love to live that day again, sing, knead, and eat the bread."

His tale formed a delightful image in her mind. Kyle as an eight-year-old boy eluded her though. She was left picturing him in his grandmother's kitchen as a grown man. Her eyes fell on his hands, folded now against his stomach. She pictured them working the dough in strong, slow movements.

"Somehow that day seems like another lifetime."

The resignation in his voice saddened her.

"What day would you relive?" Kyle turned to her.

The day I agreed to marry Samuel. Annie's hand flew to her mouth. She kept it there until she was certain she had spoken the words only in her mind. With Kyle's eyes on her, she struggled to think of another answer. "I... I'm not sure."

"Then the best must be still to come."

Annie nodded, anxious to change topics.

They soon did and she relaxed once again. The two kept their vigil, the conversation running on in spurts and lulls as they watched over the soldier lying silently before them.

7

September, 2000, *83 years later*

"It was another two hours before Private Kessel died." Grandma Annie's voice trembled. "He didn't wake at all."

Laurel fidgeted with a lavender thread on the hem of her shirt. Several questions ticked across her mind and she didn't know which to ask first. Before she could choose, she caught her great-grandmother yawning.

"I guess I am tired," Grandma Annie admitted. "What time does it say?"

"10:05." Laurel arched her back in a stretch then rose from the rocking chair. She joked, "Now it's past my bedtime."

Grandma Annie winked. "Yes, Laurie Bean, shame on you. Get yourself home and go straight to bed."

Laurel kissed Grandma Annie's cheek and promised to return the next day to continue where they left off. "I will have the hardest time waiting to hear more! But I won't be here until after seven tomorrow, as I have an appointment with clients after work. Is that too late to come?"

"Absolutely not. We'll have another late evening and really make that doctor worry."

Grandma Annie visited the restroom and then slipped down beneath the blankets as Laurel settled her into bed.

Laurel stole a backward glance as she left. The elderly woman's height was slightly diminished with age, but her long legs still reached the footboard. Her thin arms held the quilt tightly around her chest. Laurel thought she saw a smile as her great-grandmother closed her eyes.

Laurel laughed to herself, remembering her friend Connor's words when he'd stopped by her apartment before she left for

Grandma Annie's tonight. She'd told him she intended to ask about her great-grandfather during this visit. Her longtime friend didn't hide his doubt, pointing out that she'd been resolved to do so plenty of times with no result. She had shooed him out the door and down the flight of stairs to the parking lot. He seemed reluctant to leave. She realized this now, but between the rain and her desperate desire to sustain her courage, she hadn't noticed it then.

A quick check that the house lights were all off then Laurel's car rolled out of the driveway. Sometime in the last four hours every last rain cloud had dispersed. The stars were stunning and the moon lit the night like an overzealous street lamp. However, the silent calm of the drive out of Ravenna did little to settle the thoughts swirling around her mind. When she laid her head on her pillow, she fell asleep counting the hours until she could make the drive back again.

Preoccupied minds will do little to hasten the progress of the day and, though Laurel knew it, she thought of her great-grandmother, of Kyle and Chet, of Meg and Private John Kessel, and of little else all of the next morning. She thought of them while picking up her daily coffee and cranberry muffin on her short commute to Parker Advertising Executives. Even as she prepared for her first meeting of the day, she had yet to chase the distraction from her mind. The marketing necessities of a new coffeehouse still rested on the mental back burner when her coworker Robert Kennesaw strolled into her office at 9:15.

"Laurel, they'll be here in a few minutes."

"Thank you, Robert, I'll be right there." She turned from her window and the bustle of Fulton Street two stories below and noted the flashing appointment reminder on her computer screen.

"Are you ready?" Robert, the lead associate on the North Wind Coffees account, remained in her doorway.

"Yes, I'll meet you in the conference room."

Her reply was crisp, but she mustered up a polite smile for Robert before he turned down the hallway. She tried to banish the annoyance rising up at the interruption of her train of thought. Obviously, she should have her mind on her work.

Laurel navigated the meeting and the rest of the morning with deliberate attentiveness. She poured herself into brainstorming for the afternoon. An arrangement of possible flyers for the coffeehouse's grand opening held her attention, but she reserved a small fraction of her focus for the tiny clock in the bottom right corner of her screen. As it announced the arrival of five p.m., Robert appeared at her door again.

"Having a bad day?"

She shook her head in protest. "What makes you think so?"

"You're not yourself today, that's all."

Something about his comment raised Laurel's hackles.

Robert stepped further into her small office. He crossed his arms, leaning against the rag-rolled blue wall. He had the lean, muscled figure of a longtime runner. Laurel remembered describing him to her best friend shortly after starting her job with the advertising firm. *Dark blond hair, hazel eyes. Epitome of good looking. Handsome but not so handsome that it's intimidating. A smile for everyone in the room and everyone is drawn to him. He's perfect for advertising.*

Today, with his suit jacket left in his office, Robert's unbuttoned collar and rolled shirtsleeves revealed a dark tan left over from summer. He'd maintained a steady habit of friendliness in the couple years they'd been colleagues while her manner tended toward wariness. It wasn't reasonable, she knew, as he'd done nothing to deserve her uneasiness. It was a gut thing that she couldn't shake.

Robert's eyes rested on her now. "I liked your concert sponsorship idea, but you didn't really push for it with the rest of the team. That's not like you."

"Everyone has off days, Robert."

"Of course they do."

"Even you, I bet. Unless you're Superman."

"Well, I wouldn't tell you if I was."

Laurel smiled in spite of herself and then returned to busying herself with saving and closing her computer files.

Robert eventually stepped back into the hallway, calling out as he left, "I'll see you at the restaurant."

That evening, Laurel slipped away from her clients and colleagues at the Jackson Lounge as soon as professional etiquette allowed. She drove quickly home to trade her work wear for jeans, a gray Henley, and a thin blue cardigan. As she hustled between the kitchen, bedroom, and bathroom of her modest apartment, she listened to her phone messages.

"Laurel, it's your mother. Remember me? Your dad and I only moved to Chicago. I'm fairly certain our phone lines still connect. Give me a call, dear. I just want to know how my baby girl is doing."

She made a mental note to call her parents soon.

A second message began as Laurel slipped on her shoes.

"Laurel!" Her best friend Melanie Casperson's voice squeaked with excitement. "The wedding invitations arrived. They're gorgeous. I can't wait for you to see them. How about joining me for a little addressing party? On Friday? I'll provide food. It won't be that bad, honestly. Call me."

She smiled to herself as she locked her front door. As Mel's maid of honor, it was rare for her to see her dear friend without some talk of the wedding. Love for Mel, and Mel's well-matched fiancé Jace, kept her from wearying of the topic.

Within the first few minutes of her drive though, her parents and friend slipped from her mind. Instead, Laurel revisited every detail of last night's conversation with her great-grandmother. The recollection filled her anew with eagerness to hear more. Arriving at Grandma Annie's house, Laurel gave her a warm hug and slid the rocking chair closer to the bed before taking a seat.

"How was work today?" Grandma Annie asked.

"It was fine."

"That's good. It's important to enjoy work as much as you can."

Laurel nodded. "I like my job, Grandma."

"Yes? I'm glad." Grandma Annie smoothed the blanket covering her legs. "Father Taylor visited today. He and Mrs. Baxter came this afternoon and stayed for tea. Do you remember Virginia Baxter? Yes, of course you do. Such a sweet lady. Her husband passed away last winter. She brought new photos of the grandchildren."

Laurel helped Grandma Annie adjust her pillows. "Grandma, could we keep going? With your story, I mean. I'd really like to know more if that's okay."

Her great-grandmother's expression was blank and for a moment Laurel feared the century-old mind had finally weakened. Before she could remind Grandma Annie of last night's topic, she watched the older woman's face struggle to continue feigning ignorance. Finally, Grandma Annie's lips spread in a grin.

She teased, "Oh, so you are interested then? I suppose we could continue with that tale."

Laurel's head fell against the back of her chair. "It's been all I can think about today. I was terrible at work because I was so distracted."

Grandma Annie took pity. "Ok, where did we leave off?"

"Private Kessel died while you and Kyle sat with him."

They fell silent for a moment. Then Laurel voiced one of the questions that had nagged her since yesterday evening.

"Why did you care so much, Grandma?"

When Grandma Annie looked puzzled, Laurel clarified, "Why did you care so particularly about Private Kessel? How was he different from the other tragic deaths you witnessed?"

"That is exactly the question I asked myself repeatedly after he died. I've never come up with an answer that satisfies." Grandma Annie tucked her white hair behind her ear. "I think, more than anything else, I needed to care about him."

"I don't understand."

"Someone told me once that there is always a reason, if not many reasons, a person comes into our lives. Those reasons can be obvious or they can be hidden. I don't think it was what was different about John Kessel that mattered, but what was different about my reaction to John Kessel and his suffering."

"Why do you think you needed that experience with him?"

"What do they call it, Laurel, when your muscles haven't been used in too long and they stop working? What's the word?"

"Atrophy?"

"Yes," Grandma Annie replied. "Before Kyle and Chet came, I had let my spirit atrophy. I kept my emotions locked up as securely as I could manage. With all we experienced in the hospital, I thought it was better that way. I chose that way based on fear. By the time I met Private Kessel, I had begun to let a little of that emotion and sensitivity come alive again. The experience of his death opened the floodgates. I couldn't avoid feeling the pain and unfairness. At first, I wished I could. Later, I was pleased that I couldn't."

Laurel considered this ponderously.

Grandma Annie moved on, "That means we were nearly into November."

8

October, 1917, 83 years earlier

In the days following Private John Kessel's death, Annie was badgered by doubts and fears. Often she could push them away, but they came crashing in during the quiet moments. Discouragement dogged her steps as she went about her work.

Meg pulled her into an upstairs drawing room in the mansion and asked what was wrong.

"Of all our patients, I don't know why Private Kessel's death has been so difficult," Annie collapsed into a cushioned chair. "Maybe it's because we saved him, or I thought we did. After the first surgery, after we all worked together to save him when he had nearly died, I felt so proud. So victorious. That we failed actually is bothering me more than any other death we've had."

Meg's tender face darkened with worry. She sat down opposite Annie.

"I'm sorry if I've been awful to work with lately. I hope I didn't take it out on you, Meg."

At this Meg laughed half-heartedly, "You've never been awful. As crazy as it sounds, I'm a little relieved this is all that's wrong."

"Relieved?"

"Yes. Kyle thought something might be wrong with your family. He had me concerned you'd heard bad news from them, but hadn't told any of us. I'm glad it isn't about them. Is it, Annie? Honestly?"

She shook her head and narrowed her eyes, tempted to ask what else Kyle had said but unwilling to change the subject.

"Don't you ever wonder if we're making any difference? Has our work really been worth it?"

Meg scoffed but Annie, caught up in the relief of confession, pressed on, "Think of the numbers, Meg. How many don't even make it to a hospital? And the ones we nurse back to health, what do they want other than to get back to the same bloody battlefields?"

"This is what you've been thinking?" Meg sprang to her feet, looking taller than her five-feet-one-inch frame. She moved both hands to her tiny waist with authority no one would dare question. "Would you go into that ward and tell any one of those soldiers it isn't worth it? Could you look at them and decide caring for them makes no difference?"

Annie's mouth fell agape. Meg wasn't finished with her yet.

"Since we can't do enough we shouldn't do anything? I may not be able to help each one as much as I would like but I couldn't live with myself if I didn't try."

Annie knew she had no argument to make.

Meg moved to leave but stopped with her hand on the door, turning to meet Annie's eyes. Meg's voice fell to a whisper of warning, "You're beginning to sound like your fiancé has convinced you of his view on things."

The words echoed in Annie's ears. Nothing in the course of the past ten months had produced such passion in her friend. It left Annie convicted to her core.

Voicing the doubts had weakened their power over Annie. They were still dogged in their quest to darken her mind, but her exchange with Meg broke their grip. No way could Annie look one of her patients in the eye and label him a waste of her time. She struggled with that truth, fending off the despondent frustrations that sought their former foothold.

Uninterested in returning to the dormitory and not yet needed in the ward, Annie lingered in the small sitting room. Her eyes roamed over the furnishings of formal wingback chairs and a burgundy brocade sofa, and lingered on a marble statue on the corner table. It depicted a young, fairy-like child. Without distinction in color from the rest of the white stone, its large eyes conveyed boundless innocence. Then Annie spotted a small piano, behind the sofa, covered with cloth from the time the room fell into disuse two years before.

Annie moved to the instrument and gave the sheet a swift pull. Dust rose and then settled around her. She glanced about the room as if someone might find her out. Alone, as she knew herself to be, she scooted the bench forward and sat down. The rich wood still shone from its last polishing. Annie's private piano lessons had concluded six years ago, at fourteen. Even so, her fingers fell immediately to their proper placement on the keys. Closing her eyes, her hands moved instinctively. A tune floated through her mind and, with a few missteps, she coaxed a song from the instrument.

The piano was unexpectedly well-tuned for how long it'd sat silent and covered. The notes delighted Annie's ears but she tried to play them at a low volume, unsure how far the music might carry through the mansion. First, she played a classical tune; she supposed it belonged to one of the great composers but couldn't recall which one. Then she moved into a favorite from her lessons, a lilting, quick-stepped melody. By its end, she recollected the notes she missed in the coda and began again with greater energy.

"Oh!" Her hands halted above the keys.

Kyle stood inside the doorway, smiling. "I had no idea you were a nurse and a pianist."

Warmth spread across her features. "How long were you listening?"

"From here, not long. In the hallway, a couple minutes longer." Kyle's smile was steady despite her disconcertion. "I'm sorry if you didn't want anyone to hear. It sounded wonderful. I had to move closer."

"I kept forgetting notes. It's been so long since I've played."

"Those forgotten notes didn't dim your talent a whit. You play well!"

Annie thanked him even as she shook her head in objection.

"Some evenings, Madame Chappelle plays her phonograph while she closes the café. I can hear it from upstairs. She plays mostly French operas, but I'm still glad to hear them."

She kept her seat at the piano while Kyle took a few steps into the room. At a set of tall windows, he stopped with his back to her. The muscles of his shoulders flexed when he clasped both hands behind his back.

"I also came up here because Meg is rather upset. I could only get out of her that she'd been talking with you, so I decided to look for you. I expected to find you in the same mood as Meg."

Annie bowed her head. "I owe Meg an apology."

"It isn't any of my business. I was just concerned. I'm glad you're all right."

Annie wished keenly to explain, although the words were slow to come. "Meg thoughtfully asked what's been bothering me. I've been so discouraged and piled it all on her. I was unreasonable. I'm afraid she must not be thinking very well of me right now."

He turned from the window and she discerned compassion in his eyes. She recalled what Meg mentioned.

"Thank you for being concerned about my family, Kyle. There isn't anything wrong with them, only with my attitude. I've been confused and sad, thinking my time here isn't worthwhile. Despite my best efforts, men still die. Meg helped set my mind right again."

His eyes broke their gaze momentarily when she spoke of his concern. She decided against explaining further, although she'd have liked to know his reaction to the thoughts she had shared with Meg.

"It's difficult to see what effect one person can possibly have in this war, isn't it?"

The comfort of finding understanding on his part caused her chest to tighten. She stood reactively, bumping into the corner of the piano. "I'll try not to think that way anymore."

"Don't be hard on yourself. Feeling that way shows you care," Kyle insisted.

Annie nodded, stepping toward the door. "Excuse me, but I have things to tend to before my shift."

"Maybe you could play again sometime."

The request caught her off guard. "Maybe," she mumbled, and hurried from the room.

She spent the next hour in the dormitory, watching the clock so she could return to the hospital ten minutes before the morning nurses finished. She caught up to Meg outside the laundry room.

"Meg, may I speak with you?" The timid request did little to convey her earnest need to make amends.

Meg stopped in front of her, tight lipped.

"I'm sorry, Meg. I don't think I realized how low I'd let my spirits get, how much I'd let it affect my perspective, until I piled it all on you. You were right to be angry. Thank you for helping me see how ridiculous I was being."

"What you felt makes sense," Meg sounded both perturbed and tender. "Anyone doing what we do could feel that way."

"I'm writing to Samuel."

Meg's eyes lit up under the green kerchief that held her curls back from her face.

"Oh?"

"You told me over a week ago to write to him about our work in more detail, but I hadn't yet. I'm trying to be hopeful he will understand. I need to be fully honest with him about how hard it is and how much the soldiers need us. The letter isn't finished, but I started it."

"I'm glad, Annie, and you should be hopeful," Meg said.

Annie had spent the past hour writing and rewriting the first page of this letter. She chose her words meticulously, hoping to finally convince Samuel—and reinforce for herself—that she could not leave France yet. As her words detailed her days at the hospital, she found her energy for the work reignite.

"How do you stay so positive, Meg?"

Meg sighed and Annie caught a rare glimpse of weariness in her friend's posture. Meg's familiar smile reappeared quickly though.

"There's a room full of men who need me every morning, Annie. I'm glad to be here"

Annie gave Meg a long hug, thanking her for her forgiveness, and for talking some sense into her. Then Annie went on into the ward, the load on her shoulders feeling more manageable.

The shift that followed brushed against her nerves like coarse wool. Her mind lingered over the tiniest details. She saw each medication to administer, every dressing to change, and any complaint to hear as a stitch in mending the wrong she felt she'd done to her patients. An urge arose to speak with every soldier, to know their hopes for this war. The burden of reparation proved exhausting. By the time she approached Chet's bed after last rounds, Annie's muscles were weary, but her heart was refreshed.

"Long day?" Chet greeted her.

"Yes, but a worthwhile day."

"Kyle looked ready to drop too. Maybe it's the weather. He said it's getting colder out there."

"It is cold. I wonder when we'll have our first snow this winter."

"So, any preference tonight?" Chet asked as he reached for the book lying on the floor.

She was becoming familiar enough with the Psalms to have a few favorites, but none came to mind. "You pick, Chet, but make it a cheerful one, please."

He flipped open the thin volume, easily finding his choice then handing it to Annie. She read silently through Psalm 100 then began the brief verses aloud. The lovely words filled her chest like a deep, cleansing breath. She gave Chet a glad smile.

"'A joyful noise'," she repeated from the psalm. "I think that's what I made on the piano I found today."

"According to my brother, you play beautifully. I'd love to hear you sometime, maybe a fine waltz. I think I'm almost up for dancing."

"Well, I thank your brother for the compliment, but I think it will be some time before you are waltzing again. Don't hurry it."

Chet looked ready to argue. Lacking the energy to match him, she made quick business of changing the subject.

"Kyle said he's staying until you are able to travel home with him. That shouldn't be long from now. I'm surprised you haven't been transferred yet. They may not discharge you from the Guards since you're healing so well, but you could move back to Ireland until you receive new orders. They are usually more efficient with that."

"Eager to be rid of us, Annie?"

She ignored the pout on Chet's lips and said, "Your leg is healing well. I imagine you'll be on crutches soon instead of restricted to this bed. Do you still have as many headaches from your head wound?"

Chet's hand grazed the stitched scar on his temple. "Pretty often, yes, but they aren't as severe anymore."

Frowning, Annie examined the wound. The swelling was nearly gone, but the bruising remained dark.

"My main worry is that I'll never have a full head of hair again," Chet said with his mirthful grin.

Indeed, barely a stubble had begun to grow around the scar. If he wanted the scar hidden, he would probably need to keep his hair longer than before.

Nora brought their conversation to a close with a patient-care question for Annie. Annie tried not to notice Chet watch her move about the ward with the other nurse. A few minutes later, she waved goodbye to Chet and headed to her room to collapse into bed for the rest she'd earned that day.

9

November, 1917

In the unhurried hours before her daily shifts, Annie continued to battle the fears and bleak thoughts she so recently renounced. Annie could dismiss those persistently haunting thoughts most easily when she threw herself into her work, or when she headed for the trails in the woods. Her morning walks grew frequent while winter sympathetically hovered in the distance.

Kyle began joining her on the trails. He had discovered her routine a few days after she took it up. She was glad for his company and the affable conversation. She told herself the conversation was merely to distract her mind.

This particular morning displayed the last, glorious vestige of autumn. The sun emitted unseasonable warmth, effectively melting the crystal frost along their path.

"What do you miss about home, about Boston?" Kyle asked as they meandered through a birch grove.

She tried to remember what little she'd shared with Kyle on the topic. Their exchanges tended more toward his homeland than hers.

"I miss a lot of things about Boston. I miss the city. I miss its rows of brick houses and the streetcars. I miss the food. I crave a dinner of fresh lobster or any seafood at all," Annie said with her mouth watering.

"I used to walk to the docks and watch the fishermen haul in their catch. It always impressed me that they had nearly a full day's work completed by the time I wandered down there in the morning."

Her voice lifted, "I also miss the harbor. Not the docks, but Boston Harbor. The ships keep constant motion, coming and going, loading and unloading. Crews shout at each other over the gulls. It's so busy, but there's something beautiful about it. A park looks down on the harbor from a hill. I sat on the benches, as still as I could be, until I felt like all the world was moving except me."

She paused in her raptures and noticed Kyle smiling over her words. The familiarity she allowed herself with him left her uneasy, yet she enjoyed it at the same time.

"I couldn't stay still in all of that commotion," he said.

"You don't live in a city. From what you've told me, your home's surroundings sound tranquil. I might have trouble being still in all that quiet."

A fallen tree offered an easy bridge over a brook. Kyle stopped halfway across, taking a seat on the thickest part of the tree trunk. Ignoring her own hesitancy, Annie sat too, keeping a polite distance between them. She dangled her laced boots above the water. Meg asked once what Samuel would think of these morning walks with Kyle. The question flashed through her mind now, but she brushed it aside as quickly as she had when it was first asked.

Beneath their log throne, the delightful rush of water dominated all sounds, swirling over stones and coursing around a bend. Only a few conversations had been necessary for Annie to learn how carefully Kyle chose his words before speaking. She had replaced her initial impatience over his silence, with appreciation of his thoughtful care.

Kyle eventually spoke over the music of the water, "You didn't mention any names, any people, in what you missed. Doesn't your family live in Boston?" After a pause, he added, "And your fiancé?"

She swung her head to look at him.

"Meg told me you are engaged."

She couldn't muster a reply, but glanced at her left hand. She had safely stored in her trunk the ruby ring Samuel gave her last Christmas. How had she never mentioned him, not once, in Kyle's presence?

"Don't you miss them?" Kyle pressed further.

She looked for judgment in his eyes but found none. She knew the proper answer, yet couldn't get it past her lips. "I miss my brother Lee. We've always been good friends, although he's six years older. His son George will be three soon. I miss him a lot."

Kyle nodded. He picked at a loose piece of bark on the tree trunk but kept his eyes on her face.

"To tell you honestly, I don't miss the rest very much." Her hands shook with the admission. "I love my family, Kyle, but we aren't as close-knit as I imagine your family to be." She stopped short of mentioning Samuel by name. Grappling with a jumble of emotions, she hoped Kyle would not ask after him again.

With his face now turned aside, she feared his disapproval. Such candidness felt like a new, stiff coat – right, but not yet broken in.

Confronting her conscience, Annie became more convinced that pretense was not the wise choice. When Kyle stood, his smile had returned and was full of reassuring friendliness. At once, she knew she had no reason to be afraid of being honest with him. With this one fear dispelled though, a new one was taking shape.

The pleasant sunshine lasted through the week and Annie woke earlier each morning to ensure she would not be denied another walk with Kyle. Today they walked in easy silence for much of the time. Two deer crossed the path ten yards ahead, pausing to stare.

"They're lovely," she whispered as the animals dashed out of view.

Kyle and Annie moved forward, the dead leaves crunching beneath their feet.

"How are you able to stay here, Kyle?" she asked softly. She still felt awkward expressing her curiosity even though he shared details from his life readily enough.

"Two of my cousins agreed to look after the farm. They work for me during planting and harvest seasons, so they know the farm as well as anyone."

"And they're able to take care of things for as long as this?"

"Well, we'd hoped Chet's recovery wouldn't be so lengthy, but I wrote and asked them to stay on indefinitely."

She didn't question him further but wondered if he was downplaying the inconvenience of his time away.

"Anyway, the timing was rather providential," he added after a few beats of silence.

"I don't understand."

"The timing, I think, was very much God's doing." Kyle opened his hands submissively. "In more ways than I can tell you, really."

She looked up at him curiously.

He explained, "We had just completed harvesting when I received word of Chet's injuries. A month or even a couple weeks earlier and I couldn't have come right away. I helped as much as possible with storing and selling the grains before I left, but if there is a good time to leave a farm in someone else's hands, this is it. Winter is about caring for the animals more than anything else."

"What animals do you own?"

"There are twenty-nine sheep," Kyle said with a lift of his chin. "Not a large herd, but they produce good quality wool. The cattle number around fifty after last spring's calves. I also have two old plow horses, huge beasts as lovable and ornery as any horses can be. I couldn't get by without them."

"And a dog, right?"

"Yes, named Molly." Kyle nodded, his expression softening. "She's an excellent sheepdog, but spoiled since I let her keep me company in the house."

"Isn't your niece named Molly? One isn't named after the other, right?"

Kyle's laugh startled a bird from its perch in the trees.

"No, I don't think so. If one is named after the other, it's my niece. I've had the dog since before my sister even married."

They began walking back toward the hospital

"I like picturing you on your land." Annie met Kyle's eyes. She couldn't resist voicing another question. "You said the timing for coming here was good in other ways too. What other ways?"

He laughed, "I think my words were 'in more ways than I can tell you.'"

"Oh." Her gumption disappeared.

"You know," Kyle paused, then continued eagerly, "I can tell you. There is no reason I can't tell you." He stopped walking. He shook his head as if the notion was brand new.

"Tell me what?"

"The truth about why I'm here."

"You're here because your brother was wounded."

"Yes, and because it's safer for me here than at home."

Kyle began walking again but now Annie halted. His claim sounded preposterous and she laughed skittishly, "We're miles from the front lines of a war, Kyle. It cannot possibly be safer here."

He returned to where she'd stopped. "I've trained myself not to talk of these things, so it's difficult to change that now."

There was a smooth stump a few feet off the path and she took a seat there. Kyle leaned against a thick tree. She let the quiet linger until he was ready.

"While you were still in Boston, did you hear about the uprising in Ireland last year? I'm not sure how much was reported outside of Ireland and England."

"I think I might have heard something. I attended a dinner with my parents, and I remember some men from London discussed a rebellion starting in Ireland."

"I suppose to the outside world the uprising did look like the start of it all. In actuality the uprising was really a climax, fed by years of waiting. It was some men's way of making it obvious to the English that Ireland will fight until we gain independence."

Kyle dug his heel into the hard earth.

"You mean they resorted to violence?"

"They did." His reply held a tinge of sadness. "Not everyone agrees with the methods that were used, or have been used since, but most of us agree with the aim. Since the uprising the country has grown more divided though. I think sometimes we're fighting amongst ourselves more than uniting against England. Maybe it has all gotten away from us."

She tried to grasp the enormity of the unrest.

"Independence couldn't be achieved without fighting? Negotiations and other steps wouldn't eventually work?"

"Like it did for America?" He asked with a smirk.

"Fair point."

"For decades the Irish have negotiated, fought, and negotiated again. It hasn't been effective."

"Do you agree that a war with England is the only way?"

Kyle chewed his lower lip.

"It's not that simple, is it?"

"No, it isn't simple at all," Kyle confirmed.

He pushed the dirt back into the hole he'd dug with his boot. "I would not say it's the only way, but it's the course things have taken. It's one reason I hate this war so much. Just before England entered the war here, a bill had passed through Parliament that Ireland would be granted Home Rule. We would have had our own parliament even though we remained under the crown. It's far from our ultimate goal but it was such a step forward."

"That sounds promising."

"Some folks thought Home Rule would just be England's way of appeasing us, but it would at least put us on a higher plane for negotiating with them. It doesn't matter now though. The bill's been set aside with the excuse of focusing on the war and enlisting Irishmen in the English armies. Many of us expect it won't ever be taken back up."

"Even after the war ends?"

Kyle ran both hands through his thick hair. "Too much has happened in the meantime. With the uprising and all the other incidents of the nationalist leaders using violence since then, the English would be fools to grant us Home Rule now without addressing those things. So, it's not that fighting England was the only way to move toward independence, but it might be the only way that remains for Ireland."

Annie contemplated with compassion all this information, piecing together the broader picture of turmoil. "I still don't understand why you needed to leave Ireland; why the chance to come to France was actually a good one for you."

He took a step toward her. Kyle's gaze was direct. She noticed the tight set of his jaw and the twitch of the muscles in his neck.

"Why is it dangerous for you to go home?" she asked more insistently.

With a shake of his head, Kyle answered, "Because I could be arrested for the work I'm doing."

"On your farm?" she asked in disbelief.

Kyle's smile reached his eyes. "No, Annie, not on my farm. For a year and a half, I've been writing for an underground newspaper, a nationalist publication."

"That's what they would arrest you for?" The idea seemed absurd. "For writing articles they don't like?"

"Our intention is to report the progress of the movement throughout Ireland including injustices done by the English, speeches and rallies held by the nationalists, any details the public papers leave out. To report on things accurately, we attend as many gatherings, rallies, and trials as possible. Being present at these is dangerous in itself, and if we are ever found out as authors of that newspaper, what we publish is enough for the British authorities to charge us with treason."

"Kyle, that's awful! Aren't you afraid?" she asked, wishing that was not the first question to enter her mind.

He looked at the ground. "Sometimes, yes."

Then his voice rose, "But I refuse to let the fear make my choices. I spent far too long hearing about the movement and supporting it only in my mind. I'd heard about these men and read their articles for months before I got up enough courage to seek them out. Once I did though, I was all in. I knew I had to be."

She had no reply. Her mind began to wander, searching for something nonexistent: a purpose for which she had ever felt the degree of conviction Kyle clearly possessed.

Kyle's next words called her attention back to their conversation. "Back in September, the authorities published a bulletin demanding that the newspaper cease being printed. We didn't stop, of course. They had made this same demand before. What was different this time is they brought in one of my partners for questioning. It was the first time any of us had been detected."

Kyle stuffed his hands in his pockets. Each time he stopped talking, his mouth formed a severe line. "They interrogated him and held him in lockup for a few days but couldn't get a confession. So, they had to release him. Since then, they've monitored him closely, hoping to be led to our facility and to the rest of us. They call us his co-conspirators. Shortly after this happened, I received notice about Chet."

"So, you came here and kept the English off your trail?"

"Basically. Our group decided it'd be best for the big picture."

"This isn't right!" Annie's voice became heated, "I mean, it's not right that you're safer here, so near the front lines, than you are at home."

His expression said he appreciated her response, and for a moment, he looked ready to agree, but instead he shrugged.

Waves of anger, sympathy, affection for Kyle, and even jealousy at his conviction, engulfed Annie. She abandoned her seat on the stump and took to the path at a marching speed. Kyle's boots cantered to keep pace with her.

"Annie, wait!"

The demand stopped her. There was comfort in walking away though so she started again, this time reigning in her pace.

Kyle addressed her when he caught up, "Annie, you have no idea what a relief it is to have told someone this. It's exhausting to keep this in the back of my mind all the time but never let it slip out to anyone."

"Doesn't Chet know?" she asked without looking up.

"He knows, but we don't discuss it," Kyle admitted seriously. "Chet and I, we have different opinions about these things."

Annie's hands were in fists at her sides as she continued toward the edge of the woods. Confusion shadowed Kyle's features and she wished to explain herself.

"You shouldn't...it isn't," she sputtered. The words refused to come.

Kyle gently took her wrist and she had no choice but to stop when he stopped.

"Annie, I didn't know this would upset you. What is it you want to say?"

She looked down at his hand and he released her wrist. Crossing her arms and squinting up at him in the sunlight, she made up her mind. *Didn't I tell myself I wouldn't be afraid of being honest with him?*

"I want to say that it makes me mad that you have to live that way in your own homeland. I'm mad that men must be willing to die if they want anything to be better. And I'm mad that I could never believe that firmly in something, to be so willing to sacrifice my life for something." Her voice faltered, tears stinging her throat.

"You came here to work as a nurse," Kyle pointed out. "That had to take some sacrifice and standing your ground."

She swallowed more tears. "Maybe a little, but all I really had to do to come here was run away."

He had no reply and Annie didn't trust herself to say more. She continued out of the woods toward the dormitory. Kyle thoughtfully stayed a step behind until they reached the path between the buildings and went in separate directions.

November, 1917

In the days after Kyle startled her with his confidences, Annie cycled through an array of feelings on the matter. She recognized reason in every one of those feelings, but wasn't certain how to harmonize them. The weekend arrived with bitter temperatures, putting an end to any possibility of another walk with Kyle at present. Even the short distance from the dormitory to the hospital left the nurses with numb feet and red noses. Each glimpse of the wind-bent trees added to Annie's disappointment and left her wondering when she and Kyle would speak again.

Annie encountered Kyle in the hospital, of course, but each polite greeting or minute of small talk as she tended to Chet only left her with longing for deep conversation. How could comments on the weather and the day's work suffice now that she knew what lay beneath the surface of Kyle's presence? Then again, the pleasure of even the smallest moments with Kyle had her supposing the lack of time together might be exactly what was needed.

Tuesday brought a source of distraction when mail arrived. Samuel had written and all the nervousness which accompanied her last letter to him flowed back in as she examined the envelope addressed in his precise printing. The one she sent was thick with the pages designed to help Samuel walk in her shoes. Her heart sank when she unfolded the mere two pages he enclosed, the same length as his usual letters.

Even before she finished the letter, sorrow coated her heart. Besides a brief expression of hope that Annie would not face "those sorts of trials any longer than necessary," Samuel made no reference to her letter. Her waning regard for him weakened further with his apparent refusal to see the soldiers' great needs and the ways she tried to contribute to their well-being. Dwelling a little longer in her disappointment, Annie pulled the collection of his correspondence from her trunk. She untied the hair ribbon that bound the stack and toyed with it as she began reading. With each letter, she ricocheted between fiery anger and heartbroken tears.

In one moment, Annie formed the notion of writing a definitive conclusion to their engagement, but in the next moment she was stunned that she could even think it. With a blush despite no one else being present in the room, she heard her mother's austere voice: *Never react from anger. A lady is not carried away by her emotions.* Although she hated to allow it, her mother's training prevailed. She doubted she could follow through with writing such a letter, one that would eliminate the only future she ever planned for or expected.

Unprepared to consider whether that future was still desirable, Annie moved on to the other letter delivered that morning. This one came from Lee. Her brother had written only once before, shortly after she arrived in France. The surprise of receiving this second letter gave her an expectation of news and Lee did not disappoint. After a few cordial lines, he wrote of the matter on his mind.

> *Joanna is expecting! She and our mother declare that it isn't right to share such things in a letter. I knew it was exactly the sort of news you would like to hear so I took it upon myself to defy them.*

Annie pictured his amused expression as he penned these words.

> *The doctor says the new baby will arrive in mid-March. Maybe you'll come home to meet him or her soon after. Even if that isn't to be, I know you'll be eager to do so once you are free to return. By then George might understand what a "brother" is since my wife's explanations haven't taken hold yet.*
>
> *Did you know he tells everyone that his aunt is fighting the Germans?*

Annie smiled despite herself, bolstered by the precious admiration of a three-year-old. She leapt from her seat on the bed, pacing the width of her small room while she reread her brother's note. Excitement and gratitude poured into her heart. How kind of Lee to understand her need for such news.

When Meg later mentioned Annie's smile as they worked on the heaps of laundry in the hospital, she was eager to share the tidings from home.

"The mail came today. I had some wonderful news."

Meg dropped the sheets she was wringing out. They splashed back into the water. "Oh, Annie did you hear from Samuel?"

She opened her mouth, but Meg continued dramatically, "I'm so glad, Annie. I've been as worried as if I'd written that letter myself. How could he not understand? I'm certain he loves you." Meg returned to the wash with an audible sigh.

Annie set down the wet linens in her hands. "Actually, the news was in a letter from my brother."

"Oh?" Meg was much quieter.

"His wife is having a second baby. I'm just very excited for them." Spoken in the wake of Meg's assumptions, the news lost a degree of its thrill. Lee's message had entirely removed her focus from her righteous anger about Samuel's letter.

"And you didn't hear from Samuel?"

She weighed the option of lying.

"I'm sorry. I'll bet you have a letter from him by next week."

"Samuel wrote," she admitted. "He didn't exactly say anything new. My most recent letter appears to have made absolutely no difference for him."

The sadness that came with these words overshadowed even the ire she felt earlier. Meg's petite shoulders stiffened. Annie avoided her eyes, hoping the matter would be dropped.

"Nothing at all? No difference?" Meg huffed. "That's terrible."

"He doesn't understand. I tried but it wasn't enough."

"If he loves you, he should understand. It ought to be that simple." Meg gave her curls a shake. "My mother is always telling me that people are who they are, and we can't change their characters. She thinks I'm too optimistic for my own good. Samuel seems to be the sort of person my mother was talking about. I'm sorry, Annie. His refusal to understand is not your fault."

Annie turned back to her sink and they both returned to their work.

II

September, 2000, 83 years later

"Did Samuel ever understand why you stayed in France, Grandma?" Laurel asked.

Annie answered without bitterness, "No, he didn't."

"Why not?"

"For one, I shouldn't have expected him to understand entirely. A person can't comprehend war without seeing it firsthand, and especially not a person who sees that war as an intrusion on his own plans."

Laurel crossed her arms, frowning.

"The war and my choice to work overseas, and then remain there as long as I did, was a path too far from the life and values he'd chosen for himself. I couldn't have summarized it like that when I was twenty years old, but I understood eventually. I really think he expected everything to return to normal once I came home. He chose not to see how that wasn't possible, how the changes wrought by the war and my time away could not be undone."

Although Laurel nodded, she thought Grandma Annie was a bit too kind. She couldn't help thinking ill of the man. A trickle of awe reached her heart as she looked upon Annie's peaceful face. She wondered, if she were in her great-grandmother's shoes, if she could have offered Samuel the measure of compassion he himself withheld.

"Lee and Joanna had a girl, right?" Laurel changed the subject. That branch of the family tree was spoken of so little over the years.

"Yes, they did." Grandma Annie smiled brightly. "Corrine, named after Joanna's grandmother."

"That's a beautiful name."

"Yes, and she was a beautiful child."

Laurel's musings shifted to Kyle. Intrigued, she wondered whether he ever shared more details of his life with Grandma Annie. The tired shadows beneath Annie's green eyes told Laurel it was time to say goodnight though, and her great-grandmother agreed while promising to continue the tale with Laurel's next visit.

Back at work the next day, Laurel presented to her team on the progress made in plans for the North Wind Coffees grand opening.

"In all the essentials you've come to expect, North Wind will be a venue for local bands in the same way as other cafes and coffeehouses in town. But the details will set North Wind apart. We offer a strong incentive for artists and bands to perform there by booking acts on a recommendation basis. Why should they play this coffeehouse when they're regularly booked at others? Because this venue will represent a standard within the local music scene. Our booking is only offered when another act, or public quota, has recommended the band."

Laurel paused to find notes from the phone calls she made that morning. Half from nerves, half from the pleasure of sharing her ideas, Laurel's hands trembled slightly. This was always the case when she spoke to a group. She glanced around the room for a quick assessment of the team. Lewis, their graphic artist, jotted down notes on his legal pad. Nadya, another marketing associate, bobbed her head with enthusiasm. Robert, the team lead, sat across from Laurel with his elbows on the black oval table, drumming his fingertips together in front of his lips.

Laurel continued sharing her ideas, "The local music scene is a close-knit community. This morning, I spoke with several members of that community." She noticed Robert lean in with peaked interest. "Word of mouth publicity is vital to acts trying to break onto the scene. I am in contact with one of the more popular coffeehouses, two acts with whom the owner of that business put me in touch, and the manager of a local recording studio where many bands produce their independent albums."

Nadya spoke up, "This is great, Laurel. I'm sure we all assumed being a music venue would help the coffeehouse launch, but I was having the hardest time with how to distinguish it from all the others. I believe you've nailed it."

"Thank you, Nadya. Distinguishing is key," Laurel affirmed her colleague. "The coffeehouse venue always works well for small acts. Some people may not even realize there is a difference between North Wind and the others. But the musicians will realize it, and word will spread among their fans."

"Perhaps when an act is booked, the announcement and posters could include the name of their recommender. A little cross-promotion between the artists," Robert suggested.

Laurel liked it. "Another incentive for musicians to participate in recommendations. These artists often have a strong local following so cross-promotion would help widen their fan base, as well as bring in new customers to the coffeehouse when they perform."

Robert closed the team meeting with a review of deadlines and confirmed follow-up appointments with the client.

Laurel returned to her office feeling gratified. In addition to her proposal being well received, Lewis had shown them the final logo sketch. It was classy and eye-catching. Tangible progress on an account was always energizing. She had two more calls to make and several emails to answer. She might also find time to work on the logistics of the recommendation system. Laurel sent up a silent prayer of thanks for such a productive day.

In the last hour of the workday, she stood at the reception desk, waiting for LeeAnn to finish a phone call. LeeAnn Stilton had been Parker Advertising's receptionist for eight years. Maybe that tenure and the additional fact that Laurel began as a lowly intern in her last semester of college were why LeeAnn received every request from Laurel like an annoyance. Laurel was never sure why LeeAnn disliked her so much.

"LeeAnn, could you please track down a few names and numbers for me?"

"It's four o'clock on Friday." LeeAnn looked up with transparent irritation. She tucked a strand of her bleach-blonde hair behind her ear and frowned at Laurel.

"There's no rush. As long as I have them by the end of Monday, it'll be a big help," Laurel added with an entreating smile. She decided many months ago to employ courtesy in her attempts to win over LeeAnn, even when it didn't match the actual thoughts in her head. "Are you looking forward to the weekend, LeeAnn? Any good plans?"

Before she could receive what was sure to be a dismissive reply, Robert stopped at the desk and handed over a stack of papers. "Mind faxing these for me? The number is at the top but it needs a cover page. I promised them I'd send these today."

LeeAnn flashed a toothy smile at Robert, accepting the papers and saying she would send the fax before five. She turned back to Laurel, her face composed again in cool displeasure. Laurel's mouth gaped a bit as Robert walked away, tossing a thank you over his shoulder.

LeeAnn reached for the list in her hands. "I'll see what I can do."

"Thank you." Laurel walked away, deciding yet again not to waste energy on aggravation with their receptionist.

Laurel reached her office and found Robert there.

He stood near her desk, studying the framed photos on top of the filing cabinet. One captured her and Melanie at a friend's wedding. Their dresses, makeup, and hairstyles were more elegant than they had ever been before or since. Another was taken at college graduation; she and Connor stood with arms on each other's shoulders, grinning madly in their royal blue caps and gowns. Robert concentrated on the third picture, the one from two Christmases ago.

"Are you close to your parents?"

She replied haltingly, "Yes. Well, sort of."

He stood to his full height, waiting.

"I don't know if close is the right word, but I get along with both of them well enough. Mom and I talk pretty often. They moved to Chicago a few years ago so we don't see each other as much as before. My dad found a new job there right after Grandma Megan died. I think they were just ready for a change after taking care of her while she was sick."

She bit her lip to stop the stream of personal details. Snapshot memories surfaced of entire days spent happily assisting her dad with landscaping at their Kentwood home; their Tuesday night ritual of pancakes for dinner and playing board games; the three of them watching every Detroit Lions game, often with Grandpa Lee stopping by before the second half. The mental images were all collected before her teenage years. She forced the memories aside and stared at Robert's polished shoes.

"Any siblings?"

"No."

"I have a brother, six years older."

"So, you're the baby?" she teased.

"That's what my brother likes to tell me." He smiled, a mischievous glint in his blue eyes. "As far as I can see, it's served me well. Gary claims there were plenty of things I got away with that Mom and Dad wouldn't let slide with him."

She gave a quick smile in return, willing herself to relax. The personal bend of the conversation was not typical between them.

"Excellent proposal in the meeting today, Laurel," he spoke with sincerity. "Most people have a hard time thinking in behind-the-scenes PR terms. You're good at it. Most focus too much on only the most direct lines to the public."

"Thank you."

"Make sure you have a clear outline of the plan for our client meeting next week. They'll want specifics on how these actions will benefit them now and in the future."

"I will." She stepped behind her desk but didn't sit. "I'm glad the team was on board with it."

Robert opened his mouth, but then closed it. He turned again toward Laurel's photographs, picking up the shot of her and Melanie and setting it down again. His continued presence was an unnamable worry to Laurel. They were not friends outside of work, or at work, really. She sat down and spread some files in front of her, but Robert didn't leave.

"Don't you have any family in the area?"

She balked at the sympathy in his face. "Actually, my great-grandmother is still alive. We're very close."

"Really?" Robert asked with some surprise. "But your grandparents are gone?"

"All are except my dad's father. He's retired in Arizona. I haven't seen him more than twice since junior high." For the first time, she felt a flicker of distress over this sparse family portrait.

"Will you eventually join your parents in Chicago?"

"No," she answered firmly.

Robert's eyebrows furrowed into a V over his hazel eyes.

Laurel took a calmer tone. "I have no plans to move to Chicago, even once my great-grandmother passes away. I don't think a city bigger than Grand Rapids would agree with me."

"I agree completely," he said.

Laurel didn't answer. She thought she heard relief in his voice. Robert offered a parting smile and wished her a good weekend.

That evening, Laurel arrived at her friend Melanie's to find Mel true to her word of providing food for their evening of addressing wedding invitations. Lasagna was heating in the oven, filling the house with delectable smells. Chocolate ice cream waited in the freezer. They snacked on pretzels in the meantime.

Laurel described for her friend the perplexing encounter with Robert.

"I don't understand why he bothers you so much," Mel said without sympathy.

"You know the sort, Mel," she argued. "Guys who gain everything by charm. It all comes effortlessly, and they think their smiles are payment enough for anyone who falls for it."

"Guys like Marcus?" Mel rolled her eyes. "That's what it comes down to, right? He reminds you of Marcus."

"That's not it," Laurel protested.

"It sounds like that is it."

"How could you possibly think that?" Laurel found the notion disconcerting. "It's beyond me how you can compare Robert to the man who abruptly ended his relationship with me by moving to Pittsburgh. Completely different situations."

"Yes, very different. But I think that based on the things you've said about Robert, the things that bug you about him. They sound a lot like what you used to admire in Marcus." Melanie didn't let Laurel object before continuing, "Marcus used to capture everyone's attention when he was in the room. He always said the right things and looked, well, perfect."

"Maybe you should've been the one to date him," Laurel retorted.

"You used to talk about him that way. You were in awe of Marcus, Laurel, and not in any sort of healthy way. You're exactly right that he gained everything with charm," said Mel, "but that doesn't mean Robert is like him."

Laurel frowned. "You could have said something while we were together, you know?"

"I almost did many times," Mel admitted. "Maybe I should have said something, or maybe it would have made no difference. That was then. The point today is that Robert is not Marcus. Possibly, he's only trying to be friendly. It's a small office. You've worked with him for over two years, yet you barely know each other. Why are you so set against him?"

The pair of friends sat elbow-to-elbow at Melanie's computer, picking a font for address labels for the elegant wedding invitations in boxes on the coffee table.

"Robert treats all of his colleagues well. I respect him as a senior member of the team. I'm not set against him." Laurel held her hands up defensively. "But think about it, Mel. Why would he come into my office and ask questions about personal things we've never spoken of before? There had to be a reason. It felt like he was fishing for something."

"Maybe someone started a rumor that you're leaving and he's concerned. You're a strong member of his team."

"Yeah, it was probably LeeAnn." The name brought a bad taste to Laurel's mouth. She regretted the snide comment.

"Maybe he has a crush."

"Melanie, stop," she warned. The twinkle in Mel's brown eyes finally drew a smile out of her though. Laurel shook her head. "Just stop."

"You have admitted that he's good looking,"

"He is that," Laurel indulged her friend for a moment.

Mel's voice dropped into seriousness. "It's been nearly a year since Marcus left, Laurel."

Laurel concentrated on the letters beneath her fingertips on the keyboard.

"You haven't dated anyone since Marcus left."

She wanted to have this conversation about as much as she wanted to slam her hand in a car door. "You think a rebound relationship with someone in my office is the way to go?"

"There has to be a statute of limitations on a new relationship qualifying as a rebound. Like a year, maybe." Mel nudged Laurel's elbow, smiling again and ushering the tension out of the room.

"You're probably right, but there is still the matter of Robert being someone I work with. I don't think he'd be a smart choice." She mustered up a decisive tone to end the discussion. "There's also the small problem of me not liking him."

"Maybe you would like him if you let yourself get to know him."

Laurel turned back to the address labels on the computer screen. She said, "Mel, it's the weekend and I don't want to think about Robert Kennesaw or anyone or anything from work for the next two days."

As she knew she could trust her best friend to do, the subject was dropped.

The computer desk sat under a picture window in Melanie's living room. Even though she bought the house before meeting Jace, there were now marks of him throughout the one-story ranch. He had moved in some of his furniture and belongings to prepare for his moving in after the wedding. Laurel could easily picture the couple moving comfortably through the home together. It filled her heart with a shadow of longing.

Melanie went to check on dinner and called to Laurel from the kitchen, "You've spent a lot of time with Grandma Annie, even more than usual. Is she doing all right?" Mel returned to the edge of the room. She tried to push a strand of her chestnut brown hair behind her ear with oven mitts on her hands.

"Yes, she's doing well," Laurel replied. "I hope I'm that clear-minded at 103. Compared to just a few months ago, Grandma is more tired and weak. Her mind is as fit as ever though. I love listening to her talk."

"Good." Melanie turned back to the kitchen. "It must be the worst to slowly lose your sanity or your memory."

"That definitely hasn't been a problem for her," she agreed. "We've spent my visits reminiscing lately. She's shared things I never knew about her. Grandma lived quite the interesting life when she was young."

Scents of melted cheese and from-scratch tomato sauce drew Laurel to the kitchen. Mel had added a blue gingham apron to her ensemble and Laurel chuckled at the image of domesticity.

"Jace is going to enjoy coming home to this every evening."

"Well, I hope he won't always expect this." Mel gestured toward the steaming lasagna and garlic bread. "But I'm more than willing to welcome him home every night. It'll help if he finds sweatpants and a tee shirt attractive because you know that's how I like to end my days."

Melanie stood a few inches shorter than Laurel. Where Laurel was slim and straight-lined, Mel had fetching curves. Laurel knew Jace wouldn't mind the relaxed outfits one bit, and told Mel as much.

"Besides, I need him to be okay with it for the sake of my own hopes too," she added, pointing to herself. Both women were dressed in fitted sweatpants and unadorned tees.

"Well, for the sake of your hopes, I promise to keep you posted." Mel's solemn reply was punctuated with a wink.

They sat down to their feast and Mel led a blessing. She then returned with curiosity to Laurel's earlier comment. "So, you're learning some new things about Grandma Annie?"

"To say the least, yes." She swallowed a large bite of pasta. "She's fascinating, Mel. I didn't realize it, but I've only thought of her as being old. I never considered her life before becoming a grandmother or a great-grandmother. I'm embarrassed about that."

Mel only nodded, her mouth full of garlic bread.

"She was engaged to a man in Boston, where she grew up, but put off the wedding to work as a nurse during World War I."

"Wow."

"And everything she's telling me about that time she spent overseas has been surprising," Laurel said. "I had no idea about all she's experienced."

"You must be learning so much!" Mel said.

"Oh I am!" exclaimed Laurel. "And I could kick myself for not asking earlier. We have so much ground to cover."

"Did they marry once the war was over?" Mel's fork hung above her plate.

"No, they didn't."

"Hmmm. I wonder what happened."

Laurel could guess at the speculation going through Melanie's mind. She remembered the time as a young girl when she asked her mother why no one ever spoke of her great-grandfather. Her mother's answer had been brief and firm, telling her to respect Grandma Annie's choice to not speak of him and advising that times were simply different than they are now. Something in her mother's response gave rise to the idea of forbidden love, maybe even a scandal.

Laurel felt suddenly uncertain about sharing more of what Grandma Annie confided. It seemed entirely too personal, somehow. She was glad when the conversation segued to Mel's wedding plans. By nearly midnight, the labels and stamps were applied to each of the ivory envelopes and Laurel drove home to fall into bed.

12

September, 2000

"Hello?" Laurel mumbled into the phone. Sleep hung warmly on her limbs and her eyes refused to open.

"Good morning."

She needed a few seconds to recognize the chipper voice. "Connor Andrew Isaacson. It's..." She craned her neck to see the alarm clock. "It's 6:22 on Saturday morning."

"I know, sorry. Going to be a good day though! The sun is already out, practically for the first time in weeks, and I couldn't sleep."

"So neither could I?" She groaned and burrowed into the pillow. "I'm hanging up."

"Wait," Connor said. "I really couldn't sleep. I've been up since 4:30. I was wondering if you want to go hiking."

"You think I'll want to see you after this call?" She was mostly kidding and she softened her tone when Connor didn't reply. "I'm sorry. I can't go today, but maybe another time soon."

"OK." He sounded disappointed. "I just needed to plan my day. Jobs have been back-to back-lately. I don't know when I'll have another full day off."

Connor was an event and portrait photographer. His business had taken off in the years since college.

"We'll find a time."

"Yes, we will. Go back to sleep, Laurel."

They hung up and she tried to do as she was told, but the brief conversation had woken her too completely. A call this early from Connor shouldn't surprise her. Even during college, he didn't have a lazy bone in his body.

Laurel wandered out of her bedroom after twenty minutes of tossing and turning in bed, and shifted her thinking to her own day. Other than picking up groceries, there wasn't much she needed to do. When she opened the living room blinds the sight of blue sky and sunshine made it an easy decision to take a short run.

To her delight, Connor had understated the goodness of the morning. The air was fresh and damp. She swallowed it in deep breaths. Autumn was at that lovely point of subtle transition when its sun and green grass are remnants of summertime but its other colors and breezes are hinting at change. Ideal for a run.

Laurel's competitive spirit had thrived on the high school track team but now, running solo, she enjoyed observing her surroundings too much to be an intense runner. The most traffic this early on a Saturday was the entrance and exit of breakfast customers at the two diners she passed. She crossed into a park where the sidewalks hosted fellow joggers and plenty of dog walkers. Reaching the edge of the park, she turned right to loop back to her street and let her imagination occupy itself with the hours ahead.

The whole afternoon and evening would be spent with Grandma Annie. She decided to pack a simple lunch for the two of them to enjoy. How much she might learn of Annie's story today invigorated her as she covered the last few blocks to her apartment.

After a quick trip to the grocery store for the week's supplies, Laurel prepped and gathered egg salad sandwiches, freshly sliced cucumbers, and her great-grandmother's favorite mint chocolate cookies. She packed it all in a small cooler. Laurel silently thanked Connor for the early morning phone call that gave her more hours in her day. She could hardly wait to get to Grandma Annie's.

Fumbling with her keys at the front door, her purse and the cooler under one arm, she heard her phone ring. She set everything on the floor and answered the call.

"Hi, Mom!" Laurel smacked her forehead, chiding herself for forgetting to call her parents in the last few days.

"Oh, you are alive then."

"I was going to call, I promise."

"We'll never really know, will we?"

She could hear the phony dramatics in her mother's voice and played along. "Yes, I'm heartless; the worst daughter who ever lived. I don't deserve you, Mom. I don't think I can even talk to you now, the guilt is so overwhelming. How will I ever repair the damage? You and Dad have done all you can, don't blame yourself."

Erin Thomas laughed loudly in Laurel's ear, "Alright, alright, I'll forgive you this time."

"Sorry, I really was going to call, but I'm on my way out the door."

"Lunch date?"

She could practically see her mother's expectant smile through the phone. "Yes, with a wonderful, 103-year-old genius of a woman."

"Well, I can't fault you for that. I talked to Grandma on Tuesday and she said you've been visiting a lot. So good of you to do, Laurel."

"The pleasure is mine. I love my time there." She tapped her foot, ready to get on the road. "The drive is barely thirty minutes and we have a good time together."

"Alright, you better be going if she's expecting you."

"Tell Dad hello for me. I'll try calling tomorrow so we can talk more."

"Okay. Love you, dear."

"Love you too. Bye, Mom."

Once she made it out of her apartment, the drive felt shorter than usual. The highway was clear and Laurel lowered her window to enjoy the September sun. Pulling up to the one-story house with its faded white siding and weather-beaten blue shutters, she felt fresh excitement at the prospect of a whole afternoon listening to her great-grandmother unearth her memories.

Laurel unpacked the food onto the kitchen table before walking to the bedroom. "Grandma, I brought lunch. Are you hungry now, or should I put it in the refrigerator?"

Grandma Annie didn't answer. She was sitting on the far side of the bed, her back to the doorway. Sunshine streamed in, casting her shadow across the quilt. Laurel walked around bed to stand beside her. Grandma Annie had a tight grip on the edge of the mattress.

"Is it too bright? Should I close the curtains?" Laurel asked quietly.

A tear rolled from each eye onto Grandma Annie's wrinkled cheeks. Panic instantly moistened Laurel's hands and she wiped them on her jeans. When Grandma Annie lifted her head, a sheepish smile appeared, surprising Laurel.

"I'm not hungry quite yet. Go ahead and put it away for now."

Nodding, she waited, still wondering if Grandma Annie was in pain.

Grandma Annie, eyes fixed on the window again, pushed her next words out in a rush, like a child asking for an extra scoop of ice cream. "Can we sit outside today, Laurie Bean? I haven't been outdoors in weeks and then only to get in and out of Virginia Baxter's car for my doctor's appointment. It looks lovely out there."

Laurel released a breath of relief. "I'd love to sit outside."

Minutes later she had helped Grandma Annie down the back steps to the stone patio. They sat side by side with Grandma Annie tucked into her chair with a comfy blanket across her lap and a canary yellow cardigan around her shoulders. Satisfaction lit up Annie's face.

Annie's yard was small and private. King Maples marked the back corners, their leaves still the brilliant plum color they turned in summer. The old apple tree was bare, its fruitful years long gone. Cotton-soft clouds moved inconsequentially through an otherwise perfect blue sky.

Grandma Annie made no attempt at small talk. "We had best get started. There's an awful lot to tell you and I'm sure we'll be hungry soon." Her words were eager enough but apprehension tightened her features.

13

November, 1917, 83 years earlier

The wintry weekend that kept Annie indoors and off her favorite trails moved out on an eastbound wind. The extreme cold was replaced by more tolerable temperatures, but not without first making its mark. Any leaves still stubbornly clinging to their branches now fell to the crisp grass below. The ground grew harder underfoot. Even the deep green of the pines looked flat in the white sunlight. Occupants of the LaCroix property could pass comfortably between the buildings or down the road to the village if they were bundled in thick layers, but no one actually wished to be outdoors.

Like the soil hardened by daily frosts, Annie began to feel numb again, dulled on the inside. After receiving Samuel's impersonal letter and rereading his previous correspondence, she wore herself out trying to straddle the distance between her current life and the life on hold in Boston. The weariness in her emotions took its toll in her limbs as she lost more sleep from one night to the next. She blamed herself for becoming unfit for her own future. Blame did not give rise to regret though. No, she would embrace the changes wrought by serving here, by making a difference.

Still, the restlessness grew. By nightfall on Friday, Annie tossed helplessly in her bed, unable to shake the persistent distractions in her overtired mind.

"God, please, I just want to sleep. I can't think anymore or worry anymore. I need to rest," she whispered in desperation. She couldn't remember the last time she had prayed; maybe during a storm on the voyage across the Atlantic. She sat up in bed, near tears, and repeated the plea, "God, please bring me rest."

For a minute or two, she remained upright in her bed, feeling more awake now than before. Then a warming began in her chest and slowly spread until every limb felt heavy with it. Her eyelids drooped. She could only note the calmness that blanketed her before she laid back and succumbed to sleep.

She woke the next morning with new energy. For the first time in days, she felt able to resist the week's worries and doubts. She chose instead to be aware of only the work at hand and the people immediately before her.

Chet had significantly improved of late. He got up and out of bed as often as allowed. That afternoon, he approached Dr. LaCroix while Annie was nearby.

"I hope you don't mind but I've been poking around this place a bit," Chet's voice was at its most nonchalant. "I noticed that dining room down the hall. It's a shame it doesn't see the wonderful dinners you probably used to host."

Dr. LaCroix smiled at the compliment. "Yes, we had fine parties. Madame Adele knows how to cook much more than broth and potatoes."

Chet went on, winking at Annie over the doctor's shoulder, "I realize it wouldn't be a return to its former glory, but it'd be awfully kind of you to open up that room as an extra space for us fellows who are well enough to walk around a bit. Give us a little breathing room away from our beds."

Later, Annie encouraged the doctor to oblige Chet. The soldiers would be grateful. Many of them became restless after being confined for so many days. Her strongest hope, which she kept to herself, was that the new gathering space would distract Chet from his recent occupation of following her around the ward as she worked.

The dining hall Chet had discovered was a deep, spacious room, opening from the hallway through two heavy oak doors and ending with six floor-to-ceiling window panes. Dr. LaCroix instructed the butler to borrow a few nurses to dust out the cobwebs and line the walls with extra chairs from around the house.

The doctor's offering did not go unappreciated. Those who were well enough to walk unaided from the ward began frequenting the new space. Many found energy to write letters, play at cards, or competitively share stories from the battlefields. On clear afternoons, the winter sun streamed into the room granting a few degrees of extra warmth to anyone gathered at the enormous dining table.

Kyle could usually be found wherever Chet chose to spend his day, so he too became a fixture in the dining room. Annie's morning walks were now sporadic and solitary, the weather usually confining her indoors with sharp winds and an enduring threat of icy rain. She was sorry to lose the time spent with Kyle, sorrier than she liked to admit. She missed his quiet, intimate manner and their unguarded conversations.

Missing Kyle was the only credible explanation for her behavior one particular morning. Without deliberation, she walked the familiar road toward the village grocery. She reached the store, but crossed the street instead of going inside. When she entered the café, La Porte Rouge, warmth rushed over her. The huge ovens at the front of the room generously heated the whole dining area. Only three patrons sat at the tables and they watched her like an intruder at a family meal. She pressed her hands against her stomach to stop them from quivering. For the first time, she began questioning her decision to come, but the chance of escape was quickly lost. Kyle emerged near the kitchen, descending from his rented room upstairs. His surprise at seeing her across the room gave way to a bright smile. In a few strides he was in front of her.

"Good morning, Annie."

The soft greeting reached her like another wave of warm air. "Good morning. You've raved about the pastries here and I thought I might try one for breakfast."

Kyle raised an eyebrow. "Really?"

She nodded. He chose a table in the corner and she took the chair facing the rest of the room. From there she took in the arrangement of tables, with the handful of whispering customers, and the rotund iron ovens behind the front counter. The walls were neatly whitewashed, except for one covered by a mural of a country cottage with its red front door painted permanently ajar, open at the end of a dirt path.

"Most of the business is at lunch, so the selection for breakfast is small. Don't let that fool you though. Everything she creates in the morning is incredible," Kyle informed her. "I know exactly what you should try." He strolled to the front counter to speak with a woman lifting a pan of croissants from an oven. He then returned to his seat, clapped his hands together, and expressed his hope that she was truly hungry for breakfast.

"I am." Annie smiled while removing her gloves and coat, calming her nerves as best she could. "It's been days since I've spent any time outdoors. This is a good walk."

"You weren't too cold?"

"The wind isn't strong today."

"Good."

A pause in the conversation came and went as the pair began sharing their opinions of the winters in their respective homelands. Kyle described a splendid hill his family used for sledding on the few days each winter when substantial snow fell. Their talk was interrupted briefly by the bearer of two steaming, flaky pastries.

"Madame Chappelle, allow me to introduce Annie Walcott." Kyle stood to make the introduction. "Annie, this is Madame Chappelle. She owns the café and rents the upstairs room to me. Miss Walcott is a nurse at the LaCroix estate's hospital."

"Ah, bonjour, Mademoiselle!" The woman squeezed her plump hands together. "Welcome."

"Thank you. I've heard wonderful things about your café."

Madame Chappelle was a short woman, her face only slightly higher than Annie's although Annie was seated. Kindness beamed through her brown eyes and her smile. Leaning in conspiratorially to Annie, Madame Chappelle winked. "Monsieur Regan, he likes the éclairs."

Annie giggled. With a sideways look, she saw Kyle's face redden.

"You try these." The woman pushed the tray to the center of their table with a warning, "Ils sont très chauds...ah, very, very hot."

Madame Chappelle marched back to the kitchen.

Kyle handed Annie a plate.

"So, éclairs?" she teased.

He shrugged his broad shoulders. "I'm afraid so. Of course, with Madame Chappelle I never have to ask for any. She is forever bringing treats to my room for me to taste. 'Don't ask how I get my ingredients,'" Kyle imitated the woman's accented English. "'I have my ways.'"

Annie's laughter deepened, "She seems sweet."

"She's a mother to the core. Two grown sons, both stationed near the Marne, I think. Her husband is a captain in the French Army. I believe she leased the room to me just so she would have someone to feed besides the restaurant customers."

Kyle and Annie both fell silent, save the occasional expression of pleasure as they tasted Madame Chappelle's delectable pastries. The warm crusts flaked as Annie lifted them to her mouth. The first bite revealed a filling of custard and thick raspberry jam. She was certain she had never eaten anything comparable.

Kyle and Annie continued to savor each mouthful while they began to chat again.

Annie couldn't help feeling that more significant matters waited below the surface of their casual conversation. Those matters would respectfully remain there until she brought them to the forefront. Kyle wouldn't risk upsetting her.

Next time. She committed herself to it. Next time they talked she would speak again of the confidences he'd shared. *After all, what have I to be angry about? Besides Kyle being at risk of hanging for treason and the fact that I probably wouldn't be willing to hang for anything.*

"Annie?" Kyle leaned toward her. "Did you ever go?"

She had no idea to what he was referring. She shook her head, abandoning her rambling thoughts.

"You never tried snowshoeing? I've always wanted to try it, but we don't get enough good snow."

"Oh, yes, I mean...I was..." She cringed. "This is the first winter in twelve years that I won't go. My brother has taken me snowshoeing multiple times each winter since I was a little girl."

It was a decent recovery and Kyle seemed nonplussed by her distraction. An hour later, she reluctantly admitted it was time to return to the hospital. With an apology for not accompanying her on the walk, Kyle said he would be over to see Chet after he finished a few letters. Before Annie could exit the café, Madame Chappelle coerced from her a promise of returning for another breakfast.

The motherly hostess did not have to wait long to see Annie make good on the promise. Annie walked to the café another two mornings that same week.

14

November, 1917

"Is the dressing closet low on towels?" Meg split a stack of folded hand towels. She had remained after her morning shift to unpack the new shipment of supplies with Annie.

"I didn't notice, but we use so many that there is always room for more." She stood across from Meg in the sitting room that functioned as the hospital's office. "Maybe we could organize this room better. All the patient records are in one place, whether they're current or not. It wouldn't be difficult to separate them."

"And the shelves of supplies are getting messy." Meg paused, cocking her head to look at Annie over her shoulder. "You could come in one morning, I suppose."

"Yes, I could."

"Unless you're occupied in the morning," Meg continued, still watching her. "You could wait for a slow night and fit it in then."

Annie comprehended the implication and met her friend's eyes directly. "No, I'll start on it tomorrow morning."

Meg gave a shrug and returned to the linens in front of her, but the attempt at disinterest lasted only a few seconds. "Why haven't you told me about your breakfasts with Kyle? When did you start walking into the village?"

Fighting an unnecessary urge to defend herself, Annie forced a casual tone, "Who told you I was?"

"Chet did."

"I guess I didn't think to mention it. I had given up the trails due to the cold weather and was anxious to be outside again. The path to the café is a good walk when the weather is clear."

"You go for the sake of exercise?" Meg asked dryly.

"Yes." She couldn't help the smile breaking across her face. "And for the pastries, too, of course."

She described for Meg the mouthwatering delicacies at the café, but her friend was undeterred.

"Kyle happening to be there doesn't play into your decision to go each morning?"

Annie turned from the closet she was organizing to face Meg's teasing smile. "I'm not going to lie to you, Meg. You know I go to see him. Don't let your imagination run with that fact, okay. Circumstances have allowed us to become friends and I'm grateful for that."

Tucking a curl behind her ear, Meg gave her a sidelong glance and said, "They will leave soon, Annie."

"What do you mean?"

"Chet and Kyle, they'll be going once Chet receives transfer orders."

"I know that, Meg."

"Do you? Chet is doing so well. We've both said that we're surprised he hasn't been sent to a hospital in Ireland yet."

The imminence of the brothers' departure was obvious, but she was well practiced in avoiding that reality. "I do know, Meg. Don't worry."

She tried to steer the conversation away from herself. "I suppose Chet is anxious to go. He must realize there's been some delay."

"He certainly never mentions it." Meg shrugged. "But that's not the sort of thing he and I talk about. Kyle probably didn't expect to be in France so long either. I imagine he's found his time here more enjoyable than he could have planned on."

Meg's words were playful but Annie couldn't laugh. Right now, she wished only to stop thinking of the day she dreaded, when the two brothers would board a train to Ireland. Returning to the boxes to be unpacked, Annie remained silent. Meg mercifully did the same.

That same day, Annie sat in her dormitory bedroom and penned a letter home. Whether her reason was guilt, desperation, or hope (or a portion of all three), she was writing to Samuel much more often. Each letter detailed the recent days' activity, carefully balancing the grim tasks and trials with stories of healing and recovery. Samuel had written one more letter in return but it held no changes in his message. Annie was determined to continue the deluge of pages until he conveyed some new understanding in his replies. A dull ache spread through her chest while she finished today's note.

I do not write of these matters to frighten you or my family. Please do not worry for my well-being. As long as I am able to serve these soldiers, I am satisfied. I know I'm where I'm supposed to be. Knowing I am happy will make you glad, won't it, Samuel? To even my own surprise, I am not scared. The village and the doctor's estate lie far enough from the movements of the war's front lines that it isn't in obvious danger. Only yesterday, an English colonel who arrived to conduct discharges informed us that the front line shifted further east, and therefore further from our front door.

I will write again soon. Give my regards to your parents.

Yours,
Annie

Her tired eyes blurred as she folded the letter and addressed it. She would post it in the morning when she walked into the village to meet Kyle.

15

December, 1917

As Annie's visits to the café became more regular, the ensuing days were as good as any during her time away from home. They were filled with work, but her time with Kyle–their conversations and his warmth of spirit–gave her a prevailing measure of joy. Finally, she was afraid of not sharing enough and of not being honest enough, rather than the opposite. She did keep the promise made to herself to speak of Kyle's work, encouraging him to again talk of the turmoil in Ireland and his efforts with the newspaper. She was rewarded with his unreserved relief at having her as a confidante.

Alongside this enjoyment though was an inexplicable sense of dread. It refused to be shaken off. She felt she was weaving a soft rug of contentment that could all too easily be pulled out from under her feet.

Tonight's shift began with a rushed amputation of a soldier's leg before the hours ebbed into calm with no new arrivals all evening. Annie slowed down to visit with several patients instead of passing quickly from bed to bed during last rounds. When she said goodnight to the last of them, she sought Chet out to read.

He wasn't in his bed. She picked up his book and brought it to the dining hall. Walking past the long table, she ran her fingers along its glossy surface. A smile played on her lips. Chet sat in a chair below the tall windows at the back of the otherwise empty room. The canvas of night through the glass loomed over his bowed head. She thought he might have fallen asleep but when she drew closer, she saw his eyelashes meet and separate. He did not acknowledge her when she sat down in a nearby chair.

"Chet?"

His chest rose with a slow breath before he lifted his head. Chet didn't look her in the face and she was glad of this, for she couldn't help being alarmed by his appearance. His hair was in disarray, like he'd just woken from a restless nap. The silvery blue irises of his eyes were surrounded by redness. He'd been crying. His tear-streaked cheeks confirmed this. Annie was stunned. Only when his face clouded with the pain of his frequent headaches had she ever glimpsed tears in Chet's eyes. She wished immediately for his playful smile.

"I keep going over it in my mind." Chet turned his head in her direction but stared past her. His voice was hard. "I keep trying to figure it out."

"What are you figuring out?" she asked in a soothing tone.

"I'm not figuring anything out. No matter how I read it, I can't make sense of it."

She waited and when Chet eventually met her eyes it was with a look of defeat.

"I should've died out there. Patrick did, and Colonel O'Brien, and so many others. Why should it be different for me? I should have died."

Whatever she might have guessed about his demeanor tonight, this was not what she was prepared to hear.

Chet continued quickly, the bitterness thinning his rich voice. "How are any of us different?" He gestured toward the hallway. "All the guys here, I mean. Sometimes I hate them, like I hate myself."

"Chet!" She went to her knees in front of him. Her eyes held his despairing gaze.

"You know why I read those ridiculous psalms every night, Annie?"

She shook her head.

"They're some of the oldest prayers Christians have; go back long before the Christians. They should be some powerful prayers."

Their readings had not felt like prayers, but she nodded.

"I read them in the trenches because I was scared. I was always scared. A spineless coward," he spat the words out. "And once I was conscious again here, I read them to talk to God. How stupid, thinking God might explain it to me."

"You fought. You weren't a coward," she argued. "A coward runs from what he fears. You fought and almost died."

"Almost." The word sounded wishful. "Good men did die: men who weren't afraid, who had families, and who didn't just pretend to talk to God."

"And you think you should have died instead?"

"Yes," Chet shouted. He swung at the crutches leaning against the wall. They clattered to the floor.

Annie flinched as the noise echoed off every surface.

"When Kyle saw me awake for the first time, he said 'Thank you, God, you saved him!' He keeps talking about God's protection and mercy. Where was God for all the ones who didn't make it out? There were men who would have given God credit for their lives, but not me. If it was God who saved my life, it was not out of mercy."

If she had learned anything in the past ten months, it was that logic and common sense had no say in who lived and who died. She believed in a kind God but one who kept his distance. An explanation for the reach of death's hand wasn't something she'd ever sought.

Chet had looked away. Annie kept her position at his feet, watching him closely.

"I'm always afraid. The medics left me for dead in the trenches. If I had waited, they would've been right. But I was scared to die just like I was scared to fight, so I ran from death. I should have welcomed it."

"You didn't die in that battle. Look at yourself, Chet." She lifted her hand in a sweeping motion, stopping to rest it on his knee as she continued. "You aren't crippled. You have all your limbs and your mind intact. You're alive, Chet, and I cannot believe that is a bad thing."

He glared at her for a moment before his face softened. His beautiful eyes were dry now. In a sudden movement, Chet bent until he was eye level with her, his jaw set. She took a panicked breath before he leaned in another inch. His mouth barely grazed her lips before she pulled back as best she could. She was trapped on her knees, bending backward to look at him.

"You could make me glad I'm still around, Annie."

Her back stiffened. She narrowed her eyes as she saw Chet's features harden again.

"You're in love with my kid brother. That's the problem."

"I'm engaged to be married," she retorted. She twisted her body to stand up.

Chet gave no response except a scornful smile.

Annie departed the room and didn't stop walking until she was safely shut inside her room. With her back against the door she slid to the floor, hugging her knees as tears rushed from her eyes. A string of sobs rose up and she wondered what she cried for most: Chet's despair, or his accurate reading of her regard for Kyle.

When the tears subsided after some time, Annie kept her seat on the floor, her hands splayed against the floorboards. Her chest hurt. She knew Chet's actions meant the end of their friendship. She mourned that loss and grieved for Chet's survivor's guilt. Most powerful was the stinging reality that she must let go of Kyle, and everything that filled her heart when she caught sight of him or heard his voice.

This decision felt like the closing of a dam, tight and stony, around her heart. Behind the debilitating sorrow came a quiet, malicious whisper speaking of unfaithfulness and disloyalty. With Samuel's face in her mind, she wept again. She listened to the accusing voice without objection.

"I've made a fool of myself," she whispered. Whether her heart could or should turn back to her fiancé, she did not know.

16

September, 2000, 83 years later

Annie, eight decades later, had tears in her eyes over the recollected memories.

"When I woke up the next morning, I was angry. Very tired and very angry."

Laurel watched her great-grandmother closely. Clouds had returned to cover the sun and Laurel realized she was shivering in her patio chair. Grandma Annie, however, seemed to not heed the change in temperature. She looked warm, flushed by the anxiety of the memories.

"You weren't sad?" Laurel asked.

"Of course I was sad, but I couldn't bear to cry anymore. I felt stronger in being angry, so I foolishly grabbed hold of that."

Laurel felt a bittersweet understanding of her great-grandmother's words. "What did you do?"

Grandma Annie bit her lip. Her head moved slowly from side to side. "I made things worse."

Tears gathered in Grandma Annie's green eyes. Laurel worried over the weight of recounting these details.

"Let's move inside, Grandma. These clouds look like they're sticking around."

They had eaten their sandwiches so Laurel brought their empty plates and cups into the kitchen before helping Grandma Annie up the steps and to the bathroom. While she waited, Laurel stood before the oval mirror on the bedroom wall.

"I have his eyes," she whispered, her silvery blue eyes staring back from the glass. She surveyed the rest of her face and speculated what other features had held fast through three generations. She fingered a section of her glossy black hair. "That's from Grandma Annie, but the eyes are his," Laurel concluded.

She tried to imagine a younger version of her great-grand-mother. Grandma Annie took shape in her mind according to a portrait she'd seen years ago. Annie was only nineteen in the professional print. Her shoulders were straight, her chin lifted, and her hair was swept away from her face by dainty combs. The green of the eyes could not be captured in the black and white shades. She knew the photo was professionally posed but Annie's class and beauty were authentic. Laurel was certain those traits were apparent to Kyle all those years ago.

"Laurie Bean."

She jumped. "I'm coming."

When Grandma Annie was settled in her bed, she gazed into Laurel's face and asked, "What are you thinking, my girl?"

Laurel hesitated only a moment.

"In all those letters to Samuel, did you ever mention Kyle or Chet?"

Grandma Annie turned her face toward the window. "I sometimes tried but then I threw out whole pages I'd written. I could never find the right words. I told Samuel about Dr. LaCroix, Meg, and the other nurses. I shared many patients' stories, but to casually mention Chet, or his visiting brother Kyle, felt like a greater lie than not mentioning them at all."

Grandma Annie took Laurel's hand in her soft fingers. "All we ever talk about is me. What's going on with you? How is your friend, the one who will be married this winter?"

Laurel wasn't prepared for the sudden segue but answered with a smile, "Melanie is fantastic. She and Jace are such a good match. I've been trying to help with the details as much as possible. The dresses and tuxes are ready. We addressed the invitations last night. You should get yours in the mail soon."

"I'm invited?" Grandma Annie's voice lifted but then she protested, "I certainly couldn't attend. I get out and about so seldom these days."

Laurel allowed herself a little optimism. "Mel hopes you could at least come to the ceremony. Keep your calendar open for November Fourth."

Grandma Annie nodded. "That would be lovely. I'll be praying for them from here, at the very least. You know, now that I'm so comfy here, I'm afraid I might need a nap."

"Of course. I can go," Laurel couldn't keep the disappointment from her voice.

"That fresh air was just what I needed," Grandma Annie said. "Don't leave, Laurel. Stay and we'll talk more after I have a bit of rest."

Laurel gladly agreed. She wandered to the living room.

In the stillness, she noticed a scent hanging in the air. It was vaguely familiar so she supposed she should have noticed it before this evening. Other long-gone scents arose in her memory: bread in the oven, lilac scented candles, and, at this time of year, the pulp of a hundred apples boiled down for applesauce. These were the rightful aromas of her great-grandmother's home. She inhaled the house's thin scent and swiped at the tears gathering in her eyes. Age. Age and endings. She raised her chin against the thoughts. *But please not the ending part yet, Lord.*

From Laurel's seat on the couch, she looked about the room at the framed faces and dusty knickknacks, every single one as familiar to her as her own belongings. She basked in the warmth that filled this home, that had always filled any place where her great-grand-mother was present.

Laurel knew that the next hour or more would crawl at a turtle's pace. A hooded sweatshirt she had left behind two weeks ago was in the coat closet and she pulled it over her head. When she snuck into the bedroom to leave a note before going out the front door, Grandma Annie's sleep went on undisturbed.

The neighborhood was familiar since childhood, although now Laurel rarely did anything besides drive directly to and from her great-grandmother's house. The house stood far enough on the outskirts to abandon Ravenna's in-town pattern of side by side homes and small yards. Instead, the homes on this road stood with their backs to the woods and river, like Annie's house, or to corn-fields on the opposite side.

After a mile's stroll toward town, Laurel rounded a wide curve and reached the Main Street intersection. Until it crossed the riv-er and curved into town, the road didn't look main at all. Instead, it was the county highway bringing people into Ravenna from the south. At the intersection, between the blue water tower and the river, was Thatcher Park.

Laurel walked onto the grass and paused beside the gazebo, looking over the well-trodden grounds. A paved walking path looped the park's edge. Dirt trails branched off into the woods. Because Laurel and her grandparents had made frequent treks to Thatcher Park, she knew exactly which trail led to a deck beside the river. This time her feet took her to the swing set.

The black rubber seats hung motionless from their metal chains. She stared at them with an equal measure of determination and self-consciousness. Something within dared her to walk forward, sit down, and push herself up from the ground.

After only a few pumps of her long legs, she reached the height she used to work so hard to attain as a child. Her stomach jumped in a familiar way each time the swing pitched forward. A giddy feeling skipped down her spine and she laughed aloud. She folded and unfolded her knees to keep momentum, and leaned back until her hair hung in a black curtain from her head.

"Laurel?"

She sat up so quickly that dizziness blinded her for a moment. Her legs stilled, slowing the swing. She blinked a few times to see who called her name.

"Robert?"

He had donned a blue Tigers cap, jeans, and a faded, long sleeved, green t-shirt. She might not have recognized him if it weren't for that same smile she had seen every weekday for over two years. Her feet skidded on the dirt until she stopped.

"What are you doing here?" each asked the other.

"I'm visiting my brother," he answered first, "but Marsha needed some exercise."

"Marsha?"

Robert nodded toward the river where a golden Labrador bounded along the bank.

"She's yours?"

"Yes." He grinned. "My nieces wouldn't speak to me if I visited without her."

Laurel stayed in the swing, leaning into one of the chains. Robert took the next swing and twisted to face her.

"What are you doing in Ravenna?" he asked.

"My great-grandmother lives here. We had lunch together and I'll spend the afternoon with her, but she's napping now."

"What are the chances?" He kicked at the sandy ground beneath the swings. "Did you grow up here?"

She pushed the swing into slight motion. "I grew up in Grand Rapids, in Kentwood. My mom is from here though, and her parents too."

"My brother Gary's wife is from Coopersville, maybe 10 miles from here. They settled here when Gary started his business. We grew up as kids in Lansing though. I was there until college."

"Really? I didn't know that."

"Mom still lives there. She'd love it if I moved back."

"And your father?"

"He died when I was sixteen."

She fumbled over her words. "I... I'm sorry. It isn't any of my business."

"It's okay, Laurel. I don't mind you knowing." His hazel eyes were bright, his tone unembarrassed.

The thrill of flying through the air on the swing still had Laurel's heart rate accelerated. She spoke on impulse, "I used to come here as a kid. We spent so many weekends in Ravenna. I'd walk here with one of my grandparents or by myself." She looked away from his watching eyes to not lose her words. "I stopped coming when I was fourteen. Well, I still came to this park, but only to sit and read by the river or walk on those trails in the woods. Not to play."

"Why not to play?"

"I remember coming alone one Saturday at the end of that summer when I was fourteen." The memory's clarity startled her. "I sat on this same swing and told myself I wasn't a child anymore. I didn't need to play. I didn't need to fly. This is the first time I've sat here since that day."

He didn't ask why, yet the explanation fell from her tongue before she could reconsider. "My mom had a stroke in May of that year. Dad left in June. Mom spent months in therapy. You can't tell anything ever happened now unless you notice the little droop in the corner of her mouth. Dad came back more than a year later. It was the summer I stopped being a kid."

Robert laid his hand on her knee.

She stood up with a shaky laugh. "I should head back. I don't know why I told you all that."

He walked beside her to the edge of the park. "Where did your dad go, Laurel?"

She held his gaze briefly then looked back into the park over his shoulder. "I don't know."

After a pause she forced a smile. "I should go. Grandma has probably wakened from her nap by now."

"Marsha and I will walk with you."

She nodded, unable to summon a reasonable objection. Robert whistled, and the dog trotted to his side.

The mile walk was spent with Robert giving affectionate descriptions of his two nieces, banishing the awkwardness that had come over Laurel when she'd stopped talking at the park. He explained that in an attempt to protect his dog from being covered in pink barrettes, he allowed the five- and seven-year-old girls to braid his hair.

"Let's just say I'm glad I grabbed my hat when I left this morning." Robert winked and patted the blue cap.

She snatched the hat from his head. His golden hair was a hodgepodge of kinks and waves where the many tiny braids had been.

"Maybe you should've left the braids in," she teased.

He grabbed the hat back from her hands and they were both still laughing when they reached Grandma Annie's driveway.

"This is her house." Laurel moved toward the door.

Robert stayed on the road. "It was good to see you. I like surprises like this."

She waved as she went into the house. Once inside, she allowed herself a moment to admit how unexpectedly pleasant this surprise had been. Then she hustled down the hallway to the bedroom.

Grandma Annie was awake, rested, reading, and eager to talk. Carrying two glasses of ice water and two mint chocolate cookies for each of them, Laurel sat down in the rocking chair. She let Grandma Annie begin straightaway, not mentioning her stop at Thatcher Park or the companion she enjoyed on the walk back.

17

December, 1917, 83 years earlier

Annie lay in bed a long while after waking too early. She stared at the shadowed ceiling trying to avoid the start of the day. Her mouth settled into a grim frown as she eventually stood up and dressed. While she wound her hair into a practical bun, she thought how different this morning felt from the morning before. Chet's revelation intruded on every thought. One strand of black hair fought her repeated efforts to pin it back and, after nearly losing all patience, she left it hanging against her cheek. When she walked out the front door, the wind struck her exposed skin like iced needles. The dense, gray clouds hung low, more a part of the earth than the sky. Snow clouds, Annie predicted. She wrapped her scarf one more time around her neck, and marched toward the road.

By the time she stood outside La Porte Rouge, each of Annie's turbulent thoughts had come around to one single-minded conclusion: things could not remain as they were. This decision repeated itself as she tried to understand how she came to this point, to these circumstances. The voice of her heart recommended self-pity, and such was the state of her spirit when she entered the café. Once inside she scanned the room but didn't find the only face she desired to see.

"Mademoiselle!"

She mustered a small smile for Madame Chappelle.

"Quelle surprise. I did not expect you."

"Isn't Kyle here?"

Madame Chappelle shook her head, dusting flour from her plump hands onto a faded black apron. "No, no, Monsieur Regan is at Saint Geneviève church. He is at Holy Mass."

She recalled then that it was Sunday. A French Army chaplain provided services at the hospital sporadically and Dr. LaCroix attended Mass in the village whenever he could. She asked Madame Chappelle how long Kyle would be gone.

"Not long, no." She beckoned Annie toward the kitchen. "You wait for him and help me."

Madame Chappelle instructed her on rolling out the delicate croissant dough, then provided an apron. It was soon powdered with flour, as was the length of Annie's forearms. Madame Chapelle began talking of her children and their help in the café in younger years. Annie did her best to listen, making suggestions when Madame Chappelle searched for the correct English word.

In the moments when she let the woman's voice fade into the background, Annie listened for someone to come through the front door. When she thought she heard it open, she froze with unexpected trepidation. She hadn't considered what to say. If Madame Chappelle would only work silently, for a few minutes at least, she might be able to formulate the right words in her mind. Madame Chappelle seemed glad for a listener though, unwilling to forgo the chance to talk.

"And are you ready to be at home again, in America, Mademoiselle?"

"No," Annie answered before processing the question. "I mean, yes. That is..."

She was saved from Madame Chappelle's befuddled look when the front door opened, its sound unmistakable this time. The café's hostess rushed to see who arrived, and then returned with Kyle close behind.

"Oui, he is here," Madame Chappelle addressed Annie triumphantly.

Kyle was dressed in black pants and polished shoes. His white shirt was pressed and adorned with a necktie. Annie's stomach leapt when he smiled.

"I wish I'd known you were here, Annie. I would have hurried back."

"I didn't mind." She was altogether conscious of the flour on her apron and arms, the fluttering nerves in her stomach, and the lump in her throat.

118

Last night's harsh inner voice taunted her as a fool. She found she could not hold Kyle's gaze. Sadness closed in and, wanting to avoid tears, she sought out the anger she had carried along this morning. Kyle waited for her to finish the batch of croissants and wash her hands. When she moved silently to the dining room, he followed.

"I will bring coffee," Madame Chappelle called as they left the kitchen.

The pair reached their usual corner table and Kyle took his seat. Annie did not, instead passing him to stare out the window.

"Annie?"

She could picture the tender concern in his features before turning to see it.

"Has he told you details of the battle?" Annie surprised herself with a steady voice.

"Chet?"

"Yes."

"He hasn't," Kyle sighed. "I asked him once, weeks ago, but Chet said he couldn't remember much of it."

"He lied. He apparently remembers all too well."

Kyle looked taken aback, but he let her proceed.

"Chet remembers, and he's a mess over it."

"He's tough, tougher than he might admit. Chet will get through it."

"Are you sure about that?" She crossed her arms and watched Kyle shift in his seat. "Until last night, I thought he was one of the most emotionally stable patients I'd seen. But he's no different than any other young man who's seen the unthinkable. I believe his cheerful demeanor is a front to cover how upset he is about nearly dying in that battle."

"What happened last night?" Kyle stood, almost toppling his chair. "Chet seemed fine when I left."

Annie felt her face flush. When he came closer, his nearness flustered her. She searched for the simplest explanation. "He had a bit of a breakdown. He's very angry."

"Chet's a grown man. He went into the army voluntarily and knew, as much as any man can know, what he was getting into."

The unsympathetic reply was the last thing she expected from Kyle. "That doesn't mean he knew how it would affect him. He's angry that he didn't die. He feels guilty for living when he knows so many good men died. Better men, according to him."

"Chet doesn't want to deal with the choices he made. He has finally found something he can't run from."

She was utterly confounded. Her voice rose, "Chet did not choose this. Perhaps if you were as good a brother as I took you to be, you might have seen his state of mind as it truly is, instead of having to hear it from me."

Kyle's shoulders sagged. "Annie, you don't know him like I do. Maybe he hid these things from me, but I know there's more to his anger and guilt than you can understand. You need to take my word for it."

His soft tone almost broke through her forced anger. She was afraid to let that anger go.

Fists hanging at her sides, she spoke with unchecked passion, "Chet thinks he's a coward because he was afraid to die, but you're the coward, Kyle."

"I tried to make him stay. I really tried," Kyle said with agony, scuffing his heel against the white tiled floor. "Told him to take care of home, that we needed him."

The pain in his eyes reached her heart but she would not let it stop what she'd begun.

"You stayed at home, writing your articles and hiding out. You're the coward."

"Annie, please." Kyle opened his hands in front of him.

She trembled, already wishing the words unsaid.

"You don't believe that. I know you don't."

"No. I don't," Annie whispered. A sob caught in her throat. She rushed past him and out the front door.

Snow had come. The clouds released their onslaught of enormous flakes. Annie was caught off guard by the accumulation already on the ground. When she paused, Kyle bumped into her in his rush to follow her from the café.

She turned to him, snowflakes swirling between their faces. They landed on her eyelashes and melted with the warm tears now spilling onto her cheeks. Kyle's expression was more than she could endure, equal parts disappointment and tenderness.

"I'm sorry," she whispered. "I don't know what to do, what to say."

"No, you don't, but I could explain. I want to explain."

She shook her head, the decision already too final in her mind. "No, Kyle. It's all wrong."

"What is?"

"Everything. Us. Goodbye, Kyle."

Despite the hindrance of the weather, she walked away in purposeful haste. She avoided looking back for some time and when she did, the white mass of snow veiled the café as well as the man left standing outside it.

18

December, 1917

Annie's walk back to the estate was arduous. Her legs ached as she trudged through the drifting snow to the front door.

Nora met her on the other side. "Thank goodness you're here."

Annie shook snow from her shoulders and stomped it off her shoes. Sensation returned to her feet in painful waves. "What is it?"

"I was heading to find you at the dormitory. When you opened the front door, I was afraid more soldiers had come. We simply can't take any more patients."

"Nora, what are you talking about? We had plenty of open beds last night."

Nora leaned against the wall, looking frazzled. "The ambulances started coming around 6:30 this morning. There's a terrible fever going through the trenches."

"How many have come?"

"At least sixty-five this morning."

She could imagine too well the state of the main ward: overfilled with the frenzied nurses trying to decide who to tend first.

"The medics said they brought the first transports and they're taking more to a hospital further north. Most of them aren't wounded, but they're so ill they can't lift their heads."

"What can I do?" Annie's mind and body went into response mode.

Nora pushed herself from the wall. "Follow me."

Annie was prepared for chaos, but that was not what greeted her in the congested room. She faltered and stopped. Quiet. But not the kind that held peace or rest. This quiet was heavy, suspended with fear. Surrounding her was the nauseating odor of illness, sweat, and dirt. The smells made her eyes water. She forced herself to breathe through her mouth as she followed Nora again.

Moving through the rows of beds was slow going. The wide aisles now hosted extra mattresses, as did the floor spaces between the beds lining the walls. Some men were lying on layered blankets, the mattresses having run short. Shivering, incoherent soldiers. Their uniforms were soaked with sweat and any visible skin was blotchy and pale. Besides the rare exception, they didn't moan or toss about in discomfort. The sagging limpness of their limbs conveyed utter weakness.

As she stepped near one soldier's head, he opened his eyes. He appeared to try to focus on her as she paused above him, yet his bloodshot eyes remained vacant, either not reaching her or looking beyond. Annie was glad when Nora beckoned her to keep moving.

"We've begun parceling out the room with each of us taking about ten patients." Nora pointed out the sections that other nurses were covering. "For most of the new arrivals, all we can do is keep cool rags on their foreheads and necks, wipe the sweat off with towels, and get them to drink if they wake up. Dr. LaCroix is seriously concerned about dehydration."

Annie nodded, still stunned by this unfamiliar dimension of nursing.

"Morning rounds for the rest of the patients haven't been made yet, so if you'll take my post, I'll see to that." Nora waited for a nod from Annie before departing.

Tucking a steel bowl in the crook of her arm, Annie went to the sink to fill it with freshly moistened rags. She found Meg in the laundry room, working vigorously on a hill of soiled linens. Curls that escaped the pins holding up Meg's hair stuck to her cheeks, wet with the steam from the wash basin.

Meg offered Annie a weary smile. "I'm glad to see you."

She squeezed Meg's hand empathetically.

"I didn't tell anyone where you were, or where I assumed you were," Meg said, leveling a solemn glance in her direction. "Everyone was so busy here, they didn't have time to wonder at your absence."

"Thank you." There was no chance of confiding in her friend right now on all that had passed between her, Chet, and Kyle. She chased the prickling thoughts of Kyle out of her mind.

Returning to the ward, the thick silence startled her all over again. As Nora had instructed, she spent a few minutes at each bed in her section. Drying the sweat on their faces; replacing the wet rolled towels beneath their necks with fresh ones; offering a drink of water to the few who were awake; moving on.

The only two of her patients not asleep were those at the hospital due to battle injuries instead of the fever. Captain Lamoure was on his fifth day of recuperation, slowly recovering from a shot to the abdomen. He spoke a little English but merely nodded when Annie asked if he was comfortable.

Lieutenant Joseph Winfield was a new arrival. He wore American army greens and his gray hair was trimmed neatly around his pleasant face.

"Good thing I'm not tall," he piped up as she approached his bed.

"Why is that, sir?" she whispered.

"It would just mean I'd have more leg to be hit."

The sparkle of humor in his eye was a sweet morsel of refreshment. She replied in kind. "Well, I don't know, sir. If your legs were longer, the wound might feel smaller."

"A fine point."

The lieutenant chuckled until Annie began checking the wound. The fibers of his muscles tensed under her hands. Shrapnel had sliced deeply into the length of his thigh.

"I'm going to change the dressing. The cleaner we keep it, the less the likelihood of infection."

"Agreed," he answered through gritted teeth. After a pause he whispered, "Can you believe this?"

She followed the direction of his gaze. Her section of patients occupied a back corner of the long ward. From Lieutenant Winfield's bed, the ballroom stretched out before them, a runway of semiconscious men and nurses moving mutely among them.

"It is staggering," she remarked after a moment. "How bad is it at the front?"

"Terrible." Lieutenant Winfield frowned. "They're only letting the ambulances take the ones who can't stand on their own two feet. Plenty more with the fever are still fighting. We were practically stacked in the ambulance to get here."

"How quickly has it spread?"

"May have started a few weeks ago, in just a few soldiers here and there. Senior officers didn't give it much heed until the first ones died."

"I hope we're able to help now that they're bringing them to us."

"I doubt it. As long as the leaders keep the soldiers out there until the fever nearly kills them, I don't see how many will survive it."

Her distress must have shown because the officer quickly recanted, "Don't listen to me though, ma'am. I don't have the faintest knowledge of doctoring and medicine. Could be these boys will be back on their feet soon enough."

Annie began cleaning Lieutenant Winfield's deep injury. He closed his eyes, leaning his head back with a wince. The expression brought an odd thought to her mind. A forgotten image appeared of her father rising from the desk in his study after hours bent over court papers, stretching his arms above him. He would grimace and then smile a small, contented smile. As a little girl, she loved happening upon him in that moment. If he found her outside the study, he bent down for a kiss and she'd rub her cheek against the bristly stubble on his chin. She swept her fingertips across her cheek now.

"May I guess where you're from?"

She refocused on Lieutenant Winfield. "Go ahead."

"New England, I'm sure of that much."

"And can you tell where in New England?" Annie asked with a challenging lift of her brow.

"That's a little harder." He gave her a scrutinizing squint. "Although, you'd be surprised how much a person's manners give away."

"Really?"

"Definitely. Take me, for instance. I would bet my manners are much more casual, a little rougher, than the sort you're used to at home."

She leaned in to say, "Yes, but I rather prefer your manners."

Lieutenant Winfield winked. "Most people do, especially the ladies, although my wife would never admit it."

She needed to move on from his bedside. "So, where do you think is my hometown?"

"Boston," he answered with certainty.

"I'm impressed, Lieutenant."

"Don't be, ma'am. Your accent is polished, not as strong as I've heard in others, but no one sounds like they're from Boston unless they are from Boston." They both laughed before she walked away.

As the rest of Annie's patients were not in any condition for conversation, she wandered the maze of her own thoughts. Inevitably, each turn led her back to that morning's conversation with Kyle. She let her eyes search the room for him, expecting to be glad if he wasn't present. But she wanted him close by. She felt no gladness when she didn't see him in the ward and she continued to picture his face as she last saw it. Annie wanted to take back her malicious words. Everything in her heart contradicted what she said, yet she tried to fool herself that it was for the best.

I might have at least been honest. Calling him a coward. Really, where did that come from? But even as she chided herself, her chin rose with determination. *It isn't like I could have told him the whole truth.*

Annie told herself it was better this way, unkind or not, But it forced confidence at best.

Two hours later, Annie reached Lieutenant Winfield's bed again. The dead-end road of her thoughts made her glad for another chat with him. Lunch trays and midday medications were not quite ready so Annie accepted the soldier's invitation to sit down for a moment to talk.

"You've not been off your feet yet today, ma'am."

Once she was sitting, she felt the tiredness in her legs and back.

"At least your patients are well behaved."

Annie groaned at the ironic humor. Other than a few who took sips of the water she offered, the fever-ridden soldiers remained unresponsive.

"Sorry, that was in poor taste," Lieutenant Winfield added in self-reproof.

"It's all right. I only wish they'd show some signs of improvement."

He nodded but didn't linger on the topic, "Since I was right about Boston, maybe you'd like to make a guess at my home in return."

She considered the man before her: slight in stature, agreeable features, and warm, easy friendliness. His voice contained an unfamiliar, subtle accent. It reminded her of the difference she noticed between Private John Kessel's countryside accent and the more refined tones of the London gentlemen she met at society dinners in Boston.

"You're not from a city, I'm sure of that."

"Good, good." He nodded approvingly.

"Is it upstate New York, maybe near Saratoga Springs?" It was the only viable suggestion to come to mind. Her family had vacationed in the area a couple times.

"You need to think further. Leave the northeast, girl."

Annie shrugged.

The lieutenant conceded, "Michigan. I live in western Michigan, the most beautiful of all the states."

"That's quite a claim, sir."

"I am biased, I'll grant you."

Her eyes fell on the gold band on his left hand. "Your family is there?"

He looked down at his ring too, instantly beset by emotion. "Yes, they are; Ruby and our children."

"How old are the children?"

"Let's see." He concentrated as he began the list, "Arlene is sixteen, Jeremy is fifteen next month, Joseph, Jr. is thirteen, Frances is ten, and Jennifer is four. No, she's five."

She found herself slightly overcome as she imagined the brood and watched the proud father's grin stretch wider with each name.

"Do you hear from them often? I hope they're well."

"Thank you, ma'am. They are. I had a letter from Mrs. Winfield last week and the worst she reported was Jennifer losing the second of her front teeth. Silly girl is so proud of her missing teeth that she smiles endlessly!"

Annie needed to make another round with fresh towels for the ill soldiers before fetching the lunch trays. Lieutenant Winfield requested she visit again in the afternoon and she assured him she'd be glad to hear more about his family.

Much later, she walked out of the main ward, discarded her apron in the laundry, and washed her hands vigorously. The nurses would be rotating in short shifts to endure the night. It was nearly eleven and she was heading to the dormitory for a few hours of sleep.

"I don't suppose you would like to read tonight?" Chet's voice froze Annie's weary legs where they stood. He had exited the dining room on his crutches as she entered the hallway.

She veiled her uneasiness with placidity before turning to answer him. "It's late. I need to rest."

Chet's familiar smile held fast. "A short one then. Please?"

His apparent freedom from any awkwardness perturbed her. She was too exhausted to argue and realized a reading did sound desirable. When she didn't object again, he took the lead and she followed him to his bed.

"Kyle left a couple hours ago. He said he didn't want to disturb you since things are so busy around here. Said to 'give you his best.' Don't think I've heard him use that phrase before."

She realized she was staring at Kyle's bedside chair. Chet watched her with narrowed eyes, which she ignored. "So, which short psalm did you have in mind?"

"Give me a moment and I'll decide."

She sat in the chair where it stood, further from Chet's bed than she typically placed it. With Chet taking his time settling onto the bed and flipping through the pages of the book, she wondered over his behavior. No apologies, no embarrassment, and by all appearances, none of the tragic despondency of the night before.

"Here it is, very right for tonight. Short and sweet." He pointed to Psalm 121 and handed over the book.

Aware of the sleeping invalids all around them, she kept her voice low. From the first syllable to the last, she was cloaked in the only comfort she'd felt in past twenty-four hours.

"I lift up mine eyes unto the hills,
from whence cometh my help.
My help cometh from the Lord,
which made heaven and earth.
He will not suffer thy foot to be moved:
he that keepeth thee will not slumber.
Behold, he that keepeth Israel shall neither
slumber nor sleep.
The Lord is thy keeper:
the Lord is thy shade upon thy right hand.
The sun shall not smite thee by day, nor the
moon by night.
The Lord shall preserve thee from all evil:
he shall preserve thy soul.
The Lord shall preserve thy going out and thy
coming in
from this time forth, and even for evermore."[3]

At the finish Annie caught Chet staring at her.

"Do you believe that God never sleeps?" she asked quietly.

Chet fingered the stubble surrounding the scar at his temple. He looked away and shook his head. She knew she'd stirred to the surface last night's declarations. As much as she might have appreciated some forthrightness, waiting for Chet to offer it was pointless. The tension passed and his customary nonchalance reappeared. She saw it as a mask now. He began chatting about the snow, wondering how much had fallen and if it stopped yet.

Annie stole a quick glance again at the lines of the psalm, the book still open on her knees. Finished with pretending all was right, she interrupted him, "I must get some rest, Chet. I have to be back here in less than four hours."

"Of course. Go!" Chet smiled and waved her away.

Leaving the hospital, she repeated portions of the psalm's verses under her breath. "'He that keepeth thee will not slumber' and 'the Lord shall preserve thy going out and thy coming in from this time forth, and even for evermore.'"

The verses' claims were indisputable in her mind, despite them representing a wholly new idea to her. It's not that she ever imagined God sleeping. She had not imagined Him anything. Weariness, anxiety, discouragement, and loss—all were tempered by the comfort of the single aspect she felt she now knew of God: He that keepeth thee will not slumber. She undressed in her room and crawled beneath the blankets. Sleep came instantly.

19

December, 1917

Forty-eight more hours passed at the hospital with little variance from Sunday's routine. Annie and her fellow nurses worked steadily for twenty hours and then slept for four hours. Wednesday supplied some positive change as four soldiers were released back to their regiments. Their fevers had broken close to dawn and by afternoon, though still weak and tired, the men left on a transport. Balanced with the seven lives already taken by the fever though, these recoveries could hardly lighten the atmosphere in the hospital.

Even Lieutenant Winfield wasn't as talkative tonight. He stared disinterestedly at the pages of an outdated newspaper while Annie tended to him.

"You haven't turned the page since I started this dressing," she said. "Is there anything the matter?"

The middle-aged officer lifted his head to look around the overcrowded ward. "Is that a rhetorical question?" His mouth settled into a stern frown.

She didn't reply.

He rested back against his pillows. "Sorry, ma'am. Apparently, I'm the cranky patient tonight."

"It's all right, sir."

"I'm tired, that's all." He closed his eyes and the lids were especially pale next to the shadowy circles below them. "Just extra tired tonight."

Something in her gut told her to worry. The lieutenant made a point of engaging her in conversation each time she so much as passed his bed. He shared sweet memories of his younger courtship of Mrs. Winfield, and stories of the children. Annie fancied she could have recognized the man's children if they passed her in the street. He painted vivid descriptions of home, with mental pictures of Michigan shorelines and apple orchards. Tonight though, he was glum and silent.

He finally spoke up when she was ready to move on to another patient. "I've been thinking about something, Nurse Walcott."

"What's that, sir?"

"About family." He met her eyes with intense focus. "I've spent years with family, first as a son and brother, then as a husband, and then as a father too. It all felt natural, like I was supposed to have it, or even deserved it."

"We all take the good things for granted sometimes," she replied gently.

"Well, don't do it, miss. Appreciate it all, every chance you find to love and be loved. Especially focus on giving it."

She guessed at the true concern behind this heartfelt advice. "You'll see them again, Lieutenant. I promise."

He pounded his fists against the mattress, making Annie flinch.

"Don't promise me that. Only God knows if..."

The passion got the better of him and he swallowed with difficulty.

She attempted to segue the conversation. "Yesterday, you mentioned a tulip festival. What town is it in?"

"Holland. Very close to our home." Lieutenant Winfield shut his eyes. "It's right on the water."

"Well, I don't know what people do at a tulip festival, but it sounds beautiful. In which month is it held?"

The corners of his mouth lifted for a brief moment. "May."

"I hope, sir, you will be with your family for the next festival. You're right, I can't guarantee it. I will hope for it though. And maybe, someday, I'll go to Michigan to see the tulips too."

When Lieutenant Winfield raised his head to answer, his expression had softened. "You should do that. Promise me you'll look up the Winfields when you come."

"I will, sir."

The next dawn saw the first ambulances carrying wounded troops since the fever patients had arrived from the trenches. Annie and Nora took initial assessments as the soldiers were moved from the vehicle into the hospital.

"I don't know where we'll put them," Nora lamented while examining a Frenchman with gunshots in his arm and shoulder.

"We'll need to rearrange," Annie said. "Some of the fever patients can be moved to the open mattresses on the floor. The wounded men can have beds."

"At least more room will come once the officers arrive for transfers and discharges."

"Sure, but there's no way to know when that'll be."

Nora glanced her way with a worried look.

"What? Oh no, he didn't die, did he?" Annie rushed to the stretcher at Nora's feet. The soldier stared up at her fearfully. Annie was mortified by her panic and Nora still looked uneasy. "What is it?"

"Dr. LaCroix requested discharges be given swiftly. He sent the dispatch out on Monday. I thought you knew that."

"That's good," Annie answered quickly. "I hope nothing delays it."

"He also specified certain patients to be sent home, ones who won't be harmed by travel to hospitals in their home countries." Nora hesitated when Annie didn't react, then added, "Chet Regan is on the transfer list."

It took a few seconds for Annie to reply. False indifference came after an internal fight.

"Good. Chet's been well enough to be sent home for a while now. There's no reason he should remain in France."

Nora's pursed mouth and raised eyebrows said she wasn't fooled.

Annie returned to the soldier she was assessing.

Nora made a hushed, final comment on the matter, "Kyle will go with him."

The day crept along as Annie moved through her rounds. Two of her fever patients took a welcome turn for the better. Lieutenant Winfield read some lines of a letter from his wife. The recovering soldiers received only half-hearted encouragement from Annie though. She couldn't recall any details that the lieutenant shared.

The knot that formed in her stomach after Nora's statements grew tighter by the hour. She scolded herself, willing her mind to focus on her work, but every effort failed.

Five days had passed since she last spoke to Kyle. What did he think of her now? She deserved his disappointment. Is that what he felt toward her? If he'd been able to brush off the argument, not sharing her regret over what was left unspoken, she didn't wish to know.

A matter of days would likely bring the Regans' departure. The grip of that one reality closed in around her. The anxiety manifested itself as a throbbing headache and she was relieved to begin her last rounds of the night.

"They're letting us leave at eleven tonight, and not come back until the morning shift," Annie said when she reached Lieutenant Winfield's bed. "Enough of the patients are on the mend that we're only overlapping shifts by two hours now."

"Good, each of you nurses need more rest than you've been getting." His words were raspy. He lay flat on the mattress, staring at the vaulted ceiling.

She put on a smile as she reached for his wrist to measure his pulse. "I completely agree. You fellows wear us out. When I was a child, I thought it'd be a thrill to stay awake all night. Even when I tried though, I could only make it an hour or so past my bedtime before I was sound asleep."

His pulse was weak. Beads of sweat glistened on his forehead and she noticed the sheet and blanket were pushed off of his body.

"Are you thirsty?"

"Yes, thank you."

She told him she would return momentarily with a fresh glass of water then headed to the exam room, looking for Dr. LaCroix. The doctor was stitching a soldier's leg. He gestured for her to enter the room.

"Doctor, Lieutenant Joseph Winfield," she began, "he arrived Sunday with a thigh wound. He's American..."

"Yes, I remember."

"He's showing signs of infection. I didn't notice anything alarming when I cleaned the wound this morning, but you may want to look at it tonight."

The doctor paused the movements of his needle. "If it's only begun this evening, as you said, then we have time to treat it."

"I'll inform the night nurses of the change in him, sir." Annie left the room reassured.

At the close of the last hour of her shift, Annie didn't waste time heading for the front door. The pain in her head was blinding. She massaged her temples as she turned into the foyer.

"Ah!" She stumbled backward when her face met the chest of someone rounding the same corner. A firm hand supported her back while she regained her balance.

"I'm so sorry."

Annie's eyes met Kyle's and the earnestness she saw there stopped her breath. The piercing blue eyes and full lips, the waves of hair around his broad forehead, and the solid weight of his hand against her back all welcomed her to him. She had a momentary wish that he would draw her closer. Instead, his hand fell to his side and they took a step apart.

She could feel the tears coming and became afraid of what she might say. Kyle opened his mouth to speak, but Annie shook her head. Whatever he desired to say was held back. She focused on the front door, visible behind Kyle's tall frame, then moved toward it before the tears fell.

20

December, 1917

In the brief trek between the hospital and the front door of the dormitory, icy wind coursed over Annie. The fireplace inside welcomed her tear-covered cheeks. She met Meg on the stairway.

Meg's exclamations of concern came rapidly. "Please tell me something!" She followed Annie up the stairs.

Annie stood at her bedroom door while her friend halted at the top of the stairway. "I wish I could, Meg. I wish I knew what to tell you."

Annie closed herself in her room, sitting with a slouch on the bed and trying to steady her ragged breathing.

"I can't do this. I can't fix it. I can't fix it," she repeated in sullen defeat.

Trembling, Annie slid from the bed to the wooden floor. She turned herself around and rose on her knees to lay her head and hands back on the bed. Her senses perceived one thing at a time: the seams of the quilt beneath her wet cheek, the individual floorboards on which she knelt, the pain persisting in her head, the whistle of the frigid air sneaking through the window frame. Words, barely audible, fell from her lips without deliberation.

"I don't know if you care, or if you will do anything to help me, but I do somehow believe you can. I read those psalms with Chet and they say you're merciful and kind and faithful. God, I think it's the mercy I'm seeking right now." She pressed her forehead into the blanket. "Kyle is leaving. I don't know when, but it'll be soon. He won't know I love him, or that I'm sorry."

With each breath came a small sob. Fear and love possessed her equally.

"How can I make things right? Even if I felt able to love Kyle, if I had more time with him, when I think of the choice required to free myself to love him.... My family would be so disappointed. They wouldn't understand. I'm sure of it. I can't...I can't go back to the same life if I'm not the same person, can I?" She clung to the bed like the lap of whomever was listening.

"I'm not," she paused again, her thoughts slowing down. "I'm not really a new person yet, am I? But I'm not the old one either. I'm just suspended in between, I think."

Any doubt she held about whether or not she loved Kyle had disintegrated when she'd looked him in the eyes tonight. The likelihood of him leaving without an opportunity to make amends left her breathless. Annie opened her eyes, staring at the quilt under the shadow of her black hair. She lifted her cheek off the bed; watched her fingers shake against the blanket. Waiting for a response and wondering if she would hear one, she abandoned her kneeling posture to sit on the floor.

The trunk of personal items she brought from Boston stood against the opposite wall. She stared hard at its copper clasp, then crawled across the room to sit in front of it. A few stacks of clothing and packets of letters had to be removed before she found what she sought. The Bible was issued to her at an orientation meeting before the voyage to France. It was unopened and forgotten until now.

Columns of words flashed past her eyes as she moved from page to page, not yet reading any of them. She paused briefly in the Psalms, acknowledging the chapters like an acquaintance in a crowd of strangers. When she stopped again only a small stack of pages lay against the back cover.

"My little children, let us not love in word, neither in tongue; but in deed and in truth."[4]

Annie was unsure why her eyes stopped there, in the third chapter of the First Letter of John. The words gripped her with unexpected force. She read it again. *In deed and in truth; yes, exactly.*

She began reading at the start of the chapter and continued into the next chapter. Then she read both chapters a second and a third time, gaining comprehension with each reading. With each verse, the turmoil of recent days lost more of its power over her. Truth began to win. Isolated phrases leapt out from the page and she read them aloud with wonder.

"God is greater than our heart, and knoweth all things."[5]

"Herein is love, not that we loved God, but that he loved us."[6]

"Beloved, if God so loved us, we ought also to love one another."[7]

"Whosoever shall confess that Jesus is the Son of God, God dwelleth in him, and he in God."[8]

"God is love."[9]

"There is no fear in love; but perfect love casteth out fear."[10]

Each fragment laid itself out before her like finely cut stones merging to create a path she could walk upon. The realities in the Bible's words seemed obvious, yet entirely fresh. It was as if she might have known it all instinctively, but only these sacred pages could bring it to light. The limit of her present understanding did not agitate her. Rather, with the reading came peace and confidence. The thought that her desperate attempt to pray had been answered filled her green eyes with tears.

The phrase that had first struck her this evening now repeated itself in her memory: let us not love in word, neither in tongue; but in deed and in truth. After only a moment's consideration, she knew which deed must be taken up.

When the morning's white-light winter sun pulled her from a hard sleep, she rolled onto her stomach, laying her cheek on the edge of the bed to stare at the letter on the floor. It lay where she knelt in prayer only a few hours ago.

Writing the letter to Samuel hadn't taken long. The words came easily enough because she chose them with gentle honesty. She did not hesitate to commit them to paper. She was surprised at how few words were necessary. She scooped the paper from the floor and stood.

Dear Samuel,
Firstly, let me assure you that you are,
and will continue to be, dear to me. We

have loved each other according to what we knew. Since leaving Boston however, the disparity between what I knew and what I've come to know is significant. It is the difference between what I expected of myself and what I am now committed to, between what I hoped for in my life and what I now hope for, and it is truth I can no longer ignore.

In the last few months I have made efforts to communicate my experiences to you, and in that process I've discovered how different we are. I accept that you do not fully understand how I've changed while we've been apart. Continuing our engagement would be an act of dishonesty on my part, not an act of love. I have faith that in making this choice, we will both gain more happiness and blessings than if we entered into our planned marriage.

I wish you well, Samuel, and ask that you forgive any hurt I am causing you.

Always,

Annie

Her conviction did not lessen with the rereading. She sealed the letter in an envelope and carried it downstairs to the box of outgoing mail.

Upon returning to her room, Annie lowered herself to her knees. At first, no words came. She rested in the comfort of this moment with God. Her God. The specification made her smile.

"Thank you," she whispered into her interlocked fingers, "for whatever it is you have begun in me."

21

September, 2000, 83 years later

Eighty-three years after the fact, Laurel was captivated by Grandma Annie's narrative of newfound faith. Having witnessed her great-grandmother's expressions of faith at every turn, Laurel had never considered that Grandma Annie ever lived without it.

"That letter took courage and kindness," Laurel said.

"I did not end my relationship with Samuel in order to begin one with Kyle," Grandma Annie insisted, though Laurel made no comment on the matter. "I'm sure that seems like the obvious reason but, amazingly, when I wrote the letter to Samuel, Kyle was not on my mind."

Laurel raised an eyebrow and said, "He had to play into the decision a little, Grandma."

"No." Grandma Annie pursed her lips before explaining. "It finally wasn't about choosing Samuel versus Kyle. It was about who God had called me to be. The only choice was about Samuel and me, and nothing further. That's why I hadn't been able to make a decision before. I had complicated the situation with an imagined complication."

"You didn't imagine Kyle."

With a light laugh, Grandma Annie conceded. "I didn't imagine him, no. Kyle was entirely real."

They exchanged warm smiles.

Grandma Annie had more to say.

"That night, the circumstance God led me to deal with was my engagement to Samuel. I became motivated by love instead of fear. I had to decide the best way to treat that situation and only that situation."

Laurel's hands rose in surrender. "I get it."

"Good." Annie's expression was tender but she shook a finger at Laurel. "You remember that too, Laurie Bean. When you think a problem is more complicated than you can handle, you must find the decision at the heart of the matter. Never let your fears talk louder than your faith."

"I wish I could say I don't know what you mean." Laurel let her head fall against the back of the chair.

Both of them grew quiet, but the silence was interrupted by the chime of the doorbell.

"Oh, that'll be Mrs. Baxter. Virginia did mention stopping by with Mrs. Bill Jenkins." Grandma Annie was carefully lifting her legs over the side of the bed. "Will you help me to the kitchen so we can visit at the table?"

After the women were settled in the kitchen and began their reports of church and neighborhood happenings, Laurel respectfully bowed out of the gathering. She could only manage the briefest of conversations with Mrs. Bill Jenkins, who managed to bring every topic around to her dearly departed Bill's opinion on the matter.

"Girls today are simply too thin." Mrs. Baxter examined Laurel with sympathy in her eyes as Laurel tried to make her exit. "When we were young, society appreciated a solid, womanly build."

"I soundly agree," Mrs. Bill Jenkins chimed in. "My dear Bill used to worry so over our girls and all those lies in the fashion magazines."

Laurel held her tongue and waved at her great-grandmother. The women's voices carried through the house as she reached the front door.

"Annie, have you heard who has a new little one on the way?"

Grandma Annie indicated she hadn't and Mrs. Baxter quickly remedied that.

"Gary and Abby Kennesaw."

The name stopped Laurel with her hand on the doorknob. Robert would be an uncle again. Next, she heard Mrs. Bill Jenkins' solemn critique.

"Much too large an age gap between their youngest and this new baby. My dear Bill always recommended that siblings be only one to two years apart. Our own children..."

Laurel opened and shut the door quietly behind her before allowing herself a laugh.

Laurel sat at the dining table Sunday afternoon and dialed her parents' number.

"You've reached Marshall and Erin Thomas. Please leave a message and we will be sure to return your call."

The recorded greeting was her mother's secretary voice. It reminded her of childhood, when she'd call her mother at work and Erin spoke in that tone until realizing it was her daughter on the line. Laurel left a brief message, pressed the off button on the phone, and stared at it without focus. Her thoughts wandered to details of Grandma Annie's confidences. She was musing over her great-grandmother's decision to end her engagement when, from the back of her mind, she heard the priest's voice from Mass that morning. Pieces of his message came back to her.

"Are you willing to listen?" He'd asked the question again and again of the congregation. "Don't decide when and where and how God can speak to you. Listen. Everywhere, in everything, keep your ears open to the voice of God through His Word."

Laurel had done plenty of listening lately but wondered if her Heavenly Father's voice was in any of it.

RRRIIINNNGGGG.

Her whole body jumped and the phone fell with a bang on the table.

RRRIIINNNGGGG.

She laughed hard when the second ring startled her nearly as much as the first.

"Hello."

"Laurel? You sound odd."

She let her friend Connor wait while she finished laughing at herself.

"Laurel?"

Once she could talk, they made plans for Connor to pick up their favorite burgers and bring them over for dinner that evening.

When Connor arrived, he carried three sacks of food. He set them down and wrapped his arms around Laurel in a hug. They were the same height. When he released her, she placed her hands on his arms and took a good look at her dear friend, as deeply valued as Melanie though they didn't see each other as often as she saw Mel. Between their developing careers and other obligations, it was difficult to find the time. She noticed for the first time how the curve of his sandy brown hairline was receding a little above his temples.

He smiled genially at her. "It's been a while."

"It has."

He wore his typical uniform for his workdays: a black golf polo and khaki cargo pants. She used to suggest he expand his wardrobe but to no avail. As a photographer, the polo served Connor well for most circumstances letting him blend effectively into the background. The pockets of the cargo pants were useful for his gear.

While Laurel pulled two plates from her cupboard, he began sharing his best anecdotes from the anniversary party he photographed that afternoon.

"After fifty years the couple seem like one person. Best friends, finishing each other's sentences and anticipating each other's needs. It was adorable to watch."

"I wonder how someone builds a relationship like that?"

"Plenty of patience and teasing, I'm guessing."

"Well, that is what keeps me attached to you," Laurel quipped.

"What's in the last bag?" she asked.

Their plates were already spilling over with waffle fries and thick hamburgers. She sat down in front of the one she recognized as hers: ketchup, lettuce, and onions.

"Chocolate shakes." He pulled two lidded cups from the bag, a proud smile on his face.

She was duly impressed. This was about the extent of Connor's spontaneity.

"Chocolate is okay?"

"Is chocolate ever not okay?" She grinned and took one of the cups, poking her straw down into the plastic lid. "Thank you, Connor."

After he prayed a blessing for them, the meal began silently as they savored their first bites.

Connor stood. "They forgot to give me napkins. I'll get them."

She couldn't politely answer through the crispy fries she was chewing.

"How was your visit yesterday with your great-grandma?"

She swallowed, then took a sip of the thick, sweet shake. "It was marvelous. I stayed with her the whole afternoon."

"What do you do while you're there?"

"What do you mean?"

"How do the two of you pass the time? Do you read to her, or watch television, or take walks? I used to play card games whenever I visited my grandma in the nursing home."

Laurel shook her head. "Grandma Annie's eyesight is still good enough for her to read on her own. We used to do more, I guess. She's the one who taught me how to crochet, and she's to blame for my addiction to crossword puzzles in recent years. Now, we mostly talk."

Connor wiped mustard from his lip. His eyebrows were drawn together in thought. "Do you mean you finally asked her about your great-grandfather? Is that what you talk about."

Much like with Melanie when they discussed this, caution sprang up and Laurel hesitated over full disclosure. "Well, we talk about all sorts of things. Family, memories, daily goings-on, whatever happens to come up."

"And?"

She leaned toward him over her plate, excitement taking hold. "And we talk about things Grandma hasn't talked about before."

His brown eyes brightened. "She's told you?"

She opened her mouth to confirm it but paused. "No, not entirely."

"What does that mean? She only told you his first name or something?"

"It isn't that simple."

He waited while she set down her hamburger.

"Grandma is telling me much more than only about him. She's been sharing her experience as a nurse over in France. It changed her whole life. She is telling me about him too, but she hasn't actually said he's my great-grandfather." She tapped her foot on the white linoleum. "He is though. I'm sure of it."

"So, who is he?"

"Kyle Regan." The name felt sacred once spoken. She took another bite of her sandwich, chewing slowly while deciding how much to tell Connor. "He came from Ireland to France while Grandma was a nurse there. She makes him sound wonderful."

"She never married though, right? What kept them from being together?"

Laurel grimaced. "Who knows? Grandma hasn't reached that part of the story."

"It's good she's decided to share this with you." He set his food down, watching Laurel closely.

"The moments of sharing have been more special to me than I can describe."

"It's hard sometimes to know the best way or best time to tell people difficult things."

Laurel frowned, wondering if something was wrong. Connor had grown so serious with these words. Before she could decide whether to prod him for an explanation, he changed the subject.

"We've finally decided on a plan for my parents' 40th anniversary," he said, his smile returning.

"A plan everyone is happy about?"

Connor and his siblings had differing opinions on the celebration. She had listened to his take on the unsettled plans on several occasions.

"Yes," he confirmed. "This one was a collaboration between all four of us."

Connor and Laurel finished their meals while he shared the details of the reception-style party that would replicate details of the original wedding.

"Your parents will love it."

"I think they will," he replied. "You'll be my date, of course."

She was standing at the kitchen sink and turned to see if he was serious. At the sight of his smirk, her hands went to her hips. "Is that how you ask other girls out? I have a hunch it doesn't work very well for you."

She was teasing. It was a comfortable habit of theirs to count on each other when one needed a guest for an event.

"Well, it always works on you," Connor jested, then ducked his shoulder away from Laurel's swinging hand.

22

September, 2000

To all four corners, the bridal boutique was lined with dress racks. Laurel and Melanie had stopped by for final dress fittings. The burgundy hue of the bridesmaid gown complemented Laurel's ebony hair. She played with potential hairstyles while the seamstress finished pinning and measuring. After Laurel changed back into her jeans and sweater, she switched all her attention to her friend Mel as Mel exited her dressing room. "Melanie Casperson, you are flawless! There is no other word for it."

Mel turned to look at her image in the trio of mirrors edging the raised platform where she now stood. She grinned over Laurel's exuberance. "I haven't tried it on in six months. I'm not sure I even remember how it looks."

The pink blush flooding Mel's face confirmed that she had indeed forgotten exactly how she looked in the dress. The sleeveless silk gown was a simple, elegant design that breathtakingly skimmed over her curves.

Laurel sighed, "If all clothing fit that well, I'd enjoy shopping so much more."

A couple tears fell from Mel's eyes and she bit her quivering lower lip. Laurel rushed to join her on the platform, meeting her friends' uneasy gaze in the mirror.

"What is it, Mel?" she said. "You look amazing."

Surprisingly, Mel began to laugh. She wiped the tear off her cheeks and hugged Laurel. "I'm only trying on the dress and I can barely contain my joy. How will I handle being so happy on the actual wedding day?"

Laurel pulled out of the hug and grabbed her friend's hands. "Who ever said you were expected to contain it?"

The seamstress approached, waiting out the women's gushing before she finished her work. Twenty minutes later, they drove back to Laurel's apartment. She kicked off her shoes and fell across the sofa, propping her feet up on its armrest and sinking into the soft cushions. She and Melanie had spent the ride mulling over song choices for the newlyweds' traditional first dance. She worked hard to be only a sounding board in the discussion. Mel and Jace would choose the song together.

"I'm drinking your soda," Mel announced from beside the fridge. "You want some?"

She nodded. Melanie handed her a glass then sat cross-legged on the floor, leaning against the sofa.

"What are you thinking about?" Melanie asked.

"I was remembering some of the songs I used to think I'd want for my first dance at my wedding."

"For the longest time I wanted a U2 song," Melanie admitted. "I didn't care which one because any of them would work since I'd be marrying Bono."

They both laughed over the teenage dreams. When it was quiet again, Laurel forced her next words out in a low voice. "I used to imagine dancing to a Sinatra song with Marcus."

Marcus Bentley. They dated for the duration of her senior year of college and her first year at Parker Advertising. He talked of marriage with a promising light in his captivating eyes, but without ever suggesting it specifically to her. A week after their two-year anniversary of dating, he'd appeared at her office and unapologetically informed her he'd accepted a software programmer position in Pittsburgh. He'd hugged her, given her what was clearly a farewell kiss, and had not been heard from since. Afterward, she spent months alternating between striving to let go of, and fighting to hang on to, her love for Marcus. Little by little, the sting in her heart lessened and his face blurred from her daydreams.

Melanie reached a hand up behind her shoulder to grasp Laurel's hand. "Do you still wonder about him, Laurel? Do you wish he stayed?"

She took her time answering. "I did for quite a while. I know I refused to talk about him much after he left, but he was in my head for a long time."

"And now?"

"You know," she felt lighter with this realization, "I couldn't even tell you the last time I wished for any of it back."

Taking a sip from her glass, Laurel silently thanked God for answering her countless prayers after Marcus left.

Laurel left ten minutes early for lunch on Wednesday, garnering a look of suspicion from LeeAnn as she passed the reception desk. Instead of going someplace to eat, she drove straight to Grand River Books where Melanie worked as a manager. The two of them had a problem to analyze.

The bell above the door rang out loudly when she swung it open with more than necessary force. Several customers from the line of shoppers between her and the registers turned to look. Laurel spotted Melanie at the registers. Once Mel acknowledged her with a wave, Laurel wandered down an aisle to wait.

She browsed an arrangement of classic literature on sale at twenty percent off. Her eyes scanned the titles. She saw a paperback copy of *Persuasion* by Jane Austen, wedged between *To Kill a Mockingbird* and *The Three Musketeers*. Laurel remembered Grandma Annie saying once that *Persuasion* was her favorite novel and she'd read it a dozen times.

Melanie's high heels clicked on the hardwood floor as she entered the aisle. "Hey, what are you doing here?"

"I think I should buy this," she held up the copy of *Persuasion*.

"Okay."

"Grandma recommended it. She said it had everything a good story should include."

"Okay," Mel repeated. "And that's why you came here on your lunch break?"

"No, but as long as I'm here..."

They walked to the register and Mel patiently rang up the book. Laurel handed her the cash, knowing Mel would wait as long as it took for her to explain the real matter at hand.

"Robert asked me on a date," she blurted out like it was an incriminating secret.

Melanie's mouth opened slightly but she said nothing.

"At least, I think it would be a date. He asked to have dinner with me."

Melanie smoothed a few strands of her chestnut hair loosening from her ponytail. "That is not what I'd have guessed you were going to tell me."

"What would you have guessed?"

"I don't know but it wouldn't have been that." Mel came out from behind the counter and pulled her toward an empty aisle. "All right, tell me everything."

Laurel fidgeted with the handles of the paper shopping bag. "There isn't much to tell. On Monday, there was something different, something... oh, I don't know. I thought he might figure we were better friends now, after running into each other in Ravenna. He seemed more," Laurel reached for the right word, "more genuine."

"Genuine?"

"Yes. Robert seems carefree and relaxed much of the time but I've wondered if it is an act. Maybe meant to impress or to make people comfortable around him. It could be that I only imagined that about him, like you pointed out last week, but that's what I noticed missing since Monday."

"And what happened today?"

"I had barely turned on the computer this morning and he came into my office. We chatted. He asked how Grandma Annie was feeling."

"Nice of him to do that."

"Then he said, 'We should have dinner sometime.'"

Melanie's pink lips formed an O. She shook her head. "Completely out of the blue?"

Laurel nodded, still surprised.

"Well, what did you say?"

She bit her lip.

"You said 'yes'?" Mel rose up on her toes, waiting for the answer.

"Gosh, no," Laurel whispered forcefully.

Melanie sank back down, not hiding her disappointment.

"I didn't say anything. I was speechless. Robert said he 'would like to talk over dinner sometime soon.' That was the only other thing he said." She felt a fresh wave of bewilderment. "Then Lee-Ann walked into my office to deliver something. Robert looked embarrassed and rushed out."

"And you avoided him the rest of the morning until you could come rehash it with me?"

"Precisely."

"You have to go back to work," her friend pointed out needlessly.

"Yes, I do, and I will have to see and probably even talk to Robert again today." She crossed her arms. "What I don't know is what to say to him."

"Do you want to go on a date with him?"

She was silent for a few seconds and the hesitation put a broad smile on Mel's face.

Laurel answered with some annoyance, "I'm not entertaining that possibility. Do I really need to go through that again with you?"

"Maybe he's only trying to be friends though, and dinner would be fun."

This thought had crossed Laurel's mind. She'd ruled it out, however, due to Robert's reaction when LeeAnn came on the scene. "I don't want to jump to conclusions one way or the other," she spoke earnestly, "but Mel, when has a single man asked a single woman out to dinner only for the sake of establishing a friendship?"

"True, true." Mel winked. "You're simply more irresistible than you know."

"I'm serious, Mel."

"I am too. You're well worth knowing, and dating. But if he doesn't make his intentions clearer, you can only go on the impressions you have. Listen to your gut, say a prayer, and give him the answer you need to give him."

Melanie had taken up her tell-it-like-it-is voice. Laurel never argued with that voice, even when she didn't like what it told her. She hugged her friend and pointed herself toward the front of the store.

Returning to Parker Advertising, Laurel walked directly into Robert's office. His fingers were tapping rapidly on his keyboard as she closed his door. He didn't pause in his typing when he glanced up, then back to the computer monitor. She waited, tucking her hair behind her ears, straightening her shirt, until he finished. His direct gaze lacked any of the awkwardness she'd expected.

"Hey, Laurel, how was your lunch?"

I didn't eat. I talked about you and bought a book I could have borrowed from my great-grandmother. "It was fine. Yours?"

"Didn't take one, actually," Robert answered with a shrug. "I ate an apple in here to hold me over. I'm leaving early this afternoon; need to get as much done as I can before three."

There was no easy segue in sight, so Laurel went for it. "I don't think we should have dinner together, Robert."

He folded his hands on the desk. "Is that so?"

"We work well together. Running into you in Ravenna this weekend was a pleasant surprise. However, I don't think we need to be anything more than coworkers."

"I completely understand," Robert said. "You probably have a lot of things taking up your time anyway, especially with visiting your grandmother."

"Yes." She jumped on the provided excuse. "Also, my best friend is getting married in a little over a month and I'm the maid of honor. It's time consuming."

"I'm sure it is."

She tried to decipher if the smile on Robert's face was the old one she had always questioned, or the new one she had secretly enjoyed the past few days.

"Okay," she said as she gripped the door handle, "I will, um, see you around."

Robert nodded, still smiling, and turned back to his computer.

That evening, Laurel drove to her great-grandmother's house straightaway. Dinner was a granola bar and banana eaten in the car.

For thirty minutes, she replayed in her head the day's short conversations with Robert. Was she being unkind? Presumptuous? Did she possibly like the notion of saying 'yes' to Robert's invitation? She knew well her ability to allow fears and doubts to hold her back even when she should move forward. By the time she settled into the rocking chair by Annie's bed, Laurel longed for an off-switch for her thoughts on the matter.

Grandma Annie was eager to take up the story as it had been three days since they'd talked. Before they dove in though, Laurel noticed a difference in her great-grandmother. Considering Grandma Annie's typically pale visage, Laurel might be imagining the gray pallor in it tonight.

"How are you feeling today, Grandma?"

"You know, today has felt like a long day."

"We should make sure I don't stay too late then."

"That's probably a smart idea, even though there's still so much I want to say." Grandma Annie's face grew forlorn. She rested her head against the headboard. "Still so much."

23

December, 1917, 83 years earlier

When Annie pushed open the door of the hospital after her night of prayers and decisions, she felt she could burst with the goodness of the morning. She watched closely the faces she encountered, questioning if they could perceive on the outside how new she felt on the inside.

In the foyer, two nurses passed her on their way out. Down the hallway, she met another nurse and two patients. There were no reactions beyond their mumbled "good mornings" and "bonjours." Her chipper responses echoed against the surrounding walls.

When Meg arrived beside her, Annie realized how difficult it would be to explain the difference now compared to her distressed state when they last saw each other. The pair silently tied on their aprons, repeated glances begging each to speak first. She was so accustomed to Meg being the source of cheer and optimism that it was off-putting to see her friend's beautiful face tightened by anxiety.

Meg took the lead, "You're happy today."

"It's a good day."

"But yesterday wasn't?"

"Yesterday was...," Annie tried to fit the past twenty-four hours into one word, "it was a struggle."

"A struggle for what?"

"For peace of mind; for letting go of things I could no longer hang onto; for solving problems." Annie took her friend's hand. "After praying about it, I wrote a letter to Samuel to end our engagement."

Meg looked as surprised as if Annie announced the Germans surrendered. "Oh my," Meg gasped with her fingers over her mouth. "I can hardly believe it."

"Well, it's true," she said. "And I'm feeling so relieved, so right about the decision."

"Then I'm glad for you." Meg enveloped her in a hug. "You seem contented and much happier than when I saw you last night. That's enough to convince me you did the right thing."

"Thank you, Meg."

They walked together to the ward, their silence more comfortable than before.

Annie noticed Meg still sending her furtive glances.

"What is it?"

Meg fiddled with a loose thread on her apron's pocket. "You said you prayed about it. I don't think I ever heard you talk about praying."

Her heart swelled at the chance to share. "It was the first time I had prayed. I mean, I've been to church, but any prayers I said there hadn't come from my heart. Last night, I didn't know what else to do, so I asked God to help me. He did, Meg, he really did."

"How?"

"I'm not sure I know how because it's so new to me." She wished she understood more of how God was acting in her. "All I can say is that now I feel I have a guide in my heart, a better guide than just me."

Meg's only reply was a bright smile and Annie hoped it was sincere. They split up to tend to the patients.

The new light in which Annie saw everything made her eager to care for the sick men. Remembering her lack of attention last night, she tried especially hard to encourage their spirits today. Most of the patients in her corner of the crowded ward were dozing, but one Frenchman was sitting up in his bed. He smiled when she walked in his direction. His knees were drawn up in front of him, propping up an open book. A sling supported the soldier's right arm and one eye was swollen shut, surrounded by purple bruising.

"Bonjour," he called out.

"Bonjour."

"You are American, yes?"

She was relieved to hear him speak English. "I am. How are you feeling this morning?"

"Hmmm, compared to yesterday, I feel okay." He patted his bruised cheek and said, "Compared to most of my life, not so well."

"Well, we will focus on comparing it to yesterday then," Annie answered with a smile. His throaty accent was beautiful. "How is it you speak English so well, sir?"

"My mother was raised in London. She taught me English as soon as I began speaking." He extended his good arm. "I am Gerard."

She shook his hand. "I'm glad to meet you, Gerard. I'm Annie. Of course, we have met already. I've been taking care of you for several days."

"But without a proper introduction," he noted. "This is the first day you look, oh, what is the word?"

Annie raised her eyebrows.

"Welcoming," Gerard answered his own question.

"Really?"

"Yes."

Gerard was young with brown hair and light freckles covering his nose. His straightforward manner was reinforced by the steadiness in his brown eyes. He didn't look away as she searched his features for any malice in his observation.

"I apologize for not being welcoming, Gerard. Unlike you, I am doing quite well today compared to the rest of my life."

"Glad to hear it, mademoiselle. I didn't mean offense."

"There's no harm in honesty. You actually helped me. You see, I had a chat with God last night and he set me on a clearer course. It's helpful to know the difference it's made for me is affecting things in a positive way."

Gerard returned to his book with a good-natured smile, leaving her to consider their brief exchange. Annie was relieved to learn the change was evident after all, and not only to those who knew her well. She simultaneously felt troubled to realize that meant her former unhappiness was likely obvious too.

Turning to the other men under her care, she spotted one soldier straining to reach a tin cup on the tray beside him. She stepped quickly to hand it to him. From there, her eyes fell on Lieutenant Winfield's bed. It was empty, stripped of its linens. The air rushed from her lungs.

"What's happened?" she whispered.

Needing to ask that question of someone other than herself, she searched the room. Nora and Dr. LaCroix conversed near the middle of the ward. She walked toward them, her legs leaden with trepidation. Nora left as Annie reached them.

"Good morning, Nurse Walcott," Dr. LaCroix greeted her.

She drew in a deep breath and spoke softly, "Good morning, Doctor. Where is Joseph Winfield?"

"The fever took him. He died early in the morning."

"The fever?" She thought he must be confused. "No, sir, he didn't have the fever. The lieutenant was brought in for a leg wound. Remember, I spoke to you about the signs of infection he was showing last night."

Dr. LaCroix squeezed her shoulder. "It wasn't infection. His leg was healing well. He might have returned to the front in a few weeks. I checked on him after you left. He was barely conscious. I've never seen one taken that quickly, but I've no doubt it was the same fever as the rest. All the symptoms were present."

"Of course, sir, it must have been," Annie mumbled her reply. She ran her hands down the front of her apron, willing them to stop trembling.

Another nurse caught the doctor's attention and he left Annie's side. She groped behind her for something to lean on, backing up until her hand felt the cold marble wall. She leaned against it and lowered her head. Her mind traversed a terrain of emotions, observing each of them as options rather than feeling them. Anger pushed against her chest with familiar pressure.

No, no, not that. She felt the pressure release.

Next, she met with pity: pity for Lieutenant Winfield and for herself. A wave of disappointment rose up along with it. Lieutenant Winfield was another patient she had considered a friend, and whom she'd been confident was out of harm's way. Instead, he was lost within a night's time. She felt a small degree of relief that he had not suffered the fever's effects for days, like most of the men, but it was small indeed.

In light of what the lieutenant had lost, Annie found she could not pity herself. She would remain grateful for knowing Joseph Winfield, however briefly. *Thank you, God, for crossing our paths.*

Eventually in her silent ruminations, Annie came upon sadness. She stayed there and felt it blanket her with unexpected warmth. She felt the rightness of it and didn't resist it. When Lieutenant Winfield's family crossed her mind, tears pooled in her eyes. His wife would have bittersweet reminders of him in their five children. The older children would possess lasting memories of their father, but surely the youngest would struggle to remember.

Annie opened her eyes and pushed herself off the marble wall, blinking to disband the tears. When she lifted her head, she met the worried faces of both Kyle and Meg. They stood a few feet from her. The intensity of Kyle's gaze swallowed that distance. She straightened her shoulders and stepped toward them.

"Lieutenant Winfield has died," she informed them. While Kyle's expression did not change, Meg nodded sympathetically. "I'm afraid it was a difficult shock since he only came down with the fever last night."

"I'm so sorry," Meg spoke up. "He died shortly after my shift began. I meant to tell you about it, but when you came in you were so...," Meg's voice trailed off with a glance at Kyle.

"It's all right. I won't pretend I'm not sad, or horribly surprised. I am." She had to pause to swallow the lump in her throat. A notion formed in her mind, something she'd heard people say but never understood before. "It's all in God's care."

A flicker of surprise passed over Kyle's face. Annie's intense desire for him to understand her heart frightened her. *Is my connection to Kyle also in your care, God? Can I trust you with it?*

Fear threatened to dismantle the peace so recently built within. Annie clasped her hands together. "I'm going to see to my patients."

Heading straight for her nearest patient, she began checking his pulse. After taking his temperature, she spoke encouragingly to the soldier of his improvement since yesterday. When Annie turned to move to the next bed, she found Kyle standing behind her. Her startled gasp brought a smile to Kyle's face.

"Really, Kyle, do you even have shoes on? I didn't hear a single step behind me."

Kyle began to laugh but quickly composed himself. "We need to talk."

"I need to work."

Kyle didn't move despite her firm tone. "I didn't mean now. What time does your shift finish?"

"Oh, right." Heat of embarrassment spread through her cheeks. "I just started my shift."

He was smiling again, that broad, captivating smile that flustered her nerves. "Yes, but what time does your shift finish?"

"Not until eleven."

"And tomorrow you return to the regular schedule, so you'll be back on at 2 pm."

"How did you know that?"

"I checked with Dr. LaCroix. He said most of the soldiers with the fever were past the worst of it now."

"Of course, that's a tentative schedule. The nurses are always expected to be ready to help beyond their scheduled shifts. There is no way to know what could come up."

"Noted." Kyle feigned seriousness but there was a gleam of amusement in his blue eyes. "Barring an emergency then, could we plan on talking tonight when you're done?"

"Yes, we can. I can't guarantee that I won't be exhausted, but I agree with you. We do need to talk."

Kyle offered, "We can wait until tomorrow morning. You could come to the café. Madame Chappelle has asked about you every day this week."

She was bound to spend the night restlessly puzzling over the approaching conversation, so she answered readily, "No, tonight will be fine."

"I'll wait for you in the foyer."

She watched him return to Chet's bed at the other end of the ward. With great resolve and a timid smile, she focused on her next patient.

24

December, 1917

As Annie's shift ended that night she counted the clock's chimes to be sure and then tossed her apron into an empty basket and washed her hands. With even the laundry caught up, Annie knew she had no reason to stay late tonight.

Her feet took her as far as the hallway before they stopped. Kyle would be waiting in the foyer at the other end. Leaning against the wall, she stared down the length of pine floor. The light was dim, giving the floor a soft gleam to hide the rough marks of age and use. Generation after generation of the LaCroix family had called this place home, and now it was filled with strangers who wanted only to be somewhere else.

"I don't want to be anywhere else," she whispered. A wave of certainty reached all the way to her heels and she stepped away from the wall.

Kyle stood before an oil painting on the foyer wall. He was leaning in, his nose nearly touching the canvas, studying the artist's depiction of the LaCroix estate. When she reached him, she touched his shoulder. He jumped, causing her to do likewise and both of them to laugh.

"Now who's sneaking up on people?"

"The floorboards usually creak," she protested. "Although you were concentrating hard enough not to hear them."

Two night-shift nurses arrived through the front door, pausing in their chatter when they saw Kyle and Annie. Alone again, Kyle turned to her. She suspected he was waiting for some indication that she was now prepared to talk. She closed her eyes.

"I'm so sorry, Annie." His words were barely audible.

"No," she said quickly. She opened her eyes and met his. "I'm the one needing to apologize. The things I said that morning at the café were wrong and cruel." She shook her head. "I was angry, but not at you."

Strands of Annie's black hair had slipped down against her cheek. Kyle reached up to brush them back. As soon as his fingertips met her skin though, he pulled back and stuck his hands in his pockets. "I only meant about your friend who died, the American lieutenant."

She laughed, the sound taking them by surprise. Embarrassment washed over her. "Well, that was an awful start."

"I'm glad to be talking again." His shoulders relaxed as they exchanged smiles.

She felt the return of the comfortable rapport of past weeks, and the release brought by apology. Another nurse, then a patient, passed by in the hallway.

Annie made a recommendation, "Let's not talk here."

They walked up a flight of stairs and around a corner where they reached a closed door. Annie lingered in the hall while he stepped in and lit two lamps. The sitting room was cold and she shivered as she settled onto the sofa. The piano was still uncovered from her last foray into this room. That day, she'd come here in frustration and despondency. What very different emotions filled her now.

First walking to an adjacent chair, Kyle changed his mind and joined Annie on the sofa, the middle cushion left between them. She was grateful when Kyle spoke first.

"You don't seem as distraught tonight about Lieutenant Winfield as I expected." His expression was inscrutable. "When you first found out, you were more upset."

She looked down at her lap. "It was such a shock since he wasn't sick until last night. He'd become a friend."

"Like Private Kessel?"

"Yes, and no," Annie answered slowly. "When Private Kessel died it felt like a personal failure. Our work with him had made him a success story in my mind. His death was a blow to my confidence as a nurse, and to my reasons for staying here."

Kyle nodded, letting her continue.

"Lieutenant Winfield wasn't a failure, but he was a loss. This time, I'm not angry, I'm..."

"Thoroughly sad?" Kyle ventured when she paused.

"Exactly."

Kyle leaned forward enough for the lamplight to land on his face. She blushed under his bold gaze.

"You're different today," he said finally.

She reminded herself that she'd grown used to this level of honesty. Although it felt new again, it had only been a week since she'd distanced herself from him. "I am changed today. At least, I hope I am."

She spoke then of the frustrations and troubles that culminated in her desperate prayer last night. She chose her words carefully for she didn't wish to distress Kyle with details of his brother's actions or insinuations. When she described the effect the scripture passages had on her, Kyle's assured expression told her he was well acquainted with the words.

The only point on which she faltered was the letter to Samuel. It would be weeks before she received a reply from him, if he chose to reply at all. How Samuel handled the end of their relationship would not change her decision. It was finished. Still, she let the topic wait for the time being and recounted this morning's events instead.

"The lieutenant's death was distressing." Annie stood and paced the oval braided rug in front of the sofa. The need to articulate the change in her heart pulsed to her fingertips. "Yet I knew that all would be well despite something so awful happening. I just don't know how I knew that."

Her hands went to her hips and she looked at Kyle, exasperated. "I don't think I'm explaining it well enough."

"'The peace of God, which passeth all understanding.'¹¹ That's how Saint Paul described it."

She sank back onto the cushion. "Kyle, that's precisely what it is. It doesn't minimize the tragedy. But there's a sense that we aren't alone in it. God is with us there." She let her head rest against the tall back of the sofa. "'Peace that passes understanding.' I like that. What does it mean to you?"

Placing his elbows on his knees, Kyle propped his chin in his hands and stared straight ahead. "It means trusting that God's hand is on everything and everyone; that He's wiser than we are and that He is good to us. It means being okay with not fully understanding some things because you believe in God's providence. Of course, that is what it means in my soul. It's bound to mean a variety of things to a variety of people."

"And you believe all of that?"

"Absolutely."

She saw the fiery light in his eyes.

"I'm glad for you," Kyle said, "that you've chosen to turn to God, to receive His gift of faith. Now you can rely on His strength to get you through."

"Get me through what?"

"Anything," he replied and pushed his hand through his thick hair. "I've learned to think of God always surrounding me, no matter the circumstances."

She leaned slightly toward him. "I don't suppose that was an easy truth to learn."

"Do you mind if I share a few things with you, Annie?" Kyle's countenance was all hopefulness.

"Of course I don't mind." She folded her hands against her stomach, hoping to convey calmness that she didn't feel.

Instead of speaking, he rose and walked to the piano. He leaned against the curve in the instrument and folded his arms. She waited patiently, letting him gather his thoughts. He opened his mouth as if to begin, then shook his head. He lit another lamp. This one was attached to the wall directly across from Annie and as it flickered to brightness, it spread a pool of yellow light over the space between them. Kyle took a seat in the chair next to her corner of the sofa. "I'm having a hard time deciding where to begin."

Again, she waited.

"I need to tell you more about things at home."

He seemed to still need encouragement so she asked, "About your work for the nationalist movement?"

"It's more about a time before I started working for the newspaper. I'd like to explain how I became involved in the first place."

"I'd like to hear it."

His brow furrowed. "I've told you about the changes that Ireland needs, the politics of it. I suppose I made it sound only political. The decision to get involved was rather personal." His hand went through his hair again and he rubbed the back of his neck as he continued. "Even after the Uprising, my friends and I were following the movement from a distance. It was like a far-off battle, something we could pick a side on without having to do more than talk.

"Three months after the Uprising, in the summer of last year, a few of us attended our first rally. Chet went as well. It was in a town nearby and one of the movement's most prominent leaders was rumored to be speaking, so the crowd was enormous. Everyone was packed into the town square like sheep in a pen. I remember it being loud and sweltering."

Annie pictured the scene, thinking how rattled she'd be in that crowd.

"About midway through the leader's speech, the English policemen decided to get the crowd under control." Kyle's tone grew as sharp as a blade. "We heard so many stories of the police harassing the people at rallies but hadn't experienced it ourselves. The officials bullied and taunted us until some of the crowd began yelling back. A few people pitched rocks at the officers and it all fell apart from there."

She pressed her fingertips to her lips as she listened.

"The police opened fire, mostly wounding but also killing several people."

"Were you hurt?" she asked in a whisper.

"No." He shut his eyes. "But my friend Sean was killed. Sean tried to push Chet out of the way when a policeman charged through the square on his horse. To the policeman, it must have looked like

Sean was running at him. He took a shot as Sean reached Chet. The whole thing only took a few seconds and Sean died minutes later."

She reached for his hand. He squeezed her fingers. When he let go, she fixed her eyes on his face, aching to erase the pain she saw there.

His eyes opened. "Something snapped in me that day, in that moment. I couldn't look at anything the same as before, and there was no longer this imagined option of keeping to the sidelines of the fight. I was all in."

"What did you do next?" she asked with some trepidation.

"At first, I did nothing. I considered options, but mostly I ranted against the English and against God. It was a while before I calmed down enough to realize that ranting was pointless."

"Then you began writing for that paper?"

"Yes, once I made the right connections to introduce myself to the men running it."

"Has it helped at all in dealing with your friend's death?"

"It has a little, but it can't truly heal such a loss. After a few months, my purpose became broader. I think it had to or I couldn't have committed to the work." Kyle added dryly, "If I really wanted to avenge Sean, there are plenty of different groups I could join. Those would only feed my anger, not heal it. Those groups can't make the sort of difference I became determined to make."

His comment prompted a new train of thought in her head. "How did Chet react?"

The sigh Kyle released told volumes.

Annie asked gently, "Chet didn't realize his anger would get him nowhere, did he?"

"No, he didn't. I could easily have taken the same route. Chet snapped after that day too, but for him it was only anger. He never moved beyond it. Sean died protecting him. That horse was headed straight for Chet. After Sean's funeral, Chet didn't hide his belief that he should have been the one to die. He didn't think he should be glad to have survived because that might mean he was glad Sean hadn't."

The sentiments were grievously familiar to Annie's ears. Chet still didn't appear to have changed his miserable logic.

"He joined up with the Guards some weeks later. I think Chet had so much fight built up in him that he needed a physical enemy to face. The battle in Ireland is too much like a war with one side refusing to engage in the fight."

Kyle sounded worn out. He continued, "I know Chet's on the right side of things in this war, Annie. I don't want you to think I don't understand the importance of the war here. The trouble is, I have no doubt that Chet will stay just as angry and feel just as guilty when he's done fighting here. If a gun doesn't do it for him, Chet's more than capable of destroying himself."

Kyle stared at the wall across from them while Annie stared at his profile. The frustration in his voice emerged in deep creases across his forehead. His strong jaw tightened and twitched when he finished speaking of his brother. He inhaled a long, slow breath. She watched his face relax, the lines and shadows dissipating. The familiar expression reappeared, one she had seen often in the past weeks. '*Peace that passes understanding,*' she thought. Annie felt she could learn it simply by watching him.

Annie lifted her hand and pushed aside the hair covering Kyle's temple. It was coarser than she expected. He didn't pull away from her touch but when he kept his eyes on the wall instead of meeting hers, she drew back. Where ought she take them with her next words?

25

December, 1917

Annie moved across the room to the piano to think better without the distraction of Kyle's nearness. She was certain of one thing: if she asked the questions, Kyle would not withhold his true mind from her.

The lamp cast a soft gleam over the piano's keyboard. She sat down and lifted her fingers to the polished keys to concentrate her senses outside of herself. Once she began tapping out a simple melody, the clutter of scattered thoughts cleared from her mind. Kyle turned in her direction when she moved into a new song. It was a hymn she learned years ago. He stood and leaned against the wall behind her.

"That's one of my favorites," he said when she played the last chords.

"What impression have I given you, Kyle?" She spun her legs around the bench to face him.

The sudden question brought a frown to his face. "Of yourself?"

"Yes."

She stared him down, securing his honesty by her resolution. He stayed where he was, crossing one foot over the other and drumming his fingers against the textured gray wallpaper.

"Can I ask the purpose of your question?"

"I'm not certain I know it," she replied. A surge of energy pulsed through her, simultaneously enjoyable and frightening.

His eyes narrowed. The line of his mouth thinned as he deliberated.

"Don't worry too much on how to answer. Lately, I'm not sure what my impression is of me."

"All right." Kyle slapped his hands against his thighs and gave her a nod. "Two of my many observations are these: You live as you're expected to live; you think as you're expected to think. Secondly, you cannot bear disappointment and you make your choices accordingly."

"Disappointment in others or disappointing others?"

"Mostly disappointing others," Kyle's voice softened.

Heat reached not only her face but her neck and chest as well. She knew it would take only seconds for tears to come.

He had more to say.

"That's the impression you've given me, but it is not necessarily the one I believed."

"Well, it should be," she retorted. "That's exactly who I am."

"Don't be so hard on yourself."

Kyle moved to sit beside her on the piano bench. She stiffened, feeling provoked even though she was the one who asked the question.

He appeared undisturbed by her reaction. "It might be an assumption to say so, but I believe that is who you were. You are not your old self. What you shared about your prayer last night has convinced me of that, although the transformation started long before last night, didn't it?"

He waited. That he already understood so much about Annie was disconcerting to her.

"It did not happen in one night, no," Annie said as she strove to pinpoint the start. "The changes have been so gradual. If I had to name it, the first step was my decision to serve here in France."

She contemplated that day when she made up her mind to sign up with the medical corps. The memory of the evening when she told her parents was crystal clear, along with that night's unnerving sensation of the ceiling being about to cave in on her.

"Yes, that was the start of it," she continued voicing her unfolding thoughts. "Once I made that decision, it was like running down a hill when you start at pitch speed from the top; that feeling that you can't possibly stop until you reach the bottom. At dinner, I told my whole family at once. Father, Mother, Lee and Joanna, even Samuel was there. I didn't ask their permission, or for their opinions. Everything in me said I was doing what I should do and even if they remained unconvinced, I would still follow through on it. I had never approached anything that way before. Never."

"Did they remain unconvinced?" Kyle asked.

"Not my brother Lee. He was excited for me and seemed to understand why I was determined about it." A new thought dawned on her. "It was as if he knew long before I did that there was more to me than I'd shown thus far. I appreciate him for that, and I know it too now."

"Good." Kyle's serious expression transformed into a bright smile.

Annie returned to his prior question, "The rest of my family did remain unconvinced. They still are, actually."

"Even Samuel?"

"Especially Samuel," she whispered. "He thought it was a phase. A phase of what, I don't know."

"I'm sorry. It had to be difficult to leave under those circumstances."

"It wasn't hard to leave, no, but it was lonely once I settled in here." She shook her head. "I discovered I couldn't make them understand."

"And that's the crux of it, isn't it? No one can be made to understand something they choose not to see."

Kyle and Annie fell into a companionable silence. In the lull, Annie discerned a nudging in her gut; a suggestion that she couldn't find reason to argue against.

She slid her legs back around the corner of the piano bench to face the instrument. Kyle still sat the opposite way. His shoulder rested against hers and it took extra concentration to place her fingers correctly on the keys. She managed to remember the first few measures of a Vivaldi piece. The rest of the melody came easily once she began.

"I wrote to Samuel this morning," Annie said over the music, "or during the night. Anyway, I sent the letter this morning."

Kyle twisted at the waist to look at her.

She glanced at him for a second and struck a wrong note. "Our engagement is over. I ended it."

She watched him move his hand to her shoulder, then she stopped playing. As the last vibrations of the piano stilled and the room was silent, Kyle leaned back for a better view of her face.

"Are you upset?"

She lifted her eyes to meet his. "No. I've known for a while, but I had to find the courage to actually act on it. 'Peace that passes understanding.'"

"I'm glad." He stood and put space between them. "I mean, I'm glad you're okay with your decision. I'm not glad you had to make that choice."

She interrupted his rush of words. "I understand."

"And you're sure about your choice?"

"Completely."

There was firm purpose in his footsteps as he returned to her side. Lifting her hand, he held her fingers lightly while she stood. He leaned down, resting his forehead against hers. His skin was warm.

"Annie," Kyle whispered.

The sound of her name on his lips reached every nerve. She raised her free hand and rested her fingers on his neck, feeling his pulse reach the same speed as hers.

"Annie."

His tone had changed. The melancholy in it frightened her. She stepped back to look him in the eye but he didn't hold her gaze. Instead his eyes went to her hand, where he traced tiny circles with his thumb. "Chet got his transfer orders."

Then came an assault of information: Dr. LaCroix had spoken with Kyle that afternoon. Chet would be sent to a hospital in Dublin. The transport was scheduled to depart tomorrow evening. Kyle planned to leave once a train ticket could be purchased, maybe by noon tomorrow—no, today. It was already one A.M. according to the intrusive chime of the mantle clock.

"Apparently there was confusion with Chet's paperwork." Kyle was still explaining things and she forced herself to listen more closely. "The medics on the battlefield recorded him as deceased but then the Irish Guards received papers from the hospital after he arrived here. Thankfully, our family only received the report that he was wounded, yet the wrong papers must have been passed along in the Guards. That's the only reason he wasn't transferred back to Ireland sooner."

"And the only reason you've been in France for this long," she added.

"I'll stay through Sunday."

"What? Why?" The new shape of things shook her. "Chet will leave by Saturday night."

The conversation felt like crossing a chasm on a bridge she could only guess was there. If she looked down, she might find she was mistaken and plummet to the ground.

"And we'll have Sunday," he answered.

"It might make it worse, even harder, once you do go."

"It might. We'll find out together."

26

December, 1917

Annie's next task was to make it through Saturday. Her relief that she and Kyle had talked last night was palpable. The morning brought freezing rain, making it impossible to walk to the café for breakfast with him. So, in the hours before her hospital shift, Annie did whatever she could to pass the time.

She tidied her bed, cleaned her two pairs of shoes, wrote a short letter to her brother and his wife, began reading the Gospel of John from chapter one, and found a pair of scissors to try to even out the ends of her long hair. In between each distraction, her nerves and doubts knocked at the door. Annie's excitement over the day to be spent with Kyle was tempered by the looming question of how they might leave things at the close of that day.

With her hospital shift came welcome occupation. A few hours in, Kyle made it to the hospital during an interval in the freezing rain. His blue lips and windburned cheeks testified to the brutal cold. Still, he came into the ward smiling, scanning the long room. Annie couldn't resist his beckoning wave. Her steps nearly reached a skipping pace as she approached the doorway where he stood.

"Hello," he greeted her.

"Hello."

Despite the whispered greeting, Annie thought Kyle looked like she felt: like she could explode with the emotion pulsing in her chest. He took hold of her left hand, tugged it a little, and she moved with him into the foyer.

"I checked with Nora," she smiled up at him. "She agreed to switch shifts tomorrow. I'll have the whole day off from the hospital."

"The whole day," he repeated. "Why didn't we do this sooner, Annie?"

She frowned. "We couldn't. We both know that."

"I know, I know. We will choose to be thankful for tomorrow."

"Yes."

"So, Miss Walcott, what shall we do with a whole day all to ourselves?"

"I want to go to church with you."

His eyebrows rose at her quick reply. "I would like that."

"Afterwards, we'll have breakfast at La Porte Rouge. After that, I don't know. That's as far as I could think."

"Well, who says we need to plan further than that right now?"

Kyle hadn't released her hand yet. She could feel his icy fingers gradually absorbing the heat from hers. She let her eyes linger on his face, noticing for the first time some freckles on his straight nose and a long-healed scar below his hairline.

Activity outside the window caught their attention. Two military vehicles pulled up to the mansion. From the one with the French flag on its side emerged two men, a French officer and an American officer. An English general exited the second vehicle and all three strode up the front steps. The heavy door moaned as it allowed them into the foyer. Annie and Kyle continued their mute watch. The men passed by into the ward with no notice of the eyes upon them. Kyle stared at the empty space of the entryway. When Annie lifted her face toward him, he kept his eyes fixed straight ahead.

She sighed, "I need to get back to the patients."

"I know."

He caught her hand again. She saw in his splendid eyes every promise she wondered if she would ever hear aloud.

"I'll be with Chet until he leaves, but I'll find you before we go."

"And I will be sure to say goodbye to Chet anyway," she said.

"So, I will, um, see you."

The inadequacy of the words grieved her. "Yes, I'll see you."

By dinnertime, the many transfer orders and a few discharges were doled out. Two more of the fever-stricken soldiers had died in the last twenty-four hours, but the rest were recovering. Those who were consistently conscious received transfers to hospitals further from the front, and several others were to return to their regiments. Annie prayed the trenches were clear of the fever by now.

Three transport vehicles were due to arrive at eight-thirty to carry the transferred soldiers to the train depot. At eight-fifteen, Annie abandoned the linen closet she was organizing and returned to the main ward. From this end of the room, she had a clear view of Chet's bed. He sat on its edge, his weaker leg propped on Kyle's chair and the crutches lying beside him on the mattress. Kyle stood against the wall with his hands stuffed in his pockets and his mouth moving in conversation. She started toward them.

Kyle straightened from his relaxed posture. "Good evening, Annie."

"Hello." She smiled and forced her eyes down to the floor.

"Hello," Chet greeted her. He watched them with one eyebrow raised and a smirk on his face.

Kyle slipped by her, mumbling something about checking on the transport.

"So, the day has finally come," Chet said when Annie came around the bed to sit beside him.

"It has, indeed."

"Apparently, some folks thought I was dead and gone." His words dripped with sarcasm.

"But you aren't." She looked him squarely in the eyes. "I'm glad of it, you know."

"Can't blame you for that. How else would you have met my brother?"

She couldn't help laughing before contradicting him. "No, Chet, I'm glad you are alive. I'm glad for the times you've made me laugh, and for all the evenings I ended my shifts by reading the Psalms with you, and for the good you did by asking for that dining room to be opened for the patients. Your idea has built up a lot of men's spirits. It provided a way to enjoy a little of their time in this hospital."

"And you're glad that I had a brother who came all the way from Ireland to see me."

She tossed her hands into the air. "Yes, I'm glad you had a brother who came all the way from Ireland to see you."

Chet hung his arm around her shoulders. "Good. I just wanted to hear you say it."

They were quiet for a few moments. Chet withdrew his arm and stared hard at his lap. "I've never seen him in love with anyone before, but there's no mistaking it."

She bit her lip, feeling the heat spread over her cheeks.

"Kyle's the best man I know, and with this war, I've known a lot of men. I haven't been a decent brother to him. That never changed how he treated me though. I want..." Chet was at a loss for words for the first time since he'd awoken in the hospital. "He deserves..."

"I know, Chet. I really do." She continued tentatively, "You're a good man too, Chet."

He shook his head and started to recover his standard smile.

She wouldn't let him get away with it. "You were worth saving, worth protecting. Otherwise your friend Sean wouldn't have done what he did."

Tears gathered in her eyes when she saw the desolation pulling at his handsome features. He pressed his palms hard into the mattress. She could hear the transport personnel approaching from the hallway. They would be gathering the soldiers to leave for the train station.

Impulsively, she wrapped her arms around him. "Goodbye."

He relaxed into the hug after a second's hesitation, giving her a wink once they pulled away from each other. "Goodbye, Annie. Thanks for everything."

Minutes later, she watched the military vehicles pass into darkness as they drove to the village. Kyle went too, convincing the drivers to fit him into one of the trucks so he could see his brother off.

Now, all Annie had to do was wait for Sunday—their Sunday.

27

September, 2000, 83 years later

"Thank God I'd learned to pray that week." Grandma Annie adjusted the pillow behind her shoulders. "I don't know how many times I asked God to keep me focused during that shift."

While Laurel was anxious to hear about that Sunday, her brain was still mulling over Kyle and Annie's exchange the previous night. "I can't believe how much changed from that one single night of the two of you talking."

Grandma Annie smiled peacefully. "Kyle and I talked that night for over two hours. He shared so much, and I knew it was a privilege to be the recipient of it. His concerns were personal and important, not the kind of talk to share widely. As well, he was too humble to talk about himself with many people."

She hesitated, then asked, "Like you, Grandma?"

"How do you mean?"

"Is that how you felt about telling anyone all of this?"

"Don't think so well of me." Her great-grandmother's expression was all gentleness. "I made a lot of mistakes in my years and perhaps keeping this from you all was one of them. That is one thing I can't make up my mind about."

Grandma Annie's words were interrupted by a knock at the front door. It was nine o'clock in the evening. Laurel raised her eyebrows but Grandma Annie only shrugged. Laurel hustled through the small house and lifted the lace half-curtain hanging across the square of glass in the door.

"Wh-what?" she stuttered as she turned the knob. She stopped with the door half open. "Robert?"

"I'm sorry." He sounded apologetic but he was smiling. "Is it okay that I stopped by?"

"Yes, I mean, not really. It's late."

"The lights were all still on and I saw your car."

She didn't reply.

"I was at my brother's house," he added.

Laurel nodded.

"Abby gave me pie." He lifted a plate. The scent of warm berries wafted toward her from beneath the tinfoil. "I thought I could share."

She took a step back and he came inside, peering into the house.

"Let me go explain to Grandma. She might not be okay with you staying."

"Sure, of course."

Laurel left him there in the entryway. *Grandma, a colleague of mine...a friend from work...a friend....* She stuck her head into the bedroom.

"Who was at the door, Laurel?"

"You know Gary and Abby Kennesaw, right?"

"Gary and Abby are here?" Grandma Annie looked puzzled. "Why would they be coming by?"

"No, no. They aren't here, but I work with Gary's brother, Robert."

"Yes, I think I remember Abby mentioning something."

"Robert is here."

"So, you have a visitor, is that it?"

"I guess so. I'm sorry, Grandma. I certainly didn't expect him, and I can ask him to go."

"No sense in that." Grandma Annie dismissed the suggestion, pulling back the blanket covering her legs. "Somehow, I'm not nearly as tired now as I was all day. Hand me my sweater and we'll go in the kitchen."

Robert waited at the other end of the hallway until Laurel called to him. He came with the pie held out like a peace offering, setting it in front of Annie where she was now seated at the dining table.

He took Grandma Annie's hand in both of his. "It's great to meet you. I'm Robert Kennesaw. Your granddaughter and I work together."

"And I attend church with your brother and his family." Grandma Annie's eyes crinkled above her welcoming smile.

Robert uncovered the pie and asked if they would like a piece while it was still warm. Soon, Laurel was helping him find plates and forks in the cupboards.

He stopped her before they returned to the table. "Is my presence here all right?" Concern creased his brow. "I kind of barged in on you without warning. I'm not even sure what made me think it'd be a good idea. I'll leave within a minute if you want me to go."

"No, it's fine, Robert. You were unexpected, that's all." She smirked at him, adding, "Grandma is okay with it, so you might as well stay."

"Yeah," Robert nudged her elbow with his, "and it probably helps that I brought pie."

They all moaned and sighed over the deliciousness of his sister-in-law's raspberry pie. Robert kept them laughing with stories of camping with his nieces and trying to teach them to fish. At the first yawn Grandma Annie let escape, Robert graciously said his good-byes and thanked her for letting him visit. He carried the empty plates to the sink and left with a wave to both Annie and Laurel.

"Laurie Bean," Grandma Annie chided, "walk him to the door."

He was already at the front door, leaning against its frame. She noticed for the thousandth time how handsome he was and, also for the thousandth time, tried to not care.

"Thanks for letting me in."

"Tell Abby thank you for the pie."

"I will. I'll see you at work tomorrow." He opened the door to go then gave her a wink. "Laurie Bean."

She laughed and stepped outside too. "Robert," she called after him.

He turned as he reached his Jeep.

"It was good to see you tonight."

Robert climbed into his vehicle without a word but there was no mistaking the smile that spread across his face before he backed onto the road.

On her own drive home, she figured she did have one reason to be upset by his visit. Once he'd gone, Grandma Annie's energy was spent. Laurel left for the night without hearing details of Annie's last day with Kyle in France.

The next evening, at the end of a busy workday, she arrived home to find Connor sitting against her front door. He barely looked up from the stack of photos in his hands while she unlocked the apartment. She held it open until he grabbed his jacket off the floor and followed her inside.

"Connor." Laurel faced him with a hand on her hip.

"Yeah?"

"What are you doing here?"

He looked up at her with mutual confusion. "I'm picking you up for dinner."

She searched her memory for dinner plans.

"Mel and Jace are meeting us at Corvella's. Reservation is at six-thirty."

She smacked her forehead. "I completely forgot."

"Clearly."

He leaned against the edge of the dining table and continued flipping through his photographs. She walked into her bedroom to swap her blazer and camisole for her favorite white sweater and her pencil skirt for a pair of jeans. They were back out the door in five minutes. By the time they pulled up to Corvella's Restaurant, Jace and Melanie were already seated and ordering drinks.

Laurel was quick to apologize. "It completely slipped my mind and I worked a little late today."

Mel leaned over to hug her. "No worries. I figured Connor couldn't possibly be the reason you two were late, so I preemptively forgave you."

The pair chatted while Jace and Connor checked in with each other on the outlook for Detroit's basketball season.

"How is Grandma Annie this week?" Melanie asked after they'd all placed their orders with the waiter.

"She's really well. I've been over there so much lately and I've enjoyed every minute of my visits."

"She probably loves the company."

"Definitely," Jace agreed with his fiancé. "My grandma loved having visitors right up until the end. If no one stopped by, she called me at work to talk."

Melanie elbowed him, giving him a disapproving look.

"It's okay, Mel." Laurel shook her head. "Grandma is 103 years old. I'm well aware that I should treasure every day that I have with her."

"I'm sorry, Laurel, I didn't mean...," Jace trailed off, fidgeting with the cloth napkin draped over his leg.

"You don't need to apologize. It isn't like I think about Grandma dying." She was surprised at the trouble of getting the word out. "But it's something I at least know with my head will happen."

Jace relaxed.

The foursome was quiet until their waiter came to check their drinks.

"Jace and I decided where we'll take our honeymoon," Mel turned the conversation to the wedding.

"It's about time, guys." Annie was excited to hear their destination choice. "I can't believe you waited this long to plan it."

"We were so torn between the two different trips."

"Correction," Jace said as he laid his arm over Mel's shoulders. "You were torn between the two trips. I hoped all along that we would end up going to Spain."

Mel rolled her eyes at him. "It's just that since I was a little girl I planned to go to Hawaii on my honeymoon."

Laurel laughed, "You also planned to have fuchsia bridesmaid dresses and hire New Kids on the Block to play the reception."

"I'd still hire them if they worked cheaply enough."

Mel let Jace describe the trip. Jace was a high school history teacher and, fittingly, most of the details he gave were of the historical sites they'd see during the honeymoon. Laurel figured she would hear more from Melanie another time.

During the meal, Jace asked why Laurel needed to work late that day.

"The coffeehouse's grand opening is in a week," Melanie answered for her.

"It is." Laurel set down her glass of wine. "Today though, I was working on something else." She filled them in on the new account that was assigned to the same team working the North Wind Coffees launch. It was a jewelry boutique opening downtown and launching a widespread advertising campaign.

"And you're on Robert's team again?" Mel asked.

"I am. This is the first time I haven't been bumped from team to team as the junior associate in training. Being given a repeat spot on a team is a great sign for me at the firm."

"That's excellent, Laurel," Melanie commended her then added, "You don't mind continuing to work closely with him?"

"I've decided to be friends with Robert." She lifted her chin defensively when Melanie laughed.

Jace questioned her, "You don't get along with this guy?"

Before Laurel could try to explain, Melanie piped up.

"He reminds her of Marcus," Mel said, avoiding Laurel's eyes.

"You need to give up on that theory. It isn't true," Laurel insisted.

"I'll try."

Jace raised his eyebrows at the two of them, then wisely steered the conversation elsewhere.

The friends left the restaurant two hours later, their appetites more than satisfied by the delicious food. Laurel carried a takeout container of her shrimp primavera. She waited for Connor to comment on the odor the food might leave behind in his car, but he didn't say anything. In fact, he'd said little to her all evening.

"Anything wrong?" she asked once they were inside the car.

He maneuvered out of their parking spot. "Not really."

"Are you sure?"

He focused on entering traffic on the busy street before replying, "Are you bringing a date to Mel and Jace's wedding?"

"No." She rested her take-out box on her knees. "I'm maid of honor, which means I'll be busy all day with the bride. If I brought a date, he would be stuck by himself most of the time. I'd barely have time to see him."

Connor nodded. "Yeah, it'll be the same for me with doing the photography."

"Besides," she joked, "who would I bring? You're always my date-on-call, and you're already attending."

He gave her an abrupt glance, his face still serious. "That's true. I didn't know if there was someone else you might want to bring. I didn't want to assume there wasn't someone."

"You would certainly know if there was someone, Connor." She watched his profile, puzzled.

"Yeah, I thought so."

The awkward conversation was a rarity in the easy rapport they'd maintained for years. On the remainder of the drive, Connor didn't cooperate with her attempts at small talk. He brought her home and she said goodnight, still wondering what might be on his mind.

28

October, 2000

"I'll admit, I was surprised. It's been years since you stayed over," Grandma Annie remarked as she and Laurel sat down at Annie's kitchen table.

"I was trying to remember the last time. Must have been during high school or earlier."

A haphazard pile of recipe cards stood on the table between them. Laurel divided the recipes into two neater stacks.

"Yes, at least that long ago." Grandma Annie smiled fondly at her. "You spent a lot of weekends here as a child."

Laurel had made plenty of overnight visits to Great-Grandma Annie's. The two of them had always had a special bond. As well, one of the neighbors had twin girls her age, and Grandma Megan and Grandpa Lee lived a couple miles away. All of it made for wonderful memories from Laurel's childhood.

Grandma Annie held a recipe card above her head. "I've found it!"

Laurel clapped and reached for the card. "Annie's Chicken & Biscuits" was scrawled in faded cursive across the top. At least seventy years of family meals were associated with this recipe. Grandma Annie, then Grandma Megan, made the dish nearly every Easter and Christmas. It was Laurel's dad who was the chef in Laurel's family however, so the tradition had fallen to the wayside. Tonight though, Laurel planned to remedy that. She would learn how to make chicken and biscuits from Annie herself. She had called Grandma Annie to make the request before leaving her apartment, as well as ask if she could stay the night.

"I'll copy these down later," Laurel offered, picking up one of the piles of recipes.

"Why don't you keep the originals? I don't use them anymore."

Her fingers tightened around the recipe cards. Each one was written in Annie's feminine, old-fashioned handwriting. "Oh, I'd love to have these. Thank you, Grandma."

"You're welcome. Now, what can I do to help?"

"You can coach me through the recipe, please."

They got to work on the meal. Laurel listened to each of Grandma Annie's tips: the number of pinches of oregano, the most efficient way to roll out the biscuit dough, how small to chop the vegetables. By seven o'clock, neither of them could hide their stomachs' growls as savory aromas emanated from the oven. The meal still had thirty minutes left to cook. They settled for steamed vegetables and rice and agreed to save the chicken and biscuits for tomorrow's lunch.

"Of course, we'll have a little taste before we put it away," Grandma Annie stipulated with a smile. "We'll make sure it's worth eating tomorrow."

"Of course."

"In the meantime, we'll talk."

Laurel wondered if she should avoid the most obvious subject, worrying she'd given the impression lately that she only valued the visits because of the story Grandma Annie was revealing. Laurel deferred to asking, "What should we talk about, Grandma?"

"How is work? What are your current projects?"

"We're busier than usual." Laurel explained the timing of starting the new client while finishing work for the coffeehouse's opening.

"Sounds like you have a challenging week ahead of you."

"I do," she agreed. "But those are the weeks I most enjoy at my job."

Grandma Annie smiled affectionately. "You live a nearly full life, don't you, Laurie Bean?"

Laurel faltered over Annie's choice of words, "Well, it is busy right now."

"Busyness doesn't guarantee fullness." Grandma Annie patted Laurel's cheek with her fingertips.

Then Annie asked, "Did you thank Robert again for the pie? It was lovely to meet him."

"He wasn't at the office today. He left early yesterday too, which was unusual."

"Well, you pass along my gratitude when you have the chance. He seems a thoughtful man."

Laurel looked down, drawing her fork through the rice and vegetables. They ate silently until the phone rang. It was Laurel's mother, Erin. After a brief chat, Annie handed the phone to Laurel.

"Hello, Mom."

"Hi, sweetheart. How did your week go?"

They updated each other and the conversation lulled.

"We'd love to see you, Laurel. What do you think about driving down here tomorrow and staying overnight?"

"I'm staying with Grandma tonight, Mom. I planned to be here for the day tomorrow."

Erin's voice grew tighter. "If I'd known how little I would see you, I'm not sure I would have agreed to move to Chicago."

The comment cast a shadow of guilt over Laurel. "I'm sorry, Mom. Let's plan ahead and pick a weekend in the next month. I know I'm overdue to visit."

Tightness gave way to unmistakable sadness with her mother's next words. "A lot of things are overdue, Laurel. Let's talk again soon, okay?"

"Okay."

"You want to say hello to your dad?"

"Just tell him I love him, Mom."

"Alright. I'm glad things are going well with you and Grandma Annie, sweetie. Thank you for spending so much time with her."

Laurel said goodbye to her mother and returned to the last bites of food on her plate.

Grandma Annie spoke up, "Your father loves you, Laurel. He loves your mother."

She nodded, a maddeningly familiar lump rising in her throat.

"The two of you used to be thick as thieves."

She could make no reply. After a time, Grandma Annie laid her hand on top of hers. "So, are you ready to hear the rest of this old woman's story?"

Laurel exhaled her relief, "Absolutely."

Grandma Annie pushed her plate away and leaned back in the chair. She folded her hands in her lap, one finger tapping on her thigh. Laurel saw her gaze lose focus as she reentered the past.

29

December 16, 1917

Sunday, five A.M.

Annie entered the morning with extra energy. She'd slept surprisingly hard. The restless dreams plaguing her in past weeks were gone. Mass at Saint Genevieve church began at eight, but she was bathed, dressed and ready long before then. She would ride with Dr. LaCroix to the church, as long as no emergencies surfaced at the hospital to keep him there. In the meantime, she sat down at her small writing table.

Annie considered a plethora of thoughts to share with her parents. She discarded several drafts of a letter before settling on what to say. This letter was longer and more detailed than the one she sent to Samuel. Annie tried to communicate the goodness of the changes in her life and commitments by speaking of the restless dissatisfaction vexing her long before she left Boston. She focused heavily on the relief and peace gained by the seeds of faith planted by God in her heart. Whether her mother or father would understand at all, she didn't know.

Eyes closed, head bowed, she prayed for some inclination in their hearts to trust her. Please God, let this letter be welcomed by them.

The ride to Saint Geneviève was jarring and cold. Although the doctor owned an automobile, he preferred the horse.

"Horses are more reliable." He had pointed at the sleek black car half-covered by a tarp. "That thing has not proven otherwise."

So, they took the two-person carriage. She and Dr. LaCroix pulled their scarves tighter and hats lower as the horse pulled them at a steady clip to the steps of the church. The bells began to chime as Annie craned her neck to look at the huge, circular stained-glass window above the entrance doors. She was curious to see more of its colors and pattern once inside.

Doctor and nurse passed through the heavy doors. A woman in a powder blue hat played the organ. The instrument's brass pipes reached the ceiling, filling the air with each reverberating note. The windows inside the church captivated Annie's eyes. The colors and pictures, indistinct from the outside, were illuminated in here. She glanced back at the stained glass above the front door: a kaleidoscope of reds and golds with a white filigree cross at its center. The narrower panes lining the sides of the church were set deep into the wall and reached almost to the ceiling. They depicted a collection of figures and scenes from the Bible. Annie recognized a few but would ask Kyle to explain the rest.

With that thought, she lost focus on the windows and scanned the high-back pews for Kyle. He knelt in a row near the front. She began walking that way, entirely forgetting Dr. LaCroix until he placed a hand on her shoulder. He inclined his head to indicate where he was about to sit. She bit her lip, looking toward Kyle, then back again at the doctor. Sitting with the doctor seemed the proper choice. Her shoulders dropped a bit as she turned to follow him.

Dr. LaCroix winked and waved her away. "I will see you at the hospital tonight, Nurse Walcott."

An old instinct encouraged her to object and stay with the doctor as if that was her plan. Instead, she gave him a grateful smile before moving toward Kyle.

The Mass itself was unfamiliar. Most of it was in Latin, the sermon was in French, and Annie was consistently two seconds behind the rest of the attendees as they stood, sat, or kneeled. But the woman in the blue hat played the organ beautifully, and the whole service possessed a peaceful rhythm and reverence that eased her uncertain heart. At the end, the priest disappeared through a side door. Whispered chatter started to break out as the sparse congregation trickled out of the pews. When the last tremor in the organ's pipes faded, she finally turned to Kyle.

"So," he clutched his hat and smiled down at her, "are you ready for breakfast?"

"First, tell me who that is."

Kyle followed her pointed finger to one of the stained-glass windows. "Gladly," he replied.

She listened then, mesmerized, to the stories of ancient men and women of Christianity. Most she'd never heard of before, but Kyle spoke of them like his own ancestral legends.

Waiting beside a beaming Madame Chapelle were flaky croissants and cheese, salty bacon, and boiled eggs. A silver tray held a carafe of steaming coffee and freshly made éclairs. Madame Chappelle welcomed them into the warm, nearly empty café.

"Bonjour. You are too cold."

Madame Chappelle placed a soft hand on Annie's cheek. Annie hadn't realized how cold she was until she felt the heat of the café's iron ovens. She reached up and took Madame Chappelle's hand in her own.

"This is amazing." She gestured toward the table. "Magnifique!"

"Beh, oui." Madame Chappelle waved one hand dismissively. "It is nothing. You are hungry?"

They both nodded vigorously.

"Thank you." Annie squeezed the woman's hand.

Kyle took her coat and scarf. He watched the table as if the food might disappear, but Madame Chappelle broke his concentration when she grabbed him in a hug. Kyle laughed and embraced the shorter woman. When she stepped away, Madame Chappelle used a corner of her apron to wipe a few tears from her round cheeks.

"Ah, Monsieur Kyle, mon cher." She turned to Annie with a heavy sigh. "He is leaving me."

Annie's throat tightened and she looked at Madame Chappelle with compassion. "Yes, I know."

Madame Chappelle shook her head, lifting her hands helplessly, and hustled back to the kitchen.

The scene stirred up an ache in her chest she was determined to leave unexamined for as long as possible. Kyle pulled a chair out for her. With every movement, she kept him in view. She needed to memorize every detail of their day.

"I'm afraid she's grown a little attached to me," he said modestly.

"More than a little."

He cast his eyes downward, his face reddening. "She misses her children and her husband."

"With you here, it probably felt like she had one of her sons home again. I'm sure you have meant a lot to her."

Kyle's smile lightened the intensity of the air between them. "What should we try first?"

"The éclairs."

His smile widened.

They did eat the éclairs first, the luxurious custard filling melting on their tongues. Once they consumed the eggs and bacon too, Annie had no room for croissants and cheese. Kyle decided he could manage one though. Annie poured them a fresh mug of coffee while he continued eating.

Between bites, Kyle described Chet's and the others' departure the previous night. He speculated that Chet might already have landed in England and would be boarding another train for the opposite coast.

"I think I'll follow him to Dublin before I go home." Kyle pushed his empty plate aside. "See if he's been given an idea of when he will be sent back to the front. I can't imagine they'll keep him at the hospital for too long once he's off the crutches."

"Make sure you say hello to him from me."

"I'll do that."

Kyle stared beyond her shoulder into the quiet dining room.

Over her porcelain mug as she sipped her coffee, she observed the curve of his hairline, the lines of his square jaw, and the blue of his eyes. Only when she was satisfied that the image was entirely committed to memory did she break the silence. "And after Dublin, you'll head home?"

"Yes."

"To the farm?"

He nodded.

"And to the newspaper?"

Kyle's brows came together and he answered, "If it's possible, yes."

"What do you mean?"

"I don't know the state of things with the paper. It was too risky to have contact with the other men while I was here. I have no way to know if they were found out, or if they disbanded, or if the paper is still going strong." He frowned. "Who knows, maybe they lost track of us and I can rejoin the work, but it's just as possible they've kept on our trail or even made arrests."

She wrung her hands in her lap.

He laughed halfheartedly, "Maybe they'll be waiting at the farm to take me in as soon as I get home."

"How is that funny?" Her skin prickled with goose-bumps.

Kyle's frown returned. "It isn't. I'm sorry. I think the only good part about keeping the work a secret is that I avoid causing the people I love to worry about me."

People I love. The words repeated themselves in her mind.

"It has to be lonely, Kyle, with no one knowing where you are, or thinking of you while you're trying to stay safe."

"Except you, now."

She nodded, unable to push any words past her lips.

"I hope you will think of me, Annie, but I hate that you might spend your time worrying for me." Kyle took her hand. Her fingers intertwined with his and their hands rested together on his leg.

"You're well worth worrying over, Kyle," Annie assured him.

"What about you? Things will be different for you when you go back to America. How do you imagine it will be?"

She watched him spoon sugar into his second cup of coffee with his other hand. Every movement, every sound; she gathered the smallest details up like jewels. "I can't even guess. It would be one thing if I was there while all these changes happened. Breaking off the engagement, this new faith; if I was with them, I could at least know everyone's reactions."

He stretched his legs beneath the table and waved to greet a family who entered the café. "Maybe it's better this way. They have time to think it through, process what you've told them before reacting."

"Maybe, or they have time to deepen their disappointment while I'm away. I can't imagine Mother waiting even a day before writing to me after she finds out. She'll want to say whatever she would have said to me in person."

"And your father?"

"He'll let Mother write the letter. At least with her, I feel certain of what to expect. I'm much less sure what he will think of what I've done. Daddy likes peace and decorum. He likes things to be settled and stay settled. Still, he wants me to be happy. I don't doubt that."

"Then I'll pray he writes to you as well, instead of leaving you wondering."

The offer of prayer felt intimate. "Thank you, Kyle."

"You're welcome." He cleared his throat. "Will you be praying for me when I go back to Ireland?"

She looked at him, fondness swelling in her chest, but he kept his eyes lowered. "I promise you, I will."

With her answer, he raised his eyes to meet hers. She was certain they held an equal share of affection. Suddenly overwhelmed by the shortness of the day, Annie stood from her chair. Kyle released her hand as she rose. She set down her coffee cup with a loud clink against the plate.

"I'm going to thank Madame Chappelle for the breakfast," her voice shook.

Kyle called after her, "I'll get our coats. There's someplace I want to show you."

30

December, 1917

Kyle held up her coat and she slipped her arms into it. "Where are we going?"

Without replying, Kyle turned right when they exited the café. She walked quickly to keep up with his long strides down the cobblestone street.

"You aren't going to tell me?"

He shrugged. "I don't know what it's called."

"But you've been there before?"

"A few times, yes."

After a short walk and a turn off the main road, he stopped at a bright blue door. She looked up and down the street, wondering if he forgot how to find their unnamed destination.

"This is it." Kyle stepped up to the blue door.

The street was residential by all appearances. This was an unremarkable, two-story, brown brick home.

He lifted a hand toward the house. "See, there's no sign. I really don't know what it's called. I hope they're open."

When he reached for the doorknob, Annie stopped his arm. "What's inside?"

"A couple weeks ago, I told Madame Chappelle I wanted to find a gift for my niece. She gave me directions to this place. It was so interesting that I came back a few more times." He turned again to open the door. "There are no set store hours though. It's open whenever the proprietor decides to be open."

She heard the click of the doorknob when Kyle turned it and they smiled at each other. Entering the house, she realized he couldn't have explained it adequately. It was a home that was also a shop. The entryway and its adjoining rooms were furnished with simple pieces—a bench by the front door; a chaise lounge, sofa, and chairs in the sitting room. In between the furniture were various shelves filled with items for sale. Every imaginable trinket, souvenir, and type of artwork were available; delightful frivolities that Annie supposed few people could invest in during this war.

She followed Kyle at first, letting him point out particularly interesting pieces, then they roamed in different directions. She examined a collection of Moroccan pottery, each dish painted in a mosaic of rich colors. One shelf held delicate blown glass. There was an elegant swan, a pair of doves, and an intricate vase in a swirl of watery blues. She stood longest before a display of hand-carved wooden pieces. The wood felt soft. It had a slightly golden hue with darker striations running throughout. A sign on the top shelf probably explained the origin of the wood, or gave facts about the artist, but she couldn't interpret the words.

Annie picked up a hand mirror. Its handle was carved as the trunk of a tree. The artist managed to imitate the fine ridges of bark without the roughness of the real thing. At the top of the handle, the circle of glass was framed with branches extending perfectly from the tree trunk. Tiny leaves dotted each branch. She turned the mirror over and sighed with pleasure. The back was carved as the whole tree, uninterrupted by the glass. It was breathtaking in its perfect detail.

Annie thought then of the generosity of God to create people capable of making such beautiful works. Kyle approached, watching her face expectantly. She set down the mirror.

"Kyle, this place is splendid. Thank you for bringing me here."

"Thank you for trusting me enough to come along."

"What did you buy for your niece?"

He led her into another room. "I found it right away the first time I came." He picked up a small painting of a golden field full of bright red poppies. "This one isn't exactly the same, but it's very like it. Molly adores flowers and her favorite color is red."

"She'll love it."

"I hope so. I thought she might like to hang it in her bedroom."

"I think it's a detail of a Monet painting. I've seen one like it at a museum."

"That must be why I liked it so much." Kyle stood the painting back in its spot. "I always thought Monet's work looked like places where there must be peace."

She sighed, wondering if there was ever such a place.

"I'm going back in there." He pointed his thumb toward the sitting room.

"Okay." She watched his back until he was gone from the room. Sadness threatened to surface and she sternly rejected the emotion. These hours, at least, were only to be enjoyed. When she heard the church bells chime two o'clock, she went to find Kyle. Not once had she seen the store's proprietor. She did hear Kyle speaking to someone though, and found him just as a door to another room swung shut.

"Was that the owner?"

"It was. He and his wife are going out, so they're closing the shop for the afternoon. I'm sorry you didn't get to meet him."

"That's all right. Maybe I'll come back sometime."

He smiled at the idea. "You should, and bring Meg."

Back on the main road through the village, they fell into an easy, dawdling pace. All the regular shops were closed since it was Sunday but Annie enjoyed the window displays. She was looking on ahead when she realized Kyle had stopped. She backtracked a few steps to where he stood.

"This is for you." He pulled a small parcel from inside his coat and held it out to her.

"But when did you do this?"

"We were in different rooms." He nodded in the direction of the shop.

She didn't hide her smile. For someone who taught her so much about honesty, Kyle certainly had it in him to be secretive. She accepted the parcel, turning it over and over as she removed the paper.

The mirror. He must have seen her holding it longer than anything else. She ran her thumb around the frame, feeling the grooves of the branches, then turned it around and laid her palm against the exquisitely carved tree. She forced a couple of deep breaths before looking up at Kyle. He was fidgeting, tugging at the collar of his coat.

She reached up and hugged his neck. Her forehead pressed into his shoulder. "Thank you," she whispered before tears filled her eyes.

He returned the embrace. She felt the warmth of his chest against her. Their cheeks brushed as they pulled back and she took in a sharp breath. She held her mittens to her face, drying the tears. Neither of them spoke as they walked again. She tucked her hand in the bend of Kyle's elbow and saw him smile.

They wandered over to the market, purchasing an insensible assortment of food for a late afternoon meal. They ate at one of the little square tables inside the store, beside the front windows. From their seats, they watched the patrons coming and going at La Porte Rouge across the street. He pointed out a few regulars at the café: town police chief, owners of the inn where he stayed for his first nights in France, and an elderly gentleman who recently received word of his son's death in Gallipoli.

Eventually, they also crossed the road to the café. He asked her to wait while he went upstairs.

She made her way to the back of the room, in need of a moment of solitude. Outside the window on the far wall, the day's light grew dim. It would be dark soon. She felt keenly today the shortness of winter days.

With shaky hands, she straightened her skirt over her waist and hips. She'd worn her favorite one. The cornflower blue material hung almost straight instead of widening a great deal at the bottom like most of those she owned. A modern cut, according to the Boston store clerk. The slimmer shape didn't easily allow for the petticoat she added underneath for warmth but at least her legs hadn't shivered all day. The ovens kept the café so warm that she removed her wool sweater now. She smoothed her white blouse before sitting down.

Kyle reappeared at the bottom of the stairs. There was a flash of worry when he looked upon the empty spot where he last left her, then he spotted her waving from the corner. He set a wooden checkerboard on the table, its little discs piled in the middle. The board's painted squares were scratched and faded.

"I found it in the room upstairs. Have you played before?" He sat down in the opposite chair.

"Lee and I used to play in the evenings when we were younger." Annie said, laughing over the memory. "I don't believe I ever won against him."

Kyle divided up the playing pieces. "Maybe you'll have better luck against me."

For three games, she fared no better than against her brother. She and Kyle talked throughout. The appearance of the checkerboard had triggered a chain of delightful memories for her and she shared some with him: games with Lee, vacations on Cape Cod, the few details she could recall of her grandparents. Kyle was transparent in his gladness at being let further into her life, asking question after question.

"Oh my goodness." Annie lifted one of Kyle's pieces off the board after a successful move. "I won! Did I win?"

His laugh filled their corner of the café.

She stared at the checkerboard, convinced she was mistaken. "Lee will never believe it."

"If he won't, you tell him I can vouch for your victory." Kyle's handsome face was relaxed, his blue eyes radiant in the lamplight.

She loved the idea of introducing Kyle to her brother. "You and Lee will be good friends," she remarked then blushed at her presumption.

He nodded slowly. "I hope so."

The December day had passed into evening. The other customers were gone and Madame Chappelle was sweeping between the tables. She wound up her phonograph and hummed along to the brass ensemble performing a dramatic Berlioz piece.

"Are we done?" Annie asked. Kyle was piling the checker pieces on the center of the board.

"This way you finish on a high note," he teased.

She played along. "You're afraid I've broken your winning streak for good, I think."

He clasped his hand to his chest. "I promise, I do this with only your happiness in mind."

With a wink and a bow, he took the game back upstairs. After several minutes, Annie stood and walked over to the wall containing the mural of the quaint house with the open front door. Running two fingers along the surface, she felt the minute ridges of the artist's brush strokes on the plaster; so many individual movements and colors to create the whole.

When Kyle returned, he leaned his shoulder on the wall. Annie touched the petals of the flowers outside the painted house.

"It must be difficult to know where to start when you already have the whole picture in your mind." She looked over at him.

"I don't know. Wouldn't it be even harder to begin if you didn't know how you wanted it to look in the end?"

"You might be right."

"We're both right." He stepped away from the wall. "If it were easier, a lot more people would paint beautiful pictures."

She noticed Kyle held something in his right hand, tucked slightly behind his waist.

Madame Chappelle was back in the kitchen and putting a new recording on the phonograph. The music that floated into the room was a serene concoction of cellos, violas, and flutes. The notes brought to Annie's mind the Monet artwork that she and Kyle spoke of earlier. It seemed the music and the paintings might have been created from a common inspiration.

"I thought she played opera at night," Annie said absently.

"She usually does. I don't know why it's different tonight."

"Because you're leaving."

He nodded and scuffed the toe of his shoe against the floor a couple times.

She took a step toward him. He met her gaze with an intensity that tightened the muscles in her stomach.

"Annie, if your father was here, and if I knew things were safe for me at home, I'd ask you to marry me."

208

"You would?"

"I would."

"I would say yes." Her fingertips went to her mouth as she felt shock at her candid reply.

A handsome smile broke across his face. His voice remained low, "None of the pieces fit yet, do they?"

A sigh slipped out with her answer, "No."

"Still, I wanted you to know what is in my heart." He glanced at the mural on the wall, then back at her. "We have the whole picture in our minds."

Hope flowed like a faucet. She was willing to start with any little piece of that picture if they could build on it over time.

He offered to her what he'd been holding behind his back. "It's a collection of Irish poetry."

She took the slim volume, examining its forest green cover and the crisp pages. "Thank you, Kyle."

"It has some of my favorites," he continued. "They make me appreciate the country and the people. I thought, maybe, they could help you love Ireland even before you join me there."

With these last words, his voice grew even quieter. Tears filled her eyes and she could only nod her agreement.

The phonograph slowed, dragging out the notes as the record stopped revolving. They heard Madame Chappelle shuffle over to it and crank the handle until the music swelled up again in a lovely crescendo.

"Will you dance with me?"

Annie raised her eyes to see Kyle's hand extended to her. She set the book on a table before he clasped her right hand in his left and held it high beside their shoulders. His other hand rested on her waist and she placed hers on his arm. Everything was where it belonged. She felt a serenity she'd never known before now.

They glided away from the wall, Kyle leading her with sure steps toward the front of the café where there was a stretch of open floor between the counter and the tables. When he bumped against a chair and almost missed a step, she laughed but he didn't let it break their rhythm. Annie became a little breathless; his wide steps were a challenge to match in her skirt and heeled boots. When the stringed instruments eased into a slower melody, Annie let her cheek fall against his shoulder. She felt the muscles of her back slacken and relax as he pulled her to him. His fingers tightened on her waist.

The music eventually stopped altogether. After a few beats of silence, Kyle released her hand and dropped his to his side. Still holding her waist though, she remained close to his chest. She gripped the material where her hand still rested on his arm. Tilting her neck to look into his face, she reached up to push a wave of his hair back from his temple.

He bent his head lower to say in her ear, "I love you."

His breath was warm on her cheek. Her own voice shook, "I love you."

Moving his hand to her cheek, he placed a soft kiss on Annie's forehead. Her eyelids fluttered closed when his lips left her skin, then he kissed her mouth.

Seconds later, they stepped apart. Her tears would no longer be delayed. They came through her eyelashes onto her cheeks. "Will you walk me back?"

He nodded and fetched their coats.

The distance between the village and the hospital never felt so short. No matter how brief though, the walk did provide enough time for her to make up her mind about something.

"I won't be going to the train station in the morning to see you off." They stopped on the gravel path to the dormitory and faced each other.

"All right." Kyle's expression was tender.

"It would feel like our goodbye is being stretched through the whole night," she explained despite his lack of objection. "I don't know if I can endure that."

"This isn't the end, Annie." He caressed her cheek with his thumb.

"I know that."

He narrowed his eyes at her, the corners of his mouth lifting a little. "Do you?

She surrendered to a heartfelt smile. "I know that," she insisted, and saw him smile in return.

Kyle kissed her a second time; a long, absorbing kiss that she wished would not end. When it did, he wrapped her in his arms.

She hugged him tighter, his wool coat rough against her cheek.

"Goodbye for now, Annie."

"Goodbye."

31

October, 2000, 83 years later

Laurel held her breath. Her calves tingled painfully from sitting cross-legged on the bed, so she moved to the rocking chair. They had paused briefly somewhere around Grandma Annie's description of the shop where Kyle purchased the mirror, so they could remove the chicken and biscuits from the oven and then move to Grandma Annie's bedroom.

When Grandma Annie spoke of Kyle presenting her with the book of poetry, she'd picked up the volume from the bedside table. She clutched it still, holding it against her chest.

Laurel asked the one question at the front of her mind, "When did you see him again? How long was it?"

Grandma Annie looked at her, startled. "Oh, I never saw Kyle again, not after our Sunday together."

"You never saw him again?" Laurel repeated.

With a shake of her head and a mournful sigh, Grandma Annie confirmed what Laurel wished not to believe.

Grandma Annie let the cover of the book fall open on her lap. "I didn't even see what he wrote in the book until the next morning." She pressed her fingertips against the inscription, the words Laurel had read that began this odyssey of remembrance.

To Annie, with all my love between the pages.

"Sharing it all like this, laying out each memory, it seems like so much," Grandma Annie said.

"I'm not sure I understand."

"All the memories add up to more than I realized. I never saw Kyle again, but we had so much in our little bit of time together. I knew that then, when he left France and when everything that followed came to pass, but in the years afterward I began to feel it was less. Maybe to make it easier, or to continue keeping it to myself." Grandma Annie rubbed at her temples. "I don't know. I was wrong to think of it like that. To think of him like that. It was some of everything we try to collect in our lifetimes."

Laurel nodded, marveling at all that was shared since she first asked about the book's inscription. Grandma Annie spoke with so much more openness than she ever expected. When Kyle was the subject, Annie's voice was tender with love even all these years later. Laurel couldn't reconcile this candor and emotion with the decades of Annie's protection of these secrets. She added that question to the list of what she hoped to understand by the time Grandma Annie finished her story.

"Laurel, I have a dreadful headache."

Her musings came to an end. "I'll get you something for the pain."

When Grandma Annie had swallowed a dose of nighttime pain reliever and kissed her on the cheek, Laurel left the bedroom. She went to the kitchen to stow the cooled casserole in the refrigerator, then walked to the guest bedroom.

Laurel stared at the bed, the idea of sleep feeling absurd. Her mind was a spinning film reel of the scenes Grandma Annie described. Still, she slid beneath the blankets and tried to quiet her thoughts. The hours that followed were restless, and troubled by an assortment of dreams of two young lovers reuniting. When her eyes opened in the morning, she realized anew that that reunion never took place.

Grandma Annie sipped tea at the dining table, a fleece robe over her nightgown. "We had a decent shower at about six," she said when Laurel entered the kitchen.

The lush scent of recent rain came through the open patio door.

"Have you been up that long?" Laurel found a tin of coffee and started searching for filters.

Grandma Annie pointed to a drawer next to the stove.

"Thank you."

"I don't know that we ever made a pot of coffee in this house until Megan got married. Your Grandpa Lee couldn't get by without it."

"Neither can my parents," she said. "I don't drink it every day but I'm glad to have it occasionally. Is your headache gone?"

Grandma Annie touched her forehead. "It's better than last night."

"Maybe we should call your doctor," she suggested, thinking Grandma Annie looked especially weary. "You don't usually have headaches, do you?"

"No, I don't, but I don't think there's any reason to bother the doctor over it. I'll take it extra easy today."

She nodded, pondering what Grandma Annie might normally do that wouldn't be considered 'taking it easy.' "Can you handle talking, at least?"

"Oh, I think I'm up for that," Grandma Annie replied good-naturedly. "How are your parents? I don't think I've talked to your mother since Monday."

She hesitated. "We spoke to her last night, Grandma. She called while we ate dinner."

"Oh, that's right." Grandma Annie patted her hair and frowned.

The coffeepot was nearly full and she snuck it out from under the drip of black liquid to pour some. The mug she grabbed was yellow with the words, "Find Your Heart in Michigan," emblazoned on it. She was struck with a flash of impatience. How had Grandma Annie ever ended up here, in western Michigan, rather than in Ireland with Kyle?

"Grandma, why didn't you ever see Kyle again?"

Grandma Annie set down her tea. She smoothed her robe against her legs.

"Did he not write? Did he change his mind?"

"No, no," Grandma Annie waved her hands in protest. "It was nothing like that. Kyle and I wrote each other constantly. There were many letters."

"Then what happened?" Laurel added another needling question, "This is why you kept it all a secret until now, this part. Isn't it, Grandma?"

Grandma Annie rubbed hard at her forehead and temples. "I'm sorry, Laurel. I don't think I am up for this after all. I think I'd better lie down."

She felt a wave of remorse. "I'm sorry, Grandma. I didn't mean to press you."

"No, it's this darn headache," Grandma Annie said as she stood from the table and leaned on Laurel's arm to walk to the bedroom. "I don't feel pressed at all. I want you to know that. But I need to shake this headache first. After I do that I'll let you read the letters."

Grandma Annie said no more of the matter as she laid down on her bed and Laurel covered her with the blanket. Laurel considered going home, but the mention of the letters compelled her to stay. She showered, dressed, had a second cup of coffee and ate an apple before making up the guest bed. When she peeked in after all this, Annie slept soundly. So, she grabbed a sweatshirt and went outside.

The rain was long over and gave way to mountainous white clouds interrupting the sun's warmth as they marched across the sky. Beneath the maple trees, leaves danced in the strong breeze. Laurel went in search of a rake.

She was gathering her third pile of leaves when she spotted Grandma Annie, dressed now in navy linen pants and a cream colored sweater, waving from the patio doorway. Laurel smiled despite the wariness she felt. It'd likely been a month since she'd seen Grandma dressed in anything besides nightgowns or soft pajamas. Leaving the rake on the ground, she returned to the house.

"Are you feeling better?"

"Much better." Grandma Annie nodded. "Let's eat lunch."

Laurel's stomach rumbled at the mention of a meal. "I'll warm up the chicken and biscuits." She dished out two platefuls while Grandma Annie settled herself at the table.

"I was digging through my old dresser while you were outside." Grandma Annie tugged on her pants' leg. "These are one of my favorite pairs of pants. I don't know why I don't wear them anymore.

Since I stopped leaving the house for anything, I guess I lost interest in making myself presentable. My nightgown is so comfortable."

The vigor in Grandma Annie's voice and the flush in her typically pale cheeks were surprising. Laurel brought their warmed plates over with frequent glances at her great-grandmother. She dipped a forkful of biscuit and vegetables in the juice covering her plate. "Did you get this recipe from your mother?"

"Goodness, no," Grandma Annie said with a laugh. "My mother never had to cook anything. We did have a marvelous cook though."

Laurel took a long drink of milk.

"I got this recipe from Mrs. Winfield."

Laurel nearly choked. "You mean Lieutenant Winfield's wife?"

"Yes, of course."

"So, you went to see his family, just like you promised the lieutenant you would?"

"Well, naturally. When I first came to Michigan with the baby, they were the only connection I had."

It was as if Grandma Annie thought she already knew these details. "But Grandma, you haven't even told me how..."

"How I found the Winfields once I got to the state? I expected it to be harder than it was."

Laurel was wholly confused. When there was a loud knock on the front door, she jumped in her chair. Grandma Annie went on eating while Laurel walked to the door and opened it.

"Robert."

"Hi, Laurel. I was driving past and I saw..."

"My car," she finished for him. "Hi."

"Hi."

She stared at him, remembering her decision in favor of friendship. "You certainly are up here a lot."

"So are you." He stuffed his hands in the pockets of his jeans. "Maybe we should car pool."

"I drove up last night."

"Yeah, I was just kidding," Robert chuckled.

"I'm sorry. Never mind." She smiled. "I don't know if I can let you in though."

His shoulders dropped a little. "Oh, is it a bad time?"

"You didn't bring pie."

He tossed his head back with a loud laugh then put on a forced solemn expression. "For that, I apologize. I don't know what I was thinking."

Laurel moved to let him in and almost stepped on Grandma Annie's toes, unaware she'd followed her from the kitchen.

"Hello again." Grandma Annie waved Robert into the house.

"Hello. I hope I'm not intruding."

They were back in the kitchen before Grandma Annie finished reassuring him he was welcome.

"Have you eaten lunch?" Grandma Annie inquired.

"I haven't, but I'm sure my brother will have something for me when I pick up my nieces."

"Well, Laurel made this delicious meal. There's plenty left in the pan if you would like a plate."

He raised his eyebrows at Laurel, a half-smile on his face. She went to the cupboard for a plate and warmed up a large helping.

"This is delicious," Robert said between bites. He barely paused until his plate was empty.

"It's a family recipe," Laurel informed him. "Grandma always made it best."

"This is as good as mine ever was," Grandma Annie said. "You're a natural, Laurie Bean."

Robert smirked over the nickname and she caught the mischievous glint in his eyes. "Grandma is the only one who calls me Laurie Bean," she warned.

"Got it," Robert said, the smirk still in place.

After their plates were empty and they'd sat around the table for an hour of conversation, Robert admitted, "I can't stay any longer. I promised my nieces a trip to the park this afternoon."

"Then we won't keep you." Grandma Annie patted his hand.

218

Laurel carried the plates to the sink and Robert came up behind her.

"When I stopped here, I meant to ask if you would like to come along to the park."

"Oh," was all she could say before Grandma Annie spoke up.

"Laurel, why don't you go?" Looking at Robert, Grandma Annie added, "She's been visiting me since last night. She should go have some fun."

She wanted to object, but Grandma was nodding as if it was decided. "All right," she agreed, "but first Robert needs to help me with something." She pointed out the kitchen window at the piles of raked leaves and held up several garbage bags. "Would you mind very much?"

He took the bags with an obliging smile and walked to the backyard.

Once he was outside, she sat back down by Grandma Annie. "Are you sure, Grandma? I don't need to go."

"Go have a good time. You visit me so often, and I'm grateful that you do, but I don't want to be a reason you don't spend time with your friends." Grandma Annie stood up from the table, a lost expression on her face. "There was something else though, wasn't there? Something I was going to give you."

Laurel suggested what she hoped it might be. "We hadn't finished talking about you and Kyle, about what happened after he left France."

A shadow passed over Grandma Annie's face. She closed her green eyes. "No, that couldn't have been it."

"Then I don't know."

Grandma Annie sighed, "Oh well, it couldn't have been too important. You go show him where to put those leaves."

She did so, helping him carry the overstuffed bags to the edge of the road for pick-up. Robert waited in the driveway, perched on the bumper of his Jeep, while she returned the rake to the garage. He wore an emerald green polo shirt, untucked over a pair of worn-in jeans. She spotted his navy Tigers baseball cap on his dashboard.

"You ready to go?" he called.

"Is it okay if I meet you at the park? I need to get my things to-gether so I can go home afterward. Are you taking them to Patter-son Park?"

"I am. Do you know how to get there?"

She nodded and walked to the house.

"Wait." Robert narrowed his hazel eyes at her. "You're going to show up, right? This isn't you figuring out a way to skip out on me?"

"No, Robert, I promise I'll see you at the park." She gave him a heartfelt smile, realizing she was tentatively looking forward to the time with him.

"You better." He winked and climbed into the Jeep. "I know where to find you come Monday."

Entering the house laughing under her breath, she met Grand-ma Annie in the hallway.

"Oh good, you're still here."

"I need to take my bag with me since I'll go home from the park."

Grandma Annie was already walking away. "I remembered what I was supposed to give you."

In the bedroom, Grandma Annie tugged on the top of the bed-side table but didn't have the strength to move it. Laurel took over, pulling it several inches from the wall though she didn't understand why she was doing so.

"Grandma, what are you doing?"

Without a word, Grandma Annie slid a slim drawer out from the table. With that side facing the wall, Laurel had never guessed the table possessed a drawer.

"Here." Grandma Annie held out a dusty stack of envelopes, three inches thick and tied with a tattered red ribbon. "These should explain a lot."

Laurel's mouth fell agape. The letters felt like a delicate treasure in her hands, like they might crumble if she wasn't careful. The top envelope was addressed in neat printing to Miss A. Walcott, c/o Dr. Paul LaCroix.

"I think I might sift through a little more." Grandma Annie transferred her attention to her clothes dresser. She was lifting sweaters from one drawer and stacking them on the bed. "I'll see you soon, dear, all right?"

"Yes, of course you will." She swallowed and tore her eyes away from the envelopes. She hugged Grandma Annie and tried to recapture her attention. "Thank you for these, Grandma."

Grandma Annie was calm. "Should have showed them to you ages ago, I suppose." She kissed Laurel's cheek, as she always did when saying goodbye. "I certainly have read them enough times myself. I practically know every line by heart."

Robert's questioning of her intention to join him at the park now rang in Laurel's ears as she sat in her car. She glanced at the stack of letters lying on the passenger seat and drummed her fingers on the steering wheel. No matter if she was looking forward to spending time with him, nothing sounded as good as driving directly home to read every single one of those letters. She'd made a promise though. Still parked in the driveway, she was tempted to at least read the first one. She shook her head. The first would create the need to read the second, and so on. Instead, she turned the ignition key and said a hasty prayer for patience.

32

October, 2000

"This is Callie and this is Rachel." Robert turned to his nieces standing beside him. "Girls, this is Laurel."

Both of them looked at her with amiable curiosity. Rachel, at five years old, was missing two bottom teeth in her smile.

"Are you Uncle Robert's girlfriend?" Callie, the elder sister by two years, asked with an impish smile.

Robert ruffled her strawberry blond curls. "She's my friend, Callie. I already told you that. We work together." He rolled his eyes at Laurel. "Callie's not exactly shy."

"I like your eyes," Rachel said. She leaned against her uncle's leg and cocked her head. She had a crown of curls to match her sister. "They look like Mommy's morning glories."

"Thank you, Rachel." She looked at the pair of sisters and added, "I like your hair. I used to wish I had curls like those."

Rachel wrinkled her nose. "They get tangled and they hurt when Mommy brushes them."

"But she doesn't cry anymore when it hurts, do you, Rachel?" Callie interjected.

"No, I don't." Rachel grinned proudly.

Robert heaved an exaggerated sigh. "Can we stop talking about hair and go play some Frisbee®?"

They walked toward a grassy area behind the playground. Rachel slipped her little hand into Laurel's and skipped beside her. When she felt a tug on her fingers, Laurel bent down to hear Rachel.

"I don't know how to throw a Frisbee, but Uncle Robert promised to teach me. Do you know how to throw it?"

She nodded. "My dad taught me when I was your age. I wasn't very good at first though."

A frown pulled at Rachel's rosebud mouth. "I don't like not being good at things."

"Me neither." Laurel squeezed her hand.

When they reached the lawn, the foursome spread out. While Robert spent a few minutes showing Rachel how to handle the disc, Callie wandered nearer to Laurel. She squinted in the sun, a hand rising to her hip. "Laurel is kind of a funny name. I've never heard it before. It's like Laura but spelled wrong."

Robert spun around. When Laurel laughed, he lost his reproachful look.

"You know," she replied, "I used to dislike it because no one else I knew had that name. Now that's one of the reasons I like it."

Callie considered this for a few seconds. "Yeah, I don't know any other Callies." She paused, her face brightening, "Do you have any kids?"

"No, not yet."

"Do you have a husband?"

"No."

"Why not?"

Again, she couldn't help laughing at the girl's boldness.

"Let's play, ladies," Robert called out.

The game lasted less than a half hour. Rachel became alternately thrilled and frustrated as she tried her hardest to handle the disc. Laurel kept her encouraged. Callie liked to see how far she could toss each throw, meaning Laurel had to run for nearly every catch. When the girls grew restless for something new, they headed for the jungle gym and slides. Laurel and Robert continued throwing the disc between them while keeping his nieces in view.

"I suppose I should have warned you about them."

"What's to warn about?" She grabbed the disc out of the air. "I like them."

"Callie hasn't learned the art of tactfulness yet. I'm sorry if she was rude earlier."

"Not rude at all," Laurel assured him. "She's just honest in the way kids tend to be."

"Callie is that." Robert glanced toward the playground as the girls went down a slide together. "And she's a watchdog over her little sister."

Laurel's next throw fell short in front of Robert. He sat down on the grass instead of tossing it back.

She sat beside him and stretched out her legs. "You seem to enjoy being an uncle."

"Definitely," he answered at once. "Those girls are a lot of fun."

"And you're going to have a new niece or nephew, aren't you?"

"How did you know that?"

"Grandma Annie's friends from St. Catherine's were over while I was there."

Robert nodded. "Ah, of course," he said. "Don't tell my sister-in-law, but I am hoping I get a nephew."

"My lips are sealed."

Robert and Laurel watched the girls clamber up the climbing bars and wave from the top. Robert waved back, but Rachel didn't stop until Laurel waved too.

Robert rotated himself on the grass to face her and crossed his legs. "So, Laurel, how did you get your funny name?"

"What were you saying about tactfulness?"

"Is it a family name?"

She pulled an elastic band out of her pocket and lifted her hair into a high ponytail. Even with it up, the ends landed in a soft flip between her shoulder blades. "'Oh, may she live like some green laurel, rooted in one dear perpetual place.'"

His eyebrows rose.

"It's from a poem by William Butler Yeats called 'A Prayer for My Daughter.' My mom read it repeatedly while she was pregnant."

"That's sweet." His expression grew serious. "My brother said he has never prayed so hard as during his wife's pregnancies. He couldn't believe how much he loved and worried over those girls before he even met them. I don't know how a dad handles that without prayer."

She studied his face. This was the closest they'd come to a conversation about faith. Forty hours a week for two and a half years and this was how little acquainted she was with him. She had no one to blame but herself.

"What about Robert? Is there a good story behind your name?"

"Pretty standard. It was my grandfather's name and my dad's middle name." He plucked a few blades of grass from the ground beside his knee. "I always thought it was a boring name but when my dad died, I don't know, I couldn't help but take a little more pride in it."

"Is it hard to talk about him?"

He laid down on the grass, his eyes on the clouds floating above them. She spotted the barely perceptible grief in the way he chewed his bottom lip before speaking.

"I suppose it will never be easy, but it's not really hard either. He died in a car accident." His lips pursed for a moment. "He had to travel occasionally for work and was on his way home from three days in Saginaw. A driver in the lane beside him fell asleep at the wheel and ran both of their cars off the freeway."

Tears pooled in her eyes. She placed her fingers on Robert's forearm. He turned his head and, to her surprise, a smile was on his lips as he lifted his upper body from the ground.

"I used to hate talking about him. I hated telling people he was dead or describing what happened." He kept his eyes locked on hers. "For the last few years though, I love any chance I get to talk about him. I can't explain it."

Before she could encourage him to say more they were interrupted by Callie running over, breathless from playing.

"Will you push us on the swings? We want to see who can make us go higher."

They followed Callie to where Rachel waited. The sisters bounced in the seats of their swings. Robert's eyes narrowed and he raised his chin at Laurel, challenging her. They pushed the girls as high as the swings would go. Callie pumped her legs vigorously, but Rachel left all the work to Laurel. Eventually she couldn't keep up with the other pair. Having won the game, Robert eased up.

He turned his attention to Laurel, still pushing the swing with one hand. "How old is your great-grandmother?"

"She's 103."

All three of them stared at her with dropped jaws.

"You know someone who is 103 years old?" Callie marveled. "That is so cool."

"It truly is!" She nodded, grinning at their shock.

"I'd never have guessed it," Robert said. "She has plenty of energy."

"Consistently, she does, but Grandma was different today. I mean, if I didn't know her, I wouldn't guess her age to be that high either. Even so, she doesn't usually have as much energy as she had today."

"Had she been sick?" he asked.

Laurel scuffed the toe of her shoe in the dirt. "No, but her age is bound to have effects. Grandma Annie's mind is still sharp. Her memory and her hearing, they're both fine. She tires easily though and stays in bed much of the day. She was behaving so differently today."

"It may not be a bad difference," he remarked. "Are you worried about her?"

"I try not to worry, but it is hard knowing no one is there with her most of the time."

"Is she unwilling to go into an assisted living sort of place?"

"Grandma's been adamant about that for years. She says that unless she needs medical care that requires her to be somewhere else, she wants to stay at home."

"It's good you live nearby then."

Both of them had let the swings slow down.

"It's raining!" Rachel wiped a drop of water from her forehead.

Laurel looked up and felt a couple drops on her face. The clouds had turned ragged and dark. The girls hopped off their swings and they all ran for the cars. By the time they reached the parking lot, all four were out of breath and soaked. Robert spread a blanket across the back seat for Callie and Rachel to sit on in their wet clothes. He buckled them up.

"You're welcome to join us for dinner," he said to Laurel when she leaned into the Jeep to help Rachel find her seatbelt. "I'm cooking."

"You cook?" She was surprised but pleased by the invitation. Still, she knew she'd turn it down.

"Yes, I cook. It's one of my favorite things to do."

Callie chimed in, "Uncle Robert's the best cook ever. When they open the restaurant, he's going to make all the desserts."

"What restaurant?" she asked.

"Dad and Uncle Robert's restaurant," Callie replied matter-of-factly.

Robert looked at her with apprehension in his features. "Come to dinner, Laurel."

She shook her head. She was confused and curious, but the prevailing influence was Grandma Annie's letters waiting for her in her car. "Thank you for the offer, but I need to get home."

He accepted her refusal graciously, "Thank you for coming with us today."

"Thank you for inviting me." They held each other's gaze an extra moment before she turned back to the girls. She took in the wet curls and smiling faces and felt a wave of affection. "It was wonderful to meet you two. I had a lot of fun."

They grinned back at her, waving as she closed the door and dashed to her car.

33

September, 2000

Laurel made a quick stop back at Grandma Annie's house despite planning to drive straight home from the park. More than anything, she stopped there to confirm that she didn't need to worry about her great-grandmother. Indeed, Annie was still energetically sorting through old clothes and belongings in her closet.

Annie thanked Laurel for checking on her. "And I like Robert, that friend of yours," Annie commented as Laurel was saying good-bye.

Laurel gave Annie a long hug and made a promise to return the next day.

Back home, Laurel set the letters aside only until she changed into dry clothes. She tossed her overnight bag on her bed and grabbed a box of crackers from the kitchen before settling on the couch. It was early evening when she started reading and read well into the night.

Laurel gave the letters two readings. First, she read them straight through. Grandma Annie had kept the letters in order, the first being a letter from Kyle that he wrote from the train on the morning he left. The next was Annie's reply to him; and so on. Unable to move her mind to other matters or convince her body to sleep, Laurel read them all a second time. Apart from a few missing pieces, she now had the whole of Annie's story.

At the bottom of the pile were additional letters in neither Annie's nor Kyle's handwriting. Reading those after her second time through the stack gave Laurel most of those missing pieces. The clock hands moved toward two A.M. and Laurel laid herself down on her pillow with her heart struggling to contain its array of emotions.

All she knew was she needed to make it to Grandma's as soon as possible to hear her fill in the blanks.

After returning from church Sunday morning, Laurel decided to leave for Ravenna to see Annie. She retied the letters with the frayed ribbon and placed them carefully in her purse. On her way to the refrigerator to find a quick lunch, the blinking message light on her phone caught her eye.

"I'm calling for Laurel Thomas. This is Mercy General Hospital in Muskegon and you're listed as the primary contact for Ms. Annie Walcott. Ms. Walcott was transported here this morning. Please contact us for details of her condition." The woman rattled off a phone number.

Laurel was stuck on the word 'condition.' With the end of the message, she launched into motion and drove away from her apartment ten minutes later.

I should call Mom and Dad. Do I have my purse? Maybe I should call the office too, in case I can't come in tomorrow. The hospital might have already contacted Mom and Dad when they couldn't get a hold of me. Who called the ambulance for Grandma? Did she call it for herself? Should I pick anything up from her house on my way through? This is the right highway, isn't it? I'll call Mom and Dad from the hospital.

Putting the car in park at the hospital, she forced deep, quieting breaths in and out of her lungs before walking inside. At the first desk, a soft-spoken woman squinting at her computer screen told her that an Annie Walcott had indeed been admitted to the hospital after coming into the emergency room that morning, then she gave Laurel directions to the correct nurses' station.

One of the on-duty RN's gave Laurel as many details as she had available. Grandma Annie's friend Virginia Baxter came around the corner a moment later and added the rest.

"Father Taylor and I were making visits to the homebound this morning and brought communion to Annie around eight," Mrs. Baxter explained. "We let ourselves in but Annie was still sleeping.

When I tried to waken her, she was terribly disoriented. The more we tried to explain who we were, the more frightened and uncertain she became. It was so sad, dear. I tried to calm her but nothing worked. Father Taylor called the Ravenna doctor at his home, but couldn't reach him. We decided it would be best to call for an ambulance. I rode with her here."

The hospital had admitted Grandma Annie right away. "We've sedated her," the nurse added, "because she was still altered and distraught when she arrived, but she's perfectly stable thus far. We're monitoring her closely and the doctor is keeping her overnight at least."

Laurel nodded along to all the information, trying to absorb the details and slow her pounding heart rate. Knowing Grandma Annie was stable soothed Laurel.

"What room is she in?" she asked when the other women finished talking.

"Oh, I'll show you," Mrs. Baxter offered and started down a corridor.

They walked to Room 127. She had to swallow hard when she saw Annie. There were too many things that didn't belong: the white and gray hospital gown, an IV, and several electronic machines, each with its own beeping rhythm. Her great-grandmother looked terribly out of place at the center of the scene. For a split second, Laurel flashed back to herself at fourteen, standing over her mother's hospital bed while her dad paced beside the window.

Mrs. Baxter squeezed her hand. "She's only sedated so she can rest. It's okay."

She nodded, the only action she seemed capable of making at present.

Mrs. Baxter gently pushed her toward a chair beside the bed, then walked to the open door. "I'm going to see if I can find the doctor. He'll probably want to talk to you."

After Mrs. Baxter exited, Laurel covered her face with her hands, whispering, "Grandma is 103 years old. This should not feel surprising."

"When a person has aged for so many years without major health issues, a decline in health can feel extremely sudden to those close to them."

Laurel peeked between two fingers to see a doctor standing beside her. He looked like Cary Grant with salt and pepper hair.

"I'm Dr. Morland. I've been monitoring your grandmother."

"Great-grandmother," she corrected him.

"Yes, that sounds more accurate," Dr. Morland appraised her.

She straightened her shoulders and stuck out her hand. "I'm Laurel Thomas. Geographically, I'm her closest family."

The doctor's handshake was firm and brief. "Yes, you were in our records as the emergency contact," he paused before adding, "and as her power of attorney."

She hoped she didn't look as stunned as she felt.

"If Ms. Walcott is still disoriented and unable to understand her whereabouts when she awakens, you will need to make some decisions."

"What sort of decisions? She's only stated," Laurel stated the detail as if it resolved everything. She, Annie, and Erin had collectively settled on giving Laurel power of attorney because she lived nearest. It was merely logistics. All the possibilities had been discussed when Erin and Marshall moved to Chicago five years ago. Laurel only needed specifics from Dr. Morland so she could act according to what Grandma Annie wanted.

"Would you like to wait for anyone else before I explain?"

"No, thank you."

He pulled another chair over to the bed and sat down, then crossed his legs, folding his hands against his stomach. "Your great-grandmother has been fortunate for many years but when she arrived here today she showed classic signs of dementia. If she were a couple decades younger, I'd expect the onset to be slow, and possibly last for years. However, when dementia begins at such a late age, it is usually a rapid onset and a sign of an imminent end of life."

Laurel shuddered.

Dr. Morland frowned. "I'm not talking immediate, but I am talking near future. Weeks, perhaps, though there is no way to be sure. We won't know for a few days, but her brain is likely beginning to shut itself down."

"Weeks." The word was impossible to comprehend.

"The present need is to have your great-grandmother cared for every hour of the day. Depending on the progress of the dementia, she could be in an altered state whenever she is awake. This can produce erratic behavior, fear, and resistance toward caretakers."

Finally, there was a tangible decision to be made. "Is there specific medical attention that she will need that cannot be given at home?"

"No, there isn't, unless she becomes a danger to herself. I'll prescribe a sedative to be used when necessary, but otherwise she will simply need adequate attention. Your best option is a nursing home facility."

"If she is not medically required to be admitted to a facility then she will be going home. I'll make arrangements for someone to be in the house with her twenty-four hours a day," she spoke with more confidence than she felt.

Dr. Morland smiled approvingly. "I'm on until ten P.M., Ms. Thomas. The nurses will continue to monitor our patient through the night. In the morning, I will make an assessment for discharge." He left the room.

Laurel stood up from her chair. "Well, Grandma," she whispered to the sleeping woman, "I better find a phone."

She called her parents first.

"Your mother should be there in a couple hours, sweetie, if not sooner." Her dad's words brought tears of relief to her eyes. "Mrs. Baxter called here maybe an hour ago and filled us in. Your mom didn't wait long to leave. We tried calling you, but you must have been on your way to the hospital already."

"I probably was."

"Have you met with the doctor?"

"He looks like Cary Grant."

"What?"

"Never mind. Yes, I've met him."

Marshall Thomas cleared his throat twice, her father's signature cue that he was about to say something important. "Laurel, how are you doing right now? Is there anyone with you there?"

She was alone in a small family waiting room with beige wallpaper, cushioned chairs close together, and soft lighting. Laurel plopped down in the chair nearest the phone. "Mrs. Baxter is still here somewhere. She's been here since this morning. I think I'll tell her that Mom is coming so she feels free to leave."

"And how are you?" Marshall repeated the crux of his earlier question.

"I'll be okay," she said and rested her head against the wall behind the chair. "I feel caught off guard, which is crazy considering Grandma's age."

"It isn't crazy, dear. Grandma Annie is a permanent fixture in your world."

Laurel sighed and her father let the line fall silent. She knew he was giving her time to say more. She straightened her posture despite his inability to see her.

"Don't worry about me, Dad. It's only all this waiting that gets to me. You know I like it better when I have something to do."

"Will you stay at the hospital tonight?"

"I think so. Right now, I need to think of people to ask to stay with Grandma."

"That should keep you busy until your mother arrives. I'll pray you find enough people to help."

"Thanks, Dad." Ready to be off the phone, she added hastily, "Love you."

"I love you too. Tell your mom to call when she gets there."

When she hung up, Laurel wondered how to start this business of finding help. She personally wanted to be with Annie as much as possible, but knew she couldn't be away from the office until after North Wind Coffees opened. With the uncertainty of how much she was available to be at the house, or how long her mother planned to stay in town, there was no way to know how much help they needed. Then came the question, which she had no inclination to consider, of how many weeks this might go on. She needed to focus on the immediate task. Laurel closed her eyes.

Lord, please keep my head clear. You know what will be needed to let Grandma go back home, even if I don't have any idea. Jesus,

I trust in you. Please show me how to be your hands in Grandma's life right now.

Laurel recognized Mrs. Baxter's voice at a distance, speaking hurriedly about a chart of some sort. She followed the sound to the nurses' desk. Mrs. Baxter had commandeered a phone and chair there. Three nurses bustled around her as if it was nothing out of the ordinary.

"Yes, a chart," she repeated sternly into the phone. "A schedule of when people are available to come so we know who to call. If you could start on it, that would be a great help."

Mrs. Baxter spotted Laurel and waved her over.

"Okay, thanks ever so much. I'll call you again when I'm at home. Bye-bye." Mrs. Baxter finished the call and stood up to speak to her. "That was Mrs. Bill Jenkins. Did you know she went through this same thing with her sister, maybe 10 years back? Had to have someone sitting with her every hour, day or night. We talked it over. We're going to be plenty organized about it so you won't have to worry over Annie staying at home."

Laurel smiled for the first time that afternoon.

"You are bringing her home, right? I suppose I should have checked with you on that. I just know that's what Annie has wanted." Mrs. Baxter paused long enough to hear Laurel's affirmative reply. "Good, I thought you'd agree on that. Now, I realize you work during the week. Do you think we could count on you in the evenings?"

She couldn't resist the urge to hug the woman. "Thank you. You're an answer to prayers, an immediate answer."

Mrs. Baxter protested, though her smile betrayed her appreciation of Laurel's response. They discussed logistics for a while and Mrs. Baxter assured her repeatedly that the daytime hours would be covered one way or another.

"I'll go home and find out what sort of progress Mrs. Bill Jenkins is making with that chart. You call me if there's any change, Laurel." She gathered her purse and coat. "Otherwise, I'll plan to see you back in Ravenna tomorrow."

Laurel was surprised to see it was only ten minutes past three on the waiting room's clock. She felt as weary as at the close of the most stressful workday. Alone now, she walked back to Grandma

Annie's room. Sitting in one chair beside the bed, Laurel slid the other close chair enough to put her legs up. She settled into the stiff plastic seats as best as she could manage. In the next moment though, her stomach growled loudly.

She dug through her purse for change for the vending machine and her fingers landed on the bundle of letters, forgotten in the strife of the afternoon. Now their words came pouring into her mind as she studied the resting face of the dear elderly woman in the bed. She smoothed a bent corner of an envelope and let her mind wander into Grandma Annie's past.

34

July, 1918, 82 years earlier

I am well and safe and working hard.

So began every letter from Kyle since his December departure. It was his subtle code of reassurance for Annie's sake, letting her know he continued his work for the nationalist movement and remained safely undetected by the British authorities. The pages were dated three weeks prior, however, so she could only be sure that at that time Kyle was safe. The weeks in between each letter were cruelly long.

Annie had endured this cycle of anxiety and relief for nearly seven months now. Each day added to her desire to be in Kyle's presence, to see he was "well and safe" with her own eyes. The days when she neither received nor penned a letter, she plodded through a course of emotions—hope, impatience, and an uninterrupted ache both painful and pleasant to bear.

Kyle couldn't write of his work on the newspaper, or of the nationalist rallies he attended. Instead, he sent descriptions of every other aspect of his life: the seasons and landscapes in Ireland, the work on his small farm, an addition to his house that his father was helping him build, and visits from his sister, brother-in-law, and young niece. He often admitted his desire that Annie would eventually share these experiences.

Annie's replies were equally descriptive. She treasured the chance to communicate about her work in the hospital with someone who had seen the place himself. Inwardly, she dwelt on the love she had for Kyle. She dreamt almost nightly of living by his side. On paper, she was more cautious than Kyle, but still ensured that he knew what filled her heart. When doubts and stubborn fears nipped at her confidence, she reread Kyle's frequent encouragements to place her trust in God.

The letter she held in her hands this morning was received two days ago. Annie was rereading the pages before tucking it away with the rest of them. It was anyone's guess how long it would be before she received another. In the reply she'd written today, she instructed him not to send anything more to her at this hospital. When she had a new address, she would send word.

She folded the last of her clothes into the trunk, thinking with some amazement of all that happened since she came to serve here on the LaCroix estate. Annie's experiences as a nurse were enough to make her time in France life altering, but there had been so much beyond the work.

Her father's letter had confirmed for her the significance of it all. It came six weeks after she wrote to her family regarding the end of her engagement to Samuel. The sight of the envelope when it arrived, addressed in his bold printing instead of Mother's slanted handwriting, was a shock. She rummaged through the trunk now and pulled out the letter.

Annie,

I have put off writing to you with the hope that your mother would choose to do so herself. I think, with time, she will forgive you but for now she holds tightly to her anger.

My dear girl, I worry for you. Not because I don't trust that you are following what you believe to be right, but because of the surrounding circumstances. For now, you live and work in such extraordinary scenes. It is to be expected that the pain and toil you participate in daily will alter your perspective on life. I ask you to remember that these circumstances shall pass. Eventually, although the end of the war cannot be dated yet, you will come home to your life here. My concern is that then you might regret the choices you are making now. This would not be a surprise to any of us here, but you have spoken so strongly that I know it is not expected by you. I only ask that you keep the possibility in mind when you return home.

I return now to this letter after a brief pause. I must amend my earlier words, Annie. Just now, I have reread your letters from the past months. I am humbled. The changes you have spoken of in your most recent communication are now evident to me. They've come gradually over your time there, haven't they, dear girl? I am now convinced you have not acted impulsively or with muddled logic. And when I consider the words Samuel so often spoke during the past year, I apologize on his behalf for his lack of understanding and support.

As your parent, I will continue to worry over how you will readjust to life here in your home. Yet, I have new confidence in your strength of character to face that transition.

With this letter, I send my love. Write again soon and I will encourage your mother to do the same.

Your father,
Charles Walcott

Each time she read it, Annie felt the delighted surprise she'd had at the first reading. The strength she drew from knowing her father supported her decision now, even if he remained concerned, was tremendous. As far as the worry, she hoped it would be remedied once her family knew about Kyle. She had yet to mention him in any letters to her family, always promising herself that the next letter would be the right one in which to do so.

She pictured her father's face as she returned the letter to its place in the trunk. Daddy, if you only knew the unpredictable direction things have taken.

Finished packing, she left the dormitory and paused in the July sunshine to observe the mansion. She whispered the verses she had recently committed to memory from the fortieth chapter of Isaiah.

"'Hast thou not known? Hast thou not heard, that the everlasting God, the Lord, the Creator of the ends of the earth, fainteth not, neither is weary? There is no searching of his understanding. He giveth power to the faint; and to them that have no might he increases strength.'"

35

July, 1918

"You have to tell them, Meg,"

Annie made the same plea as countless other times in the last five months. Meg bit her lip while tears filled her eyes. Annie softened her tone. "Meg, there's no way around it. I know you're afraid."

Meg lowered herself with some difficulty into a chair in the foyer. Her swollen belly weighed down her petite frame. She reached up to rub the back of her neck.

Annie sat too. This conversation had gone the same way each time. Meg would insist it was impossible to make her parents understand, that she had tried to write but couldn't come up with the right words, and that she was afraid of how disappointed they were going to be. Then Meg would plead with Annie to simply be her friend, to be supportive.

Once in a while Meg added a request that Annie pray for her since she was praying so often nowadays. Annie always detected a trace of insincerity in these requests. Nonetheless, she had prayed for Meg daily for five months now, ever since Meg gave up hiding her pregnancy.

It was the second trimester by the time anyone at the hospital knew Meg was with child. Loose sweaters garnered no extra attention in the winter months and a lucky freedom from morning sickness made the pregnancy easy to conceal. Then one night in March, Meg came to her and confessed, leaving her speechless. She was then the only person in the world who knew. They went together to Dr. LaCroix the following day. Meg knew better than to think she could go without medical care.

A few of the nurses shunned Meg, refusing to associate with her more than their work required. One requested that Dr. LaCroix send Meg away. While it did take some pleading to convince him not to immediately send her back to Ontario, he let her stay with the stipulation that Meg write to her parents. Once they replied, he could make a decision. Meg promised to write the letter and in the weeks that followed, she claimed it was sent but with no reply yet. He sympathetically stopped bringing up the question and Meg felt secure in having a home at the hospital for at least the length of the pregnancy.

To Annie, she confided that she never wrote to her family. Annie was torn between loyal support of her friend and the demand of her conscience to be honest with Dr. LaCroix. Never sure it was her place to expose Meg's lie, she persistently encouraged Meg to tell him the truth.

It took a focused eye to see how the circumstances wore on Meg's good-humored spirits. When Annie caught glimpses of it, her heart ached. Meg's words were invariably optimistic, but her smile stopped reaching her eyes.

Now Meg was finishing her eighth month and Annie decided to say what must be said. She bent forward and held Meg's hands. Meg's fingers were swollen but still small. They made Annie think of a plump little child. "There simply isn't any time left to keep pretending that you have things figured out."

Meg pulled her hands back, her face distressed.

"You heard what Dr. LaCroix told us. His sister will house us until the baby is born, but then we will have to leave. Meg, you need to send word to your family." She tried to speak gently but the situation had become even more urgent now that the hospital was closing.

With the battle lines shifting dangerously closer each week, the hospital was at great risk of being taken by the enemy. Keeping patients here would be the equivalent of providing the Germans with prisoners of war.

Eight days ago the hospital staff began the work of closing its doors. They packed up medical supplies, sent patients off to other facilities, and scrubbed down the main ward. That expansive room felt strange and disconcerting once empty. The beds were still there but pushed up against the walls to leave the center wide open. It left the impression of trying, but failing, to return to what it used to be.

The mansion was empty of patients. Nora, Meg, and Annie were the only remaining nurses.

Nora had a seat in a transport to Paris. Dr. LaCroix was driving west to his sister's. He had communicated the details to her and she offered to take Meg in until the baby was born, agreeing it was not a good idea to put Meg on a ship across the Atlantic at this time. As for Annie, she refused to leave until she knew Meg would not be alone after the birth.

Meg's shoulders slouched in resignation. Her voice broke when she replied, "I lied, not just to Dr. LaCroix but to you. I'm so sorry. I was too ashamed to admit it."

"Admit what, Meg?" She took Meg's hands again, stroking the palms with her thumbs.

"I have nowhere to go."

"How do you know that, Meg? You can't without at least trying to contact your parents. I'm sure they will be angry, of course, but they wouldn't turn you away. You have said before how supportive your parents have always been."

"Didn't you hear me, Annie? I lied to you. I did write to my family and I received a reply. In fact, I waited a few months and wrote again, but they haven't changed their minds."

"Oh Meg, I'm sorry." She could guess the nature of Mr. and Mrs. Dupree's reactions considering Meg's dishonesty about the matter.

"They won't allow me back." Meg's cheeks were soaked with tears. "I've lied all along. They never supported me being here. When I left for France, they wanted me to marry a man I barely knew. I had to leave. I couldn't do it. So, I signed up to come here. I never saw my father so angry." She wiped her face with the back of her hand. "Well, that's probably only because I couldn't see him when he got my letter about the baby. My mother was the one who wrote back."

"And she said you couldn't come home? Really?"

"No, not with the baby."

Annie raised her eyebrows, waiting for more.

"They said I would be allowed back and to 'remain a member of the family,' those were the words she used, but not if I brought the child with me."

"Oh my." She sunk back against her chair, feeling sick to her stomach. "And there is no one else?"

"I thought my aunt might take me in." A new wave of tears spilled out of Meg's eyes. "We've always been close and she thought my decision to be a nurse here was brave. But now, she said I had gone too far; that she wouldn't help me bring the family down with my foolishness."

Meg looked worn out. Her eyes were bloodshot.

Annie nearly changed her mind on asking her next question, but it needed to be asked. "Have you told Chet?"

Meg's head snapped up, her fair curls tumbling away from her face. "I never said he was..."

"But he is, isn't he?"

Meg sighed. "How did you know?"

"It was only a guess," Annie admitted, "But I felt pretty sure. It made sense with the timing and why you would refuse to tell me who was the father."

Meg remained silent.

"Have you written to Chet?" she repeated.

Her friend's face twisted up with another sob. "Yes." After a few uneven breaths, Meg was able to speak again. "His letter was so short, Annie, as if he didn't give it much attention. He said he would be a terrible father; that he wasn't a good man. He said it'd be better if the child didn't know him."

Annie felt livid, if not shocked. From Kyle's letters, she knew Chet was reassigned to a regiment stationed along the Marne, where there was persistent action between the armies. Kyle said Chet talked of settling in southern France after the war was over. She knew Kyle prayed constantly for his brother to have a change of heart, but if the opportunity to have a family hadn't touched him, Annie wondered what sort of miracle could possibly be effective.

244

"You haven't said anything to Kyle, have you?" Meg asked earnestly.

"Certainly not. I only had my suspicions about Chet's involvement, and I promised from the beginning that I would tell no one without your permission."

"Thank you."

"Meg, what are you going to do?"

Meg pressed her fingertips against her forehead. "I don't know. I truly don't know."

Both of them were silent. She wished for the right words to comfort Meg, but what could be said?

"Meg," she paused until Meg looked up at her. "I have been praying for God to provide for you and your baby."

Meg looked uncomfortable but Annie continued. "Would you like to pray with me this time? I could say the words, but in your heart you can be making the prayer with me."

"I don't know what I believe about all of that."

"That's okay," she replied quickly. "Kyle said something once that helped me when I wasn't sure. He said God doesn't require you to have faith before He listens to your prayers. God is always listening, even when we're not sure about talking to Him."

Meg's shrug was enough of a yes to satisfy her. She leaned forward and bowed her head. Before closing her eyes, she saw Meg tentatively do the same.

With the sun edging into the eastern sky, Annie, Meg, and Dr. LaCroix strapped their trunks to the car and set off. Jean and Adele, the butler and cook, would follow in a carriage the next day. They were working to close up the house indefinitely. Dr. LaCroix planned to break with Annie and Meg at his sister Marie's before proceeding to Paris to serve the allied troops again as a physician.

Annie's plan was much the same. She hoped to continue in France as a nurse once she saw Meg and the baby safely set for home

– whatever home God chose to provide. The medical corps through which she came to France had given her a new assignment, but she had to resign her position with the corps to stay with Meg. She made these precarious choices while clinging to the peace and courage that filled her when she prayed about her friend's needs. She was certain her place for the time being was at Meg's side.

"We will be there by nightfall, as long as this machine works properly," Dr. LaCroix announced at the start of their drive, still not confident about his motor car.

Despite having no mechanical problems, Annie, Meg and Dr. LaCroix were still on the road as daylight waned into dusk. The last three weeks had been exhaustingly hot in the region. During the ride, Annie and Meg wiped sweat from their faces with handkerchiefs and were relieved when they saw the sun finally dip below the horizon. That small degree of relief was outweighed by impatience to be out of the car. Each jolt of the wheels against a bump or rut added to the ache in Annie's back. She could only imagine how much worse it was for Meg.

Meg kept at least one hand on her belly for the entire ride. With the jarring motion of the vehicle, the child repeatedly kicked against Meg's stomach and ribs. This made Meg laugh in the morning. She held Annie's palm against her side to feel the baby's movements, and joked that her son or daughter would loathe traveling after this one trip. Within a few hours though, it became painful. Meg winced with every bump under the wheels and kick from the baby.

The trio pulled up to a quaint country house tucked behind a grove of fruit trees at the end of a long driveway. Annie noticed how quiet the place was once the car's motor stopped. As the frontlines had moved closer and closer to the hospital, she could barely remember the last night she hadn't been able to hear the guns.

The doctor's sister Marie strode out the front door with a lantern that split the darkness. Marie was as tall and slim as her brother, but with fine, pretty features. She went to the passenger door first and helped Meg to her feet. Dr. LaCroix took the lantern and began carrying luggage into the house. Meg was soon standing, but with a half-bow from the pain in her back. She leaned on Annie's and Marie's arms to reach the door.

With gestures and explanations in French, Marie showed them a room with two narrow beds and a washstand. Meg curled onto a bed, squeezing her eyes shut against the pain.

Annie soaked a washcloth in the water she found in a pitcher on the washstand. She laid it across Meg's forehead and used another cloth to gently rub Meg's neck and arms.

"Do you want help getting out of your dress?"

"No," Meg answered, "I don't think I want to try. I'll just sleep in it."

She wanted to insist since Meg would be much cooler in her nightclothes, so she went to Meg's trunk to find a nightgown.

"Annie."

"What is it?"

"I feel so dizzy. I don't..." Meg's voice faded out.

"Meg?"

Annie hurried to the bed. Meg's muscles had relaxed as if she were sleeping. She shook Meg's shoulders, gripping them with both hands. It took a few seconds before Meg came around.

She spoke loudly now, "Meg, I'm going to get water for you to drink. I need you to stay awake until I get back. Can you do that?"

Annie kept hold of Meg's shoulders until she gave a weak, "Yes."

Meg's blue eyes were wide and blinking as she fought to keep them open. Annie hesitated at leaving the room, but she had to find Dr. LaCroix. "I'll hurry, Meg. Stay awake."

Outside the bedroom, she followed the sound of voices to the parlor.

Dr. LaCroix rose from the sofa when she came in the room. "Nurse Walcott, is there something you need?"

"I'd like to bring a glass of water to Meg."

Marie stood and gestured for Annie to follow her, but Annie continued speaking to the doctor. "I think you should check on Meg, sir. She's in such pain from the ride here. She might only be dehydrated but a few minutes ago, she passed out for several seconds."

They all froze where they stood when a fierce scream shot through the house. Followed closely by Annie, the doctor rushed down the unlit hallway as a second scream reached their ears.

The bedding beneath Meg was wet. She was curled into a ball, crying. "What's happening?" she managed to whisper before another jolt of pain hit her.

"L'enfant arrive." Marie had come in behind them.

"Oui," the doctor replied without looking away from Meg, "the baby is coming."

36

September, 2000, 83 years later

Laurel walked back toward Grandma Annie's hospital room. She'd left when a nurse came to check Annie's vitals. After visiting the vending machine for an apple and a bag of stale chips, she'd revisited the smaller waiting room with the comfortable chairs. Drawing near Grandma Annie's room, Laurel heard her name.

"Mom!" She spotted Erin Thomas at the nurses' desk in the main waiting room.

"There you are." Erin embraced her daughter. "I went to Grandma's room but you were gone."

"I needed a more comfortable chair for a little while." She took a good look at her mother and hugged her a second time.

Erin wore a red t-shirt with a pair of wide-legged black sweatpants and the white walking shoes she wore everywhere except to work and church.

"You cut your hair," Laurel remarked on the fresh bob. "I like it. It looks good on you."

"Thank you, dear."

The small talk ended there and Laurel felt the weight of the day settle on her once again. "So, you saw Grandma?"

Erin nodded. They walked toward room 127 together. "She didn't even know you were here. Is she really having that hard of a time remembering things?"

Laurel looked at her in surprise. "She's awake?"

"She was awake when I went in there."

"And she knew you?"

"Yes."

"Thank God." She walked faster.

Inside the room, Dr. Morland was explaining to Grandma Annie the events of the day and why she would be staying in the hospital overnight. The moment Laurel and Erin entered, the doctor lost his patient's attention.

"You are here after all," Grandma Annie greeted Laurel. "I really wasn't sure."

"That's because you haven't been awake while I've been here, Grandma." She bent low to give Grandma Annie's shoulders a squeeze.

"And Erin," Annie looked past Laurel to address Laurel's mother, "To think you came all this way and the doctor says I'll be going home tomorrow. So much trouble for nothing."

Dr. Morland jumped in with sternness, "Yes, Miss Walcott, but someone will need to be in the house with you at all times. I've already told you that."

Erin confirmed the doctor's words. "That's right, Grandma. I hope you're ready to have company for a while."

Grandma Annie looked miffed at the requirement. She showed no signs of confusion now. She said she couldn't remember anything of the day though and Dr. Morland explained that this was normal.

"I beg your pardon, sir, but nothing about this is normal," Grandma Annie retorted.

He smiled. "Of course it isn't. But it is typical for this frustrating situation. If you'll excuse me, I'll be back to check on you soon." He left the room.

"I can't believe they're making you stay, Erin." Grandma Annie frowned. "What about work?"

"They aren't making me, and the office will do fine without me for a couple of days. It's about time I use some vacation days."

Grandma Annie fussed with her hospital gown. "This is hardly a vacation."

Erin looked to her daughter. Sitting down on the edge of the narrow bed, Laurel tried a different approach.

"This is how it has to be," she said evenly. "Before Mom and Dad moved to Chicago we all decided together to keep you in your own home for as long as possible. It'll require us to rearrange our schedules and enlist some help from your friends, but we're only following through on what we said we would do. If we don't, you will have to stay in a nursing home from now on."

She made this last statement as if the nursing home was an option on the table. She saw Grandma Annie's chin lift; a signal of stubbornness that ran in the family.

"Yes, Laurel, you're right. We did plan for this."

Erin covered a smile with her fingers. "I'm going to find a phone and call Marshall." She nodded toward the door, indicating Laurel should follow her.

"There's a private waiting room down that hall to the right," Laurel pointed when they reached the hallway. "I used the phone in there."

"Thank you. I'm also going to call Virginia Baxter and see how things are coming along for arranging help. I didn't want to tell Grandma yet but I can only stay until tomorrow night. My backup for work is on maternity leave and my boss requested that I give him the week to find a temporary employee to cover my absence."

Laurel felt anxiety gripping her throat.

"This way, I'll come back at the end of the week and stay for as long as I'm needed. I'm sorry I can't stay this week. Between her closest friends and you, I know there will be others to stay with Grandma until the weekend."

Laurel knew her mother would stay if she could. "All right, I'm sure we'll make it work until you come back."

"I'm sure you will." Erin went to find the phone.

Grandma Annie was trying to push herself up with her elbows when Laurel returned to the room.

"Here, Grandma, use this." Laurel showed her the button to raise the bed to a sitting position.

"Well, that is nice."

She sat down in one of the hard chairs beside the bed.

"Now," Grandma Annie addressed her quietly, "You read the letters by now, haven't you?"

"Yes, I have," Laurel answered, stunned but thankful that Annie broached the subject. "I read them right away, twice as a matter of fact. But I have a few questions. They didn't contain what I expected."

She kept an eye on her great-grandmother, wanting Annie's behavior to be her guide.

Grandma Annie let her shoulders rest against the bed again. The muscles of her neck and face visibly relaxed. Satisfaction lit her face like sunlight from within.

"If I had known that it would feel this good to have someone know all I'd been keeping to myself, I'd have told it all years ago. I feel like my heart's been untied."

Laurel struggled to share Grandma Annie's joy in the unburdening of her secrets. Shouldn't Grandma Annie be anxious, afraid over how the truth contradicted what the whole family had been led to believe? Didn't Grandma Annie know she might be angry with her? Except, it wasn't anger in her heart. It was more of an unnamable, unsettling sensation that had coated her nerves for the past twenty-four hours.

"You aren't my great-grandmother."

Said aloud, it became acutely real, more real than even the moment she'd realized it while reading the letters. The fact struck her with all its force and her face contorted with the effort to keep hold of her emotions.

"Oh, Laurel." Grandma Annie's voice was pure sympathy.

Laurel rushed to add, "I mean, you are. You always have been and always will be. I know family is much more than genetics. Still, it is genetics too."

Her voice faded with these words and she waited for Grandma Annie to say more, to explain away the tumult in her heart, but Grandma Annie didn't try.

Laurel requested quietly, "Tell me about the night Megan was born."

The brief veil of serenity that had lain across Grandma Annie's face fell away. Her eyes went to the ceiling. "That was an awful, awful night. The baby was breech and Meg's labor went on for hours.

I can still picture Dr. LaCroix's expression. Every time he checked the progress of the labor or when he worked to change the baby's position, he had the same look he used to have during a surgery that was going poorly. I didn't know for whom to be more scared, Meg or the baby, and I couldn't keep my head clear enough to pray. With each contraction, Meg grew paler and weaker, and she passed out a few times. I was helpless."

The pain in her great-grandmother's voice brought Laurel closer to tears than even the story itself.

"Megan was born at 4:40 A.M. on July 20, 1918. Meg Dupree died an hour later." Tears trickled over Grandma Annie's temple and onto the pillow. "I remember feeling at the time that the minutes were passing slower than normal. Because I was watching my friend die, I suppose." Grandma Annie blinked rapidly as more tears pooled in her eyes. "Afterward though, it felt like no time at all between the labor ending and Meg dying. Dr. LaCroix said the labor was simply too much for Meg, that some women are not built to endure a birth that difficult."

"Was she conscious though? Did she get to meet her daughter?" Laurel asked.

Grandma Annie nodded. "She did. Meg held her baby, talked to her and cried over her, but her body couldn't last. She only stayed conscious for a few minutes at a time.

"Marie, Dr. LaCroix's sister, tended to her. Meg couldn't even lift her head off the pillow. I had to wrap her arms around little Megan so she could hold her." Grandma Annie broke down then. Tears streamed and her shoulders shook against the pillow. Laurel held her hand until she could speak again. "Once, when she woke up after passing out, Megan was crying. Meg tried to hold her closer, to soothe her, but didn't have the strength. She asked me to take Megan and I held her until she was quiet. That's when Meg asked me to be her baby's mother.

"Meg told me I was the only friend this baby had in the world. She begged me until I told her I would. Honestly, I couldn't process what Meg was asking of me, but there was nothing in me willing to tell her no. She told me where the letters from her family were and said I should keep them in case anyone didn't believe that her family hadn't wanted the baby. She even made me promise not to try to contact Chet."

Yesterday, Laurel had read the unmerciful letters from Meg's parents. They were two of the ones Annie kept with her and Kyle's letters. Meg hadn't exaggerated that the baby was without another friend. Grandma Megan would have been raised in an orphanage, likely in France, if Annie hadn't taken her in.

Before Laurel could ask what transpired when Annie brought the infant home to Boston, Erin returned to the room.

"Marshall says to give you his love, Grandma. He was glad to hear you were awake." Erin stopped behind Laurel's chair and rested a hand on her shoulder. Frowning at them, she asked, "What's the matter with the two of you?"

Grandma Annie wiped hastily at her eyes and Laurel lifted herself out of a slouch. They both pasted on smiles that couldn't have fooled anyone in a lighted room.

"Oh, I was just reminiscing about the day Megan was born."

Erin arched her eyebrows. "Really?"

Not knowing what she could possibly say to explain, Laurel opened and closed her mouth without a word.

"Yes, you'll have to have Laurel tell you sometime." Grandma Annie smoothed the gray blanket that covered her up to her chest. "She can tell you everything."

Laurel caught the meaningful look her great-grandmother gave her. Holding Grandma Annie's solemn gaze, she said, "Yes, I'll tell her all of it sometime."

37

October, 2000

In a dim corner of the parking garage adjacent to her office, Laurel sat in her car, staring at the concrete wall and drumming her fingers on the wheel. Her nerves were frayed from the events of yesterday and a poor night's sleep.

Last night, Grandma Annie seemed stronger and, with some coaxing, she ate most of the dinner the hospital provided. They'd watched old sitcom reruns and shared some lighthearted reminiscing. Yet, Grandma Annie's spirits were low, her face unsmiling and her words few. Laurel worried that the earlier talk about Meg and baby Megan was more upsetting than Grandma Annie let on. Laurel had waited until Grandma Annie fell asleep for the night before driving home.

Her mother stayed at the hospital overnight and Mrs. Baxter had promised to help get Annie settled at home once she was discharged. So, while Laurel wasn't needed at the hospital overnight, she slept restlessly in her own bed, waking frequently with thoughts of her great-grandmother. Erin had promised to call her with updates once the doctor saw them in the morning.

It was now two minutes after eight on Monday morning. She was late for work despite being right outside the building, and she still hadn't heard from her mother

Inside her office, she hung up the phone, having dialed all but one number to call the hospital. It crossed her mind that there hadn't been a convenient moment for her mom to call. No news is good news.

A knock sounded on her office door. Her coworker Nadya leaned into the office, knocking lightly on the doorframe.

"Good morning."

"Mornin'," Nadya greeted her and came around the desk to sit on its corner. She had a friendly smile on her face but cocked her head as she looked at Laurel. "Is anything the matter today?"

"What do you mean?"

"You didn't look very happy when you came in this morning."

If Nadya managed to read her mood when she merely walked past Nadya's office, there was no use lying now.

"My great-grandmother is in the hospital. I was there with her yesterday but since I needed to work today, I didn't stay with her." Laurel propped her elbows on the desk and sighed. "My mom was supposed to call me this morning with an update."

"But she hasn't called?"

"No, and Grandma should be discharged this morning as long as she was okay through the night," Laurel cringed at the sulkiness in her voice. "I'm just wishing I was there to help bring her home."

"I'm so sorry." Nadya's expression was kind. "I get it. My worst days at work are when one of the boys is sick and I can't stay home."

Laurel had a feeling Nadya truly did understand how horrible it was to be away from a family member in need. If she could stand to admit it, Laurel knew she wasn't needed at the hospital last night or this morning. Her mother and Mrs. Baxter would manage fine until she came over in the evening. This should have eased her worry but it hadn't.

"Have you tried calling the hospital?"

"I thought about it."

"You could take today off. It's the end of this week that will be especially full."

"I'll need to take off all of next week to stay with Grandma. I'll be okay once I can get focused."

"I understand." Nadya patted Laurel's shoulder then stood up from the desk to leave. "I hope you get a call soon. I'll see you in the staff meeting."

Laurel pivoted her chair nearly sideways so the phone was outside her vision as she worked at her computer. Out of sight, out of mind; this was a chance to test the theory.

Surprisingly, her attempt to focus was successful, for the most part. Laurel finalized the program for the grand opening and emailed it to the printing service. She proofread the ad to run in Thursday's entertainment section of the city newspaper. Still, she refused to get up from her chair all morning in case a call came through. Several times, she rotated just far enough to check that the message light wasn't blinking, despite never hearing the phone ring.

At 11:30, as Laurel made notes on the new jewelry store account for the afternoon staff meeting, her phone finally rang. She jumped from her seat and picked up the call.

"Parker Advertising, this is Laurel Thomas."

"Yes, Laurel, I have a call for you." It was LeeAnn. "Just wanted to make sure you were at your desk before putting it through."

"Thank you, LeeAnn."

"I think it might be your mom. She sounds a lot like you."

"It probably is, LeeAnn, thank you." Laurel could hear the soft buzz of the line but no click of the call being transferred to her. "LeeAnn?"

"Yeah, I'll put her through."

There was a click but only silence for a few seconds afterward.

"Mom?"

"Oh, yes," Erin answered, obviously distracted. "Laurel, I'm sorry it took so long to call."

"It's okay, Mom, just fill me in. How is Grandma?"

"She's better now."

"Better?"

"It was four A.M., I think, when she woke up. I called the nurse right away but Grandma was frightened. She hurt herself on the rail of the bed."

"What did she hurt?"

"Her wrist, a mild sprain the doctor called it. She didn't know where she was or who I was. It didn't take long for the sedative to kick in and when she woke up later in the morning, she was better; still disoriented, but much calmer."

"I hate thinking of her being so afraid." Laurel rubbed at the center of her forehead. "Is the doctor making her stay longer?"

"No, she's going home today," Erin chuckled quietly. "Dr. Morland was pretty reluctant, but you know how I can talk people into anything."

Laurel answered with a weak laugh. "When are you leaving with Grandma?"

"Mrs. Baxter is on her way. Dr. Morland wants to cover the details of caring for Grandma with at least two people. So, once Mrs. Baxter is up to speed, he'll sign the discharge form."

"I should be there, Mom."

"I will be certain you understand the instructions also," her mother answered pragmatically. "I'll stay until you get there tonight and make sure you're comfortable with everything that's needed, then I'll have to head out." Laurel heard shuffling papers and her mother sounded distracted again. "I need to go, dear, but I'll call you this afternoon from Grandma's house."

"Okay, Mom. Don't forget."

"Of course not."

The line went quiet.

Laurel wondered what Grandma Annie looked like when she was disoriented to the point of fear, and what things she said when the dementia skewed her memory. Laurel tried to picture it but couldn't imagine Grandma Annie without her trademark sharpness of mind and even-keeled demeanor.

Crossing her arms on top of the desk, she lowered her chin to her forearm. She pinched her bottom lip between her teeth and tried to think of what she had been doing before her mother called.

I was preparing notes on the jewelry store account. And waiting for my mother to call.

The computer pinged with a new email alert. Two minutes later, another alert sounded. Laurel ignored them. She stared at the marble paperweight on her desk with its inscription of a verse from First Corinthians: "Be watchful, stand firm in your faith, be courageous, be strong. Let all that you do be done in love."

She closed her eyes. *God, I can't decide what is making me feel more helpless, not being with Grandma while she suffers today or knowing her secret about our family's history. I don't have time to dwell on either anyway.* "God, please be my strength. Amen," she finished aloud.

"Amen." She heard an echo in a deep voice.

Laurel's eyes opened and looked to Robert in the doorway. With as much dignity as she could muster, she sat up straight in her chair and aimed for a don't-even-think-about-asking-what's-wrong-with-me expression on her face.

"You want to grab lunch?" Robert asked, apparently content to leave the curious scene unaddressed.

"Yes," she answered without thinking, then shook her head. "I mean, no, I can't."

He frowned, but mercifully did not try to change her mind.

"I would like to, but I can't. I might need to leave early today so I'm working through lunch."

"No problem. Do you want me to pick anything up for you to eat at your desk?"

"You wouldn't mind doing that? I would appreciate it. All I have in my desk is some stale trail mix. Let me get some cash for you."

"Nonsense. I've got it. Just tell me what kind of sandwich you like and I'll run down to the deli on the corner."

She gave him her order and thanked him again. Robert left her office with a warm smile on his face.

Laurel was grateful for his tact. She shifted her mind into planning mode, making a list of every single thing to accomplish this week, then sorting it by priority. Her responsibilities for the coffeehouse's grand opening were at the top. There was no compromising the deadline on those tasks. Beneath them was the requirement of spending her nights at Annie's. Mrs. Baxter and Mrs. Bill Jenkins had found volunteers to sit with Annie for all the daytime hours, covering much of the time themselves, but they were counting on her for the evenings and overnight.

Laurel picked her pen back up to add one more line to the list. She wrote it a few inches below the rest of the list, not knowing where to place it in the hierarchy of the week's responsibilities. *Find out how Grandma ended up in Michigan.*

38

October, 2000

Laurel checked the clock. Her ear was warm from the phone pressed against it for the last ninety minutes. The musical act for Saturday's opening was confirmed, as were the evening's extra servers. She had taken a call from the printer to answer questions about the program. While she was on that call, her mother left a voicemail to say Grandma Annie was back at home and sleeping comfortably.

Before leaving for the day, Laurel reviewed the list of businesses to visit tomorrow to deliver personal invitations to the grand opening. The invitations were in Nadya's office so Laurel walked there to collect them. On her return, Robert called to her from his office.

She stuck her head and shoulders through the half-open door. "Yes?"

"How about dinner tonight?"

Laurel considered explaining to Robert about Grandma Annie and why Laurel was leaving early today. The pressure that'd been lingering behind her eyes spread out to her temples. She wanted to laugh over the lack of energy she had to analyze this latest invitation from him.

"I can't tonight, but thank you." She offered an apologetic smile but decided to tell him about Grandma Annie the next time she saw him.

Melanie had emailed earlier and asked her to stop by the bookstore to chat after work. Laurel hurried now to wrap things up so she'd have time to see her friend before driving to Grandma Annie's. Her message light was blinking again. She punched in her security code and pressed the button to activate the speakerphone.

"Laurel, I'm sorry to be bothering you at work." Connor's voice sounded glum through the little speaker. "Is there a time this week we could meet up? We could do lunch or dinner." He paused for a few seconds and Laurel thought he'd been cut off, but then the message continued. "Or I could swing by your place when it's convenient for you. Give me a call so we can talk."

The entire message was strange. Connor's tone; the open-ended suggestion of getting together when Connor was normally so specific in making plans. She replayed the message before adding *Call Connor* to the week's task list. Then she collected her purse and jacket and headed out.

After making quick work of packing her bags for the week at Grandma Annie's, Laurel pulled up to Grand River Books. Mel spotted Laurel through the store window and met her at the door with a long hug.

"What a day." Mel sighed.

"What's the matter?" Laurel asked, then warned, "I can't stay long."

Mel's lip stuck out in a pout.

"Grandma is sick and I'm going to stay at her house all week."

"Oh, no! What's the matter with her? Wait, you're taking off of work? Isn't the opening this Saturday? I have it on my calendar for Saturday night."

While Laurel summed up yesterday's events and the plan for taking care of Annie, they walked to the staff break room at the back of the store.

"What a change from how you're used to seeing her," Mel remarked as she straightened shelves of books along the way.

"And she still is her clear-minded self when she's lucid. When she woke up yesterday afternoon, Grandma started right in on the conversation we'd been having the last time I was over."

They sat at one of the room's round tables.

"I can't believe it could change so swiftly."

"I don't know that I would rather have seen the dementia occur gradually," Laurel said. "That would have been much worse for Grandma."

"Well, I hope it doesn't get to be too overwhelming for you this week." Mel took two bottles of water from the refrigerator and handed one to Laurel. "I'll be praying for good focus for Saturday's event, and for you to have the energy to handle it all."

"It already is overwhelming." Her laugh came out more like a whimper. "Things kept coming at me today. There's so much to be done at work, and I can't stop thinking about Grandma Annie. Connor left a strange message for me and wants to get together, but didn't say why. Robert asked me to lunch and dinner. It was a weird day."

Mel stared at her. "Robert asked you to lunch and dinner?"

Laurel dropped her head in her hands. "Okay, let's not fixate on that. What is going on with you?"

"I thought you were giving Robert a chance. That's what you said."

"No, I said I want to be his friend, and I still do."

"If you say so."

"I do." Laurel insisted, "Now, tell me what you needed to talk about tonight?"

"Well, if I'd known all that was going on with you, I wouldn't have bothered you. I only needed to vent to my maid of honor. I can talk to you about this later."

"No, no. I'm here, and it feels good to think about a happy event like the wedding. But what's gone wrong?"

Mel threw a hand in the air. "Our caterer cancelled. One month until the wedding and they call to inform me that they triple booked the day and only have staff for two events. Apparently, our wedding was the last event booked so we got dropped."

"That's terrible," Laurel exclaimed.

"It is. Jace and I made a list of other caterers to contact but we know it's going to be next to impossible to book one this late, especially a good one. I'm also planning to talk to Connor. With all the wedding photography he does, I know he has connections in that whole industry. Maybe he'll know of more caterers that we haven't come across."

"Is there anything I can do?"

"I doubt it. We'll keep calling the ones on our list. I guess you can pray that a fabulous caterer miraculously has November Fourth available!"

"I'll do that." She leaned over to hug her friend's shoulders. "And if you think of anything else I can do to help, call me. I don't care how busy things are right now. I'm still your maid of honor."

The pair walked back through the store toward the front door. Laurel knew her mother had to drive back to Chicago tonight and couldn't leave until Laurel arrived. It was time to be on the road.

Laurel asked Mel a favor, "When you talk to Connor, could you fill him in on everything that's going on? If he really needs to talk this week, tell him to give me a call at Grandma Annie's in the evening. You have that number, right?"

Mel nodded and agreed to convey the message to Connor. Laurel repeated her promise to help in any way possible then she got into her car and drove toward the freeway, praying that Grandma Annie would have a calm first night at home.

39

October, 2000

As it happened, that first night consisted of the only calm hours in the next five days. Grandma Annie was sleeping when Laurel arrived Monday evening and she slept through the night. Tuesday morning, she was disoriented, but not panicked. She let Laurel make breakfast for her, ate well and then lay silently in bed until Mrs. Baxter came to relieve Laurel.

The days and nights that followed did not go as easily. Laurel came straight from work to hear reports of Grandma Annie's dementia worsening each day. She slept a great deal thanks to the doses of sedatives the doctor supplied, but when she woke, she was too often scared and inconsolable.

From Tuesday to Friday there were no lucid moments. There were many calm moments; it was not all panic and upset. But in those times, Grandma Annie relived past memories as if they were things of the present. Annie asked Laurel if she was Annie's mother, if she was Megan, or if she was Nora, the nurse Annie worked with in France.

Last night, when the medication relaxed Grandma Annie's tense and frail frame for the first time in hours, Laurel cried herself to sleep. The skin under Laurel's eyes wasn't just shadowy this morning, it was an entirely different shade from the rest of her face. When she checked the schedule on the refrigerator, she had to calculate which day it was today: Friday. Laurel felt like crying again, but from relief now. Her parents would arrive this evening.

Marshall would stay only for the weekend but Erin planned to be there through the following week or longer. The thought that she and her mother would be together to care for Grandma Annie for the next week had helped Laurel endure the last four days.

Laurel checked on Grandma Annie, who was still sleeping, then gathered her things for the day. Being out of hearing range of

Grandma's bedroom made her nervous, so she would wait to shower until Mrs. Jenkins arrived. With some minutes to pass before then, she went to the living room and picked up Grandma Annie's Bible. Laurel forgot hers at home and found this one on the bookshelves. Inside was an inscription revealing it to be the Bible given to Annie on the ship to France in 1917; the Bible that Annie read in her dormitory room the night she prayed from her heart for the first time. Laurel had hugged the well-worn book to her chest after reading that inscription.

The Psalms provided a great deal of comfort through the week—one of so many things she wished to share with her great-grandmother. Sitting down now on the center cushion of the couch, she felt the morning sun warm the back of her neck. She decided this time to let Paul's letters encourage her. Her eyes skimmed the pages of Second Corinthians until she came to a welcome passage.

"'But we have this treasure in earthen vessels, that the excellency of the power may be of God, and not of us.'" Laurel read the words in a whisper. "'We are troubled on every side, yet not distressed; we are perplexed, but not in despair; persecuted, but not forsaken; cast down, but not destroyed; always bearing about in the body the dying of the Lord Jesus, that the life also of Jesus might be made manifest in our body'[12]"

She skipped ahead a few verses. "'For which cause we faint not; but though our outward man perish, yet the inward man is renewed day by day. For the light affliction, which is but for a moment, worketh for us a far more exceeding and eternal weight of glory.'[13]"

Laurel ran her index finger back up the page and stopped on "troubled on every side, yet not distressed." She asked God for the patience and hope the words suggested.

Mrs. Bill Jenkins came banging through the front door and the peace starting to trickle through Laurel's veins dissolved like sugar in boiling water. In the years they'd been acquainted, she'd been both amused and annoyed by the proud, iron-willed woman and her many set-in-stone opinions. However, their increased interactions in the current circumstances revealed Mrs. Bill Jenkins as critical, and often tactless. Laurel wondered more than once why her great-grandmother was friends with the woman.

Patience, she repeated in her head as she waited for this morning's attack.

Mrs. Bill Jenkins set down her bag of yarn, knitting needles, and magazines. Hands on her thick hips, she came to the couch and stood over Laurel. "You know, you could take better care of Annie if you got some sleep. You look terrible."

Most of the seventy-three year old woman's hair was still a dark shade of brown, but Laurel watched a few gray strands waving, sticking straight out from the scalp. She had an urge to lick her fingers and make the hairs lie down, which in turn made her giggle and confirmed that she was sleep deprived.

"My dear Bill always said that a caretaker must take care of himself first." Her mouth clamped shut in a thin line.

Setting her Bible back on the floor, Laurel rose from the couch. She explained that she had waited to get her shower until Mrs. Jenkins arrived, then Laurel hustled to the bathroom and didn't emerge until she was entirely ready to leave for the day.

A coral pencil skirt and white blouse were the only clothes she had left that didn't need washing, ironing, or both. She hoped the weather wouldn't render the outfit insensible. Once her suitcase was repacked and the bathroom cleaned up, she ventured out to check on Grandma Annie. Annie was awake, sitting up in bed and eating a piece of toast with jam. When Laurel came in the room, Grandma Annie searched her face.

"Good morning," Laurel said timidly.

Grandma Annie took another bite of toast. "I know you, don't I?" she mumbled while chewing. "I've seen your eyes before but I don't know where. I think it must've been a long time ago."

She sighed and hugged Grandma Annie. When Laurel let go, Grandma Annie held onto Laurel's shoulder so their faces remained close.

"Your father had those eyes, didn't he? Did I know your father?"

"My great-grandfather, actually," she replied, hope filling her heart that she might be able to prompt a lucid moment for Grandma Annie.

"You have beautiful hair." Annie stroked Laurel's black hair with her fingertips.

I thought I got that from you, but I didn't. Laurel chewed on her lip.

Grandma Annie gave up puzzling over Laurel's identity and returned to her plate.

"I'll be back tonight," she said as she left the room. Grandma Annie nodded without looking up from the toast in her hand. Laurel turned away from the bedroom.

The clanging of pans and dishes could be heard from the kitchen. Mrs. Bill Jenkins was wiping down the stove and countertop.

Without looking at Laurel, her great-grandmother's friend pointed to the dining table. "Eat something before you go. Breakfast shouldn't be neglected."

On the table was a plate with two fried eggs, buttered toast, and a peeled orange. Although there wasn't spare time to sit down, Laurel didn't know how to refuse the order, nor did she really want to do so.

"Thank you," she said as she pulled out a chair. "I appreciate it."

Mrs. Bill Jenkins carried a glass of milk over to her. Laurel tried to catch her eye but the older woman looked uncomfortable. She hurried back to the sink to wash the frying pan and Laurel ate her breakfast in silence.

Finished, Laurel brought her dishes to the sink. "It was good, just what I needed this morning. I'll take the orange with me since I'm running late."

"Don't go speeding your way to work," Mrs. Bill Jenkins said in a scolding tone. "It'll only save you a few minutes and that's if you don't get in an accident."

"I'll be careful," Laurel agreed without argument. She turned to leave, stopped, and returned to where she'd stood. "I appreciate the time you've spent here this week. You're a good friend to Grandma."

Mrs. Bill Jenkins' plump face went pink. Sticking her hand into the water to release the drain, she finally gave Laurel a glance. "She deserves every comfortable minute we can give her. Finest woman I know."

The words thickened Laurel's throat. She said goodbye and walked briskly to her car, wiping tears from her eyes.

At the end of a busy workday, Laurel made the return trip to Ravenna. Her parents were there when she arrived and Marshall cooked a delicious dinner. With them taking over the guest room, Laurel was left with the living room sofa for the night. It didn't take much coaxing to convince her to go home instead to catch up on sleep.

It was an excellent plan, in theory. Laurel reached her apartment with the feeling of returning to an old friend. Taking only minutes to get into her pajamas and wash her face, she fell across her bed and hugged the mattress. Sleep came quickly, but left quickly too. One o'clock, two, and now, four-thirty; her wakefulness led her to move from her bedroom to the living room. The move wasn't likely to help her sleep, but at least it was a change of scenery.

She dragged her bedspread down the hallway, feeling her way to the couch, then laid flat on her back and propped her feet on the armrest. With her eyes closed and her body still, her mind still resisted rest. It browsed over a dozen different bits of thought.

Laurel worried over the lack of caterer for Melanie and Jace's wedding. Then her brain jumped to Connor as she realized she hadn't heard from him since his odd message on Monday. She hoped Melanie had called him as they'd discussed. Either way, she expected to see him tonight at the North Wind Coffees' grand opening.

When she rolled onto her side, something slid across the leather couch. She pulled from the space between the cushions the packet of Annie's and Kyle's letters. Merely the sight of them, with their worn edges and frayed ribbon, made her chest tighten. Every question she wanted to ask her great-grandmother, each unexpected detail found on the handwritten pages, and the dismay she'd felt as she pieced together the whole story: all of it weighed on her exhausted mind.

Laurel wiped a hand across her teary eyes and stood from the couch. "I need to sleep," she shouted into the unlit room. She shuffled back to her bedroom again and crawled into bed with a desperate prayer for rest. Finally, she fell into a heavy slumber filled with dreams of everything she hadn't wanted to lie awake and think about.

40

October, 1918, 82 years earlier

Dry leaves skirted the trees, unmoved by the meager wind coming off Boston Harbor. Annie found her favorite bench and parked the baby's pram beside it. The harbor below was quiet, most of the boats having returned to the water after bringing in the first of the day's catches. She retrieved her pen and stationery from inside the pram. Megan's chubby toes didn't reach the end of the enclosure yet, so Annie had stashed her things there. She tucked the white blanket a little more tightly around her daughter.

Daughter. She laid her hand against the sleeping baby's soft cheek. *I thought it would be harder to call you that, but it never was, not from the first day.*

It had, however, been as difficult as expected for her family to feel the same. In the months since her return from France, she experienced every imaginable reaction to her arrival with the infant. The stares and whispers of neighbors and friends were endurable, and even Samuel's refusal to meet to discuss what happened wasn't terribly distressing. Only her family's response to the situation had mattered, and that was not what she hoped it'd be. Gazing at Megan's dainty, pink lips and silky crown of brown hair, Annie was baffled how anyone could avoid letting the child into their heart.

She was honest with her family. They knew the baby was not hers by birth. They saw the letters Meg had received from her parents. Annie described to them Meg's death and the request and promise exchanged to take care of her daughter. In unguarded moments, she observed her father smitten with the sweet child. It was in his eyes and touch when he held Megan in the evenings. Even so, he insisted that attempts be made to convince the Duprees to take Megan into their home. Annie weathered these conversations patiently even as they left her melancholy. She knew, finally, that her family's approval would not determine her choices. Only once did her parents witness Annie express outrage instead of calm—when her mother dared suggest the baby be handed over to an orphanage.

The circumstances here in Boston were tolerable primarily because they were temporary. Only one enormous detail was still withheld from her family: Kyle. Their reaction to the baby wounded her heart, so she guarded her remaining secret, keeping it untainted for herself. The hopes she continued to hold hinged upon the letter she would write this morning here in the park.

Praying for the best words, she sat on the familiar bench in the familiar park, and began an unfamiliar task: writing a letter to Kyle that, for once, she didn't know if he'd be glad to receive.

> *Dear Kyle,*
>
> *As much as ever, I hope this finds you safe and well. Perhaps I hope for it even more on this occasion because of what I need to write. May I first, before saying anything else, ask your forgiveness? Before you continue to read these lines, please say a prayer to have a forgiving heart toward me.*
>
> *It has been months since I've been fully honest with you, Kyle. I have tried to reason away the guilt I feel, for you will soon see I had ample reasons for what I did not say in my past letters, but it is no use. I love you too dearly to not feel the significance of hiding these things from you.*

Annie closed her eyes to see Kyle. She pictured his endearing face, the lines of his jaw and the curve of his mouth. She imagined looking straight into his eyes. After ten months apart, she worried sometimes the memories would gradually fail her, but she could still recall every detail. With a bittersweet sigh, Annie returned the tip of her pen to the paper.

On July 20th, Meg Dupree gave birth to a baby girl. This likely surprises you as much as it did me. She kept her condition well-hidden until her fifth month and thereafter engaged my promise not to tell anyone, including you. Until the child was born, this wasn't something I had difficulty doing. After all, what business did I have to speak of Meg's troubles to you?

Everything has changed, however. Meg's family had rejected her and her child. She had no place to go once the baby was born. For months I prayed that God would provide for them, and in the end, He did. He placed me by her side. These circumstances were the real reason I returned to Boston after the hospital on the LaCroix estate closed. Again, I ask your forgiveness for my dishonesty.

Annie detailed these events more fully, including that July night so heavy with bittersweet significance. She finished with emotion welling up in her chest.

I am grieved with new tears as I tell you that within an hour of her daughter's birth, Meg Dupree died. Knowing full well that she could not recover, Meg asked me to take the child as my own. I will not pretend that I didn't feel great fear at this request, but there was also peace in the deepest part of me. I've never doubted that peace and it has not left me in the days since.

Unfortunately, my family has not been as accepting of the change in my circumstances. While I had hoped for better reactions from them, I am not unsympathetic. After all, I came home from overseas with a new baby but not a new name. Although they know the truth of the baby's parentage, there is still no escaping the stigma of how things appear to the rest of the world.

I wish this were all I needed to reveal to you, that I could finish by expressing my hope of still one day uniting my life with yours, a life that must now include this blessed girl, but more has been hidden.

Meg did have specific reasons for securing my promise not to tell you about her pregnancy. The child, my dear Kyle, is your niece. Meg wrote to Chet but he insisted rather despairingly that he was unfit to be a father and did not wish to be part of raising the child. When I think of the hopelessness and anger Chet carries around in his heart, I can't help wondering if the face of his daughter could spark a change in him. Megan is more than two months old now and has the loveliest combination of her mother's blue eyes and her father's winsome smile.

I've no idea how you are feeling at this moment. It required a great deal of prayer and trust in the Lord before I could write this letter to you. Now that I have done it, I am aware of the prayers that will continue to be necessary as I wait for your reply.

No matter how you choose to act, be confident of my unfading love. I will always be yours,

Annie

She saw the sun was much higher in the sky than when they walked from her parents' house. Megan stirred inside the pram. She folded the letter and tucked it below Megan's feet.

"I think," Annie whispered to the waking infant, "we must stop off at the post office before we go home."

41

October, 2000, 82 years later

Laurel was relieved to see on the clock that she had slept for six hours. Her stomach, accustomed to breakfast long before now, emitted an angry growl before she could leave her bed. With a good meal and a long shower, she might start to feel normal again.

She sat down to breakfast with the packet of Grandma Annie's letters beside her plate. A part of her held out hope that she was wrong, that she was remembering the rest of the story mistakenly. Laurel spread peanut butter on her toast, sliced a large apple, and took a letter from the bottom of the stack. It was one of the few written in neither Annie's nor Kyle's hand.

November 24, 1918
County Kerry, Ireland

Dear Miss Walcott,

My name is William Regan and I am the father of Kyle Regan. My wife Sarah and I have decided together to write this most difficult letter to you. I will not increase your pain by making you wait to understand the full meaning of this letter.

On Tuesday of last week, the 19th of November, our youngest son Kyle was killed in a fire. I am not sure where to begin in explaining the details surrounding his death so I will simply share everything that seems to matter to your relationship with our boy.

Since his return from France last December, Kyle has spoken of you frequently. He made it clear that he loved you and intended to propose marriage to you. It was our understanding that the delay was because of your continued service as a nurse in Europe. Once he told us you had returned home to America, we expected news of an engagement but this did not come to pass. Though Sarah often urged me to, I didn't question Kyle on the matter. Kyle was always one to speak and act in his own time.

Over these lines was a dried smattering of tears. She could not know if they came from the father who wrote the words or from Grandma Annie as she read them.

It was only one week ago that Kyle admitted to us the true nature of his work for the nationalists. Since he said you knew of it, I will not recount it here. He informed us though that circumstances had changed. In an effort to further elude the authorities, the men were relocating to another county. Kyle had been undecided about following them there but made up his mind not to go after he received your most recent letter. He said it was time to go to you and bring you home as his wife. Kyle mentioned there being important reasons for no longer delaying. As he didn't explain those reasons to us, Sarah and I would like to express our hope that you are well and still taken care of by your family.

Kyle booked passage on a ship departing on Thursday, the Twenty-First. By Tuesday, his bags were already packed. He spent that day at the newspaper's headquarters, helping the other men clear it out and remove evidence of their work. According to the papers, a small band of unionists attacked that evening. Kyle and the others worked in a room in the basement of the one-story building. Once the ground floor was set on fire, there was no way out. It is not our wish to pain you with more details.

The photograph I've enclosed was taken the summer before you met Kyle in France. He had it in his traveling case for the trip to America, so we've supposed that he intended to give it to you. Sarah also came across this collection of your letters in Kyle's home. We are returning them to you now.

For so many reasons, I wish the first communication Sarah and I had with you came under much happier circumstances. As that is out of our hands and impossible now, we take some comfort in the days Kyle had with you. They gave him such joy and blessing that there is no good in regretting them simply because they were brief. Please do not regret them, as we are sure Kyle would not if the situation were reversed.

I have thought for a while on how to end this terrible letter. I can't presume that there is any sense in pretending there will be further relation between you and our family. It is your lot to continue with your life in a new direction, and it is ours to simply thank God for the blessing you were to Kyle in his last year.

In deepest sympathy,
William Regan

Apparently, Grandma Annie had taken Mr. Regan's words to heart and moved her life in an entirely new direction: west to Michigan. The picture Mr. Regan wrote of was no longer in the envelope with the letter. Confident that it was still in Grandma Annie's possession, Laurel hoped to finally see Kyle's face for herself.

Laurel cleaned up from breakfast and folded the letter, sliding it into its yellowed envelope. Her heart was heavy yet again. She felt keenly the difficulty of setting aside thoughts of Annie and Kyle. It was time to focus on work and all that was required for a successful grand opening tonight for her clients. She shifted her thoughts there as she began preparing for the event.

When Laurel's phone rang later, she expected it to be one of her parents with an update on Grandma Annie. Instead she was surprised to hear her colleague Nadya Primmel on the other end of the line.

"Oh good, I was hoping you were still at home."

It was only twenty minutes past noon so Laurel didn't need to leave for the coffeehouse for another two hours. "How are you doing today, Nadya?"

"Do you really want to know?" Nadya groaned. "Would you believe I have the chicken pox?"

"Seriously?" Laurel plopped down on her bed.

"It's crazy, I know. I'm forty-six years old and I've never had the chicken pox. My oldest son came home yesterday with a fever and was covered in bumps by the middle of the night. This morning, my youngest woke up with almost as many bumps, and by noon they started on my arms."

"Nadya, that's awful." She strove to only feel compassion but her mind was moving with some panic through the responsibilities Nadya was supposed to cover today.

"It is. I'm already scratching like a crazy person whenever the boys aren't in the room. Hard to convince them not to scratch their bumps if they see me doing it, you know." Nadya rushed on, "I hate to do this to you but I couldn't get a hold of Robert. Obviously, I can't be there tonight."

"Of course not."

"The business cards are in boxes in my office and the banner is rolled up, I think, on my desk. I was going to stop there before going to North Wind."

"I'll pick them up. You just take care of yourself and your sons."

Nadya reviewed for Laurel her task list for the night.

"Thank you, Laurel." Nadya paused. "Um, there's one more thing you'll need to do."

"I have plenty of time," she answered. "What else is there?"

"There's the cake. I was supposed to pick it up this afternoon."

Parker Advertising had ordered a sheet cake as an offer of congratulations to their clients. The plan was to present it to the staff so they could enjoy it at the end of what had been, ideally, a successful first night of business.

"Did you order from Sugar & Spice Bakery like last time?" She calculated the few minutes of extra time for this stop.

"No, I used Kentwood Towne Bakery." Nadya waited but Laurel was busy recalculating the much longer drive. This bakery was on the other end of the city.

"It made sense at the time," Nadya explained, "because it's right on my way from home. I'm afraid my logic didn't factor in chicken pox."

She reassured Nadya again that everything would be taken care of in her absence. When they both hung up, Laurel allowed herself a mere five seconds of worry before switching into high gear. She had a gut feeling that the day's intensity was only beginning to build.

When her phone rang again while she swept a pink blush across her cheekbones, she let it ring through, then put her voicemail on speaker phone.

"Hello, Laurel, it's your dad. I was only checking in to see how your day is going. I'm sure you're plenty busy with work and other things. Everything here is, well, not fine but you know, it's the same. Grandma's been awake most of the day so far, actually. Anyway, I hope the opening goes really well tonight, dear. I'll see you tomorrow."

His voice sounded strained. She wondered if perhaps Grandma Annie was having a worse day than he'd admitted. As Laurel finished her makeup, she offered up a prayer for her great-grandmother and her parents.

Moments later, she gave her reflection a satisfied appraisal. She had paired her darkest bootcut jeans with a sheer lavender cap-sleeved top. The gossamer material hung loosely around her torso and she wore an ivory camisole beneath it. The only accessory Laurel added was a delicate diamond tennis bracelet her parents gave her the day she graduated from college. She had used a large curling iron to flip the ends of her invariably straight hair and it lay in thick waves over her shoulders, the black hue creating a lovely contrast against the pastel blouse. Not in a regular habit of giving her appearance this much regard, she felt a touch of self-consciousness over the pleasure she felt at the finished look.

Ready to go, Laurel donned a jacket and stepped out in the October sunshine ready to tackle the grand opening and all it entailed.

42

October, 2000

Laurel pulled into the small parking lot of North Wind Coffees twenty minutes behind schedule. Her car was filled with the blended scents of sugary frosting, freshly baked cake, sunflowers, and daylilies. The four splendid aromas were oddly unpleasant as a mix. When she turned the wheel to take a space, Robert exited the rear staff door at a jog. She nearly took him out with her front bumper as he came up to the car.

His questions began when she opened her door. "Where have you been? And why isn't Nadya here either? Have you heard from her? Please tell me you heard from her. I tried to call. Why didn't you pick up your phone?"

Robert sounded more desperate than accusing so Laurel replied calmly, "I'm sorry I missed your call. Yes, I've heard from Nadya. I'm late because she's sick so I had to get the things she was taking care of tonight."

"Nadya's sick? She isn't coming?" Robert's jaw went slack, his mouth half open. He ran one hand through his golden hair and stuck the other hand into the pocket of his jeans.

In his royal blue dress shirt, buttoned except at the very top and tucked in with a black leather belt around his lean waist, she couldn't even deny to herself how splendid he looked. She had to force herself to look away.

"It's all right," she eventually replied. "I brought everything. It will be a little rushed but we'll be fine."

Some of the worry left Robert's expression. She'd seen him like this a few times before, always on the day of a client's important event. No one could claim Robert's relaxed, ever-confident air was a detriment to his work ethic. He was a perfectionist when it came to meeting clients' expectations.

They each opened a back door of her car and started retrieving the items inside. After taking a minute to greet and congratulate Craig and Joan Millings, the owners of North Wind Coffees, Robert and Laurel returned to the parking lot for the cake and bouquet of flowers.

"So, what's wrong with Nadya?"

"Chicken pox."

"You're kidding." Robert halted, the handle of the car door in his fingers.

"I'm not."

His apparent shock softened as he laughed, "I knew it must be something bad if it kept her away but that's the last guess I'd have made."

"She said two of her sons came down with it and then gave it to her." Laurel picked up the arrangement of flowers. Robert slid the cake box across the backseat and she waited until it was secure in his arms before closing the car door for him and hurrying to the building to hold that door open.

"Have you had the chicken pox?" he asked.

"Yes, when I was seven. My mom says I made her wait on me 24 hours a day for 6 days."

Laurel was propping the door open with her hip but Robert stopped to lean against the building.

"I was four when I got it from my older brother. He says I was mad at him until I was five." He rolled his blue eyes. "I don't remember it so I have to take him at his word."

He looked straight at her as she laughed. The directness of his gaze brought a little extra heat to her face. She pulled her eyes away. "We really need to get in there."

"Do you still get nervous for these? The grand openings and client parties, I mean."

"Sure, I do," Laurel admitted, trying for nonchalance. "It isn't like I'm a seasoned veteran yet." She was watching the cake box in his hands, waiting for it to slip or bend as he seemed to have forgotten he was holding it.

"No, I suppose not. It always helps when you love what you're doing though, don't you think?"

Laurel nodded in agreement.

"Yeah, I think that's really important, especially considering the number of hours and days we put in at our jobs by the time we live our whole lives."

She nodded again, beginning to believe he'd forgotten both the cake and the fact that it was only the two of them covering this event. Robert finally did walk through the doorway, saying as he passed her, "Don't be too worried. The evening is going to go really well. I'm sure of it."

Wasn't he practically sweating with anxiety ten minutes ago? She imagined smacking the back of his head with the flowers in her hands.

"My brother and his wife are coming tonight," Robert spoke over his shoulder. "They'll be glad to meet you."

"Really?" Laurel raised her eyebrows, but Robert's attention was elsewhere now.

At the front counter, they presented the cake and flowers to the Millings, assuring the overwhelmed entrepreneurs that there was nothing to worry about today. When Craig took the cake into the kitchen to show the staff and Joan went to find a place to display the flowers, Robert and Laurel started on the rest of the setup.

Forty-five minutes after North Wind Coffees' official opening, Laurel stood in a corner of the dining room and appraised the scene. The stream of arriving customers was light but steady. She kept an eye on their reactions as they entered and chose their seats.

To her left was the ordering counter, cherry walnut and polished to a gleaming finish. While customers waited to make their orders, they were tempted by glass cases of biscotti, cookies, muffins, and the Millings' family recipe fruit-filled tarts. Laurel overheard orders for regular and decaf, every sort of tea, and the custom designed blends of Kenyan coffees for which North Wind was an official distributor.

From this vantage point, she faced the large dining area. The same cherry wood ran along the walls in wainscoting and baseboards. The rest of the surface was painted in cool, calming gray. Instead of booths there were patio style wrought-iron table and chair sets, some round and some square, with a couple of larger rectangular ones for groups. On the chairs were thick cushions in every imaginable fabric, color and pattern. Each table's set of chair cushions were different from the others, achieving a delightful variety throughout the room.

One corner, near the pair of bowed windows at the front, was occupied by a wrap around, burgundy sofa and two wide armchairs. A family of six was settled there with their drinks and treats. In the opposite corner was the stage. It was small and only a ten inch step up from the floor; well situated to play to the whole room without dominating it.

Already, she'd recognized individuals from three of the businesses she'd delivered personal invitations to earlier that week. Laurel introduced them to Craig and Joan, then she made small talk while they waited in line. A pair of men in suits and ties stood by the display of business cards and packaged products, skimming the brochure on specialty coffees North Wind roasted and ground here in the shop and made available for orders. Laurel was glad to see the men slip a few cards into their wallets.

"Other than the one server who didn't show up, everything has gone great so far," Robert declared as he arrived at her side.

"It's bound to get a lot busier when the music starts." Laurel beamed. After weeks of preparation and today's nerves, she was giddy with relief now that the opening was underway. Easygoing music drifted through the ceiling speakers for now and she looked forward to the live band playing from eight to eleven that night.

Robert matched her smile. "We did well. I wish Nadya was here to enjoy it too."

She recalled his earlier remark and asked, "Are your brother and sister-in-law bringing their daughters?"

"No, they're making it a date night. Dinner first, then they'll come here. The girls are with a sitter whom Gary and Abby actually have to pay for once."

"You usually stay with the girls?"

"Most times, yes."

"My parents are in town but they can't make it down here to-night." Her mouth snapped shut in immediate regret of the comment. She went on before he could voice the question that she saw in his face. "My friends are coming later. Mel and Jace should be here any minute, and Connor said he would come around eight."

He was undeterred. "Why wouldn't your parents come if they're visiting? They must know this is an important night." His eyebrows were drawn down in a V as he frowned, waiting for her answer.

"They just can't. They're busy."

"But aren't they up here from Chicago to see you?"

"Not exactly." She stared over the heads of the coffeehouse patrons and out the front windows. "Grandma is really sick and they're staying with her."

"Annie is sick? Why didn't you tell me?"

She was unprepared for his genuine concern. "I meant to tell you earlier this week. We were so busy with this event, and I guess I kept putting off the conversation."

"Do you want to tell me about it now? Or we could talk later, whatever you wish. I'm in Ravenna a lot. Is there anything I can do?"

His offer made Laurel want to hug him.

"I appreciate that, Robert, and I'll keep it in mind. Thank you." She decided to fill him in briefly. "Her age is finally catching up with her. It's dementia, of a rapid onset variety. Grandma doesn't know us when she's awake and her memories are mixed up. She hasn't been lucid for a week."

"I'm so sorry, Laurel." He laid his hand on her shoulder. It was warm through the thin material of her blouse.

She felt her throat thicken. When Joan Millings waved to get their attention, Laurel didn't hesitate to go see what was needed.

Melanie and Jace arrived arm in arm at six-thirty. By then there was barely a free chair and people took to standing on the empty stage. With no immediate task at hand, Laurel sat down with her friends on the edge of the low stage. Jace balanced a plate of biscotti on his knee and they each sipped fresh coffees.

"How is the night going?" Melanie asked, pausing in her efforts to cool her steaming drink.

"It has all come together well." Laurel felt fresh excitement when she looked around. She had yet to overhear a negative comment from any customers.

Jace lifted his face toward the bustling room. "It's packed, so that's a fair sign of success, right?"

"As long as they all come back again and tell their friends too."

Laurel finished her piece of cinnamon biscotti and turned to Melanie, about to ask if a replacement caterer was found yet. Melanie began speaking at the same time.

"Where is he?"

"What? Who?"

Mel rubbed her hands together. "Robert, of course. Where is he? I can't believe I finally get to see him in person."

Her surprise was quickly replaced by amusement. She should have guessed this would be one of Mel's priorities tonight. Looking past Mel's grinning face, Laurel caught Robert's eye. He walked in their direction. "How about I do better than pointing him out?" She winked at her best friend. "How about I introduce you?"

Robert stopped in front of Laurel, his height exaggerated by her low seat. She felt a small flutter beneath her ribcage. When she managed to break from Robert's gaze, she made the introductions.

Robert spoke first, "Are you the friends who are having a wedding soon?"

"We are." Jace reached up to shake Robert's hand. "Has Laurel plagued you with all the details and drama? She and Mel have been working like crazy."

"While your to-do list consists of: (1) show up in tuxedo, and (2) bring the ring?" Robert jested.

Jace laughed, "For the most part, yeah."

Melanie patted Jace's shoulder, adding, "Don't forget (3) comb hair, and (4) wear shoes."

"As long as the fifth thing on my list is kiss the bride," Jace said with a wink at his fiancé.

Robert lowered himself to the floor and sat against the wall. "Laurel hasn't told me anything, except that the maid of honor duties are keeping her busy."

Laurel flashed back to when he first invited her to lunch and the panic that ensued over how to turn him down. Tonight, she was feeling more afraid of herself than of anything Robert might do or say.

"Really?" Melanie said. "I thought she would have talked to you more, with how much time you two spend together."

Mel kept her eyes fixed on Robert, avoiding Laurel's aggravated look. Robert smiled back at Mel like they shared a long running joke.

"That means you haven't heard about the latest wrench thrown in the gears." Mel turned back to Laurel now. "We still don't have a new caterer. What on earth are we going to do?"

Jace took Melanie's hand. Laurel noticed Robert's eyes were flicking back and forth between each of their faces.

Finally, Robert asked, "You don't have a caterer for your wedding? When is the wedding?"

"November Fourth," Jace answered.

Robert whistled. "Three weeks, wow." He turned his head away and looked around the room.

Laurel expected him to excuse himself but instead he looked back at her, now smiling eagerly. She silently mouthed, "What?"

"Laurel, take this as a sign that you should talk to me more often," Robert said with a grin. Looking at Melanie and Jace, he clasped his hands together. "Consider your problem solved. You will have a delicious dinner at your wedding reception."

Jace raised an eyebrow and Melanie stiffened. "How?" Mel asked.

"What Laurel didn't know was that the answer to all her problems," he paused to smile at her, "I mean, the answer to this problem, was right under her nose."

"You're a caterer?" Melanie questioned.

"Not exactly." Robert's attention was drawn away. "My brother and his wife just arrived. This is excellent timing." He jumped to his feet and gave the trio a confident nod. "Please, don't worry about this anymore. We'll discuss details later."

As he walked away and Laurel watched him greet his brother, she wanted to drag him back and force him to explain. She addressed her friends, "I will find out what he's planning to do, I promise. He'll probably come back and explain it himself."

She noticed him pointing their group out to his brother and thought he'd bring Gary and Abby over for an introduction. Instead, they joined the line at the counter, talking and gesturing rapidly to each other.

"You know what?" Melanie exclaimed. "I'm not going to worry about it." She slapped her knees, bumping Jace's leg and sending the plate with the last bites of biscotti skidding across the floor. "He would not have said what he did if he didn't have a good idea. We've been praying for a solution to this problem and I'm trusting it is on its way."

Jace retrieved the biscotti from the floor, dusted it off and popped a piece in his mouth. He finished chewing and draped his arm around his fiancé. Melanie leaned over and kissed him.

Laurel stood up and brushed crumbs from her lap. While relieved that her friends chose to be hopeful, she still preferred to know the specific plan. She would check on Craig and Joan and the coffeehouse staff, then she'd find Robert to request an explanation.

43

October, 2000

Open floor space became nonexistent when the customers covering the stage had to clear out for the band. While Laurel spent the past thirty minutes chatting with the staff and eavesdropping on customers' first impressions, Robert remained deep in conversation with his brother. She tried and failed to meet his eye several times.

Now that the band was set up, Robert relocated to the edge of the stage, ready to give his official welcome of North Wind Coffees to the city's business community. Craig Millings stood beside him, thumbing through his speech notes. Laurel waved at Melanie and Jace where they leaned against a wall between two full tables, then she squeezed her way to the opposite far corner, gaining a wide view of the room.

Heads and shoulders obstructed her line of vision toward the stage. She did have a straight shot of the front door though. As customers occasionally exited, new ones entered. She reveled in tonight's success. Even when she thought of what would come in the following days—staying with Annie and likely seeing her condition worsen—her enthusiasm was undeterred. Whether from the high of the day or from some divine graces, her mind was peaceful.

Robert's voice drew her out of these thoughts as he began his speech. It took a few pauses in his greeting before the room quieted to a hum. Most people turned to listen and the customers at the front counter lowered their voices to whisper their orders. He was a natural at addressing the crowd, warmly welcoming everyone and inviting a round of applause for their hosts. Craig and Joan gave modest waves from the side of the stage. Still concentrating on Roberts' words, she let her eyes roam over the heads of his audience.

At the front entrance, her gaze stopped. Robert's voice faded like someone shouting from a departing train. She'd have done a double-take if she could manage to move at all, but there was no need to look twice anyway. Marcus Bently had walked through the door.

Marcus didn't immediately spot her, which meant she had the opportunity to look away and appear unaware of her ex-boyfriend's presence. The advantage could let her be a step ahead, able to greet him coolly once he approached, but she knew that would not be the case. She couldn't stop gaping at him. Any second now, Marcus would find her. They would lock eyes and she would...well, Laurel didn't know what she'd do. It felt entirely possible she might burst into pieces all over the brand new hardwood floor.

A group of laughing teenagers pushed past Marcus, interrupting his surveillance of the room. He turned toward the open door and smiled at someone still outside. Laurel felt a twist in her stomach at the thought that he was meeting someone here; that he didn't even know she'd be here. The sick feeling worsened though when Connor walked in and stopped beside Marcus.

She waited for shock to register on Connor's face as Marcus greeted him with a slap on the shoulder, but it didn't come. While he didn't look pleased, Connor was not shocked. As this fact seeped through her brain, a roar of laughter rose from the crowd and she jumped. This, at last, loosened her feet. She moved toward the side door that exited to the parking lot. With one more look over her shoulder before opening the door, she found Connor's eyes following her.

How could he? Laurel's first thought upon reaching the parking lot was not of her former boyfriend but of her friend. Her friend! Clearly, he knew Marcus was coming here tonight and didn't warn her. Better yet, he should have made Marcus not come at all. The anger rose like steam inside her lungs, undampened by the reality that no one was ever able to make Marcus do anything.

Marcus. She tried to analyze what she felt at his presence somewhere on the opposite side of the building's brick wall. Maybe if she could decide what she felt, then she could also decide what to say, what she wanted to hear from him, and how angry to be with Connor.

Her bare arms were chilled in the October night. She stood on the edge of the parking lot without a single idea of what to do next. Leaving wasn't an option. Technically, she was working tonight. She started pacing the border of the lot, passing in and out of the white light of a solitary lamppost. On her third turn, she heard the door open and close. Her anger flared up at the mere sound of it and she spun on her heel, planted her hands on her hips, and waited.

As expected, Marcus was there. He stopped in the center of the lamp's arc of light.

She suddenly wanted more than anything to be the first to speak. "What are you doing here?"

"Hi, Laurel."

"Why aren't you in Pittsburgh?"

"You almost slipped out before I spotted you."

"You shouldn't have come. I'm working."

"I'm glad to see you. It feels even longer than a year, doesn't it?"

Were they even in the same conversation?

"Are you happy at all to see me? Even a little?" Marcus cocked his head to the side.

She examined his face, which was as handsome as ever. The same closely cropped brown hair, combed to lay perfectly in place; same warm brown eyes she used to look into as often as she had the opportunity; same straight, unflappable posture, hands in his pockets, chin high. It was all there. He did not look uncertain, uncomfortable, or even cautious, all of which Laurel thought he should be.

She kept her hands on her hips where they were less likely to shake. "No, Marcus, I'm not happy to see you. I'm shocked, I'm angry, I'd appreciate answers, and I am not happy."

He opened his mouth, the corners curling up in a baffling smile, but before he could reply, the side door of the coffeehouse opened again. Connor stepped into the parking lot followed closely by Melanie and Jace. Melanie was glaring so fiercely at the back of Connor's head that Laurel wouldn't have been surprised if his hair caught fire.

Connor covered the ground between them in a few hurried strides. "Laurel, I'm sorry."

"What, precisely, are you sorry for?" She wanted to hear it from him.

"Ah, I, um," Connor made a feeble beginning. "I'm sorry for not telling you ahead of time that he was coming back."

Laurel drew in a long breath. Something about his choice of words didn't sit well with her. "What do you mean, 'coming back'?" Her eyes refocused on Marcus. "You moved to Pittsburgh. You're just visiting and then you'll go back. You're visiting." She spoke firmly, willing her assumption to be true.

"No." Marcus' tone softened ever so slightly. "I've moved back to Grand Rapids."

"How long have you known this?" she demanded of Connor. He hesitated and she repeated herself more loudly, "How long have you known?"

"A month, I think."

She threw a hand in the air. Connor flinched.

She turned to Jace and Melanie. "And you, did you know?"

Jace shook his head and Melanie protested, "Absolutely not, Laurel. We had no idea."

"Of course not, you would've told me." She shot another irate glance at Connor.

"Don't be too hard on him, dear," Marcus interjected. "He did try to talk me out of coming tonight."

Dear? Did he call me dear? His expression and tone were just as they used to be when they argued. She would become stubborn and combative while he laughed it off and refused to debate whatever matter was on the table. She used to label it a sign of maturity, that he was able to keep silly arguments from turning into real fights. Tonight, she found him arrogant and condescending. Maybe it was her turn to refuse to participate in the debate. With one step away from them, she left the lamppost's reach and watched them like an audience member at a play.

Jace stood apart from the rest, shifting his weight from one foot to the other. Melanie had planted herself inches in front of Connor. She was quietly berating him for not warning Laurel, to which he objected that he had tried.

Her mind wandered, recalling Connor's phone message on Monday. To think that if she had simply called him back; Laurel sighed over the choice she had made. Not that it excused his silence for an entire month, which was precisely the point she heard Melanie making. In flashes, Connor's peculiar comments and behavior in recent weeks came back to her in a new light.

Meanwhile, Marcus was still smiling at Laurel. She could tell by his misplaced gaze that he could no longer make out her face in the darkness. This allowed her to look at him directly while she decided her next question. She had plenty of them, yet Laurel's only wish was for the encounter to be finished.

Memories flickered through her mind of the two years she spent with Marcus. Unedited reality dawned and Laurel was ashamed of not seeing all as it truly was before now. His pride and self-centeredness; she could practically hear Grandma Annie speaking, instructing her on authentic love. *In deed and truth.* Marcus had offered no such thing to her, and her girl Friday dedication to him fell equally short of what she had imagined them sharing.

Laurel walked forward and her reappearance in the one source of light caused them all to refocus their eyes. Her hands trembled. "I am going to say something and then I'd like this to be over." She paused, then began with Marcus. "I don't know your purpose in coming here, what you hoped would come of showing up and taking me by surprise. I do know that it was a poorly-chosen plan. To be honest, and this is possibly the most honest I've been with myself since you moved away, there is not an ounce of me that wanted to see you again. Our relationship wasn't put on hold by your move." She paused again, straightening her shoulders. "It was ended, and that was as it should have been, I realize now. That was your choice and it cannot be undone. Frankly, I don't want it undone. When you came to my office a year ago to inform me you were leaving, I was too shocked to properly say goodbye. I'll say it now. Goodbye, Marcus."

The smile evaporated from his handsome face. His features were taut, and he made no immediate response. Laurel turned to face Connor next. She lifted her hands, but they were shaking even more than when she started, so she put them back down at her sides.

"Connor, you had a month to tell me that Marcus was moving back to Grand Rapids. I realize you're his friend too and that maybe it was hard to find the right way or time to say something to me, but even the wrong time is better than not at all."

He looked back at her miserably, his posture sagging. She knew that with time and some explanation on his part, she would forgive. This steadied her as she finished.

"You'll have a chance to explain why you put off telling me, and I can probably guess most of your reasons, but we won't be having that conversation tonight. Tonight, I'm working, and I was enjoying myself. I'd like to go back inside and continue with at least one of those things."

Marcus appeared ready to speak. A smile stretched across Laurel's face. He smiled back but she was no longer looking at him. Over his shoulder, she spotted Robert standing near the back door of the coffeehouse. She didn't know how long he'd been outside, how much he heard, or what he could be thinking, but gladness assailed her at the sight of him. The trembling in her hands migrated to her stomach. Robert watched her but didn't move away from the brick wall. When Marcus realized she wasn't looking at him, he turned to look behind him.

She looked at Melanie, who was rocking on her tip-toes. Impulsively, she hugged her best friend and whispered, "Let's leave this alone for tonight, okay. I can't handle anything more today." She waited until she felt Mel's head nodding in agreement before ending the hug.

Striving for a neutral expression, she walked past the others to reenter the coffeehouse. She was two steps from the door, and Robert, when Marcus caught up and stepped in front of her.

Marcus faced Robert with his right hand clenched in a fist at his hip. "I remember you. From Laurel's office, right?"

Robert nodded and stuck out his hand, which Marcus ignored. "Robert Kennesaw. I remember you too."

"Should've known you would swoop in as soon as I left that day, the way you were hovering outside the door after I talked to Laurel."

Laurel's jaw dropped. Marcus and Robert glared at each other.

She rolled her eyes. "I think the music has started. I'm going back inside."

"Me too." Melanie took Jace's arm and pulled him toward the door.

Once inside, Laurel miraculously found an empty chair. She forced her eyes straight ahead, watching the guitarist strum the first chords of the opening song. She made an effort not to care about the movements of the others as they came in from the parking lot. Still, there was no helping seeing Marcus pass by on his way back to the front door. He paused near her. She pretended not to notice and he took the hint. She'd said her goodbye outside; another was unnecessary. When he exited and the door closed behind him, she relaxed in her chair, releasing the breath she unwittingly held and listening more closely to the band.

In between songs, she turned her head to see the state of the room now that the music was underway. As expected, it was at its most crowded of the whole evening. When her eyes roamed back to her immediate vicinity, she jumped in her chair. Robert was now seated in the other chair at her table.

He leaned across the small table. "We need to talk."

She wasn't ready. Her mood was strangely light, whereas the conversation Robert wanted to have would be inevitably weighty. She gave him a stern look. "Quiet, I'm listening to the music."

Robert laughingly pointed out, "The guy is only talking."

"Yes, but if we listen to him, it'll make the next song more meaningful."

"Right, okay."

Mutual silence lasted through the song. Afterward, the singer stopped for a drink of water and the guitarist took his time retuning.

Robert didn't waste a second of the break before announcing, "My brother and I are opening a restaurant and I'll be done at Parker Advertising in a week and a half."

Laurel uttered a few syllables, none of which formed a whole word.

He stood, his trademark half-smile reappearing. "I'm getting a fresh coffee. Would you like anything?"

44

October, 2000

It was a full fifteen minutes before Robert returned to his chair. Fifteen minutes for Laurel to question whether or not she heard him correctly. Fifteen minutes to wonder how to respond to his announcement.

She still had no ready words by the time he sat down and slid her drink across the table. He busied himself with borrowing sugar from another table and adding a little to his coffee. Her latte gave her a point of focus. She lifted the drink to her lips but when the steam hit her nose, she pulled it away again.

"You should let it cool a while."

"Yes, thanks." Laurel took the lid off the cardboard cup, releasing a puff of spiced steam.

"So?" He raised his eyebrows beneath the hair slanting across his forehead

"Could you repeat what you said? Because I feel like I might have misheard you. It's loud in here." She knew exactly what he'd said, but hearing it again might let it sink into her brain.

"Gary and I are opening a restaurant. I'll be done at Parker Advertising in a week and a half."

"Wow. Yes, that is what I heard." She shook her head then fixed a smile on her face, feeling like a cheerleader at a losing game. "Congratulations!"

He hesitated. "That isn't really the reaction I expected."

"Why? I'm happy for you! I mean, your own restaurant, it's really exciting."

Her cheeks started to hurt. He dropped his gaze to the table so she let her face relax. What did he want her to say? That she was wondering if it was officially Take-Laurel-By-Surprise-Day today? That she could not imagine being at the office without the certainty of seeing him? The only thing she could think to do was get him talking. She touched his arm and Robert lifted his eyes to meet hers.

"Tell me about the restaurant."

He nodded. Laurel asked every question that popped into her head: the location, the size of the building, what was on the menu, the style of the dining room. For nearly an hour, Robert eagerly shared details of his long-held dreams coming true. Alexander's Table would open in mid-November on the southwest side of the city.

"My marketing background has been useful," Robert continued, "For knowing how to recommend ourselves in the neighborhood and getting the word out to businesses. Gary has left all of the advertising up to me."

"That's a lot to do alone."

"Sure, it is. But I enjoy it even more than any account I've handled. Besides, it isn't like we could hire Parker Advertising to do it if I wanted to keep my job as long as possible. I wouldn't have felt right about hiring one of Parker's competitors either."

He sipped his coffee. "It was a bonus to not use our start-up capital to hire out the advertising."

There was a risk of silence and Laurel immediately cut into it, asking how he and his brother chose the restaurant's name.

"Alexander was my father's name. He couldn't cook anything," Robert laughed under his breath. "Dad used to say that he was actually a gourmet cook, but he didn't want to make Mom feel unneeded at home. Mom chuckled every time he said it even though it was the least believable claim he ever made. If she wasn't keeping an eye on him when he was in the kitchen, Dad ruined anything he tried to make. Until he died, Mom didn't have to work. So, when we'd sit down to a meal and Dad would make a big deal over how wonderful Mom's cooking was, she would always say, 'But it's you who provides us this table.'"

Robert went on, folding and unfolding his napkin while he spoke. "When I was a kid, I never thought much about that exchange they had so often. It was like so many other routine things, and a little silly. Once he was gone, I remember realizing that no dinner would ever be the same without it. When it was time to pick a name for the restaurant, Gary and I played around with so many possibilities but couldn't settle on one. We were discussing it with Mom once and she asked if we remembered how Dad used to say that stuff. Later that day, Gary suggested Alexander's Table. It was perfect."

Laurel laid her hand over his. "It's a great way to honor your dad, Robert."

He turned his hand and wrapped his fingers around hers. She chewed on her lower lip and, after a moment, slid her hand out of his. They both took a couple sips before he returned to the topic of the restaurant.

"Gary makes incredible soups, purely from paying attention in our mom's kitchen. We're going for homestyle entrees, but with higher quality than a diner or the family restaurant chains, and some interesting variations mixed in."

"What are your specialties? You, not the restaurant itself," she specified.

Robert's head bowed with a hint of bashfulness. "I'm good at the baked dishes: lasagnas, quiches, a few risottos, lemon chicken with rice. We even have a zucchini casserole, also Mom's recipe, which you definitely won't find anywhere else."

She pictured him listing these same highlights as he networked with business offices and hotels near the restaurant. She couldn't, however, picture him in a kitchen preparing them.

"And desserts, right? Your niece mentioned that."

"They aren't my favorite things to make but my family has long expected that I'll bring the dessert for any gathering we hold."

"Why don't you enjoy making desserts?"

"Most desserts require precise measurements. Other foods are more relaxed. You can add and adjust ingredients according to your tastes or moods, experiment a little, but there's less leniency in baked desserts."

The longer his commentary went on, the more Laurel felt he was speaking a new language she'd had no idea he knew how to speak. It was disconcerting that such a significant aspect of Robert's life had remained hidden from her until tonight. She realized anew how effective her efforts had been in the last two and a half years to avoid becoming friends with him.

His face now held the same nervously hopeful expression as when he first broke the news. "Will you tell me yet what you honestly think about this?"

Her thoughts and feelings were still overlapping and intertwining inside her. She wasn't ready to impose it all on their conversation. "It really is great, Robert. It sounds like you have worked hard to get to this point." She was determined to be supportive. "And you're clearly happy."

"I am, Laurel. I am happy," Robert agreed.

"I'll miss you at the office." She avoided making eye contact with this admission.

Craig Millings stopped by to shake both their hands, thanking them for their work. Once he left them, Laurel noticed Melanie and Jace at another table. Mel waved urgently at her.

"I'll be right back," she told Robert.

She reached the table and crouched to hear Melanie.

"Did he explain yet?"

"About the restaurant?" Laurel asked with some confusion.

"The what?"

The point of the question dawned on Laurel. "Oh! You mean about the wedding dinner?"

"Yes! What were you talking about?"

"I'll tell you later," she replied with a shake of her head. She supposed now that Robert and his brother planned to offer catering through the restaurant. "He hasn't mentioned it, but I think I understand the plan to help. I'll find out for sure and let you know."

"Okay." Mel sighed. "Try to do it soon."

"Absolutely, I will." She hugged her friend.

Returning to her table with the intention of asking Robert about the wedding reception plan, her spirits took an unhappy blow when she arrived. LeeAnn, their dedicated receptionist, was perched on the seat Laurel had vacated. LeeAnn scooted the chair a few inches closer to Robert, her crossed knees angled toward him. She gushed over the coffeehouse as if Robert built it with his own two hands.

Robert smiled weakly at Laurel, discomfort evident in his features. LeeAnn, however, did not acknowledge her presence.

At the first pause in LeeAnn's compliments on the music, Robert interjected, "Laurel and the owners picked the band, actually."

LeeAnn finally looked her way. 'Oh, I figured you must be here somewhere."

"Hello, LeeAnn," Laurel said. "I'm glad you like the music."

"Well, it is rather loud in here, if I'm being honest. The room might be too small for this stuff."

Laurel smiled coolly, resisting the urge to ask if that meant LeeAnn wouldn't stay long.

Sweeping her hand through the air, LeeAnn commented, "I see Nadya isn't anywhere to be found. I've always thought she was a little too flaky to handle much responsibility on our accounts."

When Robert looked like he would object, LeeAnn added demurely, "Not that she can help it. That's just the burden of having children, especially five of them."

Laurel was incensed, and Robert shook his head at her as he spoke up. "Nadya has never given me that impression. She's dedicated to her accounts and does excellent work."

Still wishing to add a few choice words in Nadya's defense, Laurel opened her mouth, but Robert cut her off again. "In any case, she's not here because she and two of her sons are sick. It really wasn't possible for her to come tonight."

LeeAnn let the subject drop. She poked her straw at the whipped cream atop her blended cappuccino. Laurel looked around the room, hoping to spot someone else she knew. She wondered if Connor stayed after Marcus left but she didn't see him anywhere.

Swinging her legs forward to face Laurel, LeeAnn asked solemnly, "So, Robert has finally told you about his plans to leave us behind forever, has he? Can you believe it?" She didn't let Laurel answer. "I know I couldn't when I first heard of it, and then to not be able to talk about it with anyone." LeeAnn sighed and shook a finger at Robert. "I've been just miserable for weeks."

Laurel willed herself to contain her reaction. It was no longer a mess of emotions she felt but only one. "You knew?" she asked quietly. Her eyes fell on Robert. "For weeks?"

"Laurel." He jumped up from his chair and raised his hands, palms out in front of his chest.

"You told her weeks ago?"

"Only three weeks," he mumbled.

LeeAnn contributed gleefully, "Oh yes, Mr. Parker and I were the only ones who knew." She shrugged and stuck her straw in her mouth.

Robert tried to apologize, "I'm sorry, Laurel. I have wanted to tell you, and have been planning to tell you, but..."

"But you didn't. That's the theme of the night, I guess." Laurel struggled to keep her voice low and was thankful for the music and noise of the crowded room. She regretted her next thought as soon as she tried to speak it. "I thought I was...I mean, I'm... I'm..."

"You're what, sweetie?" LeeAnn simpered.

Robert ran both his hands through his hair, leaving it disheveled. "I'm sorry, Laurel."

He said it so simply, with no added excuses, that she felt her heart involuntarily soften. She loathed the jealousy that had risen up in her heart but even with a prayer for God's aid, it was difficult to silence it completely.

As Laurel debated walking away without another word, she heard someone say her name. She spun around to see her father standing nearby.

"Dad, what are you doing here? What's wrong?" She walked to him.

"This place isn't in the phone book yet." Marshall shrugged, his posture weary. "I remembered you describing where it was located and figured I could find you. It's Grandma."

Laurel stepped closer.

"She's been awake nearly all day. Even when we gave her the sedative this afternoon so she could rest, it took longer than usual to settle her down. She's all worked up over letters. She keeps asking for her letters."

"Oh no," Laurel whispered.

"Every ten minutes, she digs through the drawer of that little table by her bed. Did you even know that table had a drawer? I had no idea there was a drawer."

Laurel interrupted him, "It's all right. I have the letters at my apartment."

"Oh, thank God. We tried asking about the letters, who they were from, but Grandma didn't seem to trust us. We kept telling her who we were but it didn't help."

"I'll go home to get them right now and bring them over."

"Thank you. We waited as long as we could, didn't want to bother you, but we're afraid she won't sleep at all tonight."

"Don't worry. I've been here for enough hours that it will be okay to leave now."

She was delayed only by necessary goodbyes. She found Craig and Joan Millings in the kitchen. She offered her congratulations and praise, and apologized for not staying for the celebratory cake with the staff later.

Next, she looked for Robert. He was sitting alone now, thankfully. Before he could speak, she said she needed to leave. The realization that she didn't know when they might see each other sidetracked her briefly. She would be off from work for the coming week. By the time she returned, Robert would be down to only a few days left at Parker Advertising.

She couldn't dwell on that now. He expressed his hope that everything would be alright for Grandma Annie, and promised they would find a time to talk with each other again soon. Moving on to find her friends, she gave them only the simple explanation that she was going to Annie's tonight instead of tomorrow and they immediately promised to pray. Laurel hugged them both, then hustled out to her car where her father was waiting.

45

October, 2000

Laurel and her father stood beside her car in the parking lot.

"If I'm being honest, I don't think I can make the drive back. I didn't get to Grandma Annie's until two o'clock this morning and it's been an exhausting day." He yawned through his words. "Would you mind driving back with me and leaving your car at your place for tonight?"

"Of course, Dad, that'll be fine."

At her apartment, she made quick work of packing the necessities for staying overnight. She slipped the packet of letters into her bag too.

Marshall reclined his seat as Laurel turned her parents' sedan onto the road. He closed his eyes and she expected to hear him snoring within a minute. Instead, he asked about the grand opening.

"It was an interesting night," she replied with a wry laugh. Her mind ran through all that the evening had included, her thoughts lingering on Robert. She restricted her comments to business though. "The turnout was high, and people seemed happy with the coffeehouse. No mishaps with the band, or the food and drinks."

He was nodding, his eyes still shut.

"We gave the owners a cake to congratulate them. It was from Kentwood Towne Bakery."

At this he looked her way, a smile on his face. "No kidding? I'd almost forgotten about that place. We must have been there nine out of every ten Sundays for at least ten years. I'm trying to remember when that tradition started."

"When I was four, I think."

They both grew quiet, each knowing the other was remembering how that family tradition ended when Marshall left. During Laurel's high school years, though he was back at home with Erin and Laurel, visits to the bakery happened rarely.

She hoped he would fall asleep now.

"You've no idea how sorry I was then. How sorry I still am."

She tightened her grip on the steering wheel.

"Not a day goes by that I'm not ashamed of what I did. The fact that you never forgave me," Marshall turned his face toward his window, "that's been harder to live with than anything."

Never before had he spoken this way. She didn't say a word and he kept quiet then too. By the time they reached Ravenna, she felt she might choke on the air inside the car. Even so, she let Marshall enter the house before she got out. Tears had threatened for the past twenty minutes; the sort that would be accompanied by sobs. It took several deep breaths before she trusted herself to walk through the front door.

Her mother was sound asleep, upright in the living room chair nearest Grandma Annie's bedroom. She wore blue flannel pajamas. A thick, white blanket was wrapped around her shoulders. Sleep was clearly unintended as her makeup was still on her face and her hair was pinned back in a plastic clip.

As Laurel set her overnight bag in a corner, she watched her father place his hands on each side of her mother's face. He placed a gentle kiss on her hair then rested his forehead against hers until Erin's eyes fluttered open.

"Laurel?" Her mom's voice was already hoarse from sleep. "When did you get here?"

"Only a minute ago, Mom."

Erin rubbed her eyes, smearing her mascara down her cheekbones. She sighed. "It's been a long day."

"Is she sleeping?" Laurel asked and peered around the corner toward Grandma Annie's room.

"I think she must be. We called Dr. Morland and he said it was safe to give her one extra tablet of the sedative." Erin massaged the back of her neck as she stood up. "Let's see if she is asleep."

They tiptoed to the bedroom and Erin pushed the door open wider. One lamp was still on and Laurel noticed the drawer that was pulled out and set on top of the bedside table. She had never seen what was in it besides the letters.

Grandma Annie was asleep but, much like Erin's nap in the chair, the surrender was clearly undesired. She was halfway between lying and sitting, propped on pillows against the headboard. The ever-present red afghan lay bunched around her ankles. Erin spread out the blanket. Grandma Annie looked smaller and more fragile than ever before. The mattress seemed to swallow her slight frame.

When Grandma Annie didn't wake even as Erin repositioned her pillows, Erin ventured to whisper, "I'm sorry we made you come tonight. I guess it could have waited until morning."

"It's okay. You didn't know she'd be sleeping by the time I got here."

"Maybe if she sleeps all night, she won't remember about the letters tomorrow."

"I brought them with me," Laurel reminded her.

"Yes, but she was so upset over them, so worked up. It might be better if she doesn't remember to look for them again."

She didn't argue. Most of her hope that Grandma Annie would still want the letters in the morning was for her own benefit. She had questions and the window for hearing answers narrowed daily.

"I'm going to bed." Erin rubbed her eyes again. "Your dad has probably fallen asleep out there."

"Goodnight."

Erin left the room. The sounds of grunts and shuffling were heard as Marshall was coaxed to move from the couch to the guest bed. Laurel lingered, watching her great-grandmother sleeping. For once, she couldn't say that Grandma Annie didn't look her age. All 103 years of living were displayed there under the yellow lamplight.

Laurel's eyes fell on the drawer again, out on the table in plain sight for the first time. She took two steps toward the table. The light barely reached this side of the bed so she squinted as she bent over the drawer. Then Annie rolled over, mumbling, making Laurel jump. Shame swept over her and she stepped back. Grandma Annie's breathing stayed even as Laurel turned off the lamp and walked out of the bedroom.

Sleep did not come easily. Scenes played in her head starring Marcus, Robert, Melanie, Connor, LeeAnn, her dad. Their voices interrupted each other, overlapping like layers of a recording. When she finally did sleep, it was deep, dreamless, and silent. She awoke with a start, disoriented by the room that was not her own. It took a few moments to sort herself out.

She stretched her arms past her head to let them hang over the arm of the couch. Then sitting up, she became painfully aware that the two couch cushions had separated during the night to leave her lower back unsupported. Standing was a slow awkward movement and walking to the kitchen even worse. Once there, Laurel spotted the oven's clock.

4:12

She leaned her hips against the countertop, resting her head in her hands and wishing for a return of that drowsy, ready to sleep feeling. It didn't come, and if it was no longer time for sleeping, it was definitely time for coffee. It was a risky endeavor: opening cupboards, running the faucet, bumping into a chair twice. She stood close to the coffeemaker while she waited, keeping one ear tuned to the rest of the house.

Her coffee was down to the last swallow when she did hear something. There was a faint rustling, quiet enough for Laurel to think she might have imagined it. When it continued, she left the kitchen to investigate. The sound stopped when she passed by Grandma Annie's bedroom. The door was ajar but as there was no light on in the room, Laurel hadn't expected to discover anything there. She turned on the hallway light and immediately saw Grandma Annie's tearful green eyes staring back at her through the doorway.

Grandma Annie squinted against the sudden break in the darkness. Her face was flushed with the effort of reaching for the little drawer and pulling it onto her lap. In the dark bedroom, still lying down, she had removed each item from the drawer and spread them in a line alongside her on the bed. Hesitant to intrude but keen to help, Laurel remained in the doorway.

Sleep crackled in Grandma Annie's voice when she asked, "Do you know where my letters are?"

A minute later, the bedroom lamp was turned on, Laurel was once again seated in the rocking chair beside the bed, and Grandma Annie held the letters in her shaking hands. Laurel ached to believe it was like so many other days in past months, but she knew the similarity was superficial.

Grandma Annie clutched the letters. "I was sure they were lost. They were gone. I don't know how since I always keep them in the drawer. Only in the drawer, nowhere else." She shook her head in disbelief. "How did I lose them? Where were they gone to?"

Laurel required a silent bit of prayer before answering. Looking into her great-grandmother's blinking stare, she wondered how to explain. "You gave them to me," she whispered.

Grandma Annie gasped. "I would never."

"Not to keep," she added gently. Her pulse raced over the urgent desire to regain Grandma Annie's trust. "You lent them to me to read."

Her explanation was met with a deep frown.

"They're back now, all of them, and I promise you won't lose them again."

"And you've read them?" Grandma Annie sounded frightened.

Laurel leaned forward into the light of the lamp. She saw Grandma Annie start, so she moved back again.

"How do you have his eyes?" Grandma Annie asked in wonder. "Are you his sister? I never met his sister."

Laurel blew a long breath through her lips. This was her in, the meeting point for them on this uneven trek. Wanting to keep herself linked with Kyle in Grandma Annie's mind, Laurel leaned again into the reach of the light. "No," she answered, "I'm not his sister. Kyle was my great-grandfather."

Immediately, she knew her mistake.

Grandma Annie was miffed. "Kyle did not have any children."

"I meant Chet. Chet Regan was my great-grandfather." She fell silent then, letting Grandma Annie process this amendment. She couldn't believe how fixed it was in her mind that Annie and Kyle were her biological great-grandparents, despite spending the last week wrestling with the revelation that she was descended from neither of them.

Grandma Annie's face gradually moved from confusion to satisfaction. "Yes, that makes sense. Meg and Chet. Then Meg died. I took in Megan. Kyle died. Yes, you're very like him."

"Like Chet," she asked, "or Kyle?"

"Kyle." Grandma Annie scrutinized Laurel's features. "Yes, definitely Kyle."

"I'm so glad."

"Did you know him?"

The question caught her off-guard. Laurel had let herself believe that her great-grandmother still knew her, even if only in the remotest part of her weakening mind. Each additional clue that Grandma Annie had no recollection of her stung. On top of this, it was a cruel struggle to keep up a conversation about the past with someone who no longer had a grasp on time. Still, Laurel would try, for both their sakes.

"No, I didn't know him. You told me about him though, about how you two met, the time you had together in France, and then what happened with Meg and the baby."

"And about Kyle's death," Grandma Annie added frankly.

"We haven't talked about that. I only know what I read in the letters."

Grandma Annie considered this for a bit. "I really told you all that? I wonder why I'd tell you."

"Because I asked," Laurel forged ahead. "Grandma, how long..."

But Grandma Annie cut her off. "Why do you call me that?"

It was impossible to know what was and wasn't still intact in her memory. Laurel had assumed too much once again. "Because until a few weeks ago, I didn't know Meg was the mother of my grandmother, Megan. I didn't know you were my adoptive great-grandmother."

The creases on Grandma Annie's face deepened with her confusion. Laurel laid it out as simply as she could. "My name is Laurel, my mother's name is Erin, and her mother's name was Megan. You are Megan's adoptive mother, but until very recently no one in our family knew you weren't her birth mother."

"Yes, yes," Grandma Annie replied then. "How could you know otherwise?" Her eyes rested on Laurel's face again and she sighed, "Laurel. That's a beautiful name."

"My mother took it from a poem by Yeats. I think it's in the book of Irish poetry that Kyle gave you."

Grandma Annie's attention drifted. Perhaps she was remembering the moment Kyle gave her the book, or that whole lovely day. Laurel recalled some of it too and found it had a bittersweet edge now that she knew the rest of the story. Eventually, Grandma Annie's clouded expression broke and she seemed surprised to still be in the room with Laurel. But she smiled at her and Laurel was encouraged.

"Gran...um, Annie?"

"Yes?"

"How long after you heard, after you got the letter from Kyle's father, did you leave Boston? How did you ever decide to go to Michigan?"

Again, Grandma Annie's green eyes glazed over, focusing somewhere far beyond the bedroom they occupied. The curtains glowed with the rising sun. The clock on the dresser showed 5:42 now. Laurel hoped her parents wouldn't wake yet.

Focused as Laurel was on their exchange of words, she only now stole a glance at the long-hidden items Annie had removed from the bedside table's drawer. There were a few black and white photographs, a mirror, and a delicate chain with a ring hanging from it. The gold ring was dulled but its solitary ruby still twinkled.

A lump caught in her throat as her eyes returned to the handheld mirror. It was the one Kyle bought for Annie at the shop in France. It lay there, refracting the early sunlight, unmistakably the same mirror Laurel had pictured in her imagination. She asked to see it and Grandma Annie handed it to her with the softest smile.

"Kyle gave that to me."

"You told me about it, but I hadn't seen it before."

Laurel ran two fingers along the mirror's handle. The carved tree trunk and branches framing the glass were as intricate as Grandma Annie described. Turning it over, she marveled at the craftsmanship of the full tree carved on the back. She could imagine Kyle picking it up after Annie looked at it in the shop that day, and his joy over giving this beautiful gift to the woman he had begun to love. Tightness stretched through Laurel's chest as she thought how glad she'd be to receive such a token.

"It was four months before I could leave Boston," Grandma Annie finally answered the question Laurel had put to her. "I don't remember a lot from those months."

Laurel thought she meant that the memories were lost in the fog of dementia at present. However, Grandma Annie gave a different explanation.

"Once I knew Kyle was dead, after I received Mr. Regan's letter, I don't really know how I functioned or how I behaved," Grandma Annie said with a shiver. She then took a deep breath before continuing. "Everything is fuzzy in my memory and that's how it felt at the time too, like a thick fog settled over everything. My parents must've kept me in the house, looked after me and Megan until I recovered from the shock. Like I said, I don't remember."

Grandma Annie pressed on, the tremor in her voice gradually steadying. "Probably a month later – I know it was in January – I, well, I woke up. I can't describe it better than that. I remember feeling like I'd been asleep the whole time. When I came out of it, I felt like an empty shell. I also remember the moment everything changed."

46

January, 1919, 81 years earlier

Annie could hear a child crying; faint at first, as if through a wall, then louder and louder. The weeping child was near, she was sure of it, but everything in the room was still black. Annie even thought she recognized that particular cry. With that, reality registered, as it had every morning for the past month. She wished she didn't have to remember again each day. When would it be something she simply knew, instead of something she had to remind herself of over and over?

There were mornings when it didn't click into place as quickly. Annie would lie there on the pillow, calculating the hours until the mail might arrive and hoping today she'd receive word that Kyle was coming. He was bound to send her the name of his boat and the date he left Ireland so she could watch for his arrival. She'd awaken with these warm thoughts, content in the assurance that she was one day closer to Kyle coming for her. On those days, reality hit hard. It sucked the breath from her lungs so she couldn't even cry, which was all she wanted to do.

The other days, today included, the truth was waiting; a despised visitor knocking until she let it inside. It carried an icy air into the room. Annie pulled the quilt to her chin and wet its edge with her tears. She shook with sobs.

Kyle is gone. He's not coming. There is no ship to watch for at the harbor. He's gone. The facts pummeled her. She'd felt bruised for weeks.

Kyle was indeed gone, but there was someone, someone else in the room crying much louder than Annie. Her eyes were still closed; that's why it was so dark. When had she started requiring a conscious decision to open her eyes? She peeked out. The curtains were tied back on the east-facing window and she moaned at the brilliant sunlight. Why did they insist on doing that? Every day they made her head hurt with all the light they let in.

She saw her father sitting beside the bed. He smiled at her but his eyes were sad. The crying baby sat on his lap, her face pressed against his chest. She wore a lacy yellow dress and shiny black shoes, her pudgy legs kicking at the air. Annie reached out and laid a hand on the soft bare skin of the baby's neck. Warmth shot through every nerve in her arm. This was new—no, not new, but it'd been a long time.

The child's cries instantly lost their vigor when Annie touched her. Only whimpers came between hiccups now. Annie looked up at her father and he laid the baby beside her. She felt the switch being thrown for every circuit between her body and mind.

Rolling onto her side, she pulled Megan closer. The darling girl curled into the curve of Annie's stomach, clutching the quilt in her tiny fists. Their tearful eyes met and Annie hugged Megan so tightly that the seven-month-old eventually tried to wriggle away, at which Annie laughed. The sound stopped Megan's movements and she stared in wonder.

Annie watched Megan, Megan watched everything in sight, and Annie's father watched both of the girls in the bed. When the baby grew focused on pulling at loose threads in the quilt, Annie propped herself up on one elbow and addressed her father. It felt a little like someone else was speaking on her behalf.

"Megan and I are moving away. We have to go. Our life was never going to be here in Boston."

Charles Walcott was already dressed for work. He dabbed a handkerchief at the tear-soaked spot where Megan's cheek had rested on his shirt. "Where will you go?"

His voice was light and she supposed he was humoring her. He looked so tired. Maybe she'd talked like this before; she couldn't recall.

"We're going to Michigan."

"Not to Ireland?" Her father's dark eyebrows rose.

So that was the claim she made before. "No, Daddy, we can't go to Ireland, not without Kyle."

"And it's Michigan now?"

She nodded. She didn't know how but it was already set in her mind. Charles continued drying his shirt and straightening his tie. He looked at her occasionally with resignation in his features. She searched her heart and happened upon one distantly familiar thing: peace. It'd been a while, but she recognized it as an old friend. Happiness and understanding didn't accompany it. The peace was enough for now.

Her father stood from the chair, then bent to kiss her forehead. "I'll see you when I come home from the office."

"Goodbye, Daddy."

Annie sat Megan up on the bed. The little girl grabbed a fistful of her mother's hair and giggled.

Asking it of herself as much as anyone, Annie said quietly, "What do you think of that, baby girl? We're moving to Michigan."

47

October, 2000, 81 years later

"Just like that, you moved to Michigan?"

"It wasn't just like anything," Grandma Annie corrected Laurel.

Laurel was stunned. She couldn't fathom making such a decision based solely on, well, she didn't even know what. A sense of peace? How could that be sufficient? Then she smiled as her imagination's version of Kyle's Irish accent recited the same biblical phrase he once shared with Grandma Annie: The peace of God, which passes all understanding. She'd read that verse a hundred times over but knew her faith fell short of that which her great-grandmother had demonstrated.

Grandma Annie pushed herself into a better sitting position and smoothed the afghan over her legs. "I waited until spring to travel. The months felt like ages to me. I was so anxious to go once I made up my mind, but I suppose the time was necessary. My parents needed to see that it wasn't a fleeting, unstable whim, and I needed time to track down Lieutenant Winfield's family through the army. That was not an easy task."

"So you wrote to Mrs. Winfield and asked if you could stay with her?"

Grandma Annie shook her head, her white hair shifting where it hung against her cheeks. "It was my intention to do so but it took too long to find out the lieutenant's home address. By the time I had it, it was time to leave Boston anyway."

"You showed up at their door completely unannounced?" Laurel was incredulous. "What if they wouldn't help you once you arrived? I mean, it wasn't only you. You had to take care of Megan too."

"It seems foolish, doesn't it?" Grandma Annie looked amused. "You sound a lot like my mother did when she tried to talk me out of going. There wasn't any way for me to help her understand. She'd never done anything by the Holy Spirit's guidance."

The doubt Laurel held was assigned only to herself, not God. She knew her Bible stories well enough to know he sometimes led people down surprising roads.

"In the days after I decided to go to Michigan, I remembered all the wonderful things Lieutenant Winfield told me about the place. Maybe those conversations had been God's way of preparing me for this move. A few years later, I heard a sermon that made it understandable. The priest talked about providence, about God having everything in our lives within His care, even the things that hadn't happened yet."

Grandma Annie stared into the golden light still streaming through the curtains. "The Lord knew I would need a place to make a home long before the need arose."

"What if Mrs. Winfield didn't understand it that way? She might not have wanted to take in you and the baby, or could have been unable to help."

"You know, I never worried about that, not once."

She remained baffled. She'd admired Grandma Annie's faith for years without knowing the extremes to which it was tested.

"I worried over getting lost, or forgetting something in Boston that I'd want with me. I worried that my mother would never forgive me, which she didn't." Grandma Annie swallowed hard. "How Mrs. Winfield could help me was unclear. I was careful not to hold any particular expectations, but I was sure she would help in whatever way she could."

"What happened when you got there?"

"Let's see." Grandma Annie took a long pause. "I left Boston in early April, 1919, and reached Michigan maybe ten days later. That was only as far as Detroit. Once the train conductor found out I was new to Michigan, he told me facts and stories about the state, the Great Lakes, and every town we passed through.

"I loved everything I saw and it helped that I traveled in early spring. Each time I got excited about something outside the train windows, the conductor would remind me, 'and you haven't even seen Lake Michigan yet.'" Grandma Annie laughed to herself, "He was right about that one. It was love at first sight when I did reach the lake."

"Where did the Winfields live?"

"They were in Spring Lake. It was much smaller than it is today, so I had no trouble finding their home. I stopped at the first church I saw in town and asked the pastor if he knew the family of Joseph Winfield. It was no coincidence that the lieutenant and his family had attended that church for years.

"I took Mrs. Winfield by surprise, showing up that way, but she never suggested I shouldn't have come. I was careful not to ask anything of her. At first, after I explained my presence as best I could, all Mrs. Winfield cared about was that I'd been with her husband during his last days. She wanted to hear every detail of his time at the hospital."

Grandma Annie had a smile on her face as she recounted these memories. "It went unspoken that Megan and I were to stay with them. I'm still amazed, looking back, at how our new situation came together perfectly. Not always ideal or easy, but perfect according to God's providence."

"Did you stay with the Winfields for long?"

"For a year and a half. It was a happy time. We lived as one family. Mrs. Winfield cared for Megan as much as for any of her own children, and the children all loved having a new baby in the house. At least for a little while, Megan had the gift of brothers and sisters. All I learned from that family was priceless.

"I found work as a nurse with the town's physician. He had a little office, plus he made a lot of house calls. When he retired the next year, he arranged a place for me with a doctor here in Ravenna. That's when I moved out of the Winfield's home. A few months later, Mrs. Winfield remarried and moved to Saugatuck. Megan and I used to visit them each summer and spend a few days on the lake." She took a deep breath. "And that is how I ended up here, as you put it."

Laurel let out a low whistle. Grandma Annie had narrated it humbly enough, but Laurel perceived the enormity of the choices made. She longed to communicate all that she thought of her great-grandmother; the courage, faithfulness, and even audacity.

There was still one question buzzing around Laurel's head though. She thought she heard movements in another room, so she hurried to ask, "When did you start…" Lying? She couldn't get the word out. "When did you stop explaining about Megan's birth, or about Kyle?"

"Mrs. Winfield was the last person to whom I told the whole story; the only one who ever knew it after I left Boston." Grandma Annie's chin dropped. She rolled threads of the afghan between her fingers. "At first, I simply avoided explaining anything to anyone. I figured there was less harm in letting people believe whatever they assumed about me. The assumptions tended to run along one line since everyone in town knew I was a nurse during the war. They figured I married a soldier and he died at war. Some people tried to find out more, but I became good at giving vague answers. Eventually, it was general knowledge that I didn't speak about my past because it was too difficult. Their sympathy made it worse. My conscience never rested on that account. I couldn't see a way out of the lies, a way to start telling the truth," Annie spoke in earnest. "I should have started with Megan. It's my worst regret, and the sin I've prayed most for a chance to rectify."

Laurel's eyes pooled with tears. When she took hold of Grandma Annie's hand, the older woman's green eyes filled with a mirror of tears. She gripped Laurel's fingers.

"They're like anchors, those things we bury in our hearts. Do you know what I mean?" Grandma Annie's expression begged her to understand. When Laurel nodded, her cheeks now wet, Grandma Annie smiled a little. "I hope you do. I hope you get rid of your anchors. I wish I hadn't let it wait so long, but you must have been the chance God gave that I finally took."

The gratitude Laurel felt for being the recipient of this story was enough to split open her chest. That sharp pressure in her heart reached a breaking point when Grandma Annie said what Laurel felt she should have been the one to express.

"Thank you. Thank you ever so much."

48

October, 2000

The apple tree in Grandma Annie's backyard came down that afternoon. No storm, no wind, just the thickest, oldest branches collapsing violently under their own weight. For four hours, Laurel's father tackled the cleanup with a wheelbarrow and a saw.

"Sun's going down. He'll run out of daylight soon." Erin watched her husband through the patio doors. Laurel joined her there, leaning a shoulder against the glass. Erin asked, "Why don't you go help him? Grandma is calmed down now after the noise of that darn tree falling apart scared her so badly, and I need to get dinner ready."

Laurel had avoided her father all day, a task made easier once he went to the backyard. He could use her help though, so she went to find her shoes and a sweatshirt.

An hour and a half later both the light and the branches were completely gone. Only a rough stump remained, on which Laurel took a seat.

"Thanks for your help." Marshall pulled off his gloves. "I'd be out here most of tomorrow morning if you hadn't come out."

"You're welcome." She kept her eyes on the ground. They'd worked mostly in silence until now.

They were both in need of a shower, their jeans and shirts streaked with dirt, their forearms scratched by dozens of branches. Dinner was likely waiting on them. Rather than head inside, Marshall sat down in a patio chair. He stretched his legs out with a low groan, then bent his knees and rested his elbows on his thighs. He looked at his daughter until she met his eyes.

"I came back, Laurel. I came back." His voice pleaded with her to forgive. "It's been nine years since I came back."

"There shouldn't have been anything to come back from, Dad."

Marshall's expression was inscrutable with the only dim light in the yard coming from the kitchen behind him. "I was gone for a year, one year out of thirty-one years of marriage."

"This isn't about ratios, Dad. You were gone. You left."

He pressed his fingertips to his forehead. "I did. I know. You're right, it isn't about ratios. I don't know why I said that."

Her mouth opened to speak but she shut it against the bitter stream of words simmering in her throat. Her cheeks flushed with the ten years of waiting for this fight.

"Tell me what I can do, Laurel. What do you need me to do?"

Her words were quiet, terse. "I need you to acknowledge that you left, and by leaving you...," her voice cracked, but she swallowed her tears, "You hurt me, and you hurt Mom. You never apologized to me before now, Dad. How could you not apologize? That night when you came back and you and Mom sat me down on the couch, to be honest, I don't know which of you I wanted to slap more. Telling me it was all fine now, that we were a family like we should be, like we always had been. You were gone for fourteen months; for two summers and a full school year. I want you to explain." Her voice rose with this demand.

"I can't explain." Marshall shook his head. The kitchen light glinted off the smattering of whites in his sandy brown hair. "I can apologize, as I should have done the moment I walked in the door ten years ago, but I can't explain."

"Why not?"

"How do you explain the worst mistake you ever made? There's no excuse for what I chose; no why that will make you feel better."

"Fine, don't explain. Describe. Tell me what happened."

He rose to pace the edge of the patio. His hands were stuffed in his pockets. "Your mom and I had a fight the morning before her stroke, a bad one. It was worse than I can ever remember having before, and we'd been fighting a lot at the time. When the doctor started explaining the possible causes of her stroke, he kept mentioning 'extreme stress.' I was convinced that I was the cause, that I had done irreparable harm to your mom. I panicked, and I left. It was cowardice, nothing more. I told myself that because I loved you two, I should leave, but really my own fears were to blame. Not only had I given your mother a stroke, or so I assumed, I also couldn't fix it. I couldn't make her better. I hated myself.

"Within a week, I knew I made the worst possible choice. I tried to come back but your mother was so angry, as she deserved to be, that she told me to stay away. Said she couldn't stand the sight of me. After six months, she agreed to start talking to me again. After three more months, we decided to see a counselor together. This mistake I'd made damaged our entire relationship, everything we had built for twenty years. We were both convinced that it was better to leave you out of it, to protect you from all the pain and uncertainty. That's why you never knew we were working on things. I agreed to let you believe I was still completely absent from your lives. I didn't deserve any better."

Laurel's lower back throbbed from the uneven seat on the tree stump. Her father's words swirled dizzyingly in her head and she didn't trust herself to stand.

"We messed up, Laurel." Marshall stopped pacing, turned to face her but kept his distance of a few yards. "We thought we were protecting you, guarding you, but what we weren't doing was being honest with you. We underestimated how much damage was already done. Acting like it all was ok, moving forward without helping you deal with what happened; we were terribly mistaken. We realized that eventually. Your mom forgave me before I returned home that August, though there was a lot of healing left to do. I'm still working on forgiving myself."

Tears spilled from her eyes. She felt them running over her face, her neck, the collar of her shirt. Her father took a stride forward. When she didn't move, he took another. Then he was on his knees, looking up at her, his face a portrait of remorse. "I'm sorry, Laurel. You've carried this around all these years. Knowing what it took for your mom and me to heal from the hurt I caused, and your own hurts left untended, I'm sorry, I'm so sorry."

Anchors. She heard Grandma Annie in her mind. Laurel was bent over, her arms wrapping around his neck before he got through his last apology. There was no restraint, no stiffness as there'd been in every hug they exchanged in the last decade. The relief of it exhausted her. Her limbs felt weak. With his thick arms holding her against his chest, her words were muffled, "Thank you."

Her father leaned back placing a hand on each of her wet cheeks. "I love you, Laurel. You are more precious to me than you could ever know. I've done a terrible job of letting you know that."

"I'm going to forgive you." Laurel was surprised at the firmness of her voice. "It might take a while or it might not, I don't know, but I'm going to forgive you."

49

October, 2000

Laurel had been too tired to eat after coming inside with her father. The next morning, she woke late and rushed to be ready for Sunday Mass with her parents. They made it to Saint Catherine's with enough time for her to whisper an emotional prayer of thanksgiving before the opening hymn began. Returning to the house, they cooked a hearty breakfast together. Marshall drove back to Chicago in the evening, all three of them more at ease in their goodbyes than they had been since Laurel was a child. Peace had taken its first roots and even with Grandma Annie's deterioration, there was renewed joy in their smiles.

Grandma Annie's deterioration was undeniable though. That Sunday, each time she woke, Grandma Annie did not recognize or wish to speak to any of them. It was now past dinnertime on Monday and her unfortunate state of mind persisted. While Grandma Annie slept, Laurel remained in the bedroom. She watched the 103-year-old woman with her much younger eyes while her mind roamed through Grandma Annie's recent revelations. Grandma Annie slept more and more without the help of medication.

Laurel carefully, soundlessly slid the drawer out of the mosaic table, sat down in the rocker, and examined every item by the light from the hallway behind her.

The ruby ring hanging on a tarnished gold chain was explained in a letter from Kyle's mother, Sarah. That letter must have slipped out of the bundle before Annie had lent them to Laurel to read. She squinted in the shadowy room now to read its lines. Kyle bought the ring in Kilarney months before his death, long before he even received that last letter from Annie, and Sarah Regan sent it to Annie when she found it in Kyle's home.

She spent a long while on the photographs. There was one of Grandma Annie's nephew and niece, George and Corrine, dated June, 1921. Another was a blurred snapshot at the beach. Annie, though decades younger, was instantly recognizable; slim and tall with straight black hair lifted by the wind. Laurel knew the toddler hugging her legs must be Megan. In the picture, Annie smiled into the sun, shading her eyes with one hand while resting her other on Megan's dark, curly hair.

The third photograph was not an original print but a yellowed newspaper clipping with a French caption. Laurel counted thirty-six people clustered in the outdoor shot. Most were soldiers in uniforms of the allied armies, a few on crutches and several with bandaged arms or heads. Laurel studied the faces of each one. The year 1917 was written in pencil on the corner, but she couldn't determine if it was taken before or during Chet's stay at the hospital. She found Annie on the end of the second row. The neat bun of dark hair and formal nurse's uniform were the image of professionalism and maturity, but Annie's face was remarkably young, almost childlike. A much shorter nurse, just as youthful, with riotous, light colored curls, had her arm around Annie's waist.

Meg Dupree was beautiful. This enthrallingly pretty woman, whose every physical characteristic contrasted the looks of Laurel and the rest of her family, this was her great-grandmother by birth. She wondered what she ought to feel at the sight of Meg. She waited for a specific emotion to take shape but there was only an ambiguous sense of knowledge.

Then Laurel came to the last picture from the drawer. It was the photo of Kyle that Mr. Regan sent to Annie with his letter. For a few minutes, Laurel stared at him posed there in black and white. She pressed flat the curled corners of the waxy photograph. Eventually, she carried the picture out of the dark bedroom. Holding it up in the hallway light, her eyes traveled over every feature.

Kyle wore a dark suit, with a crisp, white shirt and a black tie. He held a newsboy style hat in his hands. Even though the photograph cut off above Kyle's knees, his height was apparent. She saw the broad muscular chest, the strong jaw and neatly cut but still wavy hair that Grandma Annie had described so tenderly. His closed-mouth smile looked gentle. The black and white picture could not do justice to the incredible color of his eyes, yet their brightness still grabbed her attention. Maybe it was her imagination, but Laurel felt she could read so much in those eyes. They were beautiful, glinting with happiness, but also cautious and pensive.

It was while she stood in the hallway, fascinated by this photograph, that her mother came upon her and asked what she was holding. When Erin's question broke her concentration, Laurel couldn't think of a reason to wait any longer to tell her mother.

She handed the photo to Erin. "This is Kyle Regan."

"Who is he?"

"Grandma Annie was going to marry him."

Her mother's mouth fell open. She leaned against the wall and looked harder at the man in the picture. She opened and shut her mouth a few times as if she did not know what to ask first.

"Could we wait until tomorrow?" Laurel spoke first. "I'll tell you everything then."

Erin nodded. She returned the photograph to Laurel's hand and walked back to the kitchen. After replacing the picture and its companions in Grandma Annie's drawer, Laurel readied herself for bed.

Tuesday dawned gray and chilly. Laurel found her mother, along with a steaming mug of coffee for each of them, waiting in the kitchen. Erin's hair was damp from showering and she was dressed in a loose sweater and jeans. She kept her silence only until Laurel drank some coffee. "So, Grandma told you about this Kyle?"

"Yes, she did." Laurel stretched her arms into the air, her knotted back muscles resisting the effort.

"Is he my mom's father?" Erin whispered the question.

The story, its names and characters and twists, had so filled her mind the past few weeks that Laurel almost couldn't remember knowing nothing of it. It was strange to hold this long-standing secret in her own memory now. The few seconds remaining of her status as secret keeper were weighty. They brought a flash of possessiveness.

"I need to tell you the whole story."

Erin settled back in her chair.

She took a more straightforward approach than Annie had done. "Kyle wasn't Grandma Megan's father, and Annie wasn't her mother."

Erin's face went through a succession of silent changes, eventually coming full circle to the look of wonder with which it began. "You're sure of that?"

"Yes, I am."

Erin said little while Laurel carefully summarized what Grandma Annie had revealed. She skimmed over many of the detailed memories that filled out the story, reasoning that her mother needed to hear the essentials while the rest could wait. She spoke while Erin made oatmeal for Grandma Annie, continued after Grandma Annie had eaten and while they washed the breakfast dishes, and didn't stop thereafter until she felt the task was finished.

It was noon by that time. Other than occasional clarifying questions, her mother had kept quiet until the end, giving little away of how she felt. As Erin left the kitchen table where they'd been sitting, she finally said, "I'm so glad you asked her, Laurel. To think that no one would have ever known if you hadn't asked."

Laurel didn't respond. She was certainly grateful for Grandma Annie's willingness to tell her the truth, but this initial reaction from her mother was bewildering.

"I mean, it doesn't change anything, but it feels good to know the truth, right?" Erin was now checking the refrigerator to pick out something for lunch.

"It doesn't change anything?" She gave her mother a sideways glance. "We aren't even related to Annie."

Erin faced her. "But what does that actually change?"

Laurel had no answer.

"I suppose we could make it change things, if we wanted to." Erin raised her eyebrows, watching her daughter.

"You mean we could look for Meg or Chet's family members, or something like that?"

"Yeah, maybe." Erin pulled a container of beef stew out of the refrigerator then reached for two bowls in the cupboard. "There would be nothing wrong with doing that but I don't think we need to do that."

"Maybe Grandma wouldn't want us to look for them." Laurel doubted this notion even as she voiced it.

"I don't think that's why she kept it all a secret. It didn't sound that way to me."

Laurel didn't think that had mattered to Grandma Annie either. The conversation was becoming hypothetical; a wish to pursue their biological family ties didn't actually exist. What did exist was a strengthening desire to identify at least one tangible difference the truth made. If it didn't change anything, if knowing the truth made no difference for them, why was it better now that she knew? What good had there been in Grandma Annie enduring that burden for so long?

As happened frequently in recent days, Laurel felt mentally exhausted. She wanted to clear her thoughts for at least a brief time.

"I'm not hungry yet," she said before Erin could dish up a helping of stew for her. "I think I'll go for a run."

"It's going to rain."

She acknowledged the solid cloud cover outside the window. "I don't mind. I'll take a hot shower when I get back."

"If you must. I'll put a bowl of this in the refrigerator for you."

Laurel was already wearing sweatpants. She layered a long-sleeved top over her t-shirt, rummaged through the coat closet for an old winter hat, tied her shoes, and headed out the front door.

50

October, 2000

The lifting and planting of her feet became a rhythm for more peaceful thoughts as Laurel took to the road. She let her eyes roam over the harvested fields and half empty trees. A mile down Harrisburg Road, the first rain drops splashed onto her skin. Forty minutes later she returned, soaked through every layer. Her thick hair was saturated beneath her hat, as was her clothing. She slowed to a walk just before the house, listening to the slosh of water in her shoes.

She was surprised at the sight of two cars besides her own parked in front of Grandma Annie's house. She recognized Melanie's red SUV, but the other was unfamiliar. A hint of a smile came to her dripping wet face when she entered the house to see her mother, Melanie, and Robert together in the living room. Mel and Robert were facing the other way but her mother saw Laurel and jumped from the chair.

"Yikes! You're dripping all over the place. I'll get some towels."

The other two looked over the back of the couch. Mel's brown eyes grew wide and she covered her mouth to muffle a laugh. Robert stood up and appeared to be enjoying the sight of her bedraggled self just as much as Mel.

"Fine day for running, isn't it?" Mel piped up.

"Yes, perfect." Laurel agreed with enthusiasm and they both laughed.

As Robert walked toward her, Laurel asked, "Did you get a new car?"

Robert stopped at the border of the puddle forming around Laurel's feet. "No, that's Gary and Abby's car. Gary has my Jeep to pick up some equipment for the restaurant."

"Why aren't you at work?"

"I only worked the morning today."

Melanie bounced off the couch and said excitedly, "Robert was explaining about catering the wedding. He and Gary are going to do it. Isn't that wonderful? We were talking about the menu when you came in."

"That's gr-great." Laurel's teeth started to chatter. She shivered like a wet puppy. "You didn't m-mention you were also offering catering at the restaurant."

Robert shrugged. "We aren't."

"They're only doing it this one time," Melanie gushed. She raised one eyebrow at Laurel. "Isn't that generous of them? I can't imagine why Robert was so willing to do it."

Robert explained hastily, "It's really a great opportunity for the restaurant. What better way to advertise than to serve our food to people?"

"Still, it's saving the whole reception from disaster," Melanie insisted. "You're an answer to our prayers."

"Glad to hear it. Although, maybe you should wait until you've tasted some samples before you decide your prayers have been answered."

Laurel wondered what was taking her mother so long to find towels. As if he'd read her rain-soaked mind, Robert said he'd see if Erin needed help.

"Wh-when did you get here?" she asked Melanie.

"Maybe thirty minutes ago, I think. He showed up about ten minutes later."

Laurel squeezed the ends of her hair, sending streams of water down to the growing puddle.

"I wanted to see how you were doing." Mel stepped forward like she was going to hug Laurel, but reconsidered. She patted Laurel's arm then wiped her hand on her black pants. "Saturday night was a bit much to handle and we haven't talked since then. I could have called, I guess."

"No, it's good to see you." Laurel smiled, realizing how glad she was to have her friend there.

Her mother hustled back into the room carrying several towels, Robert trailing behind her. "Sorry, Grandma woke up and asked for a drink of water."

Laurel accepted a towel and wiped her face and neck. "Was she calm?"

"Yes, though she didn't know me."

Erin laid towels down to make a path for Laurel to walk further into the house, then handed Laurel her suitcase.

"I'm going to get cleaned up," Laurel said.

Robert asked quietly, "Is it okay if I wait here? I can go if you want me to go."

She saw both her mother's and Melanie's nodding heads. "It's fine Robert, if you want to stay," she agreed.

Late into the day, the four of them kept company in Grandma Annie's living room. After the stress of the days and nights since the downturn of her great-grandmother's health, the easy, happy conversation was a balm to Laurel's spirits. Erin wanted to hear all the details of Melanie's final wedding plans. Mel inquired after the Erin and Marshall's life in Chicago, keen to hear Erin's opinions on moving to such a huge city. Laurel laughed over stories of her father trying to keep up his friendly, suburban manners with their city neighbors.

Robert listened to the women's lively talk. Laurel had never seen him so reserved. He smiled with amusement at the humorous tales and nodded along to most everything else, but he otherwise appeared distracted. When he was asked about the restaurant and what remained to be ready for its opening, his face brightened and he answered eagerly.

The clock's hands were nearing half past four when Melanie said she had to leave. "I'll barely make it to the bookstore by five. I'm closing tonight." She hugged Laurel and Erin. "Annie is blessed to have you two, you know."

For the first time since Grandma Annie's initial turn for the worse, Laurel saw her mother's eyes mist over.

Mel said goodbye to Robert, thanking him again for his and his brother's help. They'd already picked a day to meet to set the menu for the wedding dinner.

Erin, Laurel and Robert were left standing in the living room. Erin clapped her hands together. "I'll check on Grandma. She's been sleeping a long time."

Laurel expected Robert to excuse himself too, but he smiled at her mother before she walked out of the room, then said to Laurel, "So, you're staying here all week?"

"Mom and I are both here for the week. Dad will come over the weekend again. They'll both go back to Chicago after that, but Mom will return again after a couple days at home."

"What'll you do while she's gone and you're working?"

"We'll do what we did the first week after Grandma was in the hospital. Her friends and people from the church will take care of her while I'm at work, and I'll stay here each night."

Robert nodded, falling silent.

Laurel busied her hands with straightening the couch's throw pillows. "Are you sure you don't have anywhere else you need to be?" Realizing how rude that may have sounded, she added, "I only mean that I'm sure you didn't take the whole afternoon off to spend it here."

"I sort of did."

She set down the last pillow. "You did?"

His eyes lit up. His usual confidence, less obvious in the past hours, returned in his smile and posture.

"Why would you do that?"

"Because I wanted to know how you were doing and if there was anything I could do to help. Also, because I didn't like how things were left between us when you had to leave the coffeehouse on Saturday night. I came here to explain."

"Explain what, exactly?" Laurel asked curiously.

"Do you have any blankets we could use?"

"Blankets?" Laurel's backward step was blocked by the arm of the couch.

"We're going outside and it's cold today." Robert looked out the window. "It stopped raining a while ago. You find a blanket and I'll meet you outside."

She obliged, retrieving two blankets from the linen closet. At Annie's bedroom, she saw Erin helping Grandma Annie back into bed after taking her to the bathroom.

"Mom," Laurel whispered.

When Grandma Annie became nervous, Erin explained soothingly, "Annie, this is my daughter, Laurel. She's here to take care of you too."

Grandma Annie gave a weak nod. Laurel had to swallow a hard lump of grief before speaking again. "Mom, Robert and I will be out on the patio. Come get me if you need me for anything."

Erin smoothed the blankets over Grandma Annie's lap. She smiled at her daughter. "He's very nice. I like him."

"He's a colleague, Mom, or he was. He's...oh, never mind."

As soon as Laurel walked outside, Robert began explaining his situation at Parker Advertising.

"You see, LeeAnn only knew about the restaurant because she eavesdropped on my phone conversation and then badgered me about it." He pulled a sweatshirt over his head. "I didn't want you to think I just hadn't bothered to tell you."

They used a towel to dry off the chairs then sat down beneath the clouds passing out of view with the help of a strong, cool breeze. Laurel wrapped her blanket around her waist and legs.

"LeeAnn didn't get it out of me until after I talked to Mr. Parker. He was quite generous with me. Did you know he started his company while he was in what he'd expected to be his dream job? He said we never know what turns our lives can take if we let them." Robert shrugged off his reflective tone. "He agreed that I could stay on for another month and we'd announce my resignation later."

"That was good of him to do."

"It made the most sense too. This way the North Wind Coffees account wasn't disrupted before the opening, and I had time to consider who to recommend as account leader to replace me. Mr. Parker wanted to promote from within the company."

Laurel nodded. "It sounds like it played out the best way possible for everyone involved."

"I recommended you."

She looked at Robert in surprise. Holding his gaze as calmly as he held hers was not easy. "Thank you, Robert. I really appreciate it."

"You're welcome. I can't guarantee you'll get it, but he didn't give any sign that he disagreed with my recommendation."

"Thank you," she repeated. "It means a lot to me."

"You seem the best at keeping the whole picture in front of you when you're on a team account. That's one of the biggest challenges." He halted his comments there.

Questions and conversations in the last month had a new light spill over them as she realized he was making this decision during that time. She stared up at the afternoon sky, exasperated with herself. "That's why you wanted to know if I had any plans to move to Chicago, and why you tried to set up a lunch or dinner with me."

He didn't reply. She tried to inject a lighter bend in the conversation. "I'm glad I didn't lie and say I was in favor of moving away or wanting a new job."

Robert didn't echo her bantering tone. "Why would you ever do that?"

"I was kidding. I don't want to move away," she reassured him. "And I wouldn't lie to you. I'm glad to stay where I am."

His voice took on a low, impatient rumble. "I didn't ask you about that or try to have lunch with you because of the recommendation."

His hazel eyes were darker out here under the gray sky. She watched his profile.

He shoved his hands in his pockets and frowned in the direction of the stump of the old apple tree. "You know, my sister-in-law is always saying guys are the clueless ones."

"What are you trying to say?"

"I asked you to lunch, more than once, because I wanted to have lunch with you. I asked about you staying in Grand Rapids, because I wanted to know that you weren't going to disappear after I left Parker Advertising." His voice deepened further. "I've been patient, Laurel. For two years, I've waited. First, I had to; there was nothing to do while you were with him. Then he left and I still waited. Every time I prayed and looked for a chance, all I felt was right was to wait. No need to hurry, that's what I told myself. I had forty hours a week to be near you, to figure out how to be your friend, at the very least. What was the rush, right?"

For a second, he looked at her like he expected an answer, then he pressed on. "Except, then the restaurant happened. It'd been this hypothetical idea for way down the road, but things started falling into place and we seized the opportunity. It got to a month until I'd be done working with you and I was pretty sure I hadn't made it out of square one of even being friends. You just wouldn't," Robert stopped short of blaming her for anything specific.

She grabbed the chance to speak up. "I know. I'm sorry."

He had his elbows on his knees, hands gripped in front of him. "I got anxious. I couldn't be patient anymore. I started asking questions, trying to see you outside the office. You didn't hide that you were suspicious of me, either." He gave an agitated laugh. "That was so encouraging."

She looked at him with a new feeling of compassion. She worried over reaching the moment when he'd finish speaking and she must make more of a reply than a meager apology.

"It worked a little, I think." He met her eyes for the first time in a while. "Only a little."

He stood and moved up and down the width of the patio. "Then he shows up out of nowhere and on the same night I thought I'd finally have a chance to tell you everything that was going on. I should have given up at that point. Marcus turning up was probably a sign or something.

"You didn't seem happy to see him by any means, though, and you looked gorgeous that night," he leveled an accusing glance at her, "And we'd had such a good day working together. So, I tried anyway. I couldn't help it. I started to tell you about the restaurant first, just to lead into other subjects really. With your grandmother needing you here, I had to wait. But I'm tired of waiting."

A smile played at the corners of Laurel's mouth when Robert finally stopped. She leaned forward, setting aside the blanket she'd had over her legs.

He tapped his foot against the patio. "Are you laughing at me?"

She held up her hands. "No, no, I'm not."

"This is amusing to you?"

The tables had turned at an unrecognizable angle. She stood.

"By Saturday your efforts had worked a little. I was finally willing to be friends with you." This wasn't the most pleasing choice of words, so she added, "I finally wanted to be friends."

"What about Marcus showing up?"

"Well, that was a mess, and I was furious. I can see how you'd see it as unhelpful."

"That's putting it nicely."

"I didn't want to see him again. If he'd have asked to come that evening to talk to me, I would have refused him point blank, but I'd have been wrong."

His features narrowed into a scowl and she hurried to explain.

"Marcus catching me off-guard gave me the chance to be completely honest with myself, and with him. I didn't have time to analyze it, or run from it, or rehearse what I should say. I faced it and I cut the tie I hadn't known was still there. Maybe I'd been stuck in the same place since Marcus walked away from me." The thought was still forming as she spoke. "I hadn't moved, for whatever reason. Fear, I suppose."

"Fear of what?"

She glanced at the ground. "Where to begin?"

He nodded. "And now that you've moved?"

"Well, the things you've started to think are becoming impossible, I finally feel could be possible." She looked away but pushed herself to make one more admission. "My jealousy of LeeAnn for knowing about the restaurant before I did was enough to prove that, even if nothing else did."

338

"You jealous of LeeAnn? That's the most ridiculous thing I've ever heard."

She poked at the grass with the front of her shoe. She asked ironically, "Are you laughing at me?"

"Only a little, yes." He took one step nearer.

The moment was thick with uncertainty. Laurel felt suspended in the space between two drastically different terrains. They'd left their former, familiar ground but she did not yet know where they would land. She believed it was worth finding out though.

He reached for her hand and his touch startled her. When she pulled back without meaning to, Robert's hopeful expression weakened. She caught his hand. It was cold, just like hers. She grasped only his fingers at first, then their palms slid together. He leaned closer, his determined gaze bringing her eyes up to his.

She intruded upon the silence with one question, "What now?"

Robert replied with only a smile followed by a kiss that warmed her to her toes.

51

"O God, thou art my God; early will I seek thee:
my soul thirsteth for thee, my flesh longeth for thee
in a dry and thirsty land, where no water is;
To see thy power and thy glory,
so as I have seen thee in the sanctuary.
Because thy lovingkindness is better than life,
my lips shall praise thee.
Thus will I bless thee while I live:
I will lift up my hands in thy name."
Psalm 63:1-4, KJV

The family thanks you for your presence
and your prayers as we honor Annie's life.

November, 2000

Laurel reread the funeral card for the twelfth time. She flipped it over to a miniature print of the risen Christ. Even at this diminutive size and bent from clutching the card for a solid three hours, the familiar painting was beautiful. Her mother picked it from the funeral home's available selections, having recalled a distant memory of Annie admiring it once.

Laurel turned the card back to the text and looked at the scripture passage again. On Friday afternoon, they had read those verses together. Well, Laurel read them and Grandma Annie listened. Since Thursday of the week before, Grandma Annie had begun asking for someone to read to her. Although she wasn't awake a lot—each day it'd been for fewer hours—when she was awake she no longer liked to be left alone. Laurel wondered at what point the desire for another person's presence became so strong that it didn't matter if the other person was a stranger to you.

Laurel began with *Persuasion*. She'd planned only to read it herself that week, but Grandma Annie woke once while Laurel had it open on her knees as she rocked in the chair beside the bed. It was difficult to decipher Grandma Annie's expressions anymore as she moved and spoke so little, but Laurel had perceived a hint of curiosity over the book.

"It's *Persuasion*," she said. There was a glimmer of acknowledgement in Grandma Annie's green eyes. "It's your favorite and you said I should read it."

When she asked if she should read aloud, the corners of Grandma Annie's mouth lifted for a millisecond. So, she read the novel in brief intervals. Although she was drawn into the story, she put the book down whenever her great-grandmother drifted into sleep, and didn't pick it up until Grandma Annie could listen again.

They finished on Wednesday morning, exactly a week ago. After that, rather than finding another novel on the shelves, Laurel opened the worn volume of Psalms sitting on the bedside table. She took Chet's long-ago words to heart—the Psalms are poetry, each enjoyed individually—and chose one from the middle of the book. Between Wednesday morning and Friday night, she and Grandma Annie listened to the words of perhaps fifteen different psalms. Laurel was sure she'd never lose her new appreciation for their beautiful verses. She'd picked out Psalm Sixty-Three on Friday and read it before leaving Grandma Annie's bedroom and falling asleep in the guest room.

Sitting in the front pew of Saint Catherine's this morning, she considered how exhausting that last week had been. It wasn't a week of physical exertion as Grandma Annie was anything but difficult to care for, but it was a week of open-ended waiting. With each phone call while she was at work, and every entrance into Annie's bedroom in the evenings and early mornings, she awaited the announcement of the transition that had kept its distance for so long. Death had finally drawn near.

Virginia Baxter came over on Saturday morning. Laurel wanted to make a quick trip to the grocery store as she'd run out of milk, fruit, and hand soap. When she returned, only twenty minutes later, Mrs. Baxter met her at the door. It wasn't necessary to say it. Laurel understood.

Laurel recalled all of this as the congregation at the funeral Mass filed up to the altar to receive communion. The pianist played a somber hymn that Laurel didn't recognize. The notes were lengthened in her ears, like a record played at the wrong speed.

Her mother and father sat beside her in the hard pew, holding hands and staring straight ahead. Erin had not cried much since Grandma Annie died. At the visitation service last night, Erin kept repeating clichéd sentiments to everyone who greeted her.

"She had such a good, long life."

"At least her suffering was brief."

"She's with the Lord, waiting for us now."

Throughout the evening, Laurel fluctuated between loathing the sound of her mother's words and admiring her stoic, undisturbed composure. Laurel, by contrast, had cried intermittently since Saturday morning. It wasn't that she took time out to allow herself "a good cry," as more than a few people suggested she should. Instead, she wept at odd times: the middle of a conversation about the weather, dusting Annie's house before visitors started dropping by, or reheating a casserole for dinner. Laurel gave up trying to stifle the tears. They came of their own accord and dried up when they were satisfied.

With the wake so well attended last night, Laurel was prepared for a small turnout at the funeral, figuring the evening service was more convenient than the funeral in the middle of a workday for most people to pay their respects. Instead, the visitation before Mass this morning brought another steady line. The church was near capacity, discernible by the great sound of everyone standing in unison for the closing prayer. Laurel tried to listen to the words the priest read with his hands raised and his head bowed, but she was thinking about the notecards in her hand.

He invited everyone to sit while Annie's great-granddaughter shared some words in honor of Annie. Laurel heard his announcement and stepped into the aisle at once, her brain having processed that he must mean her. She straightened her black skirt and pulled the sleeves of her plum colored blouse down over her wrists. Behind the podium, she laid out her four note cards and folded her hands against her stomach.

I probably won't need them, she thought as she looked at the words on the cards. After staying up late Monday night to write the eulogy, she practiced it straight through three times yesterday.

Her opening remark was there in front of her, yet her thoughts wandered elsewhere. She touched her hair; it was badly overdue for a cut, which she somehow hadn't noticed until this morning when she pulled the top layers into a silver clip at the crown of her head.

Laurel fixed her eyes on the printed sentence at the top of the first note card, but other words swam around in her mind: lines from the scripture reading during Mass, from Grandma Annie's favorite passage in the First Letter of John. She couldn't shake the distraction of Grandma Annie's voice repeating those treasured verses: *If God so loved us, we ought also to love one another. In deed and truth. In deed and truth.*

Laurel looked out at the crowded church, rows and rows filled with a living collage of faces. Some she knew well, some had been introduced in the past week, and others remained strangers. They all waited on her. A few began whispering nervously to each other. Laurel found the face of her mother. Erin's eyes were wide and anxious. All the words she'd prepared rushed from Laurel's head like a stream plummeting over a hill. A moment of panic, then peace.

"I opened my Bible to the Book of Psalms a few days ago, to pick a psalm for these funeral cards." Laurel held up her creased card. "The Psalms were very special to my great-grandmother." She paused to catch hold of the point she intended to make. "I turned too many pages though and stopped on the last page of the Book of Job. Because it was in front of me, I guess, I read the last verse on that page. It said, 'So Job died, being old and full of days.'[14] It struck me as an odd way to end the story of a man with such a dramatically difficult life. All the suffering and tests of faith, and in the end, what mattered to the person telling Job's story was that Job died old and full of days."

She stacked up her index cards, not caring anymore to look at the neatly written remarks. "I had some specific things I was going to say to you this morning, but I find now that they aren't what I want to say. It's safe to suppose that Annie wouldn't have put much stock in spending our time on those details either. Most of it you could read in the newspaper's obituary. Besides, all of you were present for at least a piece of it. You all experienced at least one aspect of Annie's life. You don't need me to tell it to you.

"The only thing I believe Annie would want to be said of her is that she understood what it was to love." Laurel's eyes wandered back to the faces of her parents. She faltered when she saw her mother crying hard. She waited through two steadying breaths before continuing, "For Annie, love was never detached from sacrifice, from giving of yourself. They were linked in a way that shaped her entire long life.

"I had my last conversation with Annie three days before she died. She didn't know who I was, it'd been a few weeks since she knew who any of us were, but she talked with me anyway. I think that even though her mind deteriorated, her heart still knew a lot of things." At this point the tears surfaced, but she kept her concentration and only a few fell onto her cheeks. "It was only in recent months that I came to know about Annie's whole life. She shared with me the work she did, the relationships she had, and the unexpected choices she faced. Annie admitted the pain she still held in her heart, and the sacrifices life had required of her.

"I asked her, that last time we talked, how she carried on through the worst of it. Annie said that love is never weakened by suffering. If it isn't abandoned, then all that the bad can do is strengthen everything that is good in love." Laurel started to feel she was running out of words. Everyone before her listened intently. The task of finishing well felt urgent, but the words were not ready for her yet.

In the seconds of silence, which felt much longer, she looked into the most familiar faces scattered in the assembly. Her mother cried gently now, in a way that made her particularly beautiful.

Her father had his arm around her mother's shoulders, holding Erin softly while he watched his daughter with evident affection.

Two rows behind them were Connor, Jace, and Melanie. Connor had come to last night's wake, as well, and hugged Laurel harder than he ever had before. He stared back at her now, unaware of the gratitude she'd felt for that wordless embrace. Melanie's eyes glistened but she smiled encouragingly at Laurel.

Then her eyes stopped on Robert. He sat in the same row as her other friends, though across the main aisle and squeezed tightly between two white-haired ladies at the center of the pew. He wore a navy suit and silver tie, and his hair was combed more neatly than usual. His expression didn't change when their eyes met; it remained warm, with the sort of tenderness that lent strength to a person's features. Laurel was glad for the wide, solid podium in front of her. It kindly hid the slight shake in her knees.

Her gaze moved lastly to the framed photograph surrounded by white roses near the casket. It was an enlargement of a black and white portrait of her great-grandmother at nineteen. Seeing Annie's young face, what was left to be said surfaced in Laurel's mind.

"Maybe Annie's one real mistake was only blessing us with all the good that had already been fortified by the bad, keeping the suffering to herself. The beauty and depth of her faith—patient, strong, and unwavering as we knew it to be—is only honored when we honor all that contributed to it. For her, the call to love was higher than any other call. It was more demanding and more worthy of our lives than anything else." Laurel's voice quieted as the train of thought continued to course through her. "Annie had some chances to choose an easier route, less scary and more predictable. But as I think of all that happened in her life, I realize that once Annie set her course according to love—God's love and her own—she never abandoned that path. No matter how unexpected or even how brief the opportunities to love, Annie trusted that God was the source of each one. I think that is all Annie would hope we learned from her."

When she returned to her seat, the priest came down to the casket at the foot of the sanctuary. At the start of Mass, he'd laid a white cloth across it, explaining that it symbolized Annie's cleansing baptism into the family of God. Now he held a pewter bowl of baptismal water and blessed the casket with quick flicks of his wrist. She watched the water absorb into the white cloth. At the same time, the priest's voice rang out, clear and low, in a reverent song. Every other noise in the church stopped except for the sounds passing reverently between his lips.

"May Christ, who called you, take you to himself."

Laurel smiled, and wept once more.

52

November, 2000

A mere three days later, Laurel found herself at what stood a great distance from a funeral on the spectrum of social gatherings. Her best friend's wedding day was a blur of activity from the start. Even though Laurel was thrilled, nervous, joyful, and a dozen other things during the course of the day, she experienced it in a muddled state. She felt repeatedly startled, like her mind had to keep catching up with her senses. The joy of Melanie and Jace's wedding spilled over the more somber matters of the last week and coated its surface like oil on water, incapable of mixing in without great effort.

Sitting down after her toast during the wedding dinner, Laurel crossed her feet beneath her floor-length, wine hued dress and felt thoroughly irritated with herself. It wasn't that she was too sad to enjoy the wedding. She knew that if anyone noticed her mood, they would accept that convenient excuse. She contemplated this as she checked that the pearl plated pins hadn't slipped out from their place in her smooth hair. Sadness was not the problem. No, if there was to be just one name for it, it'd be seriousness. She had an urgent desire to laugh, not because anything was funny at the moment, but because she missed laughing.

Laurel looked around the full banquet room. Everyone's attention was split between the dinner plates and the few dozen conversations taking place at once. No one looked back at her as they all enjoyed the company of the people nearest them. She let her gaze land on the centerpiece of sunflowers on the table opposite her seat at the head table.

Melanie elbowed her and Laurel dropped the fork she'd forgotten was in her hand.

"Where in the world are you?"

"What?" She used the white linen napkin to wipe off the olive oil splattered on her fingers.

"You're staring at my uncle and I think you're scaring my aunt."

"I wasn't." The uncle and aunt happened to be seated at the table in her direct line of sight. "I was looking at everyone. They all seem to like the meal. Robert and Gary really came through tonight."

"Yes, it's delicious, but what's wrong with you?"

Laurel turned her head toward Melanie, prepared to protest, but Melanie gave her a warning look.

Mel was beautiful. Every time she looked at her, Laurel lost a breath. Her dark brown hair was curled and gathered up in a loose cluster at the top of her head. Pinned around the underside of the curls, her lace veil fell delicately over her shoulders. At last night's rehearsal, Jace gave Melanie a necklace of tiny diamonds set in three silver stars, which she wore today. The jewels danced under the soft light in the room. Her dress, of course, was perfect, and Jace's awe when Melanie entered the church on her father's arm was a precious memory for everyone who witnessed it.

At this close proximity though, face to face here beside each other, the resplendent bride was simply Laurel's dearest friend.

"Do you remember when I had a class with Dr. Ripley in my junior year?" Laurel asked suddenly.

"Um, sure, I remember."

"He was such an incredible teacher, the best I ever had. I wanted to remember every word he said, every point he made. It was the only class I recorded the lectures so I could listen to them again. I studied harder for his exams than for practically any other class, and it was only an elective."

"Why are you thinking about this now?"

Laurel tried to reason out her point. "When I got my final exam back, I had a decent grade but Dr. Ripley wrote some comments. He said I'd made no application of the material, that I obviously listened well in class but he was unconvinced that I learned what he taught."

"That's harsh," Melanie commiserated.

"It was true though." She pushed her plate away and laid her palms flat on the tablecloth.

Melanie only looked confused.

"What if the same thing happens again?"

"Are you going back to school?"

She covered her face with her hands and shook her head. "No, Mel, I mean with Grandma Annie. Everything she shared with me and taught me, what if I listened but I haven't learned?" Laurel put her hands back down and looked at Mel in earnest. She'd told much of Annie's story to Melanie in the past several days. She sighed, whispering, "I want it to change me."

"I don't think you need to worry."

"I feel like I'm making the same mistake now. I'm taking it all so seriously, trying to remember every part, but what good is it doing?"

Mel's face lost about half the sympathy it held. "Okay, first of all, it's been a week, for goodness sake. Do not judge yourself according to a week's time that's included your great-grandmother's death, her funeral, my wedding rehearsal and dinner, and now the wedding itself."

Laurel allowed a tight smile. "And second of all?"

"Second of all," Melanie leaned toward her, "if you want to see the good Annie's example has already done for you, go back at least as far as when she started telling you about her life. I doubt you'll still think you haven't changed at all."

Melanie's certainty bolstered her spirits. What differences Melanie already saw weren't obvious to her, but maybe if she had time to think about it....

"But could you not spend my wedding reception analyzing yourself?"

Her best friend knew her far too well.

Laurel laughed. The laugh felt like it was the first time she'd made a sound since the funeral. She laughed again, a little longer and from deeper within.

When the dishes were cleared away, the servers rearranged the tables to allow for a small dance floor on one side of the banquet room. The children present, in their colorful dresses and minia-ture suits, spun gleefully around the polished floor to the first few songs. Small groups of adults gradually ventured out, slightly more reserved in their bouncing and twirling to the happy beats.

When the opening notes of a ballad streamed through the speak-ers, the DJ announced Jace and Melanie Matten's first official dance as husband and wife. Everyone watched from the dance floor's pe-rimeter, snapping pictures. Jace held his bride as close as possible, leading her in slow steps around the floor.

"It is the couple's request that you join them for the remainder of this special dance," the DJ said over the music.

Laurel started walking back to her seat as a stream of couples came forward. Her father caught up to her though and took her hand.

"How about a dance, Laurel? Your mom and I aren't going to stay much longer."

They turned back toward the dance floor.

"You're not even staying for cake?"

"After that meal, I don't think I've ever been so full in my life." He put his arm around her back and they eased into the rhythm of the song.

Laurel rolled her eyes, tipping her head up to look at him. "You used to say that every Thanksgiving."

"Well, that's how good the dinner was tonight," he exclaimed. "Your boyfriend is going to have a mighty successful restaurant, I'd wager."

"Dad, I'm not sure that he's really my boyfriend."

Marshall smirked. "That's what your mom keeps calling him, so you'll have to take it up with her."

She was unable to hide the smile that came with the sound of her father using that word.

Other than a handful of sightings as he rushed in and out of the kitchen during dinner, she hadn't seen Robert all day. He'd wanted to attend the wedding ceremony but as he was needed for food prep all afternoon, there was no chance for him to make it to the church.

Once, as he passed the wedding party's table after distributing the salad plates, he slowed down enough for Laurel to hear him say, "You look incredible," before disappearing into the kitchen.

Her father interrupted these enjoyable thoughts. "I'm happy for you," he said solemnly. "Whatever might happen with this guy, you're already happier than I've seen you in a long time."

She protested, "I've been fine, Dad."

"You have been fine, but you haven't been happy."

"Well, if I'm happier, it isn't only because of Robert."

He kissed her cheek. "That's good to hear. Now I don't have to convince you to move to Chicago."

"I was never going to move to Chicago."

"Doesn't mean I wasn't going to try." He hugged her and they danced in contented silence for the remainder of the song.
As the last notes faded and a second ballad began, Connor showed up beside them. The men shook hands.

"Good to see you again, Connor."

"You too, Mr. Thomas. Do you mind if I take over for this dance?"

"Not at all." He smiled and turned back to Laurel. "I think I'll coax your mom out here for one before we leave."

She hugged him again. "Thank you, Dad."

The crowd of couples thinned out with the second song, leaving Laurel and Connor with ample room to move as they began dancing.

"Taking a break?" she asked. Connor hadn't stopped snapping photos since the reception began.

"I'll do more when they cut the cake." Connor looked over his shoulder to the cake table. One of the four waiters hired to help Robert and Gary tonight was arranging dessert plates. "Which will probably be after this song," he added.

Laurel could feel the traces of tension that hung between them since the night at the coffeehouse. It had thinned, diminished by their interactions this week and by the fact that Laurel retained none of her initial anger with him, but she knew that the friendship wasn't entirely mended.

"I know we're okay," Connor began carefully. He kept his eyes on hers. "But I still want to say how sorry I am for the way I handled the whole Marcus thing. I kept imagining how upset you might be when you found out, and I hated that I'd have to be the one to do that to you. That's no excuse though."

He'd never excelled at apologies so she felt the significance of him raising the subject.

"You know something?" She cocked her head.

"What?"

"If I had to see Marcus again and deal with him, I truly believe it was better for me to be taken by surprise."

"Really?" Connor ventured a smirk. "So, you're glad I didn't warn you ahead of time?"

"Ha! I wouldn't take it that far. No, I only think the end result was better because of the way it happened, like pulling a bandage off really fast."

He grimaced. "People always say that's the better way, but it can still hurt a lot."

"It can, but it's short-lived and you haven't wasted your energy planning how to handle it. You just do it. You react and you move on."

"I get it, and I'm relieved that's how you feel about it."

A question popped into her mind. "How come you asked me once about having a date for the wedding? What did that have to do with it?"

With a grunt, Connor asked, "Can you believe Marcus wanted to show up here at the reception?"

She stumbled, almost knocking into another couple.

"He thought it'd be romantic or something, reuniting at a wedding," Connor explained with disgust. "I had to convince him that he shouldn't be so certain you'd be thrilled to see him. That's when he decided the coffeehouse opening would be a better night to surprise you."

"Wow, thank you," Laurel sputtered when she found her voice. "Oh my goodness, could you imagine?"

"I know. It wasn't one of his smartest ideas."

The song was nearly over. She lifted her chin resolutely. "I don't want to talk about Marcus anymore, okay?"

"Fine by me." Connor was already distracted. Jace and Melanie were leaving the dance floor and heading for the cake table.

At the end of the song, Connor rushed off to photograph the couple. Laurel moved with many other guests to watch them cut into a tier of the chocolate truffle cake, then gently place a bite into the each other's mouths. Jace kissed Mel on the nose and left a dot of frosting there. Connor captured every angle and movement, looking more pleased with each shot.

Laurel caught Robert watching her. He leaned against the doorway of the kitchen. His white chef's apron had a rainbow of smears across it and his blond hair was tucked messily behind his ears. When she met his gaze, he walked to her, his smile growing with each step. Without a word, he leaned in and kissed her gently. The sensation was still thrillingly new. He turned to watch the newlyweds and slipped his arm around Laurel's waist. She let her eyes linger on his profile a moment longer.

Returning her attention to the bride and groom, Laurel considered how all the months and even years of preparations, of waiting, were suddenly over. It was all brought to an end now. As she felt Robert pull her a bit closer, she realized that summary of things only skimmed the surface. Underneath it all, she could see only beginnings.

About the Author

Carrie Sue Barnes has always adored books, and when she fell in love with creative writing in sixth grade, there was no going back. She resides with her family in Wisconsin, though she says she will always be a Michigan girl at heart.

You can read Carrie Sue's short fiction stories and faith-inspired reflections on her website, carrieinwriting.com.

Carrie invites readers to connect with her on her Facebook author page,

www.facebook.com/carrieinwriting.

Notes

1. Psalm 33:21-22, King James Version (KJV)

2. Psalm 69:15-16, KJV

3. Psalm 121:1-8, KJV

4. 1 John 3:18, KJV

5. 1 John 3:20, KJV

6. 1 John 4:10, KJV

7. 1 John 4:11, KJV

8. 1 John 4:15, KJV

9. 1 John 4:16, KJV

10. 1 John 4:18, KJV

11. Philippians 4:7, KJV

12. 2 Corinthians 4:7-10, KJV

13. 2 Corinthians 4:16-17, KJV

14. Job 42:17, KJV

51301764R10197

Made in the USA
Lexington, KY
02 September 2019